ABSOLUTE ZEROS
XANDER FRANKLIN

SEVERED PRESS
HOBART TASMANIA

ABSOLUTE ZEROS

ISBN: 978-1-925840-89-6

For my wife Kati, whose love and support made this story possible. And for every Grunt who's ever pulled watch at a static post in the middle of nowhere.

PROLOGUE:

The sun set low on a frozen dune. The wind swept lightly over its peak, feathering the air with thin plumes of snow. Caught in the waning light, they glittered orange before fading away. From the south came the low rumble of an approaching engine, with the growing creak of snow compressed beneath heavy wheels.

Vernis Baker sat hunched in the threadbare comfort of his chair, his face dimly lit by the green dials in front of him. His jaw clenched, he peered out through the scratched viewscreen of the BredRan's cab, charting a mental course through the icy dunes. Every so often, he checked the small heads-up display in the corner of the truck's screen, tracking the blips as they grew in size. Vernis eased off the throttle as the display's chirrups grew more insistent. Absentmindedly he stroked his chin, a small feeling of unease beginning to well inside him.

They shouldn't be this far. His uneasiness deepened as he glanced at the fading glow of the horizon. Vernis hated to venture out this close to night, it was easy to misread the terrain or sink in a pocket of loose snow. With so much that could go wrong, driving during the day was always better. Even when the temperature never rose above negative fifty degrees, the sun still provided some meager comfort to his solitary outings. And now that comfort was slipping away behind the drifting dunes.

They have to be around here somewhere, he thought, coming completely off the throttle to park the truck's six wheels on the peak of a large snowdrift. As the chirping of the AcuTrack display grew to full volume, Vernis craned his neck to look down in the valley below. There, spread before him, lay the shaggy backs of his wayward herd.

With a soft sigh he climbed down the rusty ladder on the side of the BredRan's cab. As he stepped off the last rung, he halved his fall with a quick step on the outer tread of an enormous tire. A small grunt escaped him as he hit the ground, snow crunching softly beneath his thick boots. He didn't like to admit it, but he was getting older, his joints a little stiffer as he crawled in and out of the massive red truck. He adjusted the thin hose under his face mask, seating it more comfortably in his nostrils.

Bending over to check the flow from the O_2 pack on his side, he breathed in, filling his lungs with the stale tang of canned atmosphere. He fiddled with his goggles, trying to seal out any gaps around the corners of his eyes. In a place this cold, frostbite sets in in seconds. Satisfied, Vernis set off down the slope, taking careful steps to negotiate the loose snow.

As he cleared the foot of the dune, Vernis returned his attention to the Gluffant herd. Up close, they appeared like so many hills of thick white fur, rippling softly with the sway of their tremendous bulk. He stepped forward, a few of the great beasts chuffing in the wintry air, their breath escaping in small clouds of steam from flared, black nostrils. Vernis slowed down as he neared them, his approach already causing the nervous stamping of wide, hooved feet. Some of the males tensed, warning him off with a shake of their massive horned heads. Vernis wasn't concerned about the horns, largely vestigial, they were little more than a relic of a time well before domestication. They came from a time when their ancestors roamed mighty plains before being shipped halfway across the galaxy and bred to grace the tables of the ultra-rich. Stepping past patches of polar lichen, Vernis put his hands up to ease the herd. Though generally docile, Gluffants were large and unpredictable enough to require caution, especially when working alone.

A few yards from the crowded herd, Vernis still puzzled over why they had come this far. There was plenty of lichen in the valley, but it wasn't appetizing enough on its own to draw them away from their normal range. It was a meager foodsource, and the Gluffants still required supplementation from nutricubes for their daily essentials. *I bet there's a methane vent around here,* he thought. Vernis searched the walls of the valley for a tell-tale crevice. Despite needing oxygen, albeit in much thinner concentrations than humans, Gluffants would search out methane vents from time to time. Gathering near them and breathing the vapors in, they would become dizzy and disoriented before they staggered off. The effects could last for an hour afterwards, one last act of natural rebellion, an instinct unquashed by centuries of genetic manipulation. Vernis sighed. If there was methane nearby it might explain why they had come to this valley, but it further complicated his work. He set his mind to the laborious task of relocating the herd, making peace with the fact that he wouldn't return home until well into the night.

Taking aim with his handheld scanner, he began syncing the radio collars around the beasts' thick ankles with the AcuTrack base unit mounted in the cab. Moving methodically, he set about checking and logging each one of the great creatures, ensuring that the herd had remained intact in its migration. He wove around the circle, taking care to catch the smaller young on the edges. Most of the calves would be allowed to grow to the enormous size of their parents, but a select few would be culled early, fetching a steeper price at market for their tender meat.

Abruptly he stopped; there was a shift in the herd's behavior. Formerly loose, the group had tightened their circle, with the males forming a rigid perimeter. The young no longer wandered near the edges, now sequestered within the center. The wind shifted slightly from the north, and a few females let out a low bellow from inside the circle. Vernis tensed. He'd been a rancher for twenty-five years, and he'd learned to take his cues from the shaggy beasts.

He paused for a few beats, assessing his surroundings as best he could from within the thick layer of his overcoat and thermal mask. The dying light drew long shadows over the valley, the glare from the ridgeline shining directly into his goggles. Seeing and hearing nothing, he circled the herd again, trying to catch a better glimpse of what had set them on edge.

He stopped again as he neared the head of the group. The wind had shifted, this time coming in from the east. The bellowing ceased, replaced with an ominous silence from the nervous beasts. *It must be northward,* he thought, changing direction to investigate further. Vernis strode with purpose towards a hummock of loose snow, confident that whatever the problem was, it lay on the other side of the hill. Sheathing his scanner, Vernis unslung the long rifle from his shoulder. Archaic by present standards, the kinetic weapon had been in his family for generations, and he took comfort from the knurled wood stock in his hands. As he crept towards the hill, his eyes swept left and right, searching for signs of anything unusual.

Vernis began to circle the snowdrift when he caught a glimmer of orange from the corner of his eye. Turning to face the hill, he drew closer, attempting to pinpoint the origin of the orange shimmer. A few feet in front of it, Vernis lowered his rifle, perplexed. The mound shifted slightly, and too late Vernis realized his mistake. Too late he turned to run, dropping the rifle in the deep snow.

He was caught by a broad sickle claw at the end of a nimble fore limb. Though it happened in seconds, Vernis had enough time to register the power and ferocity of the clawed arm as it yanked him through the air. His last view was of his panicking herd outlined against the twilight sky, before he was dragged past the serrated teeth of the enormous, hungry maw.

A plaintive cry arose from the valley, carrying the collective terror of the herd below. It echoed softly out on the wind-sheared dunes, mixing with the light idle of the abandoned truck, before being swallowed up by the rushing wind.

CHAPTER 1:

It was dawn, and an alarm chimed from a distant console in remote station AZH-01. It was dawn, and someone was getting their ass chewed.

"I don't *fucking* believe it," said Sergeant Ramos. The swarthy, grim-faced man looked back over a broad shoulder. "Do you believe in miracles, Lieutenant?"

The Lieutenant crossed his arms, a wry smile on his pinched, freckled face. "Depends on the miracle, Sergeant."

"Well I must've been graced with the divine sight, able to see the dead!" the Reed-Sergeant continued, the frown-lines of his face deepening as he spoke. "Or at least I hope I'm seeing the dead. Because the *only* reason two of my fine troopers have failed to get off site in their allotted seven minutes, is if *they* have *fucking died!*"

Sergeant Ramos paused, staring down the two young men before him. Private Li and Special-Trooper Reming, for their part, concentrated intently on the blank space of wall behind the non-commissioned officer, level and slightly above his shoulder.

"Well?" he asked, broad, olive hands sweeping the air aggressively towards them. "Have. You. *Died?* Have you left this mortal plane? Am I talking to two *fucking ghosts?*"

Reming shifted nervously where he stood. Li offered a shallow cough into the back of his hand.

"Well either I'm looking at two dead men, or I caught a glimpse of the future and have seen two troopers about to die. Either way, you have exactly three seconds to depart this floor, or you will be *fucking departed.*"

Reming and Li both blinked, turning their attention back to Sergeant Ramos.

Lieutenant Preston leaned in, his thin face momentarily occupying the blank space over the Reed-Sergeant's shoulder.

"I think that means you should go," he added helpfully.

"Now!" thundered Sergeant Ramos.

Reming and Li took their cue and scrambled, a tussle of arms and legs suddenly possessed with a singular and distinct purpose: moving rapidly away from their impending demise. As the clanging of boot-heels receded down the hall, Sergeant Ramos shook his head. Turning back towards the Lieutenant, he chuckled as they walked down the alloy hallway. The officer offered a shrug. *What are you going to do?*

Reming climbed the last rung of the white-painted ladder, leaping over to land in the patch-worn seat. In the driver's seat across the cab, Li buckled the straps on his five-point harness.

"This some *bull*-shit," Li said, drawing out the first syllable as long as possible.

"Uh-huh," grunted Reming, settling in to secure his own harness.

"Why is it always us that gets caught with these bullshit alarms?" the young Private asked, pressing the ignition. "Every time I try to sleep in, fuckin' alarms."

"Every time," Reming agreed, toggling the switch to open the bay door.

Li nudged the throttle forward.

"And every time, I think to myself, 'It's alright, just a few more minutes, then I'll get up and respond.' And every time, there's Rammin' Ramos, jumping in my ass."

"Straight up in it," echoed Reming. "Just a thirty-foot long jump, deep into your ass."

"Nights never has to deal with this bullshit," said Li, as the massive vehicle rumbled forward. "Sergeant Wingo is so chill, all he does is game. Doesn't give a fuck how long a response takes."

"Yup." Reming nodded, reflecting on his most recent string of devastating losses to Buck-Sergeant Wingo in *Altar of Combat.*

Mighty wheels crunched in snow as Li pulled out of the bay. Turning south to align with the waypoint on his screen, he sighed.

"Nights never has to deal with *any* bullshit."

Unknown to Private Li, the subject of night-shift, and the degree of bullshit with which they may or may not be dealing with, was being discussed at that very moment in the Command Den.

"Damnit," Sergeant Ramos muttered to himself, rifling through the papers scattered on the black-topped desk.

"DAMNIT!" he shouted, holding the pages in the air for Lieutenant Preston to see. "Look at this shit, LT! Look at these sorry excuses for InReps! Yesterday's is missing the timestamps, and there's two from last week without location IDs. He never logs their fuel 'spenditures, and all of his training statements are canned entries. Wingo never checks these things, and I heard he's letting them break scram-times."

Sergeant Ramos paused for a breath, clenching his broad-set jaw.

"That's it, if Wingo lets this bush-league shit get submitted again, I'm gonna wake his ass up and make him eat them!"

Lieutenant Preston shifted his eyes from the blue-and-white glow of his terminal screen. Eyeing the papers brandished in the hands of his beleaguered Reed-Sergeant, the officer smiled.

"I don't see why you still print those out," he said, attempting to defuse the volatile Sergeant. "They're easier to edit while they're still in the console."

"It's a tactile thing," grumbled Sergeant Ramos, undeterred by the sudden change in subject. He leveled a heavy hand at the officer, crumpling the papers slightly. "You wouldn't get it. If you were stationed on Avina when the Troubs came in and the power went dark, scratchin' our orders on paper with fuckin' ink, *maybe* you'd understand. That was real shit then, like the cavemen."

"Sure," Lieutenant Preston said, turning his attention back to his screen. Softly, he added, "But this isn't Avina, is it?"

Deflating slightly, Sergeant Ramos dropped the papers back on to the sparse alloy desk. Grabbing his mug with his last ounce of indignation, he looked up just in time to be infuriated once again.

"Bright mornings, gentlemen!" Sergeant Sikes announced as he walked through the door. "And how are we welcoming another day at AZH-01?"

"Still surprised I haven't put a gun in my mouth," Sergeant Ramos muttered under his breath. Catching the disapproving eye of the Lieutenant, he corrected himself, adopting the stilted maxim of the Inter-Stellar Coalition Forces. "I mean, with temerity and enthusiasm to carry out this dutiful tour!"

He raised the mug of SimuCaff to his lips, trying to shield his disgust for the Senior-Sergeant.

"And you, my fine commanding officer?" continued Sergeant Sikes, turning his broad, toothy smile towards the Lieutenant. "What level is your morale today?"

Wincing at the formulaic, canned platitudes, Lieutenant Preston wondered if the Senior-Sergeant had always spoken in ICF clichés, or if twenty-three years of service had driven military jargon and protocol so far into his brain that they replaced all other patterns of speech.

"Excellent today, Senior," he replied. *As excellent as it could be when you're assigned to the furthest remote post the ICF has to offer.*

"Great, great," Sergeant Sikes absentmindedly said to the floor. Looking up again he asked, "And the troops? They are well? How is Private Khalil? Is she re-adjusted?"

The mug in front of Sergeant Ramos' face hid his pained expression well. Working ahead of the Reed-Sergeant's cutting remarks, Lieutenant Preston forced himself to answer in a careful, neutral tone. "They're good, holding tight. Special-Trooper Rania is...fine. She's pushing through her next development volume. She's trying to focus on her studies."

"Although if you really wanted to know about them, you could always come see them in formation," Sergeant Ramos added, barely keeping the disdain from his voice.

A long pause stretched between the three. For a split second, the beaming smile faltered on the Senior-Sergeant's pale, bloodless face. In a flash, it snapped back into its well-worn position.

"Yes, well, of course. I would love to. I just have to finish the quarterly weapon calibrations in the armory." Sergeant Sikes turned to leave, adding as he hurried out the door, "I would hate for there to be any complications during our next firing qualification."

"Of course, that would be tragic," said Sergeant Ramos, sipping casually from his mug.

"I'd hate for him to actually give a shit," he muttered, just low enough for the officer to hear. Lieutenant Preston clasped his hands behind his head and shrugged, *what are you going to do?*

The wind whipped across the frozen plains, picking up a few flakes of snow along the way before depositing them on the hairy back of an enormous beast. The Gluffant paid them no mind, as it ignored most things unrelated to the passage of food from the ground and on into the four-chambered gut. With a single shake of its massive head, it cleared the snow from its delicate ears. Satisfied, it returned to the pressing task of grazing on lichen, pausing only to stare directly at the sun. The Gluffant scratched at the ground with a great, wide hoof, clearing away more snow to reveal the lichen underneath. Many days had been spent like this, eating lichen, staring at the sun, scratching the ground to find more lichen. The beast was consistent in its desires.

A low rumble reached the animal's tufted ears. As the sound grew in volume, the Gluffant paused in its chewing, raising its shaggy head. It fixed a beady, black eye on the north, watching the silhouette grow in the distance. A long, squat vehicle with a hexagonal cab approached, speeding towards the Gluffant on eight, heavy-treaded wheels.

As the vehicle grew closer, the rumbling grew louder, mixing with the squeaking crunch of snow compacted beneath large wheels. The Gluffant observed through dull eyes, mentally contrasting the size of the vehicle to its own, formidable bulk. At nearly five tons, there was very little that could intimidate the great beast, but it noted with slight unease that the eight-wheeled vehicle continued to grow in size as it approached. The rumbling increased still further, and the Gluffant shifted its feet nervously.

The vehicle drew abreast of the beast, riding on wheels fifteen feet tall. Abruptly it turned, angling towards the east and moving away from the shaggy-backed creature. As it watched the vehicle diminish in the distance, the Gluffant relaxed, content in the present superiority of its size. Derisively it snorted, before resuming its daily routine once again.

Private Li and Special-Trooper Reming bounced along in the crowded cab. Propelled forward on eight great wheels, the *Massive Modular Utility Transport, Category: All Terrain*, abbreviated as the MMUTCAT in standard Inter-Stellar Coalition Force doctrine, was well equipped to tackle the harsh rigors of AZH's icy tundra.

Outfitted with all manner of active traction systems and colossal, honeycombed wheels, there was little in nature that could stop the fifty-ton vehicle once it got up to speed. Although costing nearly five million credits and taking twelve years to develop (all necessary in order to encompass the vast array of features inserted by top ICF brass at different stages of the design process), very little was spent in the way of softening the suspension or improving the thin-cushioned seats. Operator comfort was deemed an expendable luxury by a headquarters leadership that would never experience riding in the vehicle they demanded.

Reming and Li bounced again in the hard, plastic-cored seats, jostled by the MMUTCAT's sudden encounter with a small rock.

"Easy Li," the ruddy trooper chastised, rubbing a hand on the tender beginnings of a fleshy love-handle. "My ass wasn't made for this abuse."

"That's 'cause it's made of candy," snapped the young Private. "Now, you want to shut the fuck up and let me drive? You bitch an awful lot for someone with a revoked license."

This was true. Special-Trooper Reming's complaints *were* significantly more frequent when compared to the other troopers of AZH-01, especially after having his driving privileges formally revoked early in the tour when he rolled the unit's newest MMUTCAT on its roof.

"You know that wasn't my fault! I was swerving to miss a Gluffant."

"Whatever, man," Li replied, momentarily thrown against the nylon harness by the massive truck's contact with a shallow pothole. "All I know is that they recalled everyone onto wake status to fix that shit. It took *both* the other MMUTCATs to bail you out, and the new one's *still* dead-lined after the rollover."

"Whatever, it was just a mid-model upgrade," the Special-Trooper said turning back to the window. "It wasn't even that much nicer."

The reply was terse and accusatory. "I heard it had the deluxe seats. Heated *and* cooled."

Reming sat silently, observing the passing snowhills through the viewscreen. After a few minutes, he spoke again.

"Man, why is it always Echo-3? Takes almost two hours to get there."

Li grunted in tacit agreement. "MinMap says we're almost there."

The soft blinking of the heads-up display had grown more insistent as they drew nearer to the sensor tower at site E-03. A chirrup indicating the tower was a kilometer ahead was hardly necessary as the vehicle cleared the summit of a large hill. A thin spire rose on the plain before them, red lights blinking along its side.

"There it is," Li sighed. "Let's get this shit done."

Rania bint Khalil sat cross-legged at the foot of her bed. Alone in the dark, she assumed the lotus position. All was still around her, save for the quiet lilt of the *Qur'an* recited through the speaker on her dresser. She breathed in deeply, quieting her mind to all except the measured cadence of the *ayah*. She concentrated on the sound, trying to separate the recitation into the few words she understood. The first line was the easiest, it was the same opening for every *surah*, but after that she struggled to connect the ancient words to understanding in her mind. Her great-grandfather had been a *Hafiz*, one of the last few to memorize the holy book and recite it in its entirety. She wondered what his voice sounded like, if it held the same passion as the speaker in the recording. She could feel her concentration slipping, the words sifting like sand through her fingers.

With a grimace she gave up, distracted by the illumination of a small blue light and a notification sound not unlike a bubble being popped. Rania opened her eyes, sighing a little before she spoke.

"Stop playback. Answer call."

The singing stopped, replaced with a soft whirring as the computer complied. A second bubble pop let her know the transmission line was connected.

"Special-Trooper Rania, what's your need?"

Her question was met with the abrupt howling of the wind, filling the quiet confines of the dark room.

"Uh, yeah. Rania? It's Li. We're out at Echo-3 and we can't get the infra alarm to reset." Li's voice was muffled, barely able to get his words in over the sound of the wind.

"Did you check the field rings? Are the beam-gates open?"

"Uh, yeah, and we cycled the dampeners."

Rania winced. Cycling the dampeners typically implied applying direct force to the delicate electronics with a heavy, blunt object, usually the butt of a rifle.

"Hey, is that Rania?" Reming's voice joined the line; just like Li, his voice was muffled, barely breaking in over the wind. "Tell her we need her. The stupid thing is broken, and it won't reset. Just tell her she's the best, that we suck, and she's the only one who can help. She'll like that."

"Rania? It's Li again. We suck and we need you."

A small smile crept on Rania's face.

"What's the weather like?" she asked.

"Fuckin' cold," said Li.

She rolled her eyes. "I mean the weather conditions. I need the specifics."

"Uh, there's no snow, temp reading at negative sixty degrees. And it says windspeed is thirty-five knots."

Rania frowned. "I have to get authorization for travel in anything over thirty knots."

"Please Rania, it's hard broke. We need you."

"*And?*"

"*Annnd,*" Li sighed. "You're the best."

"Perfect," said Rania, smiling once again. "Help is on the way."

Rania's next call was to a decidedly less personable recipient. Taking a quick breath, she steeled herself and ordered the computer to dial the Command Den. A soft whirring filled the room as she readied herself. The bubble popped, and the line opened.

"Command?" she inquired.

"Speaking, what's your request?" the taciturn voice of Reed-Sergeant Ramos filled the line.

Fuck, Rania thought to herself. She cleared her throat and forced the words out as quickly as possible. "Sergeant, I have a call coming in from Echo-3, they can't get a reset. They tried what they could, I think it might be the DMT."

"And?" came the curt reply.

"Wind speed dictates command approval prior to dispatch. Respectfully requesting permission, Sergeant."

Silence filled the room for a few moments.

"Granted."

And the line clicked off. Rania released the breath she wasn't aware she had been holding. She stood up, shrugging on her boots and the mottled gray jacket of her uniform. As she passed by the mirror on her way to the door, she paused. She pulled back her curly black hair into a quick ponytail, secured with the small, elastic band she wore on her wrist. Another quick survey ensured she'd captured all the loose ends, and wiped off a smudge from the end of her angular, bronze nose. She nodded in approval and stepped out the door.

Li hopped from one foot to the other, crossing and uncrossing his arms in the cold. He shivered in spite of the thermogenic layers of his standard-issue *Cold Weather All-Purpose Layer* (known by ICF doctrine as the CWAPL, known by ICF troopers as the *crapple*). Li tugged at his facemask, double checking that the liner of the hood sealed properly along the edges. He shivered in the wind.

"Reming! How *the fuck* is it this cold? And why *the fuck* are we still *here?*"

"I know man," the Special-Trooper replied, "this shit always breaks on us."

Li continued his hopping, attempting to keep feeling in his toes. Mashing the temperature dial on his CWAPL, Li subjected the button to his growing frustration.

"And how. *The fuck.* Does this *crapple* never work?" Li spat, continuing his furious assault on the jacket's controls.

"Fuckin' A." Reming agreed, crouching down in the space between two of the MMUTCAT's wheels. He rubbed his arms, glancing up and spying a Gluffant about fifty yards away. The Gluffant stared back at the two small and shivering forms, calmly chewing its cud. Reming eyed it with suspicion. Normally docile, the massive beasts were sometimes unpredictable--he'd even heard one of them charged a MMUTCAT head-on during the previous crew's tour. The drivers were unhurt, save for some mild whiplash, and the vehicle was left without a scratch, but it took the troopers nearly a week of hard scrubbing to clean the guts from the big truck's grill. Li chose this point to look up, finally noticing the hairy beast in front of him.

"Fuck man! Where'd that come from?" he stammered, stumbling backwards.

The Gluffant continued to stare, benignly chewing. A mild sneeze shook the snow pile off its great shoulders.

"Why are they always here? Don't they have packs they roam in?"

"Herds," Reming corrected. "And it's the sensor site. They're attracted by the methane it runs off of. Gets them high or something."

This was a continual problem. Gluffants had been known to damage sensor sites from time to time, sometimes knocking a tower completely over just to get the methane tubing that powered its intricate sensor infrastructure.

Li rolled his eyes beneath his mask. "Did you learn that in your biology class?"

"Classes." Reming corrected again, idly drawing in the snow with a thick-gloved finger. "I took a whole semester of xenobiology, you know, before I dropped out."

Despite the praise and constant support of his enthusiastic mother Special-Trooper Reming's promising career as a xenobiologist was tragically cut short after just one semester, when he was first introduced to alcohol during post-midterm celebrations.

"Whatever, man, it just better stay the fuck over there," said Li, ducking his head to block the wind.

"I wonder where Rania is?"

At that moment Special-Trooper Rania was completing the final pre-flight checks for her DC-12 *Solo Skimmer*. The thin, torpedo-shaped craft perched lightly on spindly landing gear, with four swept wings lending the ship an appearance not unlike a dragonfly flying in reverse. Laying forward in the cockpit seat, she gripped the knobby rubber of the twin throttles. Lightly easing them forward, her heart leapt as the small skiff raised off the ground. Flying a *Solo Skimmer* was one of the few perks of her job as a sensor technician, which necessitated expedient travel to tricky dispatches.

Light, finicky in rough weather, and difficult to repair, the small ship was nonetheless highly maneuverable, especially in a thinner atmosphere like AZH. Thanks to its twin scramjet boosters mounted towards the aft and its wide-differential ailerons, the DC-12 was able to fly at mach-seven, perfect for traveling quickly to distant sites. Rania adjusted her goggles, seating them firmly over her blue-green eyes, before she slammed the levers forward and launched into the snowy wastes.

Back at sensor tower E-03, Special-Trooper Reming was mercifully spared from Private Li's continued complaints by the approaching sound of a small jet craft. Standing up in the MMUTCAT's arched wheel-well, he shielded his eyes and scanned the horizon for the fast-moving ship. He spotted the telltale white trail left in the wake of the DC-12 as it hurtled across the sky. The scream of the jet's exhaust grew louder before tapering off in a series of quick puff-puffs, the ailerons fanning out repeatedly to brake the thin craft. Slowing to a stall, the twin jets pivoted downwards, holding the *Solo Skimmer* in a controlled hover. He could just make out Rania's ear-to-ear grin as she deftly maneuvered the craft to the ground. Reming watched her trade the flight goggles for an ICF facemask before she unsealed the cockpit and disembarked. There was a little strut in her step as she approached the two troopers.

"Took you long enough," Li said.

"I had to request permission," she fired back. "Maybe *you* shouldn't have broken it."

"We didn't," Li began to protest, gesturing to Reming to back him up. Reming just shook his head and resumed crouching between the wheels. *It's too damn cold to argue*, he thought.

Rania walked to the foot of the tower, opening up the screen of the ScanTool strapped to her wrist. After syncing with the tower's subsystems, she began her diagnostic check, softly clicking her tongue as she checked the lines of code. Confirming her earlier suspicions she snapped the ScanTool closed, walking closer to the frozen ladder rungs on the north side of the sensor. She climbed the tower, pausing only briefly to knock some ice off the next rung before continuing upwards. She stopped roughly fifty feet in the air, hooking one arm around the ladder and opening the side latch with the other. Removing the line coiled on her belt, Rania connected the wires from her ScanTool to the sensor's interface porting. She typed one-handed for several minutes while Private Li paced the ground below. Satisfied with her work, she removed the wire, locked the hatch and proceeded back down the ladder. She hopped to the ground from the last two rungs.

"Well?" Li inquired. "Did it reset?"

"Yep," Rania confirmed, head in the air as she walked back towards the skiff. "It was the DMT, bogged down because of the irregular atmosphere readings. It's fixed now."

"We good?" asked Reming as the two approached.

"Yeah, we got resets, now let's get the fuck outta here," Li said.

Reming glanced at the setting sun before fixing his gaze on the DC-12. "It's a long drive back, and I'd hate to miss evening formation, any chance we can hitch a ride?"

Rania shook her head, unsealing the cockpit's bubble canopy. "Sorry boys, you know the rules, you gotta be licensed to take that flight.

"Maybe you should apply for a cross-train, try testing for the Electric Corps," she added, swinging her leg into the *Solo Skimmer's* cockpit. "You only need an ARMs score of twelve-hundred."

The cockpit sealed close around her as the boosters ignited, gently lifting the light skiff into the air. Li and Reming watched it turn north before jetting off into the distance.

"Twelve-hundred? Shit, son," Li drawled. "Maybe if we added our scores together."

CHAPTER 2:

"Sheridan drew this today!" James Saint-James beamed through the monitor on the Command Den desk. "It's a friendly monster wearing a *scary* mask. She used tissue paper to add texture to the mask. Used the glue all by herself!"

As James fumbled to present the artwork to the camera, Sergeant Ramos ran a swarthy hand through his graying, black hair. Rubbing the back of his neck, he scrutinized the mass of brown and orange blobs on the screen. Unable to distinguish the friendly monster or the scary mask, he gave up with a sigh.

"Looks great dear," agreed Sergeant Ramos.

James continued enthusiastically. "Isn't it? She has a real talent with mixed-media, she's definitely going to be an artist. She has a vision for each canvas!"

Sergeant Ramos drew his hand from his neck to begin rubbing his eyes. "That's what you said about Silvestre, and he hasn't touched paint since he was seven."

"Silvestre never used mixed-media," James chastised. "Besides, you should see him on the field, he drives after the ball with such passion!"

Sergeant Ramos snapped his attention back to his husband.

"I know!" he said gruffly. "I've seen him on the VidScreens."

"Yes," James Saint-James acknowledged, a touch of sadness to his voice. "But he can't see you."

Sergeant Ramos grumbled non-committally.

"How's the job going?" he asked. "Any news from the Small Council?"

"Nothing so far." James noted the change in subject but allowed it to slide. "They're still debating the funding requirements for expansion in the Karnassus theater. Some of the minority representatives are questioning the utility in further commitment to the planet's pacification. They'd rather starve them into compliance with sanctions."

"Sanctions cost less, fewer lives too," remarked Sergeant Ramos.

"Fewer ICF lives maybe, but it'll cost the colonists tenfold when their organic supplies start running out and people go hungry," James said, his gray eyes flashing as his voice rose. "Sanctions mean my journalists are cut off as well, we won't be able to access the story on the ground."

"No new stories means the public loses interest," the non-commissioned officer mused, leaning back in his chair.

"And no public interest means the Coalition gets a blank check to do what they want," said James, a blond lock from his ponytail falling forward as he spoke. He tucked it behind his ear without thinking. "Just like what they did to Avina."

"Just like Avina," replied Sergeant Ramos, his voice trailing off.

"But I'm assigning Deckly to continue coverage of the Council chambers," James concluded, successfully bringing his husband's focus back to the conversation. "Sheridan has a recital Tuesday evening. They're performing *The Howling Orchids of Doctor Manasta*. She's playing Beatrix."

Sergeant Ramos furrowed his brow.

"That's a little advanced for her, isn't it?" he said, rubbing his broad, olive chin. "She's only four."

"Five-and-a-half," corrected James, the blond lock of hair falling forward again. "And she's had the lyrics down for three weeks. The show is at 21:30, Earth Standard Time. You should tune in."

After a beat he added, "If you're not too busy."

Sergeant Ramos sighed.

"I'll see what I can do," he offered, trying to head his husband off before the argument escalated.

"You should," James remarked stiffly. *You're her fucking father*, came the unspoken implication.

"I'll see what I can do," the NCO repeated.

A few minutes of silence stretched between them, as vast and deep as the distance between Earth and AZH.

"Anyway," Sergeant Ramos said, breaking the silence at last, "we're expecting some storms over the next few days. Linknet access is expected to go down, I probably won't be able to talk. I'll call you as soon as it comes back up."

"Of course," said James, "do what you can."

Brightening, he added, "I love you."

"You too," came the flat reply. Sergeant Ramos closed the window containing his husband's smiling face, severing the connection with a small pop. Wearily, he stood up from his chair, cracking his back as he brought his mug of SimuCaff to his lips. He set the cup of bitter brown liquid next to the monitor, smoothing his carefully styled hair in the reflection from the blank screen.

The Lieutenant looked up from across the room.

"Evening formation?"

"Yes, sir," came the terse reply.

"Alright then," replied the officer, standing up from his chair. He reached for his uniform jacket hanging from the hook on the wall. "I thought the storm forecast was for next week?"

"I know," said the Reed-Sergeant brusquely, heading out the door. "Let's get this shit done."

For the fifth time that day, an alarm sounded in Buck-Sergeant Kyrghizwald's room. The soft clanging, like wind chimes in a swift breeze, rose in tenor as the alarm continued. Bleary eyes fluttered open, then closed again. As the alarm increased in its insistence, a single, watery, blue eye snapped open. Attempting to focus on the illuminated numbers blinking on the desk, the eye narrowed and closed again. It took thirty seconds for the time on the display to permeate his sluggish brain, and another thirty seconds for the resulting panic to spread through the rest of him.

Shit, Sergeant Kyrghizwald thought, bolting out of bed. *Shit, shit, shit, shit shitshitshitshit*. Newly thawed, his thoughts began racing in response to the present crisis. The time showed 19:02, evening formation had already started. His eyes darted around the room in a frenzy. *Where?* He thought to himself, searching for his boots as he pulled on his mottled grey pants. *Where, where, where wherewherewhere?* His right boot was standing upright by the foot of his sink, while he located his left in the dusty confines of the crevice between his bed and dresser. He thrust his hand through the gap, straining to reach his errant footwear. His heart racing, Sergeant Kyrghizwald offered a half prayer up to the vague god of his ancestors, a jumbled mutter located midway between a stuttered imploration and a primal grunt of need. As his fingertips brushed the top of the boot, Sergeant Kyrghizwald let out a whoop of triumph, snagging the laces and dragging the troublesome shoe out. Hopping on one foot, he strained to loosen the laces and slide the boot on.

Having successfully achieved a state of dress, Sergeant Kyrghizwald stumbled to the door, glancing at the mirror as he passed. Baggy eyes noted the shadow of stubble covering his weak chin. Running his hand over his scruff, he weighed his options. *Late and looking like dog shit*, he debated internally, *or miss it entirely but look clean?* In the end, he chose the side of expedience, hoping to avoid the full brunt of the Reed-

Sergeant's wrath. *Late was forgivable*, he reasoned rushing out the door, *absent was indefensible.*

Reed-Sergeant Ramos stood at attention in the center of the large room. Poised motionless, he surveyed the troopers formed in rows before him. With a grim expression, he pulled the clipboard in front of him and began calling roll from the paper sheet.

"Private Almar?"

"Present," came the reply from a dark-skinned youth in the front row.

"Private Godrey?"

"Present," replied a short trooper with blond hair.

"Private Konrad?"

"Here," a low voice emerged from a towering trooper in the back.

"Private Konrad?"

"Sarge?" Craggy brows furrowed as the question rolled out.

"Get a haircut son. This ain't the Commando Raiders, you need to be clean-cut. Not walkin' around with that fucking mop like the spokesman for *Delia*."

"Rog," came the laconic reply.

"Private Li?"

"Present."

"Private Li, you and Special-Trooper Reming have the distinct honor of cleaning out the RationVendor after evening chow. Courtesy of breaking scram-time this morning."

Oooooh, arose a chant from the crowd. "You just got rammed!" a voice called from the middle row. Reming sighed, staring a hole in the back of Li's head.

"Can it!" barked Sergeant Ramos, resuming his call for attendance. After working his way through the remaining Privates, he began in on the Special-Troopers.

"Special-Trooper Rania?" the Reed-Sergeant asked.

"Present."

"Good work on the DMT error today, thanks for the quick turn on those resets," the Lieutenant interjected.

Rania straightened in formation, a small smile forming on her face. A glance at Sergeant Ramos quickly stopped her, withering under his glare. With a note of irritation at being interrupted, the Reed-Sergeant continued. He terminated his roll with Senior-Troopers Joelson and Leonard. The latter causing a slight twitch in his upper lip as he considered the stale musk emanating from the weapons technician. His attention was drawn away from the ever-present nature of Leonard's oily funk by the arrival of Sergeant Kyrghizwald, slinking through the door in the back of the room. Biting back his frustration, Sergeant Ramos continued on with the daily announcements.

"We had two alarms today, Echo-3 and Quebec-9, both got resets but this is the third time Echo-3 has gone off this week. We may need a code change."

There was a groan from the crowd, code changes meant a seventy-two hour stay at the site, shivering in the cold as the sensor programming was manually replaced, line-by-line.

"The forecast shows clear skies, with temps in the low negative sixties, and some drifting snow. It's low threat, but make sure you're watching for light pockets."

The warning was heeded by all present. Loose patches of un-packed snow, light pockets could stretch up to a half-acre and shift right from under a trooper's feet. It was even said that a MMUTCAT was swallowed up by one on a previous crew's rotation.

"Coalition Republic News states the conflict continues on Karnassus. There was sub-orbital bombardment yesterday on a Vickys camp just outside the city of Taneria. The bombardment was intended to take out their viceroy, but ScanDrones have not yet confirmed."

Sergeant Ramos paused to assess the glassy-eyed stares of the men in front of him.

"Finally, we're coming up on firing quals this week. Senior-Sergeant Sikes will be inspecting the weapons prior to accepting them, mirror-shined or you don't turn in."

Another round of groans emerged from the impatient crowd.

"Questions?"

Hearing no response, Sergeant Ramos snapped the clipboard crisply to his side.

"Dismissed!" he thundered.

As a unit the troopers stiffened, took one step back and then abruptly turned around. The formation broke up as everyone rushed to leave. Sergeant Ramos turned to join the line of unit leadership gathered off to the side of the room.

"Bombardment, huh?" inquired Sergeant Kyrghizwald, walking up with a dopey grin.

The Reed-Sergeant took in his slovenly appearance in sections, eyes cutting up and down from the junior NCO's unshaven face, past the wrinkled uniform top, and terminating in an untied right boot. Sergeant Ramos reddened, looking to the Lieutenant for permission to unleash a suborbital bombardment of his own upon the poor Buck-Sergeant. Lieutenant Preston cocked an eyebrow, a twinkle in his brown eyes. He nodded as if to say, *do what you must, but don't destroy him, we have to work with the tools we have.* Sergeant Ramos nodded grimly in reply before turning to face Sergeant Kyrghizwald.

"Sergeant K," the Reed-Sergeant spat, hooking an arm around the Buck-Sergeant's shoulder and walking him away towards a corner of the room.

"Yes sir?"

"You mind explaining how in the *fuck* you thought you could be late today?" growled Sergeant Ramos. "And how. In. The. *Fuck.* You walked into *my* formation looking like the Saturday morning leftovers from *Madame Bertran's Pleasure Palladium*? Give me an excuse, ANY excuse, why I shouldn't bust your ass to chipping ice off the hull-grates with your fingernails?" Sergeant Ramos' voice rose on the last line, threatening the Buck-Sergeant with the slipping bonds of his barely controlled fury.

"No excuse sir," Sergeant Kyrghizwald's voice was stammering and contrite. "I overslept, it won't happen again," he offered, staring at the floor.

Sergeant Ramos sighed with an air of weary disappointment. Sergeant Kyrghizwald was erratic, on his best days he was motivated, quick to hustle, and stayed well on top of his troops. Other days his performance was far less stellar, barely getting through a shift without catching hell.

The Reed-Sergeant reflected briefly on his first meeting with Sergeant Kyrghizwald. Bright-eyed, newly-minted as a Buck-Sergeant, Kyrghizwald seemed like a spirited addition to the leadership team, an enthusiastic infusion of energy into a nightshift that desperately needed it. After a brief introduction, Sergeant Ramos had scuffed that bright-eyed sheen when he christened him 'Sergeant K.' *It's bad enough I have to read that word soup on your chest,* he'd said at the time, *ain't no way I'm gonna fuckin' say it.* He had watched the light dim a little in Sergeant K on that day, but he was confident at the time that the junior NCO would rebound in spite of Sergeant Ramos' lack of encouragement. Now he wasn't so sure, concerned that he had misjudged the young Buck-Sergeant and failed to lead him properly.

Sergeant Ramos snapped from his reverie. Looking back at Sergeant Kyrghizwald's ashamed face, he relented.

"Not again," he admonished bluntly.

The dopey smile returned to Sergeant K's face.

"And as punishment, you can go find out why Special-Trooper Leonard smells *this* time. And fix him."

Sergeant Kyrghizwald's face fell with this last bit of news. Sergeant Ramos left him to join the others, a small measure of warm satisfaction kindling in his heart.

The clatter of trays mingled with the dull roar in the dining hall. Steel forks scraped on alloy trays as troopers eagerly shoveled in their evening meal, pausing to chatter and gossip between bites. A screen in the corner displayed a constant stream from the *Republic News Network*. Senior-Trooper Joelson waited in line for the RationVendor, tapping a tuneless, staccato beat with his hands. As the line shifted forward, he stopped just long enough to adjust the wire-rimmed glasses perched delicately on his ebony face.

Satisfied, he stepped up to the giant, rectangular appliance, inserting his tray into the slotted receptacle below the order screen. He pondered his decision, sussing out the better of the two choices. On a whim he selected 'Beef Wellington,' and the sound of mighty gears combined with soft clanging within the great box. A small hatch opened and out plopped a soft grey brick, quivering on the tray with a texture resembling an underdone pastry crust. A second hatch opened and a jiggling sphere of amber liquid dropped to the tray, lightly contained in a glucose shell. Joelson observed this activity, unimpressed. With a small sigh he picked up his tray, turning to face the rows of aluminum tables and benches. Spying an open seat he walked over, easing into the space between Private Almar and Special-Trooper Reming. Dipping his head in a brief prayer, he picked up his fork and began to eat, sliding into the conversation of the troopers around him.

"It has to be a fucking cosmic joke to call *this* lasagna," Private Li said in disgust, poking a fork at the orange cube on his tray.

"What? Not your taste?" Almar inquired dryly, cutting a thin slice of cube with his fork. "I thought the RationVendor was perfectly calibrated to produce the exact flavor profile of the item requested."

"Just close your eyes, then you won't be able to tell it's not lasagna," Joelson offered.

"That's not the fucking point!" Li scoffed. "I shouldn't have to cut off my core senses to enjoy some fucking chow here. It's an organic printer, it can make literally anything! So why would I settle for this shit-pile?"

"Budgeting," Joelson mumbled, his mouth full of food. "The simpler food structures are non-proprietary, and this way they ensure consistent nutritional supply."

"Not if I don't eat it," sniffed Li.

Joelson shrugged, adjusting his glasses before resuming his meal. He looked up just in time to see Special-Trooper Rania take an open seat across the table.

"Look out everyone, it's the 'Hero of the Day' here to brighten the lives of us lowly mortals," Private Almar teased. Holding his fork in pantomime of a microphone, he adopted the stilted speech of the *Republic News Network* anchors.

"Tell me madam, did you ever think you'd make it this far, to achieve heroic status, triumphing over the alarms of Echo-3? Say, you wouldn't happen to have any words of wisdom to share with the lowly folks back home?" Almar held the fork outward.

Swallowing a bite of grey mush, Rania opened her mouth to reply, a mischievous gleam in her eye.

"Affirmative Trevor, absolutely," she remarked, mimicking the clipped speech of ICF brass. "It was a brave day. A singular day. A day we faced a singular challenge, bravely. As always, I was lucky to have the support of the lowest enlisted," she said, tipping a wink at Reming and Li. "Truly, our backbone in this great force. I am always lucky to stand on their backbones to accomplish the mission. And as I always say, 'Unity in Duty, Duty for Unity!'"

That last line brought a wave of eye-rolling from the table. Nobody enjoyed the ICF's sanctimonious new motto.

"You know what I don't get?" Li said, pointing an accusing fork at Rania. "Why is it we all call you by your first name? You're the only one here that goes by their first name. Why is that?"

He paused, thoughtfully chewing his mouthful of food.

"I mean," he swallowed, "I have a first name too, but ain't nobody call me Alfonse."

Privately, Private Li hoped that *his* first name would catch on as well. He hated being addressed by his last name, ever since boot camp, when drill sergeants used it as the foundation of some truly abominable puns. *'Private, you better move your ass quick-Li.' 'Private, I want to see your boots shining spotless-Li.'* On one occasion, he was treated to a particularly inspired bit of hackneyed linguistic butchery after he dropped his rifle in the middle of marching; *'Private, get your head out of your ass! You gots to be more careful-Li.'* And so, always on the hunt for a relenting in ICF standards, he hoped that this may be his moment of recognition.

Blank looks greeted him instead.

"She's Arab," Private Joelson stated with the patiently confused tone of someone explaining the delineation between toast and bread.

"So?" Li protested. "I'm Chinese, what's the point?"

"The point is that Khalil isn't her last name," Lieutenant Preston explained, passing by the Troopers on his way to the leadership table. "It's her father's. 'bint Khalil' is 'daughter of Khalil,' so we address her by *her* name, not his."

The officer walked on, leaving Li to puzzle over the diversity of Earth cultural conventions. Rania looked down at her half-eaten plate, grateful that someone else was able to explain this time, instead of just her. She glanced up and flashed a warm smile at the leadership table, fading once again when she caught the disapproving stare of Reed-Sergeant Ramos. *What is his deal?* she wondered, *why does it seem like he hates me?*

Sergeant Ramos harrumphed before returning to his plate. He firmly disapproved of women on remote tours. They'd been banned from serving at the outer posts when he was first assigned to remote duties, nearly ten years ago. Shortly thereafter, the ban was lifted thanks to lobbyist pressure on the ICF brass. Considered a politically expedient means of appeasing the Large Council, Sergeant Ramos saw nothing but discord in their decision. *They sacrificed standards for good press*, the Reed-Sergeant thought, *and we've reaped nothing but trouble ever since.* He'd had issues in the past with female troops shirking duties or getting involved with a supervisor. This current crew lost the only other female trooper two months ago, a weapon technician named Regina Belle, when she became pregnant by a Private on her shift. *It took a month to arrange her transport back*, he noted, angrily stabbing his fork at his plate, and *we still don't have a replacement.* His musings were interrupted by a loud clanging from the corner of the room, and the cheering whoops of troopers nearby.

"Three… four…five," grunted the slab of a trooper in the back of the room, veiny arms straining to seat the heavy bar in its place on the rack. Standing up from the bench, Special-Trooper Early bowed before his closest audience, sweat dripping down the edge of his crooked nose.

"How much was it?" inquired the Lieutenant.

"Five-sixty," beamed Early. "Not bad after five sets of bench," he added with mock humility, slapping his thick chest. Sitting down by Joelson, he took a hearty swig from a bottle of SimuWhey, barely grimacing at the chalky aftertaste.

"How can you drink that stuff?" Rania asked incredulously.

"You got to want it," said Early, brushing imaginary dust from his broad shoulders.

Li prodded the massive trooper in the side. "Wouldn't SynthGro be easier?"

"SynthGro is cheating," grunted Early. "And I heard it shrinks your balls."

"Myth," came the lumbering voice of Private Konrad from a table over, idly scraping at his plate.

"It speaks," Reming intoned softly to the others at the table.

"Did you learn that in the Raiders?" Reming called back, loud enough to be heard across the room.

His question was met with a non-committal grunt, as the scarred, red face turned once again to the task of inscribing lines in his alloy tray. Reming studied the hulking Private's mottled complexion before returning to the conversation at his table.

"Why do you work so hard?" he asked Early, his eyes still on Konrad. "Trying to push away your problems?"

"Going on the touring circuit when we rotate back," Early shrugged. "And the lower gravity makes it easy to get soft."

"Can't get soft if you've never been hard," guffawed Sergeant Wingo from the leadership table, slapping his flabby belly.

I bet that's the tagline to your shitty life story, thought Sergeant Ramos, eying the Buck-Sergeant with distaste as his bulk rippled within the confines of his uniform. With a morose sigh, he pushed his tray away and stood up, walking away from the table. *What a waste of a fucking uniform.*

The RationVendor loomed over Private Li and Special-Trooper Reming. A monolithic tower of smudged black screens and flat grey panels, the years of use showed in the layers of scratches, dents, and grime; battle scars from its grueling tour of duty with the Troopers of AZH-01. The machine emitted a low hum from underneath a layer of dust, crackling softly with malignant energy. It stood before the troopers like the altar to a malevolent god, determined to reap the sacrifice of their sweat and free time. Private Li took a step forward.

"This shit is fuckin' gross," he declared.

Special-Trooper Reming nodded in agreement.

"I fuckin' hate this. This is bullshit," continued Li.

"I fucking hate this bullshit," he added for good measure.

Reming grunted in affirmation. Dropping his bucket and sponge, he stepped forward to the right side of the machine, taking up a position on the back corner. Li shook his head and did the same, placing his hands on the opposite corner. Bracing themselves against the wall they began to push.

They heaved at the great machine, ignoring the screeching as stoppered feet clawed into pale alloy tiles. Grunting, sweat beading on their brows, little-by-little they heaved the appliance forward, creating a foot-wide gap between the panels and the wall. Gasping in triumph, they rested against the wall, wiping their faces on their shirt sleeves. Li opened his eyes, kicking out at the back panel in his frustration. His foot connected with the brushed metal, jarring something loose from deep within. It fell with a soft plop, and a dozen cockroaches streamed out from beneath the machine.

"Aw, sick," Li noted, exhaustion tempering his disgust.

Reming leapt to his feet. Shuddering, he swept his hands down the front and back of his pants, sweeping away imaginary insects, while he stared in horror as the real ones scrambled away to crevices between the wall and floor. His heart still racing, he briefly contemplated running back to his room and burying his head under his covers.

"I should go," mumbled Reming, wide eyes still searching the crevice under the huge appliance. "I could get my ZapGun..."

Modeled after the tesla rifles from the late twenty-second century, the Metam Zapgun fired a small bolt of electricity arcing a few feet to strike errant cockroaches, flies, or sting beetles. Fifty kilovolts was usually enough to smite even the most robust of inter-stellar pests.

"That gimmicky piece of shit?" Li asked incredulously. "Naw man, no way you're leaving me to deal with this shit by myself."

"They're just roaches," he added, tying a rag around his mouth and nose. "You should be used to them by now."

Numbly, Special-Trooper Reming nodded. Though the Coalition Republic was uniquely cognizant of the threat posed by invasive species, having learned the disastrous environmental lessons of the twenty-first century, even the strictest decontamination protocols suffered from limitations. Able to halt the spread of zebra mussels, gray rats, and even the common housefly, the Coalition took great pains to avoid seeding other worlds with the virulent scourges of Earth. Less out of respect for the indigenous environment than from fear of swift breeding pests rapidly evolving on a foreign world, the Coalition Republic wielded the full might of its regulatory authority to tackle the thorny issue. By and large they were successful, with one notable exception: *Blattella germanica*, the German Cockroach. Swift, omnivorous, resilient, able to flatten its body to sneak through crevices a fraction of an inch wide, and uniquely adapted to life within human-occupied spaces. As inter-stellar travel expanded with the possibilities of faster-than-light technology, the cockroach was right alongside man every step of the way, a constant companion in his quest for galactic colonization.

Still shivering slightly, Reming bent over and retrieved his bucket of supplies. Tying a rag around his face, he gave Li a thumbs-up, steadying himself for the task. Private Li nodded, then leaned forward to apply his HexTool to the stamped screws on the panel. Glancing back, he noted the lingering twitch in his partner's hands.

"I know," he said, muffled through the coarse cloth rag. "Let's get this shit done."

CHAPTER 3:

Dawn crept over AZH-01, bathing the thick metal dome in a halo of golden hues. The stale air of the station was still, redolent with the weighted silence of the early morning. Private Li lay sprawled on his bunk, anchored by the firm gravitational pull a warm bed exudes on an exhausted body. A thin line of drool traced a path from his pillow to his open mouth. The room's only sound came from the tinny ringing of music played through a small white earpiece, dislodged during one of Li's periodic shifts in position. A muffled snore punctuated the placid quiet of the room.

A harsh klaxon split the air, exhibiting all of the genteel civility of a glass terrarium falling on a hardwood floor.

'ALERT, ALERT, SHIP DETECTED, TIER-3 THREAT ASSESSED,' came the automated voice, implying the sense of urgency one has when discovering the smashed terrarium previously contained twenty-six furious, red scorpions.

Li's eyes snapped open. He kicked aside his blanket, the alarm message pounding in his ears. As he dragged himself upright, he experienced the tumultuous emotion typically reserved for a beleaguered entomologist counting only twenty-five recaptured red scorpions. *Son of a bitch...*

"Son of a bitch!" shouted Special-Trooper Reming, throwing his controller against the wall.

"That doesn't count!" he snarled, shouting at Sergeant Wingo through the voice chat.

"Everything counts," Sergeant Wingo crowed as the alarm message paraded across the screen in his room.

"I was so close too, I had you this time," lamented Reming, as *Altar of Combat*'s loss screen flashed across the monitor on the wall.

"Horseshoes and hand grenades," Sergeant Wingo offered helpfully, a broad smile splitting his jowls as he watched his win ratio tick up by one.

"Yeah, yeah," sighed Reming, terminating the voice chat. Pulling on his boots, he tucked the laces in loosely around the cuff. *It better be legit this time.*

The hallways were awash with the thuds of troopers clamoring to their posts. Boots rang off alloy floors as the alarm continued to sound. Mug of SimuCaff in hand, Reed-Sergeant Ramos strode purposefully towards the control room. Catching sight of his reflection in the dull shine of the alloy wall, he paused briefly to smooth his hair back in place. Every graying swoop in order, he grunted and strode on, propelled by the vengeful energy of a seasoned NCO.

"Move your ass!" he barked, brushing past a harried trooper. He took a swig of his mug, quaffing the bitter liquid without slowing his pace. He reached the swinging doors of the control room, throwing them open as he swept in. As he moved to the center deck, Sergeant Ramos took up a position alongside the lieutenant, surveying the flurry of activity around them.

"What do we got, sir?" he asked, sipping from his mug.

"Tier-3 ship," replied Lieutenant Preston, crossing his arms across his chest. "No details yet."

The Reed-Sergeant observed the quiet discomfort on the officer's face. Looking out from over his cup, he snapped at the nearest trooper.

"Joelson, get me a visual, now!"

Senior-Trooper Joelson looked up from his monitor. "I'm trying sir," he said, concentration beading on his brow.

"I got it, Sarge," called out Sergeant K, rushing across the room to assist the Senior-Trooper. Sliding into the seat alongside Joelson, Sergeant Kyrghizwald began typing furiously at the keyboard.

"What's going on?" asked Buck-Sergeant Wingo, tumbling through the control center doors.

"Ship detected," the Lieutenant answered.

"Tier-3," added Sergeant Ramos.

Shuffling up to the center deck, Sergeant Wingo stood abreast of the other two.

"Have we got a visual?" asked the Buck-Sergeant absentmindedly, hitching up his pants.

"Not yet," came the Reed-Sergeant's irked reply.

"Working on it!" hollered a flustered Sergeant K.

"We're working on it," confirmed Lieutenant Preston, tamping down the unease in his voice.

The three stared at the blank screen encompassing the wall before them, silently willing it to life. After a moment the wall-sized monitor glowed blue, a small loading bar appearing in the left corner.

"Got it!" shouted Sergeant K. "Should come up any minute now."

The three watched the loading bar's progress with impatience, each urging it onward. As it neared completion, the screen flickered black, dashing their hopes in the process. Sergeant Ramos cursed in frustration.

"Worthless, cheap-ass, pile of ICF shit!" the Reed-Sergeant spat. "It's 2332 and we're still making due with outdated shit from the twenty-third century!"

Turning towards the Lieutenant, he composed himself once again.

"You know, LT, if it's really a Tier-3, we should have the weapons primed."

"Good point, Sergeant," acknowledged Lieutenant Preston. "Have the troopers start prepping the Ion Array."

"Right away, sir." Sergeant Ramos leaned over the railing of the deck, barking orders below him. "Leonard, head to the core station. Start setting up the initializers!"

Leonard nodded, the oily Senior-Trooper making his way to the nearest exit.

"Rania, go with him, see to it if he needs help," ordered Sergeant Wingo, asserting his place in the leadership conversation.

"NO!" Lieutenant Preston shouted, interrupting the troopers furiously working around the room. Thirteen sets of eyes swung to the officer. He regained his composure under the weight of their stares, swallowing before addressing the bewildered Buck-Sergeant. "That won't be necessary."

Reed-Sergeant Ramos glared at the perplexed gape on Sergeant Wingo's face.

"We need her here to man the sensor console," he hissed through clenched teeth. "Private Li will go with Leonard to assist."

Rania let out a small sigh of relief. Li groaned, dragging his heels as he followed after the Senior-Trooper. He wondered what vengeful god he could have offended that would continue to visit such punishments upon him.

Special-Trooper Reming jogged along the narrow corridor, bathed in flashes of amber light. His boots clanged against corrugated tile floor while overhead, the alarm continued its mournful wail.

'TIER-3 THREAT ASSESSED, ALL PERSONNEL TO READY POSITIONS'

Reming ambled onward, propelling himself with the languid ease of someone stretching the boundaries of the word 'hustle.' He turned the corner, breath escaping as a series of slow, measured sighs. Ahead of him, a line of troopers queued before the armory. Seeing his goal, he dropped the pretense of running, sauntering up behind the broadly sweating back of Special-Trooper Early.

"What's the word, Early? Legit or not?" Reming asked, without even the courtesy of being winded.

"Dunno," rumbled Early, turning his thick neck to reply, the back of his shaved head still flushed from exertion. "Alert popped off, and I ran. Got here as the line started up."

"Did they open the window?" inquired Reming. "Or is Sikes not back there yet?"

"Window's open," called Private Almar from farther up the line. "Sikes is just taking his sweet-ass time."

"He better get moving," Reming said dryly, rolling his eyes. "I'd hate for the attack to be over, and I'm still standing here waiting for a rifle."

Shifting to peer around Early's thick body, Reming searched up and down the line.

"Where's Konrad? Isn't he supposed to help during weapons issue? Speed this shit up?"

"Haven't seen him," answered Almar with a shrug. "Maybe he's on a Raider mission?"

"I heard he's out hunting Gluffants with a spoon," another trooper called out at the front of the line.

"He's probably already on the ship, snapping Vickys' necks," chimed a voice from the middle.

"Maybe he's prepping the weapons array," Early offered, wiping the sweat on his brow. "I heard the Raiders qualified him to fire the Ion Cannon single-handed."

"Or maybe the big oaf was trapped by the fear-shits as soon as the alarms started," grumbled Reming under his breath.

The Commando Raiders were the ICF's elite special operations unit tasked with carrying out the toughest missions in any environment. Molded of myths and legends, they rained fire upon the Coalition's foes, accomplishing daring exploits under odds that defied the imagination. Their missions were covert, kept under the tightest secrecy for years after a conflict ended or whenever a Raider retired with a lucrative tell-all lined up. They were celebrated, heralded by soldiers and civilians alike. They drank for free at any bar on any ICF installation. They boasted the best equipment, with an operating budget so classified it was only approved by the Small Council. Their unit logos adorned the walls of children throughout the Coalition Republic.

Their training was secretive, their capabilities untold. No one knew for sure how many Commando Raiders were even serving at any given time. Their selection pipeline sported a washout rate of ninety-five percent, with twenty percent of prospective recruits dying in the process. These were the acceptable operating conditions that forged the pinnacle tip of the ICF's pointy spear, creating a force more capable than any other in man's history.

Private Konrad was a relative newcomer to the unit, arriving just before they tripped out. Older, scarred, and taciturn, it was rumored that he'd served a campaign with the Raiders before being transferred to work remote tours. Private Konrad was a mystery to the troopers of AZH-01. The younger troopers puzzled over his enigmatic origins, and chased down the meaning between his scant words. The more experienced troopers gave him a wide berth, figuring if there was any truth to the rumors, he was probably trouble. Special-Trooper Reming just thought he was an asshole.

Reming groaned in exasperation as the line shuffled forward, at least one trooper having succeeded in retrieving a weapon from the slow hands of Senior-Sergeant Sikes. A clatter arose behind him, forcing Reming to turn. He caught sight of Private Konrad sprinting towards the armory, arms held stiff and out, pumping with furious purpose. Coolly, Reming observed the flush behind the crisscrossing scars of the youth's face, sweat dripping from the craggy brows. Konrad stopped midway down the line, composing himself with an audible crack of his neck. He strode to the front, offering a dismissive snort to the other troopers before disappearing behind the door next to the armory window. *Oh good*, thought Reming dully, *a hero arrives in our time of need.*

Private Li dropped off the last rung of the ladder onto the grated walkway of the access tunnel. Side-stepping the oily drip of condenser water, he looked back up the chute at the huffing form of Senior-Trooper Leonard, still halfway up the ladder. Not for the first time that day, Private Li sighed in frustration. He'd volunteered to go first, if only to avoid being trapped above the sweaty Senior-Trooper, hanging from the ladder as he was slowly engulfed in the miasma of Leonard's exertions.

He wasn't sure which direction led to the weapons array. He needed the more experienced trooper for that information. Underneath the curved metal dome of AZH-01 stretched a warren of crisscrossing hallways, corridors, and tunnels. Designed from a standardized template to be employed in any alien environment the ICF decided required the dedicated application of trooper manpower, the station stretched nearly five kilometers across. It was developed to house and maintain an expeditionary force of up to ten thousand, but on the frozen planet of AZH at the edges of Coalition space, the vast station was put to work serving less than thirty troopers, with hundreds of its rooms and hallways empty and unused.

And so Li waited, tapping his foot as Leonard descended with all the practiced grace of a hippo negotiating stairs.

"You can do it man," he called up indifferently. "I believe in you."

After waiting another minute, Li called back up the shaft. "Hey man, which way is it? Left or right?"

"Left," came the breathy response from Leonard, struggling down another rung.

Li nodded in appreciation, weighing his options in abandoning the weapons technician. After careful contemplation, he shook his head. The station was just too big, he reasoned, and he'd only been to the Ion Array once before. Besides, the initializers for the Ion Cannon's main array were complicated, and Li lacked Leonard's years of experience. With another sigh he resigned himself to staying put, awaiting the arrival of his perspiring charge.

Reed-Sergeant Ramos paced along the center deck of the control center, stopping alternately to strum his fingers impatiently on the railing. Lieutenant Preston waited with his arms still crossed, occasionally shifting his weight from one foot to the other. Buck-Sergeant Wingo stood beside him, his arms crossed in a facsimile of leadership presence.

For the third time that morning Sergeant Ramos raised his mug to his lips, noting with extreme displeasure that it was still empty. He cast his eyes around for an object on which to vent his frustrations. He spied a short trooper with black hair passing by the deck.

"Johnson, go and get geared up," Sergeant Ramos ordered. "We may need you to do a manual reboot from outside the dome."

"Sir?" the puzzled trooper asked, pointing to himself. "I'm not Johnson, I'm Smith."

"I'm Johnson," called another dark-haired trooper from across the room, peeking up from behind a desk.

The Reed-Sergeant glowered at both men, castigating them for their impudence. The diminutive troopers quailed beneath his punishing glare.

"Fine," he accepted in clipped acknowledgement. "Smith, *you* go get geared up for a manual reboot outside the dome."

"And Johnson," he added, gesturing with his empty mug. "You go with."

Satisfied, Sergeant Ramos renewed his grievance with the emptiness of the main screen.

"Joelson, Sergeant K! It's been twenty minutes, how do we not have a fuckin' visual read?"

Senior-Trooper Joelson popped up from under his desk, his shoulders draped in a mess of wires, glasses askew.

"Working on it, Sarge. There's some kind of connectivity issue with the subspace cameras. The feed isn't processing from the suborbital tether."

He paused to halt the slow escape of his glasses from the bridge of his dark nose. "We're attempting a manual patch-in to see if that redresses the connectivity."

Sergeant Ramos grumbled in acceptance. He turned his attention to the Special-Trooper seated at the desk below him.

"Rania," he began. "What's the sensor picture look like?"

Special-Trooper Rania focused on the readings flowing across her glowing monitor. She took a deep breath before answering.

"PMZs indicate it's a *Vaunted* class ship. Based on the size and potential armament, the subsystem classifies it as a Tier-3 threat. Right now it's hanging out just beyond stable orbit."

"Why would they do that?" asked Lieutenant Preston, pulling his attention from the empty main screen.

"They might be banking their solar sails," she answered. "Or they might be scanning the surface for geo-terrain intel."

"Or they might be the advance scout for a larger force," growled Sergeant Ramos.

"Or that," affirmed Rania, swallowing hard before continuing. "Unfortunately, I can't tell intent from the sensors alone."

The officer nodded, thanking the Special-Trooper for her input. He mused over this latest development, running his hand over his pointed chin. His reverie was interrupted by the arrival of Senior-Sergeant Sikes, pushing through the swinging doors.

"Bright mornings, gentlemen!" Sergeant Sikes called out, striding towards the center deck. "What level is our morale today?"

A grumbled reply muttered forth from nine indifferent throats. Sergeant Sikes maintained his cheerful, toothy smile, never wavering as he mounted the stairs of the deck. "What is it?" he asked.

"Tier-3 ship," responded Sergeant Wingo, grateful to exercise some amount of his limited expertise.

"Great, great," replied Sergeant Sikes. "Do we have a visual yet?"

A groan arose around the room. Lieutenant Preston turned his attention to the Senior-Sergeant. He cut back his initial reply, noting with some amusement that the vein in Sergeant Ramos' forehead had begun to pulse angrily.

"Not yet," Lieutenant Preston said through a wry smile. "But we're working on it."

The officer turned his attention back to Sergeant Ramos.

"Any word from Leonard and Li?"

Private Li swung down to the next level from the safety railings along the stairs, feet never touching the steps. Alighting on the grated floor, he looked back at his grunting colleague. Senior-Trooper Leonard made his way cautiously down the stairs, hands gripping each rail tightly for support. Looking ahead, the access tunnel opened up into a large vehicle bay. As they headed towards it, they were greeted by the soft sounds of a struggle echoing tinny in the hollow chamber. Private Li stepped into the bay with Leonard right behind him, blinking timidly in the brighter light. The sounds came from two petite men, one wrestling to assist the other in pulling their CWAPL over his head.

"Yo, Smith, need any help?" Li asked, waving as he passed the tangle of troopers.

"It's Johnson," came the stifled reply, the rest lost in a muffled struggle with the thick-hooded garment.

"Whatever, man," said Li under his breath. "The *crapple* goes on first, then the face mask."

Leonard and Li proceeded into the hallway adjoining the bay. Nearing their destination, Li picked up the pace, breaking into a light jog and putting some distance between himself and his partner. Leonard struggled behind him, breath coming out in gasps as they came upon the door to the Ion Array. They entered into a small room, covered floor to ceiling in paneled displays. Li approached the nearest blinking console as Leonard leaned against a cabinet to recover. Much to his disappointment, Li was made instantly aware of how small the room they occupied was, and how tightly he was confined in with the Senior-Trooper. He sighed, resolving to try breathing through his mouth.

Four men stood on the center deck of the control room, bathed in the blue glow of the main screen. Eight eyes tracked the careful progress of the loading bar in the left corner, tracing its path to the right. A notification sound not unlike a bubble being popped echoed over the quiet efforts of the troopers in the room.

"Answer call," declared Lieutenant Preston, opening up the communication line.

"Control? This is Li."

"Go ahead Li, whatcha got?" the Lieutenant inquired calmly.

"Initializers are up and running. The Ion Cannon is prepped, sir. Just need a visual feed for targeting."

"Excellent," said the officer, letting out a calming breath. "We should have visual on screen any minute now. Good work, thanks."

Lieutenant Preston closed the conversation with another bubble pop, turning to Sergeant K for confirmation. Sergeant Kyrghizwald nodded and gave the officer a thumbs-up. Briefly the screen went black, before being replaced with the fuzzy image of stars. Applause rang out with a smattering of cheers as the visual feed focused on a squat, beetle-shaped ship, hanging in the space above planet AZH. The room was silent as everyone inspected the screen with bated breath, ten sets of eyes searching for meaning behind the ship's appearance. The Lieutenant was the first to speak.

"Joelson, try and zoom in on their colors, I need a better visual of their markings."

Senior-Trooper Joelson hurried to comply, enhancing the image to highlight the pictograms on the side of the ship's hull. As the image coalesced into greater detail, the control room waited on tenterhooks.

"It's a mining barge," announced Lieutenant Preston suddenly, recognizing the logo of three dashed lines across a crescent fish. "Banking sun before their next jump in the shipping lanes. It's okay everyone, just a false alarm."

A wave of collective relief rippled across the room.

"Pack it in folks, nothing more to see here," Sergeant Ramos declared as troopers across the room began powering down their monitors. Sergeant K and Joelson exchanged high-fives before clearing up the mess of wires surrounding their desk.

"Good work everyone," Lieutenant Preston concluded. "Leaders, to the Command Den for after actions."

Once in the Command Den, Lieutenant Preston stood before his NCOs, digital tablet in hand to take notes.

"Alright," he opened. "General situation was a Tier-3 threat assessed against an Orbyx Mining Barge based on readings from the initial PMZ sensors."

He looked around the room as heads nodded in confirmation. He continued.

"Initial response was positive-mixed. Our alarm readiness was active, but it took thirty-seven minutes to get a visual, and that was after necessitating a hardline re-feed."

Lieutenant Preston paused, turning to address Senior-Sergeant Sikes.

"How was the arming response?" he inquired. "Did we get weapons issue done in our allotted time?"

"It was great, great," replied Sergeant Sikes, his pale eyes darting around the room. "Weapons issue was as smooth as could be, expedient and without delay!" he added, voice lilting up.

Lieutenant Preston paused, scrutinizing the face of the senior NCO. Sergeant Ramos scoffed, chuffing softly into his fresh mug of SimuCaff. Lieutenant Preston shook his head and continued, ignoring the Senior-Sergeant's odd reply.

"So that's the third false alarm this quarter. Do we need to recalibrate? Turn down the PMZ sensitivity?" he asked, addressing the room once more.

"The sensors are right where they should be," offered Sergeant K, speaking for the group. "You don't want to turn them down and risk missing a smaller class ship."

"Better a false alarm than no alarm," gruffed Sergeant Ramos in agreement. "Keeps the troopers engaged."

"Absolutely, Reed-Sergeant," interjected Senior-Sergeant Sikes. "These false alarms are a challenge for the men. After all, 'discipline needs challenges, challenges breed unity. And unity in duty, duty for unity!'" he finished, voice rising once again on the back of the ICF's slogan.

Sergeant Ramos could not contain his disgust, staring daggers at the Senior-Sergeant. Lieutenant Preston interrupted, cutting off the Reed-Sergeant before he had a chance to respond.

"That's all well and good," Lieutenant Preston acknowledged, attempting to defuse the room and bring the conversation back on track. "But the troopers are still going to be frustrated. They signed up for action, and they aren't getting any."

"They came to the wrong place for that," chuckled Sergeant Wingo. "Ain't no action at the Snowglobe in the seven cycles I've been here."

"He's right, LT" sighed Sergeant Ramos, shifting the focus of his displeasure. "AZH-01 is about as far from the fight as you can get."

Lieutenant Preston swept these objections away with a wave of his hand.

"Nevertheless," he declared. "We are here for a reason. We're the only installation capable of hosting a surface-to-space Ion Cannon in remote space, and we're the only deep-detection sensor point between the outer ring and the core Coalition system. We're the last chance to detect and defeat threats to the Republic before they enter the core system. That includes Karnassus, so as far as I'm concerned, our work is one in the same with the ICF fight against the Vickys there."

He paused before adding, "It's easy to lose track of that though, so we may need to remind the troopers at the next formation. Show them that we value their work. Make sure our lines of communication are clear."

The gathered leaders nodded in agreement, pledging to ensure no trooper was forgotten in the scope of their efforts.

Private Li walked down the alloy hallway, searching for answers on his way back to his room. He'd waited in that claustrophobic room for as long as he could hold his breath. When the amber lights stopped flashing on the wall and he still hadn't been given the order to fire, Li surmised that it maybe, just possibly, it might have been a false alarm. Lacking any new communication from the control room, he set out for more sleep or more information, whichever came first, leaving Leonard to power down the Ion Cannon alone.

As he wandered through the halls, he began to pass troopers headed back from the armory. Catching sight of Special-Trooper Reming, he hustled alongside to pepper him with questions.

"What's the word, Rem?" Li asked.

"False alarm," said Reming, heading towards the chow hall. "Orbyx Mining Barge, but the visual feed was too slow. So we genned-up for nothing."

"Again?" Li questioned, crestfallen.

Reming nodded, plodding ahead in his quest for breakfast. Li slowed behind him, stopping in the hallway.

"When am I going to see some fuckin' action around here?" he asked the empty walls.

The creature hustled along the frozen expanse, leaping to cross a narrow ravine. It was cold, far colder than it had ever been before. Its usual range terminated along the southern shelf, where winter was a season to be endured, not this ever-present state of being. The creature surged ahead, summiting a frigid dune, its breath escaping in steamy gasps from the shimmering orange vents along its side. It despised the cold, insomuch as it could hate anything, but it felt an instinctual resistance to the prolonged discomfort of the snow-plagued steppe.

Still it pressed on, broad face to the wind, a mobile hill propelled by a singular drive: hunger. It stopped at the top of the peak, clicking its sickle claws in quiet contemplation. It surveyed the plains before it, taking in the sounds and smells carried to its senses on the winds. Food, it thought, a virulent and angry yearning churning up from inside its vast belly. The food was far more plentiful than it could have thought, substantial herds of hoofed beasts, slow and dimwitted from their years of domestication. The creature relished their hunting, ambushing them in a rush of terror and a flurry of hulking, white fur. The young ones were easiest, as they strayed from their parents' side, but even the older males posed little threat.

The creature studied the plains, reaching out to envision the currents of activity before it. It detected prey below, another one of the slow moving herbivores, this one staggering around a crack in the earth. This prey was far simpler to find than any in the southern latitudes, where the creature stalked swift, meager meals among the fungal forests. The creature opened and closed its cavernous jaws, scythed forelimbs clicking in anticipation. Charting a course towards its next hunt, it hopped along down the snow-capped ridge. There was food here, far more than a thousand years of evolution would have led it to believe. Supply was ample enough, able to briefly satiate its pernicious hunger.

But that was not why it ventured north, so far past its usual range. As it wandered down the icy crags to its next hunting position, it looked ahead to the north. There, on the northern edge of the horizon, came THE GLOW. It dwarfed anything it had ever sensed before. It was THE GLOW that drew it onwards.

CHAPTER 4:

Snow crunched beneath honeycombed wheels as the MMUTCAT churned ahead across a moonlit plain. A plume of dust and snow rose behind the behemoth, brick-like machine, kicked up by the spinning of eight, immense tires. The still, frigid air filled with the low rumble of the engine, punctuated by the occasional squelch of rocks driven deeper into the compacted ice. Bouncing along in the cab, Special-Troopers Reming and Early were locked in the most important strategic discussion of the twenty-fourth century.

"Teddy Roosevelt could beat a Striker 526 in a fight."

Reming snorted. "That guy from the vidplays? How?"

"He was smart and strong," Early announced, as if the argument was a foregone conclusion by those points alone. His eyes remained on the frozen landscape, measuring his course along the blinking waypoint.

"He's from the 1900s!" exclaimed Reming. "I don't care how smart he was, he's not going up against a hundred tons of Coalition firepower and surviving. It has six tempered-beam cannons *and* a mini-Ion Array. Roosevelt would be glassed from a hundred miles away."

"Nuh-uh," countered Early, bald head bouncing along in the crowded cab. "He started the Rough Riders. They'd outflank it."

"It's got polyreactive armor!" Reming protested. "And he had what? A *gun*? That shot *bullets*?"

"He'd find a weak spot," Early explained calmly, still focused on the viewscreen as he guided the massive vehicle between snow hills.

"It's the ICF's main battle tank! It doesn't have any weak spots!" Reming cried out, throwing his hands up in frustration.

"Sure it does, they just don't tell you where they are," said Early, leaning in with a conspiratorial whisper. "They want you to believe it's invincible so you feel safe when you're riding in it. Do you really think the ICF has your best interests at heart?" Early tapped two fingers on the side of his shaved skull.

"Besides," he said, "Roosevelt hunted tigers."

Reming snorted in disbelief. "How tough could a tiger really be? They've been extinct for two hundred years."

"He hunted bears too," the big trooper added.

Reming fell silent, chewing over this latest information. One of the last remaining megafauna, bears remained a scourge on the outskirts of every major Earth city. Six hundred pounds of claws, fangs and mottled fury, bears posed one of the few natural threats to man. Each year was marked by a few hundred attacks, every event sensationalized in explicit, colorful detail by the *Republic News Network* anchors.

"Anyway," Reming contended after thinking a moment. "Didn't he have tuberculosis or something?"

"Asthma," Early corrected "And he beat it."

The burly trooper took a deep breath before launching into another one of his rare, rambling, intermittently insightful, baritone monologues.

"That was his whole deal, never accept your limitations. Embrace the 'strenuous life' to overcome any challenge. It's why he was the greatest. He was a hunter, then a soldier, then a politician. We complain when we don't get the posting we wanted or the Linknet is down. Life didn't go his way, *so he made his own*. When they didn't let him in the army, *he made his own*. When they didn't let him lead the party, *he made his own*. Nothin' stopped him, not sickness, not a bullet, *nothin.*' He wasn't satisfied with what he had. He climbed the mountain in front of him, just because it was there. It's the climb that measures a man, the drive. And it's the drive we should all push for."

A pause stretched between the troopers as the MMUTCAT rumbled along. Reming was taken aback by the second longest stretch of words he'd ever heard from the traditionally succinct Special-Trooper.

"A Striker is a helluva lot harder to beat than a mountain," insisted Reming after a moment, turning away to look out the side viewscreen. "You're just ate up with him 'cause of that screenjob they did a few years back. That whole series was exaggerated, I mean, it had him riding a moose for fuck's sake."

"He could beat it," Early declared with finality. "He's the toughest man ever."

"Was," corrected Reming. "And that's if he existed at all, you can't believe everything off the vidplays."

Rania stood very still in the center of chaos. Slender hands on her hips, she surveyed the piles of loose pages, rumpled clothes, and scattered gear. Her CWAPL lay crumpled in the corner, her boots were in a tangle under the chair, and her goggles hung precariously from the edge of her desk. She sighed, stepping back and kicking over an empty bottle.

Every year she swore that she'd get organized, that now would be the time she buckled down and cleaned up her act, but it had been like this ever since she was a little girl. Many times her father would come behind her, sweeping her up in a tight embrace. *Alhamdu lilleh Rania,* he'd say, *I thought that haboob had carried you away!* She'd look at him in bewilderment, asking what he meant. *The sandstorm, ya eini, the one that destroyed your room! I was worried it had taken you with it.* She'd rolled her eyes then, but she missed it now-- missed hearing him chastise her with words from the old country. He was the last one she knew who spoke Arabic, the last one who still prayed. She wished she shared that with him--his sense of purpose and connection. No matter where they went, he could always turn to Mecca.

A knock at the door interrupted her reveries. Working around a swaying tower of technical manuals, Rania made her way towards the furious rapping, kicking aside another empty bottle to crack open the door. Li stood in the hallway, hands still hammering the air where the door used to be. He was looking over his slight shoulder to Senior-Trooper Joelson, still staring absentmindedly at the ceiling. Turning back to the open door, Li stopped knocking.

"Vidplay?" he asked, heart-shaped face splitting into a lopsided grin. "Linknet came up long enough to download *Demonster House IV: Bedlam and Breakfast.* Almar's already in, and Joelson said he's still got some popcorn left from his last care package."

Rania looked back at the anarchy of her room, perpetually locked in a violent revolution against good order and discipline. Weighing her options, she acquiesced to the crushing pressure of their offer.

"Sure," she shrugged, shutting the door behind her. *I can always clean tomorrow.*

Lieutenant Preston sat alone in the dark, staring a hole into the white expanse of his monitor screen. His chin rested in his hand, index finger pointing up along his temple. His other hand idly tapped the seat of his chair. The title of his thesis yawned back at him in bold black letters, while the small cursor shouted at him from the edge of the line. He stared it down, intimidating the thin, blinking, black line. In a flurry of motion he snapped his hands to the desk, fingers flying over the terminal keys. *Enter*, he tapped, a new line started. He rapped the space bar twice before leaning back in his chair to survey his work. He scowled at the blank page before settling in to massage the bridge of his nose.

The lights flickered on in the Command Den, triggered by the motion of Buck-Sergeant Wingo and Reed-Sergeant Ramos stepping through the doorway. Lieutenant Preston looked up from his hands, grateful for the distraction.

"That's it! I'm fucking *done!*" shouted Sergeant Ramos, gesturing wildly with his empty mug. "Do they think this is a fucking game?" he asked the room, the mug cutting a wide swathe through the air.

"I mean, kind of, I guess," protested Sergeant Wingo. "They're here, they're bored, they think it's funny." He raised his hands in a shrug.

Sergeant Ramos stormed over to the SimuCaff brewer, pausing halfway to jab at Sergeant Wingo with his mug.

"Do *you* think it's funny?" His dark brown eyes narrowed to vengeful slits.

"Oh no, not at all," the Buck-Sergeant sputtered, raising his palms and shaking his head. "I just get it, that's all. It's not ok. It's disrespectful."

"And?" probed Sergeant Ramos, cocking an eyebrow.

"And, it's demeaning?" Sergeant Wingo offered, stalling on the first word as he grasped for an answer.

"AND IT'S PREJUDICIAL TO THE DISCIPLINE OF THIS UNIT!" thundered Sergeant Ramos, the hot beverage sloshing out of his mug.

"I almost think you enjoy this shit," he hissed, shaking his hand and scattering drops of the scalding brown liquid on the floor. A small cough drew their attention to the back of the room. Lieutenant Preston looked back at both of them with an inquiring raise of his eyebrows.

"What's the noise, boys?" he asked.

Sergeant Ramos dropped his shoulders with a final shake of disgust.

"Sergeant Wingo found more graffiti in the East Hall." He turned back to pour more SimuCaff from the carafe.

Lieutenant Preston shifted his gaze to the thickset Buck-Sergeant.

"Someone scratched another 'E' into the marker sign," explained Sergeant Wingo, still cowed from the Reed-Sergeant's outburst. The Lieutenant nodded, comprehending at last. Graffiti had been a recurring problem at AZH-01, with troopers expressing their thoughts on the station with the addition of the letter 'E' at the end of the title marker.

"I'm fucking done with this shit, LT," Sergeant Ramos continued. "The next time I catch one, I'll have the whole crew scrubbing this station with their fuckin tongues. Then I'll…"

Lieutenant Preston tuned out the rest of the Reed-Sergeant's ever-more inventive stream of punishments, turning his attention back to his barren thesis. 'AZH01E,' the officer mused. The station's amended name was used frequently as a moniker for both the command staff and the troopers posted on the remote, frozen installation. *I guess that makes me the king of the assholes...*

Special-Trooper Reming dismounted the MMUTCAT's cab, pivoting from the last rung of the white-painted ladder to the oversized wheel. Special-Trooper Early needed no such acrobatics, gently lowering his substantial bulk from the ladder into the snow. Straightening against the wind, they both turned to walk to the frozen spire.

"It had to be Quebec-7," carped Reming. "Oldest piece-of-shit out here."

"Uh-huh, and you know there's another skitter nest in the exhaust vent," Early pointed out.

"Not again," whined Reming. "I thought they made Konrad take care of that shit last time. After he failed his upgrade exam."

"Guess he didn't," huffed Early, lumbering ahead towards the tower. "He probably had something better to do."

Reming cursed under his breath before mushing through the frozen slog. He managed one step in the deep snow pile, discovering with some dismay that his other foot was stuck fast.

"Ah sick," he noted with weary disgust. "I landed in Gluffant shit."

"Need help?" asked Early, trudging out against the blowing snow. "I can lift you out of there."

He contorted his body to flex through the thick suit.

Reming considered his options before shaking his head.

"Nah, I got it," he said, sitting down in a huff. As Early stomped over to the sensor tower, Reming leveraged his full strength towards extricating his boot. *I'm fucking done with this shit.*

Back in the warm confines of the Command Den, Lieutenant Preston continued his struggle against the blank pages of his research. In the background, he paid half a mind to the escalating war stories swapped between Sergeant Wingo and Sergeant Ramos. The latest series concerned the antics of Senior-Sergeant Nix, the previous tenant of Sergeant Sikes' office.

"Did I tell you about the time he responded to a possible Tier-2 naked?" guffawed Buck-Sergeant Wingo.

Sergeant Ramos snorted into his mug.

"No! Where was I during that?" he coughed, wiping his face with the back of one swarthy hand.

"Oh, this was about two years ago," answered Sergeant Wingo. "You musta been home on leave."

The Lieutenant's ears perked up--leave in the middle of a tour was rare indeed, usually only reserved for personal emergencies.

"Right, right," confirmed the Reed-Sergeant. "Back in 2330."

"Anyway, there we were," began the Buck-Sergeant, "middle of mid-shift, must have been about 0200. All of a sudden the alarm comes out of nowhere. It's a Tier-2, so everyone is freaking out. LT Baxter, you remember him, with the slicked-back hair? He was freaked, shaking so bad I had to grab him a chair to sit in on the center deck, dragged it up the stairs myself."

Lieutenant Preston sighed, he had heard a few stories about his predecessor, none flattering. It was always difficult to take over a new unit, especially when the previous regime erased most of the mystique of the officer role. The Buck-Sergeant continued, voice rising as he laid out the scene.

"We're all scrambling, here and there, trying to figure out if we should prep the Ion Array or send a distress call back to command." Sergeant Wingo slapped his knee with a fleshy hand.

"We're waiting for the main screen to come up. Every sensor is telling us it's at least a *Solomon* class ship, maybe even more than one. Definitely a pucker moment as we wait for visuals."

Sergeant Ramos nodded, swept up in the junior sergeant's story.

"Then the screen comes up, and it's just a comet, coming from some deep-range orbit, passing through the outskirts of the sensor field. We're all breathing a sigh of relief, even LT is calming down."

The Buck-Sergeant paused for dramatic effect.

"We're all patting ourselves on the back, just happy we're not gonna die, when in runs Nix! He's got an R-91 in each hand, sweatin' like he just ran a marathon, wearing nothing but his boots!"

Sergeant Ramos spat out his SimuCaff.

"No way!" he choked out, setting his mug down to clean up the mess. "Nothing but his boots?"

"On my life," swore Sergeant Wingo. "You should have seen it, Nix sweatin', dingus hangin' in the wind. The LT bugged out. He just kept stutterin' 'Sergeant Nix, that is *NOT* an acceptable uniform!' We couldn't believe it." Sergeant Wingo sighed, wiping a tear from the corner of his eye.

"I miss Nix," Sergeant Ramos admitted. "He was salty, but he gave a shit." Sipping from his mug, "That's a trait rarer each day."

"Yeah, I miss him too, poor guy. Cockroach allergy right?" Sergeant Wingo asked, still holding his sides in laughter.

The Reed-Sergeant nodded. "Yep, not a lot we can do about it. There isn't an ICF post that isn't crawling. Allergy means a one-way ticket to an early retirement."

"You remember what he said on his way out?" Sergeant Wingo asked.

"Of course," a sly smile crept across Sergeant Ramos' face.

"Kiss my black ass goodbye!" they shouted in unison, smacking the table and startling Sergeant K as he walked through the door of the Command Den.

"N-n-not to bother you," Sergeant Kyrghizwald stammered, winding his way around the giggling NCOs. "But I just got done talking with Johnson about the next supply drop."

Lieutenant Preston looked at Sergeant K in confusion.

"Johnson?" he questioned, "Isn't he on days? What's he doing answering the CommNet this late at night?"

Sergeant Kyrghizwald paled, adding further contrast to purple bags set deep around his watery eyes. *He looks like he got road-hauled behind a MMUTCAT*, thought the Lieutenant, *must be one of his 'off' days*.

"S-s-sorry sir, I must be mistaken," sniffed the junior NCO. "Must have been Smith."

"Easy mistake to make," acknowledged Lieutenant Preston, hoping to bolster the fraught Buck-Sergeant. "You were saying?"

"Yes, uh, the supply drop. The next one," sputtered Sergeant K. "Smith says it's going to be delayed by at least a week. The transport freighter got held up waiting for a subspace lane. They won't be in position for the orbital supply drop until middle of next week."

The Lieutenant grimaced, sweeping a hand through his short red hair. *That's going to hit morale pretty hard. The troopers count on those shipments.* Not to mention, he was still waiting on a package of his own, a rare copy of the film series that formed the subject of his research. He thanked the Buck-Sergeant for the update, dismissing him with a wave of his hand. Sergeant Wingo and Sergeant Ramos turned back to their discussion, chatting again on the inspiring audacity of Senior-Sergeant Nix. Lieutenant Preston returned his attention to his monitor, his paltry paragraph of text mocking him for his efforts. With a sneer of disgust he signed out of the monitor. Standing up to leave, he resolved to get some rest before the next shift. *I can always write tomorrow.*

Special-Trooper Reming pried the occluded nest off the exhaust grate with a final heave of his crowbar. Off balance, he fell backwards into the snow, chest heaving from the effort. Special-Trooper Early watched him with bemused detachment, no offers of assistance this time.

Standing up, Reming dusted the snow from his thighs, marching back up to the tower with grim resolve. His path was blocked by a cat-sized blue arthropod, rising up on multi-jointed legs. It swiveled its black eyestalks towards him, gnashing its jaws, and buzzing its carapace with alien fury. Without missing a beat, Special-Trooper Reming walked up to the Snow-Skitter and punted it aside, sending its clicking limbs careening into the nearest snowbank.

Annoying, but not a threat, *xenoarthropoda terenix*'s mandibles were only used for grinding, perfectly adapted to scour the native lichen from the icy ground. The only fauna known to be indigenous to AZH, the Snow-Skitters were largely ignored by the colonizers from earth, both the two-legged and four-legged varieties. The only danger they presented came from their obnoxious habit of building nests in warm areas, particularly the tempting heat exhaust vents of the sensor towers. Created from an amalgamation of rock chips and the Skitters' cement-like feces, the nests were difficult to chip off, requiring painstaking work to hammer them away.

Special-Trooper Reming didn't reflect on the existential questions raised by a space-faring interloper disrupting the natural habitat of native species--he was just pissed that it was him who had to do the hammering.

"Fuckin' Konrad. Raiders made him too fuckin' *special* to do his fuckin' job," he grumbled under his breath.

"Yup," agreed Early, without looking up from his ScanTool. "I'm almost done debugging the infracodes."

"Great. Phenomenal. Out-fucking-standing," barked Reming, punctuating each word with a swing of his crowbar. "Wouldn't want you to utilize those great, big muscles you're always going on about," he snapped.

Early chuckled and shook his head, still poking at the codes displayed on his ScanTool. Reming kept swinging, cursing under his breath the whole time. He paused to wipe the flecks of nest from the goggles of his mask, panting as he sat down in a bank of snow. A lone Snow-Skitter watched from the top of the hill, buzzing with reproach. Reming heaved a chunk of ice, knocking the alien crustacean off its perch. *I'm alone on a planet of assholes,* Reming mused to the wind.

Alone in the woods, the woman stumbled forward, eyes wide with fear. Her breath came in short gasps, steam escaping towards a heaven encircled by the knotted branches of blackened trees. Tears ran down her muddied cheek, mixing with the blood from a gash on her forehead. A mournful howl arose behind her, pitiful in its wavering cry, like the hungry call of an immense infant. She swung her head back and forth, long tresses of blonde hair matted with twigs and leaves. She scoured the darkened woods for danger, panting in the grips of her terror. The howl came again, closer this time, seeking her out. She cast her eyes down the three branches of the forked path, desperately searching for a way out of her waking nightmare.

The woman froze, the camera paused in a dramatic close-up of her wide, blue eyes. The image held fast on the wall screen of the leisure den. Three options unfurled below the woman's eyes, as a thin orange line emerged in the center, shrinking rapidly to indicate the timer's countdown.

"Go left," suggested Private Almar. "Back towards the lake."

"No way man," Li said, running a hand through his spiky, black hair. "The lake has the *Kappa*, she's dead for sure."

"What about the middle?" offered Joelson, passing the bowl of popcorn. "Isn't that where her car is?"

"Yeah but that ending is boring," protested Li. "She just gets in it and drives away. The final shot is her at home, hugging her step daughter."

"I'm lost," confessed Rania, taking a handful of popcorn. "Didn't she get away during the first *Demonster House*, why would she go back?"

Li rolled his eyes, snapping his fingers to pause the timer bar. He turned in his seat, eager to educate his boorish squadmate.

"She got out in the canon storyline for *Demonster House I*, but if you watched the side plot for *Demonster House III*," Li said, adding extra emphasis to the titles' numbers, "you'd've seen that she goes back to recover her great aunt's amulet and break the spell of the demon ledger."

"That's dumb," said Rania. "If I survived a blood-draining death cult, I'd never go back to their hostel. Even *if* their biscuits got great reviews."

"Totally," agreed Private Almar from his chair across the room. "I'd write to the small council and get the whole house glassed from orbit. It's the only way to be sure."

Private Li threw up his hands in frustration.

"You're all missing the point! She can't spread awareness of the cult because that increases the strength of their power!" he cried.

"That's convenient," mumbled Joelson.

"Right?" argued Rania. "If that were the case then how come the cult doesn't advertise? Take some money and purchase a sky-banner or a print pop-up? Raise their own awareness so their blood god comes sooner?"

"Because," Li countered, shaking in irritation. "Because their message can't be committed to paper, we learned that in *Demonster House II: Concierge of Carnage*."

Waving his hand in the air to restart the video, he turned to the screen in a huff.

"We're going with the far right," Li declared, selecting the last option on the screen, "back to the winding cavern."

"What about the cult using a *video* commercial?" quipped Joelson through a mouthful of popcorn.

His suggestion was met with 'oohs' from around the room. Li threw his head back, sighing in exasperation. *There's no reaching these people,* he thought to himself. The others ignored the woman's plaintive cries on screen to discuss the minute difficulties in getting a cursed teleplay past the Republic's censors. *They just don't appreciate good art.*

Reming and Early climbed into the MMUTCAT's cab, settling into the patch-worn seats. Reming slammed the door shut, stripping the mask off his sweat-drenched face.

"SimuWhey?" Early offered, holding out a bottle of chalky beverage.

"No, thanks," said Reming, pulling out a box of candy and leaning back in his seat. "Wouldn't want to get too big and challenge you for your title of Mr. AZHOLE."

Early snorted, chuckling as he strapped in for the ride home. Pressing the ignition, the MMUTCAT shook to life, the low rumble of its engines filling the night air once again. As they headed west, back towards the station, they watched the rising of AZH's second moon, an orange glow bright against the darkened sky. As he nudged the throttle forward, Early turned back to his miserable compatriot.

"Mind if I play a little country?" he asked, swiping the screen on his portable speaker.

"Whatever, man, just wake me when we're home." Reming closed his eyes as he turned towards the side viewscreen. Watching his partner slouch into some meager comfort, Early shrugged, setting the glowing blue speaker down as the cabin filled with the twang of acoustic guitar. Turning back towards the front, he cracked his thick neck, settling in for the long ride back. *Some people just don't appreciate art.*

CHAPTER 5:

With bated breath, four troopers held their position. Watching, waiting, they scanned the dim cavern for the enemy they knew would come. It dropped from the ceiling suddenly, silently, a grimacing silhouette of bristling weapons and snarling ferocity. With palpable menace, the figure turned against the stalwart troopers huddled behind a low wall and charged their position. Rifle fire crackled through the air, peppering the silhouette with dime-sized holes, each perfectly round with edges that glowed orange. The enemy drew closer, impervious to its wounds, stopping just a few yards shy of the clustered troopers in the center of the room. A chime sounded through the cavern, the din of a brass gong ringing through the singed air.

In one fluid motion, two troopers slunk into a prone position, bracing their rifles in a crook on the wall. With practiced ease, the remaining troopers held fast, continuing their barrage and concentrating fire on the target's center mass. The prone troopers resumed their shooting, shredding the enemy's head with precision fire from their supported positions. A second chime sounded, clanging like giant brass marbles rolled in a sack. Cool eyes watched as the figure's progress stopped, torso swinging softly. It tore in half, ragged and frayed along the outline of a particularly dense grouping of shots. They watched the orange edges fade to black, glimpsing hollow sky through the cluster of holes in their enemy. Small smoke trails curled up from their shredded foe, mixing with the acrid tang of ozone and burning tires.

They did not have long to savor their triumph. Amber lights flashed along the concrete walls as a foghorn blast cut through the stale, seared air. A dozen silhouettes dropped from the ceiling, shifting and rotating as they set upon the troopers. Sweat ran in rivers down brows steeped in concentration. Across the room the troopers reacted swiftly to engage these new threats, each concentrating their fire on a section ahead of them, working to align their optics with the rapidly moving targets. The enemies' muzzles began flashing with light, spitting beams of infrared against the resolute troopers. The troopers ducked lower, maximizing the meager cover offered by their wall, each attempting to shore up targets in the glowing reticules of their optics.

A trooper went down on the left, his helmet marked by a well-placed shot from a particularly aggressive enemy. His cries of pain rose above the crackle of superheated fire, body twitching on the ground. The nearest trooper shifted position, bringing his R-91 to bear as he worked to close the gap opened up along their flank. The figures drew closer, taking fewer hits as they twirled around each other. They encroached upon the center troopers' position, threatening to envelop them. Bitterly the troopers hung on, drops of sweat sizzling on the burning muzzles of their weapons.

A voice rang out from another position, far right of the troopers grouped behind the wall. It rose above the din, echoing over the broiling sputter of particulate crossfire.

"Gotcha, bitch," cried Special-Trooper Early, pulling the trigger of his SLW-18.

For a brief moment the whole room brightened, bathed in red light. A thick beam erupted from the barrel of Early's bulbous cannon, surging ahead with a rumble like distant thunder. *Bwwwrrrrrrmmmm* echoed across the chamber, the laser cutting a fist-sized hole through three of the targets. Grunting with effort, Early shifted the immense bulk of the portable cannon, dragging the beam to cut through two more silhouettes. A small alarm chirped from the screen mounted on the side of the weapon's buttstock, indicating the rising temperature of its internal components. Early released the trigger, gasping as he lowered the heavy rifle. Like a snap of the Almighty's fingers, the beam of light winked suddenly out of existence. Small flaps opened up on the weapon's side, venting jets of superheated air down the four-foot expanse of barrel. Early pulled the *Squad Laser Weapon* back behind his own wall, throwing his substantial bulk down behind cover as the gun cooled. Panting from the strain, the burly Special-Trooper gave a thumbs-up to his assistant gunner. Private Almar nodded, kneeling to bring the barrel of his R-91 over the wall and cover them.

Cheers came from the four troopers in the center of the room. With newfound energy they fired up their rifles, engulfing the remaining targets in a rapid barrage of accelerated neutral particles. They tore through the remaining silhouettes, pausing only briefly to eject expended batteries and slam in new ones. As the last target ignited under the troopers' bombardment, another chime rang through the air, like a church bell rolling down a hill. The lights came up, illuminating the firing range. Helmeted heads popped up from behind covered positions, like meerkats peeking up on the savanna.

Reed-Sergeant Ramos strode through the empty hall with the Lieutenant in tow, rubber heels clicking on the worn concrete. Neatly side-stepping around the charred remains of the ICF Qualifier targets, Sergeant Ramos approached the four still huddled behind their low wall. He stood over the splayed form of Private Li, favoring the groaning trooper with a smile of paternal recognition. The Reed-Sergeant crouched down and extended a hand to Li, helping the young trooper to his feet on wobbly, jellied knees. Private Li stood briefly upright, took a tottering step back, and promptly reeled over to vomit on the dusty floor.

"Neural lock-up's a bitch, ain't it? Next time keep your head down, don't peek up so much when you're covering a low sector," Sergeant Ramos admonished, placing a hand on the trooper's heaving shoulder.

He looked the young Private straight in the eyes, adding softly, "Dying sucks, don't do it."

Stepping past Li to address the remaining troopers, Sergeant Ramos breathed in deep before launching his evaluation.

"Alright chuckle-fucks, let's break this cluster down step-by-step and see where it went wrong."

The Reed-Sergeant aimed a flattened, knife-like hand in the direction of the nearest chuckle-fuck.

"Reming, watch your trigger squeeze, your shots were all over the place. Keep it slow and smooth and you won't burn through so much ammo."

He swung the knife-hand around, slicing through the air as he rounded on the next trooper.

"Johnson, time your reloads. You never swap a battery at the same time as your flank mate, you keep the firing steady as a unit." The Reed-Sergeant pointed at the trooper's weapon for maximum effect.

Confusion crossed Private Smith's face. Across the room, Private Johnson stood up from his position alongside Private Konrad.

"Over here sir," he said, waving.

Sergeant Ramos snorted, beside him Lieutenant Preston began chuckling. The frown deepened on the Reed-Sergeant's face. He moved to address the troopers in the far left position.

"And what the fuck were *you* doing this whole time?" he unloaded on them. "You call that sorry shit-show flank protection?"

Rounding on Private Konrad, Sergeant Ramos jabbed the edge of four fingers in the scarred trooper's broad chest. "And you, firing no shots the whole round? Were you waiting on a personal invitation?"

Private Konrad regarded the Sergeant with dull eyes.

"Lining up a kill shot," he answered flatly.

A vein twitched in the Reed-Sergeant's forehead.

"That ain't your fucking job! This *ain't* the Raiders and you *ain't* some solo sniper! You provide covering fire as part of a unit, forget your job, and it's the *unit* that suffers!" Sergeant Ramos thundered, gesturing back at Private Li.

Konrad eyed Li as he braced against Reming, wiping bile from his mouth on the back of his sleeve. He shrugged without taking his eyes off the shaky trooper. Sergeant Ramos curled his lip in disgust. Determined not to lose the momentum of his critique, he wheeled away to address the rest of the team.

"Early, you've got to come in sooner with that *slaw*, don't wait for the stars to align before engaging to suppress."

The big trooper nodded. Timing was a critical skill in a squad's heavy gunner.

"And make sure you're dialing the focus for that beam, you have to match the terminal point to the specific target distance." The Reed-Sergeant gestured to Private Almar, "Your AG has a range finder equipped just for that. Dial it too near and you risk thermal bloom, too far and you over penetrate your targets."

He pointed at a black line etched along the wall of the firing range. The slagged concrete terminated inches from the low wall Johnson and Konrad still stood behind.

"You gotta mind your back-drop, over penetrate and you might have friendly fire."

Special-Trooper Early bobbed his shaved head, the criticism settling on his broad shoulders. Witnessing his effect on the young trooper, the Reed-Sergeant softened.

"Good communication with your AG though," he grumbled. Sergeant Ramos completed his tour of the room with a return to the four troopers gathered in the center position.

"Joelson, I need more command out of you. You're almost a Buck-Sergeant-- I need you to act like one. You know what needs to happen, so *lead* these assholes and make it so."

The Reed-Sergeant looked to the Lieutenant, inviting any additional critiques the officer might have to share. Lieutenant Preston shook his head, he knew better than to interrupt the Reed-Sergeant with his own ideas on the troopers' efforts. Sergeant Ramos pivoted away from Senior-Trooper Joelson, addressing the group as he headed towards the door.

"As we all learned from Private Li, those sensors in your training gear aren't just for show. You have to be smarter to avoid taking a hit. Utilize cover, use effective fire and movement, and you might just live through the real thing."

They left the troopers to collect their gear, proceeding past them out the door in the back of the range.

The troopers sprawled out in the dusty cleaning room, each seeking a comfortable position on the dingy alloy tile to strip their weapons. In short order the air was filled with mechanical clicks as latches were undone and dust covers opened. Metal on metal rasped as barrels were twisted and removed before being held to the light for inspection. Brass brushes were dipped in solvent, then bent to the pesky task of scraping ionized deposits built up inside their barrels.

Li looked up from his rifle, stretching his back while sighing.

"This is *bull*-shit," he groaned, ensuring he was loud enough to inflict his dissatisfaction on the other troopers.

"Join the ICF, they said. You'll shoot guns, they said. Action and adventure guaranteed," grumbled Reming, still bent over his R-91. "Recruiters never tell you about this shit when you're signing eight years away."

"Quit your bitching," drawled Early, lumbering past them with the SLW-18 cradled in his hands. He eased the fifty pound cannon on its thin, metal bipod before flopping down beside it. "At least the R-91 is light."

"That's what you get for being so big," mused Reming, brushing deposits from the particle emitter in the rifle receiver. Looking up, he adopted a sage expression and intoned with half-lidded eyes, "With great muscles, comes great responsibility."

Early snorted, twisting the barrel clockwise and drawing it out. Li eyed the massive weapon with a mix of admiration and envy.

"Aren't heavy gunners guaranteed a combat tour after their second security detail?" Li asked. "At least then you get to do some real shit."

"Ain't no guarantees in the ICF," grunted Early, polishing the lenses in the SLW barrel. "You either get someplace or you don't."

Li sighed, smearing grease on his cheek with the back of one hand.

"I didn't sign up for this shit. I wanted to go to Karnassus, do some real fighting."

Li's announcement was met with non-committal grunts around the room. "Join the club buddy!" was the only response, offered by a trooper in the back. Li looked around grasping for any conversation he could find.

"Joelson," he said, pointing his brush at the Senior-Trooper. "C'mon man, what did you join for?"

Joelson looked up from his rifle, smudging his glasses as he pressed them up the bridge of his nose.

"I was home-schooled my whole life, no Coalition assistance. When I turned eighteen I left. I wanted to travel, see something new."

"I thought you needed a special permit for that?" Li asked, pointing to the wire-rimmed glasses perched on the Senior-Trooper's nose. "What was it? Some kind of religious thing?"

"Nah," answered Joelson, checking the R-91's nooks and crevices for additional dirt. "Mom never trusted the Coalition after they liquidated her research department on Avina. Pulled me out of Republic school when I was seven. Hence the glasses--can't get the Coalition to pay for optical surgery without school enrollment."

Joelson took off his glasses and breathed on the lenses, wiping them off with a rag from his pocket. "When I joined the ICF, I'd worn them for so long they were comfortable, so I stuck with 'em."

Li nodded, turning his attention back to his rifle.

"I also joined for Karnassus," Smith offered, raising a hand from across the room.

"No one cares!" snapped a trooper by the door.

An alarm chimed softly from a monitor overhead. Sergeant Ramos and Lieutenant Preston strolled through the door, hustling the troopers to respond.

"Reming, Li, you're on deck for this one. It's Alpha-2," Lieutenant Preston said while Sergeant Ramos marshalled the troopers to their feet. Reming sighed, dropping his brush to snap his rifle back together.

"How come it's gotta be us?" asked Li, shoving his cleaning kit back in his locker. "Why can't the ICF use one of their kill-bots for guarding this shit?"

"Because then we wouldn't have our steady supply of trooper bitching," snapped Sergeant Ramos. "Which as we all know is the unlimited power source that fuels the ICF fleet."

"It's because of the cold," Lieutenant Preston answered, injecting a calm voice amid the mix. "Their hydraulics don't work as well."

This was not true. *Ground-Based Autonomous Sentries*, GBAS in ICF doctrine, *kill-bots* in common parlance, were actually quite resistant to all manner of temperature extremes. A perk of their reinforced armor, they were exceptionally capable of operating in any contested environment, bringing their armament to bear through rapid mobility on six double-jointed limbs. The only real drawback was their exclusive licensing and production by a particularly litigious defense contracting company, which stipulated that GBAS's could only be maintained by a certified company mechanic. Paying multiple corporate technicians for years of duty on remote assignments was quickly calculated to add an additional zero on the end of the ICF's yearly operating budget. As such, the decision was made to staff each remote post with ICF troopers, who, bitching aside, were a fraction of the cost of a unionized maintainer.

Lieutenant Preston didn't know any of this, but he was always loathe to appear ignorant in front of the troopers. Only twenty-four, he was the same age as many of the Senior-Troopers, a fact he kept secret as best he could. As such, he always made sure to offer an intelligent explanation to any enlisted seeking information, regardless of the gaps in his own knowledge. Better the trooper be wrong than he be seen as a 'green Lieutenant.'

Li was ignorant of the internal discussion filtering through the mind of his Lieutenant, but he was acutely aware that his own ass didn't fare so well in the cold either. Shrugging his rifle over his shoulder, he hustled out the door after Reming. *Fuckin' recruiter*, he grumbled, *I didn't sign up for this shit.*

The Gluffant stood solemn, alone on a snow-swept plain. It was massive, even for its kind, weighing in at seven tons. A majestic bull, blessed by fortuitous genetics with an extra half-inch to the length of his curved horns. The great bull thanked his forefathers when he put on full weight and his horns came in longer and thicker than those of his peers. He was the largest of his herd, and amongst his kind he was a benevolent king. He carried his weight proudly, regally, surveying the landscape and ruminating over his mastery of the domain. These were unusually complex thoughts for one of his breed, but today was an unusual, extraordinary day.

Perhaps it was the sun, the Gluffant mused, chewing over a mouthful of cud. He fixed a beady, black eye upwards and stared as hard as he could. The bull confirmed that it was still bright orange, still hanging out of reach, but noted that it seemed to be shining far brighter today. Unusually, encouragingly, bright.

Or perhaps it was the lichen, he considered. He had awoken with the sunrise as usual, letting out a rumbling, low bellow to announce to the world that it was, in fact, daytime. As he rose to his feet on broad, umber hooves, he had noted with considerable delight that he'd fallen asleep in an immense patch of lichen. He chewed on it thoughtfully, mulling over the fortunate circumstances that had blessed him by combining his favorite things; eating and sleeping. *No*, the Gluffant thought with a great shake of his shaggy head. He had awoken many days surrounded by lichen, the result of falling asleep while eating the night before.

It had begun at dawn, or so the bull reckoned, when he woke up to no ill-effects from the day before. He had gorged himself the day before, happening upon one of the spindly towers that denoted a ready supply of the vibrating air. He had bumped the tower then, as his kind had done many times before, shifting the steel supports with his immense bulk and exposing the piping in its base. He could still feel the surge of elation he experienced when he set about to chew on the piping, drinking in the intoxicating vapors as they escaped. Normally this was proceeded by discomfort the next day, shaky steps, ringing in his ears, and an unpleasant lurching in his stomach--penance wrought upon him by the capricious auroch gods. But not today. Today he woke up feeling strong. Immovable. Mighty.

The Gluffant's musings were cut short by a low, mechanical rumble growing steadily louder. The great bull turned a beady, black eye towards the west, noting the developing brick-like shape arriving on eight swift wheels.

The chirruping display on the MMUTCAT's viewscreen grew more insistent, announcing that their target destination was less than a kilometer away. Private Li prodded the screen, stabbing at the twinkling icon with one finger as he sought to acknowledge and mute the annoying display. In spite of his efforts, the icon only grew louder, its electronic razzle reaching a fever pitch.

"I know, I know! I can see it for fuck's sake!"

Li continued his futile jabbing of the dancing announcement.

"Can't you shut this thing up?" he asked, turning to his partner in the left seat.

"It's Gen III. After the update came out they won't let you mute them anymore," Reming said, dumping a handful of candy in his mouth.

"Why in the fuck would they do that?" Li demanded, pounding the screen with the palm of his hand.

Reming shrugged. "Some trooper probably fell asleep while driving, so they installed the beeping to keep us awake."

Li gave up, slumping back in his seat with an exasperated sigh.

"Gluffant ahead, don't hit it," the ruddy trooper said, pouring more candy into his hand.

"I see it," snapped Li, glaring back at his copilot. "Who the fuck could miss something that big?"

The Gluffant stood still as the imposing vehicle drove around him. The great bull watched it stop several yards short of the spindly tower, still cocked at a leeward angle from his activities the day before. The prodigious Gluffant observed it park, watching two figures climb down from the cab and stroll towards the tower. They were animated little things, jabbering to each other as they wrapped a chain around one of the tower's support beams, connecting it back to the vehicle's winch. Placidly, he watched them climb back into the hexagonal cab, set the vehicle in reverse, and pull the tower back into alignment. The small ones clambered out of the big truck, still chattering to each other as they walked to the tower, tools in hand. The bull noted that their actions appeared to have unearthed a fresh patch of new lichen, scraped up by the recession of the enormous wheels. Curiously, the small ones appeared to take no notice of this, repeatedly bypassing the tasty lichen to carry an assemblage of pipes and material back to the tower. The Gluffant was perturbed by this casual disregard of one of life's great pleasures, and set about to investigate further.

Li closed the shield on the arc-welder, severing the connection to the thin plasma stream. He straightened up, stretching his back after hours of crouching in the snow. Wordlessly he handed his tools back to Reming, who snapped them neatly in place in their maintainer box. Li hopped from one leg to the other as he stretched, shaking out the pins and needles.

"Fuck," came the voice behind him.

"What?" Li asked, interlocking his fingers and raising them up, palms to the sky.

"The Gluffant, man. It's standing in front of the truck."

Li sighed, dejectedly turning to face this latest misfortune. It was worse than he feared. There it was, the big one they'd been so careful to avoid earlier, leaning on the MMUTCAT, its massive hind end planted firmly on the front bumper. It stared at them with dull, black eyes, chewing slowly.

"We have to move it," said Reming, announcing the obvious as a call to action. Li groaned, trudging towards the shaggy beast, cursing his recruiter the whole time.

The Gluffant watched the small ones as they approached, still nattering back and forth. He paid them little mind as he continued his scraping and chewing, they were far too small to challenge him for dominance of the herd. He swallowed hard, chuffing in the crisp cold air. He was immensely pleased his curiosity had paid off, discovering incredible comfort when he leaned his hindquarters on the warm front grate of the vehicle. He sat firm, a king upon his throne, with abundant food in front of him and ample warmth behind him. The great bull watched the peevish buzzing of the small ones as they drew in closer to his thick, matted hide. Still he ignored them, continuing his grazing with tranquility.

"I'm telling you we have to move it!" shouted Reming, gesturing with both hands from the beast towards the proper place that Gluffants should be.

"That. Is not. In question," hissed Li, narrowing his eyes behind his mask. "But do you have *any* fucking idea how to do that?"

"I dunno, fucking push it for fuck's sake!" shouted Reming, throwing his hands in the air.

"I ain't pushin' it!" bellowed Li. "YOU fuckin' push it!"

"We. Need. A plan," Li said, stabbing a finger into the palm of his hand. "Figure it out, *Special*-Trooper."

Reming scratched his head through the hood of his CWAPL.

"Alright, alright," he said, raising his hands to placate the agitated Private. "We'll use the truck. Start up the MMUTCAT, and we'll use it to push it away."

Li eyed the immense beast doubtfully.

"Why don't we just back up?" he asked. "Then we can just drive off and leave it."

Now it was Reming's turn to sigh.

"We can't just leave it here, it'll just bust up the sensor tower again. We have to scare it off."

Li raised a finger in protest, opening and closing his mouth several times as he grasped for a counter-argument. At last his shoulders slumped, defeated.

"Alright," he sighed, "we'll push it."

Once inside, the MMUTCAT fired up, grumbling to life as Li prodded the ignition. The two troopers strapped into their seats, cracking their necks in nervous anticipation.

"Ready?" Li asked, his hand on the throttle.

Reming nodded. Li nudged the throttle, torque building in the great wheels as the electric motors revved. The MMUTCAT's rumbling grew louder.

But it was to no effect.

The Gluffant sat firm, enjoying the increased sensation of vibration through his behind. He sneezed in the bright sunlight, thick ropes of mucus flaring out from his wide nostrils.

Li pushed the throttle further, gritting his teeth. Reming sat frozen, watching the viewscreen, still cradling a handful of candy.

Nothing changed. The mammoth beast remained steadfastly planted on the front bumper of the big truck.

"What the fuck, man?" said Li, releasing the throttle. He pounded the dash in frustration.

"I know man, I know." Reming tossed the handful of candy in his mouth, chewing thoughtfully.

"Try the siren?" he offered after a beat.

Li stared at him, bewildered.

"What fucking siren?"

"You know, the distress siren, the one for emergency signaling," said Reming, forcing the words around a mouthful of candy. "It's the switch under the dash, with the safety cover."

Still perplexed, Li felt under the MMUTCAT's dash, locating the plastic cover and pulling it up. He paused, letting out a deep breath, before toggling the red switch.

The cabin erupted with the furious cacophony of the emergency klaxon. The troopers watched through the viewscreen as the field of snow was bathed in alternating flashes of amber and crimson light. A wailing cry poured out of the speakers along the MMUTCAT's sides, undulating with the wavering of the emergency lights. Li jammed his hands over his ears, trying to lessen the noise pounding in his head.

But it appeared to have worked. As the caterwauling started, the Gluffant leapt up, snorting and shaking his huge, horned head. The great bull had never encountered something so horribly sudden in all its life, and tore off down the snowy steppe in fear.

Reming let out an elated whoop, fist pumping in the air as Li killed the emergency siren. They high-fived, reveling in their success. The young Private pointed at the viewscreen, a wide brown streak framed in the snow, tracing a path towards the fleeing beast.

"Yo man, I think it shit its pants," Li snickered.

Reming looked to the screen, appraising the brown trail with laughter that turned to dread.

"No," he whispered, undoing his harness and scrambling out of the MMUTCAT's cab. "No, no, no, no, no, no…"

Li stopped laughing, following after his distressed squad-mate. The front of the truck came in view as he rounded the corner. Li clapped his hands to the back of his head, sinking to his knees in despair. The entire front of the cab was splattered with thick, brown streaks, hardening quickly in the frigid air. Reming had dropped his muttered protests in favor of silent, full-body cursing. It would take hours to clean the mess up. He kicked out in frustration, scuffing the frozen ground with the heel of his boot. *I'm going to murder that recruiter.*

CHAPTER 6:

The creature was still, huddled at the base of a growing snow pile. Patient. Waiting. Hungry. The scent of prey drifted past, borne aloft as the wind whipped across the desolate landscape. A stale musk, with floral notes of rotting vegetation, told the story of the large herbivore upwind. The smell only deepened the creature's predatory resolve.

It drew its powerful limbs in closer, shivering in the frigid air. Coarse bristles, mottled in grey and white, rustled together across the creature's thick back and muscular hind legs. It wondered, in so much as it had any capacity for thought beyond blind hunger, if it should move. If it should leave these glacial lands and return to its hunting grounds in the south, where the arctic chill was confined to finite seasons. The prey was good here, far larger and more satisfying than any the creature had known before. They were docile, senses dulled and diluted. They made a grand meal, so long as it was patient.

But the cold still cut through its thick hide. The snow still threatened it whenever it stood still, at the mercy of being buried by an intemperate blizzard. It was true the prey was larger, but so too was its hunger, whet by constant struggle against the starker chill.

Only THE GLOW kept it resolute. THE GLOW gave it reason to drive forward, in thrall to its dazzling brilliance, illuminating the horizon. It was closer now. The creature felt it in a sense deeper and more basal than smell or sound. The creature felt THE GLOW in its very being. The pull of it was tantalizing, its power drawing the creature forth along its shimmering spiral wave.

But the creature was not there. Not yet. The creature was here, being buried slowly by the growing snowdrift behind it. It was alone. Alone except for its hunger.

The wind picked up again, the musk was stronger now. There were new notes this time, fleshing out the prey in the mind of the creature. It was a heifer, swollen and pregnant. The pain of hunger stabbed through the creature, a flash of urgent need through its deep belly.

It tamped down this urge, the urge to leap and chase, and waited. Chasing was for the summer months, when the sun was warm and the prey was quicker. Winter was for waiting, of biding time and saving strength. Now was the time to sit and stay.

The creature was right to be patient. The Gluffant trudged through the deep snow, a craterous trail of fractured ice in its wake. The big heifer weaved, meandering drunk, oblivious to the threat ahead. She had been fortunate to stumble upon a methane vent earlier, breathing in her fill. She was fortunate to have found a thick patch of lichen and eaten so well, still giddy from the intoxicating vapors. It was a fortunate day, or so the Gluffant thought.

The creature stopped its shivering. The low bellow of the Gluffant reached its ears. It sat silent, motionless. Only the faint shimmer of orange from the vents along its side betrayed it as something other than it appeared, as yet another outcropping of snow.

The Gluffant marched ahead, aimless, wandering down the worn tundra path. Her vision spun, distracted by the shimmer of sunlight reflecting off the icy ground. She ambled between two snow-dunes.

The creature struck. Swift. Violent. Merciless. Its face split wide, revealing a cavernous maw of serrated teeth. It pounced, engulfing the Gluffant's shaggy head in one immense bite. Toothy jaws clamped down behind the base of the Gluffant's skull, stuck fast in the matted, woolly hide. She struggled in its grip, trying desperately to pull back, but the creature held her firm, her wounded cries trapped in the inky crush of its mouth.

Still the Gluffant fought on, digging her hooves into the ice as she pulled against its grasp. But she was growing tired, her thrashing weaker as the creature's hold remained still firm, resolute. Exhausted, the Gluffant dropped to her knees, sides heaving from effort. At long last she stopped her straining and lay still.

The creature released its grip on the Gluffant's neck, sitting back on its thick haunches. It appraised the bounty before it, sizing up the great feast. Sickle fore-claws clicked with anticipation as the creature evaluated how best to butcher the large beast. It made up its mind quickly, slicing off a front leg and shoveling it in the expansive, toothy mouth with a deft movement of its forelimbs. The creature worked fervently, slicing and shoveling, gorging itself in its drive to satiate the hunger within. Full at last, the Gluffant's corpse dismembered and scattered by the fury of its appetite, the creature raised its head to the snow-swept sky. Its triumphant roar echoed through the valley, claiming its kill for all to hear and know.

Lieutenant Preston sat alone in the Command Den, framed in the backlight of his monitor screen. A few days had passed since his last attempt in wrestling with his thesis, but he had been furiously busy. There were InReps to edit, trooper evaluations to complete, and his officer quarters had twice needed a thorough cleaning after an errant cockroach crawled across his nose in the middle of the night. The subsequent dusting of his room the next day was also necessary. Pressing concerns such as these had stalled Lieutenant Preston's writing progress, but what else could be expected of a young officer in command? He was at the mercy of his inescapable responsibility.

Lieutenant Preston tapped a quick beat on the desk with his fingers, rereading his progress so far.

Within the speculative confines of twenty-first century fiction, the Alien *series is notable for its atypical subversion and metaphorical casting of psycholiminal spaces. Though miscategorized by many art historians as a romantic exploration of gender integration into interstellar exploration (something that was quite unheard of for centuries of interplanetary travel) a deeper intertextual reading of the series, as a whole, reveals a primary component of brutality, horror and sexual violence. Ridley Scott can be seen to...*

Lieutenant Preston leaned back in his chair, running a hand through his short red hair. He'd had a burst of creative energy when he first sat down, churning through the first two sentences with ease. But he remained frozen on the third line, unable to fully compose exactly what Ridley Scott could be seen to do.

It had always been this way for him. He loved the research side of academia, tearing through books and articles, poring over frames of ancient films. The research spoke to him; he always started a project by wading into a sea of information, waiting for the lines and connections to materialize before him. It had served him well during his undergraduate studies. The twenty-first century was awash with primary source work. Film reviews, directors' commentary, analytical thinkpieces written from the perspective of a contemporary audience, all of it scattered across the fragments of the Old Linknet. It was all out there to be uncovered, so long as you had the patience and creativity to sift through generations of noncompatible technological artifacts.

But reading and understanding the material was never enough, he thought, *you always have to commit it to the page.* That was the part

Lieutenant Preston despised, having to condense all of his observations into a single document, then submit it for review by the stodgy monolith of the University Graduate Standards Committee. He loved exploring the metaphorical fears expressed in twenty-first century filmography, watching hours of grainy videos, distorted around the edges from hundreds of years of file compression and re-extrapolation. He loved the contrast of the older films, characterized by limitations of light and effects technology. They had color, they had depth, as creators scratched together stories with their most primitive tools.

Lieutenant Preston excelled at academic pursuits, so when he had joined the ICF to pay for his master's degree, he thought for sure he would commission into the Historical Corps or even the ArchForce Subset. He never would have guessed the ICF would make full use of his art history degree as the commander of a security-sensor platoon.

He hadn't lost hope yet. His cross-train window would open in two more years, and he was still able to pursue his Master of Arts, albeit remotely. Lieutenant Preston stretched, rolling his shoulders before placing his hands on the keyboard. He flexed his fingers as he thought through his next line. *Ridley Scott can be seen to…*

Sergeant Ramos burst through the door, tripping the lights on as he did. Startled, Lieutenant Preston shot up out of his chair, rubbing his eyes as they adjusted.

"Sorry LT," Sergeant Ramos said, catching sight of the officer's discomfort. "But Almar just got word of a direct line comm request over the Linknet."

Sergeant Ramos paused, looking intently at the blinking officer. "From Headquarters."

Lieutenant Preston nodded, settling back into his chair. He selected the communications program on the desktop, tapping the screen to initiate the interstellar video call. His thesis was replaced with a full screen image of the ICF logo, a silver eagle with two planets clasped in its talons, a thorny wreath encircling the outstretched wings. The image fluttered across a blue background as the program awaited the connection on the other line.

Lieutenant Preston let out a short breath, steeling himself for what was to come. The image blinked out, replaced with a dour, bald man seated at a large, mahogany desk, surveying the screen from beneath bushy eyebrows and an imperious grey mustache.

"Good morning Colonel Belevoir," Lieutenant Preston began, "I was–"

"Greetings Lieutenant," interrupted the mustache, "it has been twenty-eight days since your last call, and we wanted to check in on your post's status."

"Yes sir, absolutely, and so I–"

"Now as you know, remote posts are considered the first line of defense for the Coalition Republic," the Colonel continued, "and as such we make it a top priority to ensure their wellbeing and discipline at all costs."

"Of course sir, I was just reminding the troopers that–"

"And we cast a critical eye on the unity and moral cohesion of the security platoon, the platoon being the backbone of the Inter-stellar Coalition Force."

"A top priority for us sir, always–"

"And so we have reviewed your after-action report." The Colonel paused in his address, allowing the magnanimity of his speech to carry over through the screen. Lieutenant Preston swallowed his next words, staring back at the stern commander on screen. They sat together in silence, an interminable time stretching between them. At last Lieutenant Preston cleared his throat.

"Yes sir, and I–"

"We have reviewed your after-action report," the Colonel announced, interrupting the young officer once again. "Though it would appear that your mobilization efforts were in full compliance with established standards, we have noticed an uptick in false alarm reporting from your station."

Lieutenant Preston said nothing, waiting for the Colonel to finish.

"There has been a marked increase in commercial traffic bypassing the primary shipping lanes and opting for longer, less well monitored routes," the mustache declared, quivering slightly at the trimmed ends overhanging his lips. "We at ICF Command do not have a full sight-picture of the cause of this uptick, but rest assured, our intelligence sources will get to the matter in prioritized time."

Lieutenant Preston knew better than to comment, 'prioritized time' was headquarters code for projects that would be pursued after all of the current priorities were completed, just so long as new priorities didn't arise in the meantime. It typically meant a time between next week and the inevitable resolution of mankind's desire for enacting war.

"But in reviewing your post's efforts, we have noticed a few disturbing trends." The Colonel paused again, casting an appraising eye over the young officer.

Lieutenant Preston shifted in his seat. "Trends sir? What kind..."

"It would appear that your report fails to include the ICF standard conclusion address at the endpoint of each section," Colonel Belevoir proclaimed loftily, his eyes cast to the space above the monitor on his end.

"Your report failed to include ICF forms 293C and 17N annotating a page index and a catalog of regulations referenced during the incident. Most disturbingly, you appear to have utterly neglected to number the appropriate pages on both the top-right and lower-left corners."

Lieutenant Preston sat rigid in his seat, studiously maintaining a neutral expression.

"Such mistakes are seen as within the typical range for first-term platoon commanders, but it should be noted that this conversation will suffice as your annual mentorship feedback. You will have to take more care in the future that your reports do not continue to reflect such a callous disregard for good order and discipline in your unit. Further submissions of this caliber will be rejected for correction."

Lieutenant Preston chewed on his lower lip; he nodded once. Satisfied, the Colonel resumed his address.

"Finally, we wanted to inform you that AZH-01's bi-annual inspection has been scheduled for September 19th. Due to the remote nature of your posting, we will be utilizing a class-II inspection drone series. It will arrive via orbital drop on the 18th. They are entirely self-sufficient, but you will need to assign a trooper to follow the inspector and open doors for it, ensuring full access and compliance. Your station's pre-inspection self-assessment will be due on the first of the month. Do you have any questions?"

"No sir, we'll be ready for it," replied Lieutenant Preston.

The Colonel nodded. He terminated the communication with a wave, and the image on the Lieutenant's screen was once again replaced with the somber faced eagle of the ICF. Lieutenant Preston rocked back in his chair, kicking away from the desk and unleashing a wordless shout of frustration. Reed-Sergeant Ramos cast a look of sympathy from across the room.

"Don't worry, sir. I'll get the troopers after it," the senior NCO insisted. "We'll get this shithole spotless before the inspectors."

Lieutenant Preston said nothing, despondently pushing his chair in a circle with one foot.

"Why don't we grab some chow?" Sergeant Ramos offered, walking over to the officer and placing a hand on his shoulder. He leaned down to eye level with the glum Lieutenant. "We can war-game this inspection with Sikes and Wingo."

Lieutenant Preston sighed, accepting the Reed-Sergeant's proposal with a conciliatory nod. He slumped up from the chair, and together they headed for the door.

Rania bint Khalil faced her challenge with resolute silence. She stared down the mounds of developmental studies material stacked around her, sizing up the volumes of technical manuals for weaknesses. Tentatively, she drew a loose-bound packet from the top of one stack. She stared a hole in the cover, reading and rereading the title before opening it up and thumbing through the pages. She battled within herself, forcing her concentration on the page as she attempted to commit the formulas and code expressions to memory. She turned the page, words skipping off her eyes and sliding off her brain. Rania gave up with a sigh, tossing the study packet back on the stack. She'd gone through the trouble of printing them out on the advice of a friend from sensor technician school, something to the effect of inked words being easier to read than a screen. Dragging a hand down her face, she took stock of the piled pages scattered around her. Rania couldn't help but feel that no medium would help her tackle this sea of information. *I need a break, clear my head.*

Standing up from the middle of the stacks, she stumbled, artfully dodging the loose bottles and precariously stacked binders. As she made her way to the door, she caught her reflection in the mirror, grimacing at the strands of tangled, fly-away hair. Rania stopped to brush her curls, smoothing down the top into a semblance of order. *It'd be so much easier with a hijab*, she mused, brushing away at the knotted ends. Her great aunt Huda wore a *hijab*, the last one in her family. Rania's mother had always told her that it took strong faith to make such a commitment, and that she should never wear the *hijab* lightly. *But mom was always so fond of her own hair*, thought Rania, remembering the countless times she watched her brush it before going out, carefully styling the dark brown locks into a wavy cascade of tightly bound curls. Rania dropped the brush and studied her own hair, long and smooth on top, but descending into a chaotic tumble near the ends. She sighed, gathering the ends in her hand and pulling them into a loose ponytail in the back as she stepped out the door. *I guess that will have to do.*

The chow hall was awash with the clanging of trays and the chatter of troopers. Rania sidled up to the line behind the RationVendor, stepping forward to make her selection. *'Roast beef and carrots'* or *'enchilada supreme'*? She weighed her options carefully. *Do I want the brown cube of jelly mush, or the light orange?* She sighed, making her selection and waiting as the RationVendor shook and grinded in its labors. A fat brown cube dropped from the machine's trapdoor, depositing on her alloy tray with a wet plop. *The finest food for ICF's finest*, she thought as she walked over to the metal tables. As she settled in to her seat, she drifted into the troopers' conversation.

"And then we get around front and the entire cab is covered in shit!" said Li, waving his fork in the air for added emphasis. He drew circles in the air, tracing the outline to show the exact degree in which the MMUTCAT had been covered. Li's fervid descriptions were met with riotous laughter from the other troopers, with Private Almar starting to choke on a forkful of 'enchilada supreme.' Early thumped him on the back, clearing his throat while Li continued his colorful tale. Rania smiled, *and that's why it's better to fly, less shit to clean up.*

"We scrubbed for hours. I thought it'd never come off," added Reming, cutting into his partner's story. "And the worst part was that when we got done, we had to finish cleaning our weapons."

"No!" Early gawped. "Sikes still made you clean after all that?"

"Wouldn't even let us change our clothes before turning them in," Reming confirmed, swearing by his raised hand. "He just stood there in the doorway and watched us as we cleaned, still covered in Gluffant shit."

"Fuckin' zoomie," replied Almar. "I bet that room smelled almost as bad as being trapped in the Ion Array with Leonard." Troopers around the table murmured in support. Rania grew cold at the mention of the name.

"No way man," joked Li, "nothing compares to Leonard. It's this weird, half-foul, half sweet thing, and it sticks with you. It's unreal, it smells like, it smells like…"

"Like dead flowers," Rania interjected.

A hush fell over the table. She could feel the weight of their stares as she picked at her food.

"Yeah," continued Li, trailing off as he studied her. "Yeah, just like that. Like…"

"Like rotting lavender," said Rania, completing his sentence but ignoring his questioning look. Her thoughts were punctuated with flashes of unpleasant memories, *the staccato beat of the shower on bare tiles, the feel of the coarse towel on her face as she dried, her confusion over looking up and seeing Leonard leaning against the wall.* She fought back against the swelling tide within her, tamping it down as she stood up from the table, the thought of eating suddenly repulsive. Her face flushed as she fought to contain her roiling emotions. Slamming her tray into the cleaning receptacle, she stormed out of the hall under the crushing pressure of their silent gaze.

Once in the hall she broke into a run, chasing her way back to her room. She slammed the alloy door once she got inside, her chest tight, breath coming out in short, fevered gasps. Tears ringed the corners of her eyes as she slumped against the back of the door. She hated this feeling, *like an egg with a cracked shell, any quick move and it'll all come spilling out.* She pounded the back of her fists against the cold metal door. *No! He doesn't get to do this to me, not now, not tomorrow, not anymore!* She pushed up from the door, wiping a tear from each eye. She stood in resolute silence, quieting the emotion as she shook first her arms and then her legs. She composed herself, swallowing hard. *I'm going for a fucking run.*

Back in the cafeteria, the conversation slowly returned to the seated troopers. The shock wore off and murmurs grew in volume as the troopers picked up where they'd left off, forks clinking on trays and chatter rising. At the leadership table, Sergeant Wingo renewed his conversation as if nothing had happened, eagerly recounting the general cleaning mayhem that preceded the last inspection.

"And so there I was, mop in one hand, dirty drawers in the other, when LT Baxter rounds the corner," explained Sergeant Wingo. "And so I say to him, 'Trust me. Sir, *I ain't your guy!*'"

Sergeant Wingo erupted in laughter, slapping a fleshy palm on the alloy table. Sergeant K joined in, coughing as he choked down his electrolyte beverage. Reed-Sergeant Ramos offered only a derisive snort, far less impressed with the Buck-Sergeant's story than Sergeant Wingo was with himself. Lieutenant Preston said nothing, morosely pushing the scraps of 'enchilada supreme' around his plate. Unlike the others, he'd seen the expression on Special-Trooper Rania's face as she rushed out the door, an expression he'd seen only once, about two months ago.

Rania reached a hand for the rusty ladder to the station's running track. Nearly four kilometers long, the three-lane ring of rubber coated catwalk encircled the upper dome of station AZH-01. As she summited the ladder, Rania wiped the accumulated grime on the sides of her shorts. It was the only space dedicated to running in the whole station, and was consequently one of the least used pieces of equipment. When they volunteered their own time to work out at all, most of the troopers were far too concerned with building muscle to engage in 'skinny-work' like running. Besides that, the track was dirty, the unfortunate repository for dust and grit circulating in the station's air vents. It was also hot, the result of warm air collecting near the top of the dome.

And so she knew she would be alone, climbing past her own greasy handprints, leftover from months of her thrice weekly ritual. She hopped over the railing at the top, landing deftly on two feet, and stopped to catch her breath after the climb. The oxygen was thinner here, blame the poor circulation, but that helped make up for the lower gravity. As Rania shoved away from the railing's edge, she pushed herself hard, launching into a swift sprint across the creaking walkway. She drove through turns, legs and arms pumping furiously with each bound. She tore across the straightaways, feet rebounding against the light rubber. She ran on, and replaced the vortex of noise in her head with the pounding of her heart and the panting of her breath.

Alone in his quarters, the Lieutenant watched the screen intently, pausing and unpausing the video as he jotted down notes on the tablet in his hand. He set the tablet down in his lap, reaching for his mug with one hand and waving to start the video with his other. His fingers coiled around the ceramic handle as he brought it to his lips, breathing deeply in the warm steam rising from the cup's contents. He savored the charismatic notes from the bitter liquid, closing his eyes as he tipped the mug. Real coffee cost a fortune, with only a few dozen farms even capable of raising the heirloom trees. He'd been fortunate indeed, finding a discount supplier through the family farm of a friend from the Aegis University Art School, able to receive pounds of the dark roasted beans for a tenth of their retail cost. It had been that very friend who had introduced him to the magical beverage when they'd been cramming for finals.

Ever since then Lieutenant Preston couldn't stand to drink SimuCaff, a hollow approximation of the majesty he'd once tasted. But even at a discount his three-pound bag still cost nearly a month's salary, and so he used it sparingly, sealing it away in a vacuum canister, brewing only in times of necessary focus or inspiration.

And so he drank some now, as he sat down to watch *Alien 3* for the first time. He'd seen transcripts of the director's commentary, read critical articles by journalists from the twentieth century, even a few compendium analyses by those that reviewed the eighteen-part Alien series in its entirety, at the end of the twenty-first century. But Lieutenant Preston had yet to watch it, difficult as it was to find a copy of the much-maligned film in a file format he could even begin to decipher. Seeing it now, he was surprised by the artistic direction of the film, whose disjointed tone and narrative stakes laid bare its troubled development history.

Lieutenant Preston watched the screen as the protagonist, Ripley, was shoved against the infirmary wall, sobbing in the face of the advancing Alien threat. As he watched it push closer, dripping and wet, its oblong black head mere inches from the heroine's face, he couldn't help but tighten his grip on the mug. *Is this how she felt?* he wondered, thoughts sprouting unbidden in his mind like mushrooms in the dark. *Was she afraid as she huddled against the cold bathroom tile?* He sipped again at his coffee, but he found the taste to be stale, acrid against his tongue. He blanched, swallowing hard and emitting a sputtered gasp. Lieutenant Preston snapped his fingers, pausing the video as he pounded on his chest to clear his throat. He turned back to the frozen image, reflecting on the events of two months ago.

He was only two months into his command when he heard about it, that something had happened to Special-Trooper Rania, and it involved Senior-Trooper Leonard. It had come to him third-hand, relayed to him by Sergeant Wingo, who'd overheard a comment from Special-Trooper Belle, shortly after she'd found out she was pregnant and would be transferred home. Lieutenant Preston had listened hard to the Buck-Sergeant, trying to fill in the gaps in his winding, scant story.

He'd called a leadership meeting at once, assembling the NCOs and drawing on them for insight and advice. They brought in Special-Trooper Belle and had her retell as much of the story as she knew. Belle alleged that Rania had been showering alone when she came out and saw Leonard in the locker room. Rania was surprised to see him after she had locked the outside door (standard practice whenever females used the showers in the station) and asked him to leave so she could finish changing. According to Belle, Leonard had refused, reaching his arms around her and attempting to kiss her instead. Rania had pushed him away, but Leonard got mad, shoving her against the bathroom wall and licking her face. Rania had wriggled out, still wet from the shower, and escaped the locker room to flee down the hall, still naked. After her story, they dismissed Special-Trooper Belle, ordering her not to discuss the matter with anyone else while they conferenced over the facts at hand.

There was little, if any, evidence to the story--nothing physical to prove the event had transpired. They examined Belle's details, trying to reconcile it with what they knew about the troopers involved. Senior-Trooper Leonard was odd for sure, but it was difficult to fathom him a rapist. Sergeant Wingo noted that the Senior-Trooper had been posted at AZH-01 for four years now, with no previous history of issues. Sergeant K agreed, Leonard had difficulty making eye contact with anyone, let alone having the confidence to force himself on another trooper. Reed-Sergeant Ramos raised the question of how an out-of-shape, doughy greaseball like Leonard would even be able to pin Special-Trooper Rania, who was widely known to be in excellent physical condition.

This then brought the subject to Special-Trooper Rania, who was relatively new to the unit, arriving on the same transport as the Lieutenant. Not much was known about her, save for her love of fitness and general aptitude for the job, able to get resets on even the trickiest alarms (Sergeant Ramos had scoffed at this, labeling her efforts adequate at best). She'd been on the station for only two months, with only Belle as a friend or confidant. She was an unknown quantity in their minds, and it spoke volumes to them that she had failed to bring her own allegations of misconduct to the attention of the leadership team.

Instead, it was argued by Sergeant Wingo, these allegations came from Special-Trooper Belle, who, he reminded the group, had a habit of exaggeration and poor work performance. This was most likely a misunderstanding, some small happenstance that spiraled in rumors and needed to be handled. Reed-Sergeant Ramos agreed. He'd seen this type of thing before in a previous unit, when a trooper had professed his love in a public and embarrassing manner and was rejected. That trooper had leaned in for a kiss and been slapped for his efforts, all the more shocked when the female trooper had called him out to her leadership for his inappropriate conduct.

Then, as now, the Reed-Sergeant argued, they had to weigh the magnitude of the incident against the potential damage to the unit. Senior-Trooper Leonard was their lead weapon technician, soon to be their only one after Belle rotated home. It would take months to arrange his replacement, in which case they would be combat ineffective should a real incident occur. Senior-Sergeant Sikes clamored to join this train of thought, citing the considerable damage posed to unit cohesion by the exposure of an incident such as this. These types of incidents were detrimental to morale, as they undermined the ICF's image of good order and discipline. Sergeant Sikes claimed to have seen reports of units that were disbanded after a scandal such as this, with their leadership removed from duty. Surely, he argued, it was not worth dissolving the unit over a slight misunderstanding.

And so the Lieutenant wavered, listening to the counsel of his NCOs, men who boasted decades of experience in service to the ICF. He took in their arguments, weighing their statements against his own reasoning. He felt lost. The ICF had never discussed a situation like this in the Officer Training Academy, which had mostly been spent learning combat tactics and paperwork management. All he wanted was to get through this two-year tour, get his degree and cross-train into the type of service in which he felt most useful. All he needed to do was get this unit through the next two years in one piece. He shook under the magnitude of his decision, his two months of experience paling before the careers of his Sergeants. And in the end, he crumbled, acquiescing to the logic of their reasoning.

He had ordered Senior-Trooper Leonard be placed on night-shift, separating the two so they wouldn't cross paths when they worked. He'd ordered Sergeant Ramos to sit down with Leonard, straightening out the trooper where necessary to ensure this type of thing never happened again (to this Sergeant Ramos heartily agreed, growling that Leonard wouldn't be able to lift his arms after he was done with him). As for Rania, Lieutenant Preston had directed Senior-Sergeant Sikes to reach out to her, offering counsel and guidance in case she needed it. The important thing, he told them, was that they provided her the support she needed. The NCOs nodded in agreement, affirming the importance of assisting the new trooper as she adjusted to the unit. Lieutenant Preston had dismissed them then, hoping that would bring resolution to the incident.

But it hadn't wrapped up so neatly, not then, not now. Even though she'd never discussed it with him, always working with a smile on her face, he couldn't get past the nagging doubt that all was not as well as he'd hoped. He'd seen the look on Rania's face when she left Sergeant Sikes' office, full of pain and disbelief, mixed with an undercurrent of betrayal. He'd been drawn back to that look, reflecting on it time and time again. And so he sat, alone in his room, his coffee growing cold in his hands as he stared at the frozen image of Ripley harassed by her alien demons. He thought about the look on Rania's face today, and wondered now, as he had then, if he was the one responsible.

CHAPTER 7:

The stars stretched out before the ICF freighter, a limitless field of glowing pinpricks, like a flashlight shining through holes in a great, black, blanket. The freighter sped through empty space, cubist dream of duty modules, bristling antennae, and boxy shipping canisters bolted around a central, tubular fuselage. Captain Daniels stood on the bridge of the *Hendrix*, surveying the shipping lane ahead through the viewscreen mounted floor to ceiling. She stared out at the inky void, dark, flat, and impenetrable. Pop culture always showed hyperspace travel as dynamic, all glowing streaks of stretched starlight, the reality was much more mundane. The universe was just too big, the distances between stars and planets far too great. The view from outside was always static, just points of light painted on a blank, black canvas.

'Astrological Flattening' was the name given to explain the effect. When you're traveling at hyper-speeds across the vast emptiness of space, it renders the illusion that you are standing still, stagnant against the galactic backdrop. *A romantic term for the blisteringly mundane,* thought Captain Daniels, sipping from her mug of SimuCaff. It was yet another disappointing disconnect in her life as the Captain of an ICF ship. Her dream ever since she was a little girl, she had longed to sail on starlit waves, tracing a path through the cosmic glitter of the Milky Way. *But ships don't sail, they hang,* she mused, *transfixed, appearing motionless.* You started out in one place, typed in your coordinates, and in a few months you were in another, with no tactile sensation to impart the billions of miles crossed in between. *Like going to sleep in your bed and waking up in another country.*

She had fought hard to earn her commission, rising through the ranks through grinding practice and besting her peers' evaluation scores time and time again. And time and time again, she had made it abundantly clear to her superiors that she had earned a command assignment, as soon as possible, and that she wouldn't take no for an answer. Captain Daniels sighed into her mug, blowing waves in the bitter, brown liquid. ICF Command had listened to her all right, granting her a full command almost a decade ahead of her male peers. It just happened to be as the commander of a deep space transport freighter, a not-so-subtle hint that she might have been better served waiting her turn. *And keeping quiet when her Command School Professor reached his hand up her thigh during a leadership feedback evaluation*, she thought, a grim smile playing out on her face.

She sipped again at her mug, enjoying the silence of the bridge. She was alone except for the soft clattering of keys from her navigator, his eyes grimly focused on the glowing monitor at his desk.

"We're coming up on the drop point, Ma'am," said Senior-Trooper Briggs, cutting in over her reflections. "StatServe say t-minus fifty seconds for our launch window."

Captain Daniels nodded. Supply runs to the outer-rim weren't particularly difficult, the onboard navigation computers controlling all of the fine details of throttle, direction, and guidance. There were no surprises in the shipping lanes, codified interstellar routes purposely designed to be devoid of obstacles or astronomical objects. The only real command decision she had to make was to authorize the supply launch, blasting a capsule of mail, ordinance, and logistical materials at the precise trajectory to land at their destination along the remote posts as the freighter whipped through at ten-lightyears per second. *And even that part could be outsourced to a computer if the ICF bothered to update their policy standards.*

Briggs looked up at her questioningly, awaiting her verbal approval to initiate the launch. Captain Daniels took one last sip, finishing her drink and resting her mug on the alloy railing.

"Go for launch," she sighed.

Briggs nodded, hammering out a quick command on his monitor. Captain Daniels turned away from the screen, clinking the mug along the railing as she headed for the door. *Glad I was here to serve the Coalition,* she thought, ducking her head as she walked through the bulkway. *Only the best get to command.*

A white light flashed along the freighter's side. The capsule launched in a jet of flame, a white and grey drum capped in a blunted cone exploding from the shipment tube like a roman candle. It hurtled through the empty void, spatial dampeners slowly unfolding as it went, guiding it on track to a sparse outpost on the outer-rim. Onboard guidance trimmed throttle and adjusted pressure as it made its way to the frozen pole of AZH. As it breached through the atmosphere a trio of red and grey parachutes deployed, slowing it further in the thin atmosphere. A fourth parachute stuck fast in its canister, the product of failing quality control standards in the recently commercialized ICF production facility.

The barrel-shaped capsule arched across the hazy sky, a trail of burning ozone dragging out behind it. The nose cone glowed bright orange, heating tiles straining under the atmospheric friction. A parachute tore off, leaving the capsule unbalanced and fluttering in its descent. It hurtled towards the planet surface in a lazy spiral. The capsule impacted the frozen ground at three-hundred miles per hour, awakening a herd of nearby Gluffants and sending them stampeding off in a hooting panic of thundering hooves. The capsule dug a wide crater, casting a wave of dirt in the air and burying itself deep within the tundra's soil. Only the top of the thirty-foot capsule was visible, stamped with a battered and charred sign that announced in bold red letters, 'ICF Property, Handle With Care.'

The molded plastic was cool along Rania's cheek. She shifted in the *Solo Skimmer*'s narrow cockpit, prone against the molded, tempered seat, feet firmly hooked in the dampener stirrups. Her grip was tight against the knobby rubber of the throttles, turning them forward as she trimmed the direction of the ailerons with a light twist of her wrists. The windstream howled outside the cockpit, a few inches above her. Only a thin layer of clear poly-plex formed the bubble canopy, giving the pilot unparalleled visibility in all directions, but leaving it vulnerable to scratches and chipping.

Rania's DC-12 was showing its age, a constellation of pinprick craters peppered the cockpit front, courtesy of the sudden hailstorms common in AZH's fickle polar climate. The long, angular prow of the *Solo Skimmer* was pitted and marred with years of impact from aerial debris, dragging long scrapes in the muted gold and grey paint. The skiff's belly was awash with gouges and scrapes, scarred from almost a decade in service to young, exuberant sensor techs. It was also covered from bow to stern in a loving layer of polish, carefully applied by the detailed ministrations of its current pilot.

The small craft tore across the frozen sky, buffeted here and there by ebbs in the windstream, a pocket of water vapor building on the forward edges of the four swept wings. A grin stretched across Rania's face as she reveled in the joy and exhilaration of flight. She dipped and wove the small craft, playing with the freedom and deft maneuverability of the DC-12. Spiraling into a loose roll, Rania crossed over a MMUTCAT below her crawling back to post. *Sometimes it pays to be a sensor tech*, she thought, righting the craft and soaring over the empty tundra. The waning sun shone through the arctic haze, glittering off ice crystals in the air and bathing the sky in a golden glow. *Who else gets the chance to see something like this?* She sighed, content, and headed back to the station.

Far below the gleeful zooming of the enthusiastic pilot, Private Li and Senior-Trooper Joelson tumbled along in the MMUTCAT's impact resistant, barely cushioned seats. They slammed against the unyielding chair backs, thrown momentarily in the air by the collision of the MMUTCAT's enormous wheels and an abandoned Skitter nest.

"Fuck me," Li muttered, rubbing the back of his head where it smacked against the stiff plastic backing.

"And that wasn't even a big one," observed Joelson, calmly returning his glasses to the bridge of his nose. "The bigger nests grow ten feet across when a whole colony gets together. Hit one of those and you're liable to snap an axle and drop a wheel, internal motor and all."

"Is there anything in this place that doesn't suck?" Li snapped, dropping his hand to the throttle control.

The MMUTCAT rumbled to the top of a ridge, hanging on the edge of the peak before tipping forward. As they drove down the draw, the snow covered plain stretched before them, stark white and beautiful. Joelson looked out over the frozen landscape, the wind swirled with a dusting of snow gathered from the heaped dunes, glittering in the light of the setting sun.

"Sometimes the scenery's nice," he said.

"Fuck the scenery."

"I like it, it's open and the air is clear, you can see for miles," said Joelson. *Not like on Earth.* After what happened on Avina, his mother had resettled in Buenos Aires, taking comfort in the anonymity afforded by the bustling megacity. Joelson had spent considerable time retreating to the rooftop of his ninety-story apartment complex, brushing aside the soot and pigeon feathers to lay out and look up at the murky sky. The city was chaotic, claustrophobic, the gnarled mass of human activity pressing down on him whenever he walked the humid streets. But up there, out of sight of the endless expanse of crowded towers and away from the ceaseless chatter of the city, he'd spent hours watching the roiling clouds of rust colored haze.

The first time he saw stars was when he joined the military, looking out the window as the preorbital transport broke above the smog layer. As the rocket pushed through the dusty cloud and into the sunlit upper atmosphere, it seemed like the future opening up before him. He'd been hesitant when he was first assigned to remote posting in the outer-rim, picturing a labyrinth of closed-in walls and sunless rooms. Joelson had brightened when he arrived, relishing the chance to venture out and answer alarms. *Anything to see the sky again.*

Joelson gazed out at the barren expanse, dotted with hummocks of snowy dunes. A herd of Gluffants stampeded to the west. "I like the quiet too. Peaceful."

"That's just code for 'nothing fucking happens.'"

Joelson shrugged, allowing the younger trooper to stew in his bitter mood. It had been a long day, a trip out to Bravo-05 for faulty heat exchanger, and two trips out to Foxtrot-01 for a feedback loop in the PMZ codes. Li's short, spiky black hair was matted with sweat, an errant tuft sticking straight out from the back. Li ran a hand over to smooth it, only succeeding in disturbing the placement of another clump. The day had truly started off wrong when Senior-Sergeant Sikes had cornered him in the hallway, telling him that he hadn't scored enough hits during weapons firing to retain his quarterly qualification, necessitating a re-firing after his shift ended. He would be joined by Private Konrad, the surly ogre being the only other trooper to shoot less than Li did.

The thought of losing his precious off-time to spend hours alongside the scowling, scarred giant infuriated him. Bad enough he had to re-qualify with Konrad, but he'd also have to do so under the simpering gaze of Sikes, enduring the Senior-Sergeant's vague, contradictory instructions and endless collection of recycled ICF clichés. It formed the frustrating foundation to the shit-stacked day Li was having, a nagging reminder that even after he answered the sensor alarms, he'd still have more work waiting back at the station. It had him questioning every decision he'd made in the year and a half since his eighteenth birthday, furiously analyzing which one led him to this frozen, puckered asshole of an installation.

Joelson looked back from the viewscreen, studying the tightness in Li's jaw, his clenched grip on the throttle handles. *I remember those days, when it seems like the entire world is set out to piss on you.* Joelson had gotten into a few fistfights back in Buenos Aires, swift, tussling scraps in the dripping alley behind the bicycle repair shop. His mother had always chastised him afterwards. *Life will always try to pick a fight with you, but it doesn't get better by going out looking for one*, she'd say while patching up his scraped knuckles and icing his bruises. She'd had plenty of practice herself. Dr. Patricia Joelson had been a minor-ranked cage-fighter for nearly a decade, saving her winnings to afford a degree in Aeronautical Bio-Engineering. Joelson was only a few years older than the impetuous Private, but his time at AZH-01 had mellowed him. Here, amid the swirling snowfields and quiet predictability of sensor-security operations, he found his center.

But he knew better than to provoke the sulking trooper with advice or observations. *'Acceptance comes in time'* was another one of his mother's favorite sayings, usually given in response to one of his vented frustrations. Joelson stared ahead out the viewscreen as the top of the installation's alloy dome crept into view on the horizon. He afforded Li space as they drove together in sullen silence.

"Daddy, daddy did you see me singing?" Sheridan's exuberant face pressed in close to the tiny camera, filling the monitor screen on Sergeant Ramos' desk. "I hit all my notes daddy, even the really high ones!"

The video feed fogged slightly as Sheridan breathed on the camera, pressing her words through the Linknet connection. She turned her head, looking away on the screen and pressing her ear against the monitor on her side, waiting for his response. Sergeant Ramos smiled through his hands.

"Of course honey, I caught it all through the VidScreen. You were amazing as Beatrix, good flute work."

"*Daaad*, it's a piccolo, *Bensen* plays the flute," she corrected.

"Right, of course, and you were the best," Sergeant Ramos backpedaled. "That's why you're my favorite daughter."

"I'm your *only* daughter," said Sheridan, rolling her eyes at the screen. Shifting gears she said, "When are you coming home? Are you gonna be here for Christmas? Daddy J said I can get a new fish from the store, 'cause Professor Bubbles went back to the ocean. Daddy J told Miss Deckly he didn't think you would even call."

The smile faded from Sergeant Ramos' olive face. On-screen he watched James Saint-James pull Sheridan back from the monitor, lifting her out of the chair and depositing her next to the desk in their study.

"Alright dear, that's enough for now," James said, patting her on the head and turning her towards the door. "Why don't we leave Daddy C alone so I can talk?"

James lowered his voice in a conspiratorial whisper. "That way we can talk about your presents, but only if you play in your room."

Sheridan's green eyes lit up at the mention of presents. She ran out the door, long black hair streaming behind her. James Saint-James flopped down in the chair, swiveling to face the monitor.

"She really loved that fish, it's a real shame bettas only live a few years." He turned his eyes to the screen with a lopsided smile.

Sergeant Ramos grunted, his expression pure granite. The smile faded from James' face, a weariness creeping in around the corners of his grey eyes.

"It's also a shame you couldn't catch the performance on livestream, the recorded playback always loses fidelity on the high notes."

Sergeant Ramos shifted in his seat, running a hand through his graying, black hair.

"I caught the VidScreen. I couldn't get live feed because of the snow–"

"Yes, the snowstorm, I know," snapped James Saint-James, a blonde lock slipping out of his careful ponytail. "But there wouldn't even be a snowstorm if you hadn't taken a fifth tour! Every other security trooper does four before they rotate back. Everyone else but *you*."

Sergeant Ramos dropped his hand. "I told you it was my only choi–"

"Choice. I *know*." James Saint-James shook his head, shoulders slumping as if under a heavy weight. Softly he added, "But it's a choice you made for both of us."

Sergeant Ramos leaned back in his seat, refusing to look at the screen. Lieutenant Preston poked his head in the doorway, mouthing the word "Formation?" and pointing at his watch. The Reed-Sergeant nodded, turning in his chair to face the screen. He opened his mouth to speak.

"Something just came up, I know." James cut him off with a raise of his hand. "Go run formation, we can pick this up again some other time."

Sergeant Ramos nodded, leaning in to say goodbye.

"It's always some other time," muttered James, severing the connection with a wave of his hand. Sergeant Ramos stared at the black screen, his jaw opening and closing silently. Scowling, he pushed himself from the desk, jumping to his feet from his chair. He snatched his mug off the desk before storming out the door, pages fluttering on the clipboard clenched in his hand.

Lieutenant Preston leaned against the wall of the formation room, the matte-grey alloy cool through his uniform jacket. It was large and open, empty save for the hustle of troopers milling about as they waited for evening formation. Crossing his arms, he caught snippets of conversation amongst the pockets of troops. Off to his right, Special-Trooper Early, Private Smith, and Senior-Trooper Joelson were locked in discussion on the finer points of Gluffants.

"I'm telling you, I had a Gluffant steak at a bistro in London," said Private Smith.

Early snorted. "Bullshit. Gluffant flank goes for three grand a pound. We had a few old, dairy Gluffants back on the farm, and *I* haven't even tried it."

"I did too." Smith stood firm. "I had it rare, with scallops and fire-roasted potatoes."

Early scoffed. Joelson humored him.

"What did it taste like?" he asked, accommodating the younger trooper.

"It was like music made out of meat," the excited trooper sputtered. "It was smooth and soft. It fell apart on my fork."

Early snorted, shaking his head over Smith's insistence. *It was probably just pressure-grown beef steak*, Lieutenant Preston smiled to himself, *I've never even tried Gluffant*. The only meat to still come from living animals, Gluffant steak fetched an exorbitant price at the market, where it was seen as the ultimate in luxury. It was priced high enough to be completely out of reach of the common masses, raised and cultivated exclusively to feed the carefully curated tastes of the ultra-rich. *The kind of people whose family names are on the marquees over banks and on the sides of ships*, the officer mused. Even the ranchers were a rare breed, coming up in the insular industry through family ownership of legacy herds. It was said that each herd was sponsored and insured by venture capitalists, in the way that gold mines were at the turn of the twentieth century. Lieutenant Preston tuned back in as the conversation shifted to the logistics of capturing one of the local Gluffants.

"I'm telling you we just grab a little one, or an old one that was going to die anyway," pleaded Smith. "That way you both can try it and know I'm not lying."

Early and Joelson appeared to be mulling it over.

"Bad idea, the herds are insured by the Coalition Republic," said Lieutenant Preston, stepping in quickly to curtail the conversation. "Each Gluffant is tagged and recorded, so the Coalition can safeguard the farmer's investment. That's why they're always raised near ICF outposts, for the added protection."

This was not true. By and large the Coalition Republic cared very little for the investments and expenditures of small businesses in general, let alone a boutique herd raised for the glittering tables of old-money establishments. But at a forty-percent tax rate at market sale, Gluffant meat served as a small but profitable source of revenue for the Coalition government. Though there were few enough herds spread throughout ranchlands scattered around the galaxy, each Gluffant represented at least three tons of taxable meat, making them more than worth the minor hassle they provided to troopers on remote posts on the outer-rim. Lieutenant Preston didn't know any of this, but he still believed in the benevolent good provided by Republic governance.

The troopers nodded, mulling over the information the officer provided. Private Smith opened his mouth to ask a question, but was cut off when Private Konrad shoved past him, an apology half-growled in his wake. Lieutenant Preston frowned at the arrival of the testy trooper, noting his stubbled face and the churlish swing of his arms. The officer was well aware that a number of troopers in the Security Corp had begun service as Commando Raiders, making their way into the career field through cross-trains for any manner of reasons. He hadn't reviewed Konrad's records yet, but he doubted that any amount of time in special forces granted someone license to act so poorly.

He broke away from the group of troopers, walking over to the Buck-Sergeants gathered loosely near the doorway. The officer approached Sergeant Kyrghizwald, pleasantly noting the Buck-Sergeant's bright eyes and chipper expression. *Must be one of his good days.* When he reached the NCOs he outlined the problem, identifying the trooper in question and the disreputable state he currently inhabited. Much to his surprise, Sergeant K volunteered to take care of it, marching off to confront the ill-mannered trooper. Lieutenant Preston and Sergeant Wingo watched the Buck-Sergeant confront the sour Private, sharing jokes at the expense of the junior NCO's animated expressions and gestures. Their mirth was short-lived as Reed-Sergeant Ramos arrived, darkening the room with his mood. He strode to the center of the formation room, drawing his clipboard up in his hand, calling the unit to fall in as he commenced with roll. As he made his way through the list of names, he stopped at the list of Senior-Troopers.

"Senior-Trooper Joelson," he announced, his gravelly voice echoing over the gathered troopers.

"Present, Sergeant."

"Congratulations trooper, promotion listing just came out. You made Buck-Sergeant."

A smattering of applause rang through the room, punctuated by small whoops and cheers. "Fuck yeah Joelson!" called a trooper in the back. Joelson smiled, his chest puffing out a little where he stood in formation. Sergeant Ramos' face was grim.

"Guess we'll get more command out of you whether you're ready or not."

Joelson's smile faltered, he snapped his focus into place, standing at attention a little straighter than before. Sergeant Ramos huffed, then continued with announcements.

"Hailstorm in the forecast for the next two days, ensure you're wearing helmets on top of your normal protective gear. Coalition Republic News states that the Small Council has approved resolution for further sanctioning of Karnassus following the failure of accurate orbital bombardment. The resolution goes to the Large Council next week to deliberate on the specific goods and industries affected."

The Reed-Sergeant paused, looking up from his sheet to survey troopers' response. He was satisfied with a few nodding heads, and continued.

"Finally, supply drop came in today." More cheers broke out, along with the light titter of whispered conversation. Sergeant Ramos paused, waiting for the troopers to settle down, his face taut in scowl.

"Early, Reming, I need you to take a MMUTCAT out and pick it up tomorrow morning. It came in fast and hot, so you'll probably need to tow it out of the crater. Take cables when you go, and the plow in case you have to dig it out. Expect to be there a while."

Early nodded. Reming sighed, he'd been hoping to grind through another few levels of *Altar of Combat* on his day off. He also needed to do laundry. The dirty pile in the corner was in severe danger of achieving sentient life.

"Sergeant, can I go with?"

Sergeant Ramos looked up from his papers, catching sight of Rania raising her hand from the second row.

"Why?" he asked, glaring at the Special-Trooper.

"I've never ridden in a MMUTCAT before and it might give me a new perspective. Besides, I want to help."

Probably just wants to get fucked, the Reed-Sergeant surmised, narrowing his eyes at her from behind his clipboard. To his surprise, she returned his gaze, staring him straight in the eyes and ever so slightly lifting her chin. He considered his words carefully, turning over the most crushing 'no' he could think of. He opened his mouth to respond.

"I think that's a fantastic idea," said the Lieutenant, cutting in over the Reed-Sergeant. "An excellent way to bridge the gap between Sensor Tech and Security Troop. Rania, you can ride with Special-Trooper Early out to the supply drop."

Rania broke into a smile, looking back at Sergeant Ramos. The Reed-Sergeant glowered, but he knew better than to supersede an officer. *Fine, let her get knocked up like the last one.* Reming let out a sigh of relief, his day off was back on track.

"Fine," said the Reed-Sergeant, acid etching his voice.

"But Reming goes too."

The MMUTCAT rumbled across the tundra plains, the refrigerator-shaped vehicle chugging along over the squelching ice. Clouds drifted in the lazy sky, casting long shadows where they passed in front of the sun.

Special-Trooper Early kept the throttle steady, guiding the immense truck towards the blinking waypoint on his heads-up display. Reming sat with arms crossed in the passenger seat, chin tucked to his chest in defiance of the beautiful day. Rania stared through the viewscreen, harnessed to the cloth jump-seat in the truck's massive interior bay. She ran her fingers along the nylon restraining belts, humming tunelessly as she did.

"So..." she said, breaking over the silence in the cab. "This is life as a Security Trooper."

She bopped her head around, slapping her hands on her thighs. "Is it always this quiet?"

Reming sighed, turning away to face out the side viewscreen.

"Not always," Early answered. "Sometimes we talk. Or play music."

Rania nodded, still tapping away at her thighs. *I never realized how slow these things were.*

"What kind of music?" she asked at last.

"Oh, lots of stuff," replied Early, looking back over his shoulder while he drove ahead. "Joelson likes classic rock, Almar digs Castilian pop, Li likes NasCore, and I'm a country boy.

"But some people aren't music fans," he added, nodding over at Reming.

"I'm a fan, I just hate that western crap you always play," Reming huffed, still facing out the viewscreen.

Early nodded good-naturedly, still driving ahead as the MMUTCAT bounced along the frozen wastes. The cab was silent again.

"You know," said Early, "I'm something of a musician myself."

"Yeah?" Rania brightened. "What do you play?"

"A little guitar, a little bass. Mostly I sing though."

Turning back towards Rania, he favored her with a droll smile. "I wrote a song for a girl I met during our stopover in Tamarin. Want to hear it?"

Reming started up in his chair. He waved frantically at Rania from over Early's broad shoulder, mouthing the word 'No' as hard as he could.

"Of course Early, I'd love to." A cheerful smile crept across Rania's face.

Early blushed. Turning back towards the front, he rummaged under his seat for his speaker. Pulling it out, he thumbed across the menu screen, making his selection with a tap of his thumb. He set it down in the center console, a few seconds of chirruping bird song playing as the speaker queued up his song. Impatient, he prodded at the speaker with a meaty index finger. All at once the cabin erupted with the discordant wail of drawling song, playing over the poorly tuned twang of an acoustic guitar.

I've been aroun' a long, long time/ Just a partner searchin' fer a crime/ Saw you there, now yer on my mind/ Sweet like an orange, but ain't got no rind....

Rania forced a smile as the atonal lyrics rang in her ears. Early looked back at her, an eyebrow cocked and questioning. She gave him a thumbs-up and bit her lip, gritting her teeth as the chorus started.

Don't you know it's truuuuuuuuuuuuue...That I love Judy bluuuuuuuuue...Nothin' I wouldn't doooooooo...I'm just glad she knewwwww...

Reming clawed at his face from the passenger seat, covering one ear while he jammed the other against the abrasive plastic of the headrest. *I'm in hell, I'm in hell, I'M IN HELL!* he shouted in his mind, desperate to drown out the pestilential singing. As the MMUTCAT wound its way to the crater, the anxious wailing seeped out from the cab. Mixing with the soft rumbling of the engines, it drifted through the plains on lazy winds.

CHAPTER 8:

The metal dome glowed in the soft light of a new day. Filtered through the passing clouds, a quiet dawn radiated on the broad expanse of curved metal, sparkling on the pockets of snow deposited by the shifting winds. The four trails of red lights unwound from the communication spire centered at the top of the dome. They blinked in muted unison under the deeper sunlight of the morning. The second and third lights of each trail illuminated out-of-sync with the rest, the result of inexperienced repairs after a hailstorm many years before. A family of Snow Skitters bathed in the warm steam emitted by a hull grate, scuttling about on segmented legs as they jostled for the best position. It was a quiet day. A new day. A day of rest.

It was not to be.

'ALERT, ALERT, SHIP DETECTED, TIER-3 THREAT ASSESSED.' The automated voice split the air with the casual grace of a venereal disease diagnosis being broadcast over a waiting room speaker. It echoed down the alloy halls, announcing in time with the flashing amber lights. 'ALERT, ALERT, SHIP DETECTED...'

Private Li snapped an eye open. Seeing nothing but darkness, he quickly shut it, grinding his head further under the muffling embrace of his pillow.

'...TIER-3 THREAT ASSESSED.' The clashing alarm bored its way through his downy shield, penetrating and reverberating in his skull. Li ground his teeth, using both hands to pull the pillow tighter around his head. His inner thoughts formed an ouroboros of circular aggravation and protest. *Not today, it's my day off. Not today. It's my day off. Not today! It's my day off. Not! Today! It's. My. Day. Off!*

But still the alarm persisted, as calmly indifferent to his pleas as a free clinic desk clerk midway through her double shift explaining that test results are accurate to an error rate of .00002%, and that the odds were not in your favor of being the exception.

86

As the klaxon continued to echo in the dark confines of his room, Li was forced into the sobering realization that the alarm was not, in fact, a fevered figment of his exhausted imagination. Due to the forces of cosmic injustice clearly at play, he was most likely going to have to respond, regardless of today's status as his day off. This alarm, much like a diagnosis of venereal disease conducted at a free access sexual health clinic, would not proceed to disappear simply by ignoring it. Li tore the pillow from his head, flinging it across the room as he sat upright. It was going to be a long day.

'ALERT, ALERT, SHIP DETECTED, TIER-3 THREAT ASSESSED.' Rania looked up as the amber lights began to flash up and down the narrow hallway. A loud crash arose from Reming's room as she passed, the unmistakable sound of a game controller shattering against an alloy wall. A door swung open on her left as Li stumbled out, hopping along as he struggled to pull his boots on. Troopers began filing out into the hallway all around her, rubber soles clanging on the metal tiles. Rania broke into a light run, hustling to keep up with the press of troopers. She spotted Early jogging up ahead, smaller troopers flowing around the hefty trooper like a creek around a stone.

"Headed to the armory?" she asked, catching up with the musclebound soldier.

He nodded, thick arms swinging stiffly at his sides. "So much for breakfast."

Joelson pulled up alongside them, toothbrush still in his mouth.

"Think it's legit?" she asked the Senior-Trooper.

Joelson shook his head, pulling the toothbrush from his mouth. He stuffed it in his pocket, wiping his hands on his pants as he ran. "Probably just another Orbyx miner."

Early snorted in agreement, rolling forward like a lowland gorilla. Rania nodded. She was getting the hang of the station's rhythm. She and Joelson peeled off to the left, leaving Early as they headed towards the swinging doors of the control center. They pushed through the double doors, bowling over Private Johnson on the way in.

"Sorry!" she gasped, stopping to help the fallen trooper.

"Move it Rania!" Sergeant Ramos barked from the center deck. "We need those PMZs up ASAP."

"Sorry Smith!" She left him behind as she rushed to her desk.

"I'm not..." began Johnson, dusting off his pants without looking up, but she was already gone.

Reming grumbled along in the armory line, still fuming from his videogame's excruciating interruption. He'd been inches from a save point when the alarm kicked off, freezing his terminal connection and breaking his concentration. He'd woken up early and spent all morning slugging it out through *Altar of Combat*'s dreaded water stage, dodging traps, AI enemies, and the interference of invading players like Sergeant Wingo. Reming had just managed to weave past the last Dreadnot, dodging the swift-moving enemy's tendrils and leaping onto the floating platform. He was three steps and a leap from the last checkpoint, finally saving his hard-earned progress after hours of work. Then the alarm began.

He regretted smashing his controller, chucking it across the room in a fit of rage. He'd picked up gaming when he arrived on station almost four years ago. Like Li, he joined the ICF for the action-packed adventure his recruiter promised. *Kick some ass, get paid, and maybe pick up a girl or two on a distant colony.* What he got was two tours on AZH, a planet so far outside of the action that it didn't even have a proper name, just an alpha-numeric designator left over from its initial cataloguing by Coalition survey drones. Reming had tried to make the best of it when he first arrived, throwing himself into every alarm and response. But time is a relentless wheel, and as the days turned on, the repetitive cycle of life on AZH-01 became crushingly apparent to the earnest young trooper. The longer he spent on station, the more he recognized the immutable forces that controlled his destiny, and the more he retreated into the competitive, challenging digital world. The grinding was the same, but at least the progress was tangible.

Good thing I ordered a new one, hopefully this bullshit ends soon. They had retrieved the orbital shipment late last night, dragging it out of the crater and back to the installation. Unpacking a supply drop was a highpoint of morale, so they always waited until after evening formation the next day so everyone could be present. Until that time, his progress in the game was stalled, but if they wrapped this alarm up early he might be able to borrow Sergeant Wingo's controller and ensure the day wasn't a total loss.

The line shuffled forward as Special-Trooper Early sidled up to the armory and heaved his SLW-18 through the window. He cradled the massive laser in his hands as Private Almar walked up to retrieve his assistant gunner pack with spare batteries and range finder. Early heaved the unwieldy weapon over his shoulder, draping his arms over the stock and barrel to keep it in place. They stepped off down the hall together, joining the other armed troopers waiting in the formation room.

With their departure, the line shifted forward a few steps, then stopped. A few paces ahead in line, Li groaned in exasperation. *You and me both, buddy*, thought Reming.

"Is Konrad up there?" he asked the young trooper.

Looking back, Li shrugged. "No fuckin' clue. All I see is Sikes, lecturing each trooper before he hands out a weapon."

Fucking figures, he never passes up an opportunity to hear himself talk. Reming slumped against the cool alloy wall, leaning his head on the hard metal. He looked around for Konrad's lumbering, scarred mug, cursing the ICF for entrusting alternate armorer duties to the ill-tempered Private. *How come that bastard's never around when he's needed?*

"How come we never have visual feed when we fucking need it?" Sergeant Ramos demanded, pounding his hand against the center deck's railing. The control center below him was a frenzy of activity as troopers hustled to and fro, each working hard at their post or attempting to look busy enough to escape the Reed-Sergeant's wrath.

"We're working on it," answered Lieutenant Preston, placating the ornery Reed-Sergeant. He looked over to the desk with Sergeant Kyrghizwald and Senior-Trooper Joelson, huddled in earnest discussion as they spliced wires together.

"Any minute now," he added, catching Joelson's eye. Joelson nodded and gave a thumbs-up as the wall-sized monitor flickered to life. The loading bar in the top left corner surged across the screen, completing its path to the right in record time. The screen went black, then returned with the image of an Orbyx Mining Barge unfurling its golden sails to catch the sun. The room relaxed as the red and orange markings came into focus on the scarab-shaped hull. Lieutenant Preston breathed a sigh of relief. Any false alarm was a good alarm.

"Alright folks, pack it in," Sergeant Ramos ordered, as troopers around the room reached to close up their terminals. He swung down from the center deck, clearing the ladder without touching a step. Landing deftly on both feet, he pivoted crisply and headed to the hallway.

Sergeant Wingo pushed through the double doors, streams of sweat pouring down his face.

"Do...we have...a visual?" he wheezed. He doubled over, bracing his hands on his knees, pulling the breath through his wide-open mouth.

"Got it covered, Wingo," said Sergeant Ramos, neatly sidestepping the portly Buck-Sergeant. "Just a mining barge, we're on to after-actions."

Lowering himself to eye level with the panting NCO, Sergeant Ramos whispered in his ear. "And if your tubby-lovin', gravy-swillin', lard-ass misses another fucking alarm, I will double-time you until you *fucking die*."

He patted a hand reassuringly on the Buck-Sergeant's heaving shoulder, then turned and walked through the swinging doors.

In the Command Den, the room was abuzz with playful chatter. The NCOs grouped loosely around Lieutenant Preston, still tapping away at his tablet as he jotted down the preliminary findings for the incident report. Senior-Trooper Joelson shifted nervously as he leaned against the black-topped, polymer desk, crossing and uncrossing his arms. The lone junior enlisted in the room, Sergeant Ramos had grabbed him in the hallway before he could sneak off to the chow hall. *'You're about to sew on Buck-Sergeant, time to join the men's club,'* he'd said.

Once in the room Joelson had taken up a position outside the main circle, wary of his proximity to so much concentrated leadership. *Caution: exposure to leadership may be fatal in high doses*, he thought, but he knew his carefree trooper days were drawing to a close. When he'd tested for promotion last fall, he'd been excited, hoping to bring the changes he'd yearned for as a Private. Now, in the Command Den, surrounded by sergeants and officers, he was made acutely aware of his overwhelming smallness within the vast machine of the ICF.

A cough from the Lieutenant drew his attention back to the center of the room. "Alright gents, let's get start–"

"Bright mornings everyone! Another satisfactory standardized security situation!"

Senior-Sergeant Sikes strode through the door, interrupting Lieutenant Preston as he did. His charm and enthusiasm beamed out from a wide, toothy smile, but his pale eyes rang false. The other men were silent, shifting in their chairs. The Senior-Sergeant pushed into the room, undeterred by their underwhelming response, and took up a seat next to Lieutenant Preston, still flashing his cold-rolled, standard-issue smile. Sergeant Ramos locked eyes with Lieutenant Preston, a silent conversation passing between them, filled with contempt for the Senior-Sergeant's veneer of calculated pleasantries. Lieutenant Preston returned his attention to the group.

"As I was saying, let's get this after-action done. General situation was another Tier-3 assessed against a mining barge. Sergeant Ramos, how would you qualify the response?"

"Mediocre."

Lieutenant Preston looked up from his tablet at the gruff Reed-Sergeant.

"Care to elaborate?" he asked.

"Visual feed is still shoddy," clipped the Reed-Sergeant.

"And?" Lieutenant Preston waved his stylus in the air, drawing out his question.

Sergeant Ramos sighed. "And we didn't test the Ion Array, and our loudspeaker still doesn't annunciate in the vehicle bays, and our response times are slow. Lacking *effort*." He punctuated his last sentence with a fixed stare at Sergeant Wingo. Sergeant Wingo looked up at the ceiling, twiddling his thumbs and pointedly avoiding the Reed-Sergeant's gaze.

Lieutenant Preston nodded, and turning to Sergeant Sikes he asked, "And the arming? How'd it go?"

"Great, great!" The wide grin flashed again. "Expedient and without delay!"

Lieutenant Preston looked hard at the senior NCO, trying to read past the textbook phrases and years of ICF conditioning.

"Are you sure? I heard we had some issues with the line. That it took forty-three minutes and we didn't get all of the weapons out before we terminated the response."

The smile faltered, dipping around the corners.

"Buck-Sergeant, what did you think?" the officer asked, looking past Sergeant Sikes to Senior-Trooper Joelson. "What did you hear from the troopers about the arming response?"

Joelson looked up from his hands, eyes shifting nervously back and forth from Lieutenant Preston to Sergeant Sikes.

"I, uh, I," he faltered, his mouth suddenly dry.

The Senior-Sergeant favored him with a wide smile, pasted under eyes of silent pleading. Lieutenant Preston inclined his head, encouraging the young man to speak. Joelson looked to Sergeant Ramos, who favored him with a stiff nod. He swallowed, and found his voice.

"Sir, I, uh, I think arming is a consistent problem in these responses. The line is slow, the troopers barely get their weapons before we end up terminating the response, and then they spend up to another hour turning back in at the window."

Sergeant Sikes' eyes glittered, his gaze turning glacial and cold. Joelson avoided looking at him, focusing on Lieutenant Preston's warm smile, and continued.

"Sir, it's because we only have one window open for the majority of the time. Konrad is the only one we have as an armory alternate, and he...he isn't always first to the window. We'd be a lot better off if we certified more people to help out."

Joelson swallowed again, a little easier this time.

"We'd probably be able to halve our arming time just by training up a few other troopers. We could even do it on both shifts, to speed up the response further."

There was a smattering of murmured agreement as he looked around the room, Sergeant Sikes glared at him, livid that the young trooper had dared offer criticism. Reed-Sergeant Ramos nodded once, favoring Joelson with a half-smile. Rubbing his chin, Lieutenant Preston mulled over the Senior-Trooper's words.

"Alright," he said at last, bobbing his head in agreement. "I'm putting that in the report. Let's make it happen."

Joelson breathed a small sigh of relief, still studiously avoiding the daggers Sergeant Sikes shot his way.

"On to the next agenda, this inspection. It's coming next month whether we like it or not."

The Lieutenant paused, setting down his tablet to address the gathered leadership.

"Sergeant Wingo, I need you to assign someone to guide the inspector drone. Apparently it needs doors opened."

"Roger that sir, I'll get on it." The stout sergeant agreed.

"Sergeant K, I need you to organize the InRep files, make sure our terminal spaces are legible."

"Yessir." The pale-faced Buck-Sergeant confirmed, rubbing the dark circles around his eyes.

"Sergeant Sikes, I need a double-check on those weapons. They need to be 'white glove' spotless. Make sure we don't lose quality control when we add in new armorers."

"Yes, sir. With temerity and enthusiasm I carry on this dutiful tour!"

Sergeant Ramos ground his teeth.

"And Joelson."

Joelson looked up, surprised to be included in this conversation.

"There's a lot of cleaning to be done between now and then, I need you to organize the working parties. Divvy up the tasks and designate responsibilities."

Joelson's face fell, he knew firsthand how much everyone hated working parties, and he would have to be the one to assign cleaning jobs to his friends. It was a responsibility he didn't relish.

"Alright gents," Lieutenant Preston concluded. "Another solid day down. Let's get back to work."

The leadership team broke and headed for the door. As he passed, Sergeant Ramos clapped a hand to the shoulder of the crestfallen Senior-Trooper.

"Cheer up, Buck-Sergeant," he said, walking out the door. "Everyone hates NCOs, might as well get that out of the way early."

The supply capsule loomed over the troopers gathered in the vehicle bay. It was tilted oddly on its side, singed nose cone pointed at the sky in a forty-five degree angle, the charred heating tiles filling the bay with the faint smell of burning tires. The grey and white canister bore the scars of its abusive journey. The barrel-shaped body was rough and dented from its impact with the planet surface, soil still caked in clumps around the rear. Long gouges trailed the underside, with rocks embedded here and there in the hull, courtesy of being towed behind a MMUTCAT for miles along the tundra plains. A single red and grey parachute remained, the other two torn off as it was dragged out of the deep crater it dug through the soil. It was a shabby, pitiful sight, but a celebrated one. The troopers gathered with chatty anticipation around the vessel of their hopes and happiness.

Reed-Sergeant Ramos and Lieutenant Preston stood off to the side of the main body, surveying the battered package with careful eyes.

"Looks a little rough," the officer said at last.

"Rough? Shit, sir. It looks like the last ship off Avina," remarked Sergeant Ramos. "Did those fuckers have to send it through an orbital barrage on its way here?"

Lieutenant Preston ran a hand through his hair.

"Think it's safe to open?"

The Reed-Sergeant sized up the beaten-down supply pod, rubbing his broad chin thoughtfully.

"They were built to withstand heavy impacts," offered Sergeant Ramos, pulling his hand from his face to point out the salient structures of the craft. "The interior is lined with shock dampeners and hydraulic buffers, and the nose cone is supposedly insulated with high-heat ceramic tiles. Coming in hot like it did, there's probably damage to the dampeners, the interior is probably smashed to shit, and the fuel tanks might be leaking into the side wall. The first two ain't bad, but the fuel could be ignited if we trigger the wrong electrical relay. They're designed to survive with contents intact regardless of condition. But as you can see," he paused, gesturing to the fourth parachute still lodged in its tube, "quality control has declined a bit since the design phase."

Lieutenant Preston nodded, taking in what the Reed-Sergeant had said. He looked back over to the crowd of troopers excitedly discussing the contents of the supply drop. These canisters were a godsend, the station's lone physical connection to the outside galaxy. The care packages, Linknet purchases, and fresh food supplies were a breath of fresh air whenever they arrived, and everyone was much more tolerable and patient in the days after an uncrating. *Besides*, he thought, *they're already here, they've seen it. I can't take it away now and pretend like it got lost along the way. They'd riot.* Lieutenant Preston sighed. It'd be another month before the next supply drop, and this one was delayed already. He'd rather risk a fiery explosion than spend another month trapped here with a crew of surly troopers.

He waved to Sergeant Ramos. "Open her up."

Crowbars found their purchase along the battered door of the supply capsule. Four troopers heaved with all their might, straining against the deformed metal. One by one, they popped the heat seals around the doorframe, prying the capsule open inch by inch. The metal creaked and groaned, railing in protest at this latest abuse. More troopers moved in, led by Special-Trooper Early, and put their backs to the task of levering the door open. A mighty struggle ensued, man against stubborn metal, but the weight of numbers favored the troopers. With one last steely scream, the door ripped from its frame, falling to the ground and clattering on the concrete floor of the bay. A cheer went out among the gathered troopers. Two troopers climbed into the capsule, thankfully intact, no fuel spills or interstitial hydraulic contamination. Sergeant Ramos formed the remaining troopers in a line to receive the boxes, and began ordering the capsule's unpacking.

Hours later, the task was completed, all the boxes and crates stacked neatly in the chow hall. One pile sat aside from the others, a large stack of crates meant for one of the local ranchers. Supply drops being both expensive to conduct and capable of carrying several tons of material, it wasn't uncommon to lump shipments together as long as they were bound for the same hemisphere. Tomorrow they'd have to assign some troopers to drive out, ferrying the boxes to the ranchers nearby. It was a job no one relished. The ranchers were insular and ornery, and there were decades of friction built up between them and the ICF troopers, mostly on account of the troopers' frequent harassment of the ranchers' Gluffant herds.

Troopers milled about, gathering in clumps and pointing out the boxes with their names. Sergeant Ramos cleared his throat, the room going silent as all eyes swung in his direction. He nodded and the crowd swept in, troopers excitedly pulling boxes from the stack, peeling off into the corners of the room to open their prizes.

"Feels like Christmas morning," Lieutenant Preston remarked, standing alongside the senior NCO.

Sergeant Ramos grunted in agreement. "Every time."

Early and Reming were first in line, snagging their boxes and hoisting them overhead, wading past their fellow troopers as they snagged a spot along the wall to sit. Eager hands ripped the taped seals along the corners of their packaging, reaching inside and pulling out handfuls of sterile packing material. Reming felt deep inside and found his prize, a limited edition *NiteScope Delta* gaming controller, with custom printed thumb bezels and integrated microphone.

"No more headset!" he grinned.

Early was also ecstatic with the contents of his box, broad shoulders quivering with glee as he pulled out the latest volume of his bodybuilding idol's serial memoir: *The Heaviest Weight is the Heart.* The plastic box containing the flash drive with the book's digital files was awash with full-color pictures from the life of author Stavrom Bearsur; bodybuilder, environmentalist, and inter-galactically renowned gourmet chef. Early held it at arm's length, carefully admiring the shimmer of the holographic text in the fluorescent lighting of the dining hall.

Private Li sidled up to the two men, a package carefully tucked under both arms. He dropped to the ground, splaying his feet out beside his fellow troopers. He ripped into his own package, drawing out a box of *Shirley's Synthetic Brownies* ('No chocolate, but made with REAL love!') and a pair of triple-thick SynthWool socks, courtesy of his caring mother, Jia Li.

"Nice," remarked Reming. "Those'll come in handy."

Li nodded, breaking the seal on the sweets and pulling out a diminutive brown puck. He popped it in his mouth, savoring the artificial flavors. *Just like home*, he thought.

"Not opening the other one?" asked Early, still admiring the flash drive's packaging in the light.

"Naw man, savin' it for later. Never know when the next drop gets delayed," Li said around a mouthful of brownie.

"Smart thinking," agreed Rania, walking up to the boys and grabbing a spot on the wall. She slid down, dropping into a crouch as she opened her own box. "I just wish I was that patient, I always have to rip into mine as soon as I get them."

"Patience is a virtue in time," sang Joelson, walking up to the group. "At least that's what my mom always said."

He grabbed a spot on the other side of Rania, dropping a stack of packages on the ground.

"What's with the haul?" asked Reming, eyeing the tower of wrapped parcels.

"Mom heard I got promoted, wanted to send me things to celebrate with."

He opened up the first box, pulling out a bottle of non-alcoholic SimuChamp and a handwritten note. He adjusted his glasses on the bridge of his nose, skimming his mother's loopy printing. A smile crept across Joelson's face as he folded the letter and tucked it safely into a pocket. He reached farther into the first box, pulling out another three green glass bottles.

"Looks like you got enough to share," said Rania, her hands full of packaging. "SimuChamp isn't cheap. Your mom must be very proud."

"Although not enough to send you the good stuff," sniffed Reming, eyeing the bottles of the sparkling, non-alcoholic beverage.

"She knows the packages get scanned before they arrive. She wouldn't want me to get in trouble right before I sew on the next stripe." Joelson carefully lined the bottles by the wall before settling into another package.

"Smart lady," coughed Li, forcing his words out around the chewy, brown mass cementing his back molars. He worked his jaw hard, beating the synthetic sweet into submission through the sheer will of his chewing.

"Smartest woman I ever met," Joelson said, pulling a crate of popcorn out of the second box along with another handwritten note. As he unstuck the letter from the box, a picture fluttered to the ground, faded and creased around the edges.

"Oooh, is that your dad?" Rania snatched the picture off the tile, angling it for the group to see. "He looks so young."

"Looks strong," said Early, noting the dark-skinned man's broad shoulders and impressive, cannonball biceps. "Good arms."

"Yeah, I take after my mom," agreed Joelson, gesturing to his long and lanky form.

Reming set his controller down, looking hard at the image in Rania's hand. "Dig the mustache, very retro."

"Both he and my grandfather had one. Mom said it made them look cultured, more mature." Joelson reached for the picture, taking it in his hands and admiring his father's youthful spirit and infectious grin. He didn't know much about his father. He'd died back on Avina when Joelson was very young. That mustache was what he remembered most about him--that and how his smile always seemed to spread throughout a room. The picture showed him shaking hands with a Representative from the Small Council, receiving an award plaque in the other hand and laughing into the camera, the background filled with the ornate trappings of the Capitol Award Center.

"I wish we could have beards," said Li, swallowing hard on the last of his brownie. "My Uncle Tuto had a beard, and he looked badass."

"Too bad ICF won't let you 'cause your mask wouldn't fit right," said Rania, picking up her package again. "Not that I really have that problem."

"No worries, neither does Li," snorted Reming. "Can you even grow one?"

"Fuck you, man," scowled Li, punching the older trooper in the shoulder. "My beard is thick like your sister's."

"Doubt it. Unlike you she has to shave *every* day," snickered Reming, rubbing his shoulder. The group shared a laugh at Li's expense, with Early offering a reassuring pat on the young Private's outstretched boot.

The laughter froze in Rania's throat as a familiar smell drifted by, cloying and sweet, with undertones of rot. She stiffened as Senior-Trooper Leonard walked past, her chest constricting slightly. He sat down at a table directly across from them, bobbing his head to a tune only he could hear. He looked up from his package, locked eyes with her and waved, a penknife still in his hand from opening the box. Rania went cold, avoiding his gaze and staring at her feet. Joelson reached out a hand, but she turned away, shaking her head.

"I'm fine, it's ok," she stammered. "I, I think I'm going to go back to my room, get back to studying."

She rose and walked away stiffly, fists clenched and jaw tight. Joelson watched her go in silence, wishing he had better words to say.

But Joelson wasn't the only one observing her. Senior-Sergeant Sikes watched their exchange through calculating eyes, paying half a mind to the conversation surrounding the Leadership table. Sergeant Wingo was in the middle of another one of his stories, barely getting through the words as he stopped to laugh at his own recollections. *The inanity of fools, so focused on themselves, devoted to reliving their own meager triumphs.* He thanked the blessed ICF that he only had a year and a half left, then he could retire. A quiet ranch house on a distant colony, a lifetime pension and a personal MedStation for his home. *No more counseling whiny troopers with their petty personal problems, no more trivial debates with boorish fellow NCOs, no more currying favor with buffoonish officers.* They were all beneath him, and he salivated at the day he would finally be rid of the constant, galling tar of puerile worthlessness. *What do they know about the purity of service? They know nothing of the sacrifices I've made to fulfill the ICF's needs, to keep this installation a singular unit.* Sergeant Sikes nodded along with Wingo's story, laughing along at the appropriate punchlines. *But I would burn this place to the ground if it meant retiring from here a minute sooner. And all of you inside it.*

He shook his head, a thin smile stretched across his face. He watched Rania stand up, brushing aside Joelson's hand as she left. *Still, a ranch could get lonely without a proper companion.* As an ICF weapons administrator and counselor, he was well versed in the psychological complications that arise from long-term isolation. His decades of service in remote tours had given him little opportunity to find a wife of his own, and the decision to allow female troopers to serve at the remote installations had been approved less than a decade ago. They were just becoming a regular feature of the security-sensor platoon.

He leaned in to the Lieutenant, touching his elbow to draw his attention.

"You know, Sir. I do believe Special-Trooper Khalil might still be experiencing some distress."

He kept his voice low to avoid interrupting Sergeant Wingo's latest bumptious anecdote. He pointed to Rania before drawing the officer's attention to Leonard, who was currently working his way through a fistful of SimuJerky, chewing hard with his mouth wide open.

"I should sit down with her again. To better gauge her morale level and establish a pipeline for better integration in the unit."

Lieutenant Preston nodded, concern furrowing his brow.

"Of course, Senior. Whatever you think is best."

CHAPTER 9:

"I'm telling you, they explode."

"Dude, shut the fuck up. No they don't." Reming jabbed his fork into the pile of pale grey mush on his tray.

"They do. Almar said he and Godrey drove through a valley two nights ago by Lima-2, and one exploded."

"Almar and Godrey drove by Lima-2 and watched a Gluffant explode?" Reming cocked an eyebrow at Li from across the table.

Li dropped his shoulders, pushing his pile of mush around on the tray.

"Well, no. They didn't actually *see* it explode, they just drove past and one *had* exploded. It was just parts scattered everywhere." He perked back up again, sweeping his hands around to emphasize the dismemberment's extent. "Leg here, horn there, fur scattered all over."

"And so they just assumed it exploded?"

"What else could it be? Only thing that eats them is us, and the ranchers' slaughterhouse is all the way by Foxtrot-7."

Reming considered the young man's point, drawing figure eights on the tray with his fork. He set the utensil down and stared hard at Li.

"Alright, smartass, even if I buy that, why would a Gluffant explode?"

"Methane."

"Get the fuck out of here man!" said Reming, slamming his hands on the metal table.

"They do! They eat the methane to get high or whatever," Li insisted.

Reming shook his head at the trooper's ignorance. "They breathe in a little, yeah, but they don't just fill up on methane, walking around like a shaggy Hindenburg."

"A what?"

"You know, man. Hindenburg. From the vidplays. The giant, flaming balloon or whatever."

Li nodded in understanding. "Oh, yeah. The 'Ole the humanity' one."

"That's it," said Reming before resuming his poking at the tray. He chased a suspiciously round lump through the pale, grey 'Beef Stroganoff.'

"What are we talking about?" asked Joelson, making his way to the table. He set his tray down next to Reming while Early sat down by Li.

"Gluffants," answered Reming. "Li thinks they explode."

"They do!"

"They don't!" hissed Reming. "Shut the fuck up!"

"Ah." Joelson nodded, sliding a fork into his pale blue cube of 'Fresh-Baked Blueberry Oatmeal.'

"Almar says he saw one explode two nights ago," said Early, taking a swig from his orange electrolyte beverage.

Reming sighed, throwing his hands in the air. Li let out a whoop of triumph, dancing in his seat. Reming dropped his head to the alloy table and began banging it softly. He looked up to see Rania swing in on the other side of Li, sweat staining her shirt and dripping off her face.

"Gross. You couldn't have showered first?" Li leaned away, giving the sweaty trooper a wide berth.

"Sure, because *I'm* what's unsanitary here." Rania jerked a thumb towards a solitary cockroach crawling up the wall behind them. Reming stiffened on the bench, his skin suddenly crawling. He regretted leaving his Zapgun in his room. *Would it be weird if I strapped it to my thigh?* He ran through the difficulties in crafting a holster for the diminutive pest disposal weapon.

"Good run?" asked Joelson.

"Not bad, six miles," shrugged Rania, digging into her own blue cube.

"Too far," said Reming, shaking his head. He stepped away from the table, the thought of eating suddenly repulsive. "You can't run from your problems."

"Watch me!" called Rania as his back was turned. She returned to the mushy remains of the blue cube on her plate. *I wonder if this is what disappointment tastes like?* She shook her head, shoveling down the 3D-printed organic 'food' and paying half a mind to Joelson explaining about the coming inspection.

"So it's next month. I'll need everyone to meet up in the formation room after chow."

Rania nodded, still focused on her food. This was her first inspection, but sensor techs were rarely affected. Working in such a precise, technical field meant that very few inspectors were remotely qualified to check on her work. As long as the sensor systems still ran, it was generally assumed that she was performing her duties well. Besides, it's not like she had any weapons to keep clean. She nodded along as Joelson fielded Early's questions on the inspection preparations. *Guess that's what you get for promotion, the burden of knowledge and planning.* Sergeant Kyrghizwald drifted into view, lethargically walking his tray to the leadership table. His watery blue eyes were set deep in the dark circles under a mess of disheveled hair. *Rough night?* she wondered. *He looks in worse shape than me.*

Buck-Sergeant Kyrghizwald was in a fog. Dragging his way over to the table, he set his tray down next to Sergeant Wingo and flopped onto the long bench seat.

"Rough night, Sergeant K?" asked Lieutenant Preston, scanning the Buck-Sergeant with a look of concern.

"Long," he replied. "Still cataloguing the InReps."

Lieutenant Preston nodded, worry still on his face. Sergeant Kyrghizwald lifted the jiggling sphere of electrolyte beverage and drank deep, chugging it down with hard, violent gulps. He drained the empty membrane and set it down on his tray, wiping his mouth on the back of his hand. Feeling slightly more human, he turned his attention to the brick of 'Lasagna' on his tray. Sergeant Wingo was thoroughly engaged in discussing Special-Trooper Early, and his apparent status as a musician.

"So yeah, LT, you gotta hear this song," laughed Sergeant Wingo, leveling a plump hand at the officer across the table. "Top five in the 'Worst Things I Ever Heard' category."

"What's it on?" asked Lieutenant Preston, a bite of gray mush jiggling on the fork he held in his hand.

"Some chick he met when we stopped over in Tamarin," answered the Buck-Sergeant with a snort. "Apparently he caught the feelings real bad. Inspired the inner poet in him."

Sergeant Ramos grunted, dismissing the wasted energy.

Lieutenant Preston nodded along. "I'll have to check it out. Do you have a copy?"

Sergeant Wingo positively grinned. "Of course, sir. Half the unit does. You know these things spread fast."

"Happy to share it with you," he said with a wink.

Lieutenant Preston turned to Sergeant Ramos. "I heard Special-Trooper Belle had her baby yesterday. A little boy."

Sergeant Ramos grunted again, nodding in acknowledgment of the good news. Across the table, the smile sagged a little on Sergeant Wingo's face.

"Did she?" he asked, trying to mask the concern in his voice. "But that's too early, right?"

"A little, yeah," admitted the Lieutenant, failing to read the change in the Buck-Sergeant's tone. "But she was at six months, so they were able to get him stabilized in an incubator."

Sergeant Wingo nodded, stroking his double chin. The conversation quickly turned towards the upcoming inspection, with Lieutenant Preston expressing some apprehension about the two MMUTCAT's sitting non-operational in their vehicle bay.

"Don't sweat it, LT," said Reed-Sergeant Ramos. "We already document deadlined MMUTCATs in our monthly VINReps. We wrote up the accident report for Reming's rollover when it happened and we backordered the heat cycler for the other last month. Should come in on the next supply drop, but until then, don't worry. The way these things work, everything's gravy if it's on paper."

The officer nodded, his fears put slightly to rest. These inspections were no joke, he heard of more than one officer's career being abruptly derailed by a poor report. In tech school he'd even heard tell about a Lieutenant who was discharged after his unit failed one. He walked into his colonel's office as the commander of a platoon, received the results, and left as a civilian.

Sergeant Ramos read the unease still lingering on Lieutenant Preston's face.

"Don't worry, sir," he said, "This is my third inspection. We'll be fine. Besides, we've got our top troops on the cleanup."

Senior-Trooper Joelson stood before the assembled troopers, shifting his weight on the balls of his feet. They grouped in a loose circle in the bare expanse of the formation room, chatting away in small cliques. Unconsciously he adjusted his glasses on the bridge of his nose, a slight shake in his hands. He clenched a fist and drove it deep in his pocket, forcing himself steady by pulling out and unfolding his tablet. His notes on the work assignments swam in his vision on the screen. He closed his eyes, took a deep breath, and released it slowly, opening his eyes as he did. He looked out on the mass of troopers and cleared his throat loud enough to draw their attention.

"Alright everyone, we have an inspection coming up, so I put together the list of work details to get things ready."

A loud groan rose out of the collected troopers, Joelson ignored it and kept going, fixated on the words on his screen.

"They want a deep clean now, with maintenance cleaning weekly until the inspection. But don't slack off on this one, since they'll be coming around to inspect by 2100 Sunday. They want 'white gloves' on this."

The grumbling from the crowd deepened, Joelson kept on track, neatly sidestepping the fact that as a new NCO he would swiftly be leaving the lower enlisted ranks and joining the leadership collective of the eponymous 'they.'

"Now I tried to be fair in this, so everyone is set up with a partner. I tried not to double-tap anyone who's had that working party before."

Joelson paused, looking up from his tablet to read the faces of the crowded troopers. He felt pinned under the magnified weight of their stares. He turned back towards the tablet and began reading his list of assignments.

"Godrey, Early, you've got the chow hall and the RationVendor."

"Rog." Early bobbed his big, shaved head.

"Reming, Li, you've got the showers and bathrooms."

"Aw c'mon," whined Li.

"Hush!" Early cut him off, nudging the young Private with a broad shoulder. "Let'm speak."

Joelson breathed a sigh of thanks for the burly Special-Trooper. Pointing at the next two troopers in the group, Joelson continued down the list.

"Johnson, Konrad, you've got the armory."

Konrad grunted, a touch of color coming to his scarred face. Private Smith raised a hand.

"Uh, Johnson's over there," he said, pointing to a trooper in the back of the group. "I'm Smith."

"No one cares!" called a voice from the back.

"Let's get this done!" called another.

Joelson shook his head, his glasses sliding further down his nose. He adjusted them and addressed the short, young trooper.

"My bad. Smith, *you're* with Konrad for weapons cleaning." He nodded his head towards Private Johnson. "Johnson, you and Almar are slotted to take the farmer crates to the Gligman Ranch. It's the one by Lima-1. It's a bit of a drive, and I know you're working shift tonight, so if you tackle this you won't have to clean."

Johnson and Almar nodded, the sting of being forced to meet the local ranchers lessened by the knowledge that at least they wouldn't have to scrub anything. Joelson worked his way down the list, divvying up the remaining work among the rest of the troopers. He paused when he got to the last name on the tablet screen.

"And, Rania," he said at last.

"Yes?" She looked up. It seemed like all the cleaning to be done had already been assigned. She'd been wondering if she was left off the list by accident, but apparently even a sensor tech isn't immune to the ICF's insatiable hunger for working parties.

Joelson looked at her over the tablet screen. "I need you to tackle the control center, policing up the wiring and dusting. There's not too much, but you'll be handling it alone."

Her brow furrowed. It almost seemed like she was getting off too easy.

"And," he added, "Sergeant Sikes wants to sit down with you beforehand. Something about working on unit integration."

Fuck. She knew she was getting off too easy. A chorus of 'Oooohs' came from the crowd of troopers. Sergeant Sikes was weird enough from a distance, speaking exclusively in ICF approved idioms and demanding mirror-shined polish on every trooper's weapon before turn in. He had an odd intensity in his eyes when he spoke, a piercing stare that clashed with the wide smile plastered on his face. It always seemed like he was looking straight through you without actually seeing you, like he was never actually present during the conversation. The effect was off-putting.

Her last meeting with him had been less than pleasant, a 'reconciliation mentorship feedback session' as he termed it, forced upon her in the wake of the incident with Leonard. It had come out of nowhere. She wasn't even sure how leadership had found out about it, although she suspected that Belle told them, since she was the only one Rania had confided in. All she knew was that one day after formation, she was ordered to have an appointment with the Senior-Sergeant, with no discussion of how or why. It had been awkward, his stilted speech crisscrossing over the incident that was still fresh and painful in her mind.

She remembered spending the meeting on the verge of tears, finding herself lost in his flurry of clumsy doublespeak. *And now I get to do it again.* Rania shook her head, clearing her thoughts and tuning back in to the conversation. Joelson had just finished sketching out a cleaning timeline with the other troopers.

"Alright then," he addressed to the crowd of troopers, "Any other questions?"

"Yeah, I got one," said Reming, raising his hand. "What's up with that shadow on your lip? Is that like some dirt or something? Do you need help brushing it off?"

Joelson cringed as the weight of the crowd's attention focused on his upper lip. A second chorus of murmurs drifted out as troopers in the back craned their heads to see what Reming was talking about.

"Oooh," Rania's eyes widened. "Are you growing a mustache? Like your dad?"

Joelson blushed.

"Everyone, has their posts so, uh," he stammered, "Dismissed!"

He turned on a heel and sped out the door, the room echoing with laughter behind him.

Herman Gligman stood alone on a low, snowy ridge. The valley stretched before him, the sun sparkling off patches of ice. A stiff wind rippled past, tugging at the corners of his thick snow suit. Herman adjusted the lining of his fur-lined hood, seating it firmly around his insulated goggles. He took a deep breath from the oxygen tube running under his scarf-wrapped face and sighed, content in the majesty of the morning.

He shouldered his pack and took a step down the snow-packed dune. Ahead of him, a dozen Gluffants ambled in the morning light, bellowing to each other and scraping for lichen. Herman slipped the AcuTrack from a holster on his belt and began syncing their radio collars. He checked the herd into the database in the small tablet, downloading the vitals on each animal from the collars around each beast's massive ankle. He scrolled through a few on the small touch-screen, satisfied with what he saw.

"You want me to make you some lunch?" a voice whispered in his ear. "Or are you gon' be out all day?"

Herman smiled behind his wooly scarf. Henrietta took great care of him, keeping him whole over their thirty years of marriage. A woman willing to give up everything and move to a frozen wasteland on a planet in the outer-rim was a rare find these days. And Henrietta had seemed genuinely delighted to join him on the family ranch, taking to the arduous, humble work with grace and charm. She seemed to have a real knack for sales, always working a better deal on the Tridman Slaughterhouse and sourcing out the best buyers for their premium Gluffant steaks. Herman knew she was the one when he first brought her out to the ranch on AZH. She caught her first sight of a Gluffant on that day, a young heifer of three years, stark white with a shock of blond in a zig-zag patch on her huge, shaggy head. Henrietta had rushed over, mouth agape under her many layers, and reached out to pet the great beast, earning a snort of appreciation when she scratched behind her ears. Henrietta fell in love with their herd then, and Herman with her.

She was always so good about taking care of their immense charges. Brushing the tangles out of their thick fur, prying out sharp rocks occasionally lodged in a hoof. Not that Henrietta took any less care with him. She was always fussing whenever he came home with a bruise from an errant kick, splinting his ribs one time when he made the mistake of standing between a bull Gluffant and his cow. She was good to him, better than he deserved, and when he woke each morning before sunrise and saw her lying next to him, it warmed his heart for the day to come.

Herman tapped the headset under his hood, opening up the thin microphone that stretched under his oxygen line.

"No dear, I'm fine. I've got a few of the new calves to tag before I set in."

He turned and looked to the south, his cottage was marked from the steam rising in a cloud from the twin geothermal generators. From this distance it looked so small, so quaint, but it held his whole world.

He tapped the headset again. "Although I wouldn't say no to a bowl of your world-famous chili."

"I can do *that*." The voice whispered in his ear. Herman smiled at the way she sang that last word, drawing it out in a lovely melody. He turned back to the herd, his attention once again on the task at hand.

He spent most of the morning tagging and checking the rest of the herd. A considerable amount of time was spent in chasing the three calves that dropped this week, still prancing about on clumsy new legs. He wove in and out of the herd, careful around the testier bulls, but by and large was ignored by the hulking beasts. It was the smallest ranch on AZH, just him and Henrietta, so the herd was used to his presence. They paid him little mind as he set about his work. It was well into the afternoon when he'd finished, the sun just beginning to set over the ridge.

He turned south and headed home, trudging along in thick snow boots. He passed by the barn his great-grandfather had built, a wide, open-floored structure for the Gluffants to take shelter in during the worst winter storms. He patted the metal wall as he passed, pitted and worn by decades of windstorms and blizzards. While it had weathered all manner of trials on AZH's unforgiving North Pole, there was still a dent in the east side from when his father had driven the family BredRan straight into the wall as a young boy. They still had the faded, red truck, tucked away in the small garage by the cottage generators. It was one of the older models, with four snow tracks instead of wheels. It had been kept going for decades after the company had phased the model out, maintained by patient hands.

Herman whistled as he walked, the sunset bathing the grey roof of his house in a warm amber glow. He could see Henrietta through the window, dancing along as she flitted about in the kitchen. He saw the steam rising out of the pot on the stove and imagined the spicy, garlicky smell of its bubbling contents. It had been a long day for Herman Gligman, but a good day, and his heart was full as he stepped to the door.

The creature watched from a small hill, squat and hunkered against the snowy dune, its mottled grey and white hide blending in perfectly with the snow-swept steppe. Its coarse bristles wavering lightly in the wind, further distorting its outline against the icy backdrop. It was still. Patiently waiting as it surveyed the quiet scene before it. The wind picked up, carrying with it the smell of a herd a few miles north. More of the same prey the creature had been feasting on for a month, the creature ignored them.

Below its perch on the modest hill, was a glow. It was not THE GLOW, which was still many miles off on the eastern horizon. But it was A glow. THE GLOW still called to the creature, a beacon of primal desire drawing it further and further. THE GLOW held promises for the creature, the promise of a meal beyond its imagining. Though there had been no shortage of prey here, still the creature yearned. THE GLOW whispered to the creature in its sleep, pulling it ever forward. 'Come with me,' it said, 'and you will never be hungry again.'

The creature shivered, either from cold or from the sheer pleasure of the thought. THE GLOW was everything to the creature, but it was not the only thing on the horizon. That was why the creature waited, watching the lesser glow below it. It was a smaller glow, but still substantial, shining brightly against the bleak emptiness of the barren landscape. The creature watched as something walked towards the lesser glow. Its two-legged gait was slow, unhurried. This prey was new to the creature, its smell foreign, covered in flat synthetic odors. The creature was intrigued, curious as to this new prey and its relationship to the glow. It watched the prey approach the source of the lesser glow, lax and careless to the dangers of this world. The prey approached the lesser glow and after a moment in front of it, disappeared inside. That was enough for the creature. It leapt from its perch, bounding silently down the hill, curiosity and hunger rumbling through its belly.

CHAPTER 10:

The MMUTCAT rumbled across the open plain, eight enormous tires churning on the fresh packed snow. The air was quiet, still, the wind having died down after the snowstorm the night before. It was quiet inside the boxy cab as well, the only sound coming from the soft drone of the engines filtering through the bare metal floor. Privates Almar and Johnson rode in silence, staring out at the icy tundra through the front viewscreen.

"So..." said Private Almar, breaking the quiet hum of the cabin. "Are you the one that grew up on Avina?"

Johnson rolled his eyes. "No, that's Smith."

Almar nodded, his eyes still on the front screen. "So you're the one dating that girl in freight logistics?"

Johnson couldn't keep the weariness out of his voice. "Nooo, that's Smith, too."

Private Almar bobbed his head, still searching the viewscreen to avoid any light pockets on the ground ahead. He didn't want to risk the MMUTCAT getting caught in one of those patches of un-packed snow. The last thing he'd want is to be trapped for hours waiting on a tow.

"Ok, but you're the one that plays cello. In the café band, right?"

"No!" snapped Johnson, pounding a fist into his other hand to punctuate each word. "That's. Smith."

He leaned back in his chair, a frustrated sigh escaping from his lips. He stared up at the rough headliner on the ceiling.

"Why can't anyone tell us apart?"

Almar shrugged, still focused on the road ahead. "Dunno man. You're both short white guys with dark hair. And you're both new."

"And there was that time you wore Smith's jacket during a Tier-03."

"That was one time!" Johnson sputtered. "Our laundry got mixed up!"

"Try a new look?" Almar offered with another shrug. "Maybe grow a mustache like Joelson?"

"I can't," sighed Johnson. "It comes in patchy as hell. Looks like shit."

"Shitty mustaches get remembered," he said without looking at the younger trooper. Johnson mulled it over as the cabin lapsed again into silence.

Minutes passed in the quiet hum of the MMUTCAT cabin. Private Almar kept ahead on the course marked by his MinMap, following the blinking icon to the rancher's home.

"So..." Almar began again. "You like music?"

"Yes?" Johnson rolled his eyes back at the other trooper. "Who *doesn't* like music? People always ask that question, but the answer is dumb. Everyone likes music! It's a basic human trait!"

"Whatever, man," said Almar, already bored with the conversation. "You wanna listen to something or not?"

Johnson deflated immediately, shoulders slumping as he leaned back in his chair.

"Sure. What do you have?"

Almar cocked an eye at the young trooper, sizing up if he was done with his petty little outbursts. Satisfied with what he saw, he jerked a thumb towards the passenger seat.

"Speaker's under the seat. It's loaded with tons of stuff, classic rock, trimble, rap, NasCore, blues, country."

He paused in his genre litany, dropping his voice in a conspiratorial tone. "It's even got Early's song on there."

Johnson's eyes widened, he looked back at the older trooper. "You don't mean..."

"Yep," nodded Almar. "Wanna hear it?"

Johnson grinned. People had been talking about this song for almost a month now. He still couldn't picture the muscle-bound Special-Trooper as a romantic or a musician, but the awfulness was legendary throughout the unit. He had to hear it for himself. Johnson reached under the padded seat and pulled out the small blue speaker. He thumbed across the menu screen, searching for the right file.

"What's it called?"

"Original Song: Judy Blue; by the Earl of Lovin' You."

Johnson thumbed across the screen, finding the file at last. He selected it and set the speaker down between their seats. The cabin was silent except for the sound of birds chirping from the speaker. He looked at Almar, tapping his hands on the armrest as they waited. A few seconds passed, and the cabin was split with the ear-wrenching thrum of a poorly tuned acoustic guitar. They cringed together as the drawling tones of Special-Trooper Early cut in over the 'melody,' his tortured lyrics out of sync with the rest of the song. They laughed along at the winding chorus, particularly his attempt to rhyme 'misconstrue' with 'Pentateuch.' As the six-minute song finally came to an end, Johnson was doubled over in laughter, clutching his sides. He looked over at Almar, who was trying to focus on keeping the truck straight while he wiped tears from his eyes.

"That was so much better than I ever imagined," said Johnson, finally catching his breath.

"Yeah, really gives you insight into the mind behind the muscles," agreed Almar.

"That went on forever. How could he find that many rhymes for blue? Did he just pull up a rhyme app on his tablet and scroll down the list?" laughed Johnson, throwing up his hands.

Almar shared the laugh, weaving the massive vehicle between the dunes. "Dunno man, my favorite was *'locked up my heart with your jiu jitsu.'*"

They settled back into the quiet of the cabin, the steady noise of the engines filling the air as they stared back out the front viewscreen. They bounced along the rocky plain. After a few minutes Johnson turned back to Private Almar.

"Funny how inspired he was by that girl. We were only on Tamarin for two weeks."

"Strong body, strong heart," Almar acknowledged with a shrug. "How long do you really need to fall for someone?"

Johnson turned back to the viewscreen, still tapping along on the armrests.

"What about you? You ever feel that inspired?" he asked after a few beats.

Almar shook his head. "I dated a few people in college, but nothin' that serious. Usually done when I got too busy or caught up in shit. You?"

"Yeah, once," admitted Johnson. "I met him in Chicago before I shipped out. He's an architect back there."

His voice trailed off, thinking about Brent and the life he'd left behind. He'd been on leave after tech school, making full use of the few months he had before deploying to the outer rim. Johnson had met him when they bumped into each other in a café near Cicero Avenue. He had spilled a SimuCaff latte all over Brent, dousing him in the hot beverage. Red-faced and beside himself with apologies, he'd kept offering to buy a new shirt for the attractive young man for his trouble. Brent had only smiled, dabbing the stains all over his clothes with a red and blue checkered handkerchief he kept in his back pocket. Brent had bought Johnson a new latte with his phone number written on the side in tight, neat letters. Johnson had been smitten, calling Brent almost immediately the next day. They'd bonded over their love of Chopin, street-cart Gyros, and their mutual hatred for political cartoons. Brent had even offered to let Johnson live with him before he shipped out, allowing him a reprieve from the friend's couch he'd been crashing on for a few weeks.

Johnson sighed. Brent had said that he would wait for him, and they'd talked a few times over the Linknet. But the days stretched on without him, and Chicago was a busy town, with fickle winds.

Almar read the change in the younger man's face. "Cheer up man, you get six months leave between tours. And three tours, and you get to rotate back to a different duty."

He patted a hand on the young trooper's shoulder. "If he's that special, he'll wait."

Johnson nodded, appreciating the support but withdrawing his shoulder from under the hand all the same. Silence filled the cabin again as they both stared out the viewscreen to the snowy valley ahead.

The MMUTCAT rolled along on eight, honeycombed wheels. It bumped and bounced along the tundra waste, wheels lifting in time over rocks and Skitter nests, flaring up on independent, articulated suspensions. Inside the cabin, Private Johnson had come to a startling realization.

"So wait, you're not Arab? Like Rania?" he asked, cocking his head in surprise.

"Naw man. Spanish and Cherokee," Almar said with a laugh. "But lots of people get it wrong. I guess the name is Arabian, or was, don't know."

"Huh." Johnson sat back in his seat, puzzling over the vast spread of surnames. "But you *do* have a bachelor's?"

"Yep," said Almar, tapping the blinking icon on the MinMap. "Digital Development, out of Oxford."

"Huh."

Johnson looked out the side viewscreen, watching snow dunes drift on by.

"Then how come you're not an officer?" he asked, still looking out the side.

"Too much hassle," shrugged Almar. "I figured I'd do my eight, get out and go back to school. Full ride for my P.H.D."

"Huh."

The MMUTCAT rolled past an exceptionally large Snow Skitter colony, Almar artfully steered around the porous, cement-like boulder. He'd enjoyed school, especially working in the abstract worlds of digital theory and design. He never felt adrift or lost there, always surrounded by likeminded scholars and stern encouragement from his academic advisors. Before he graduated he'd started research on an ambitious project to code a computer using Cherokee syllabary instead of Latin Script or Binary. He'd hoped to use it as a way to bridge the knowledge of his ancestors with an enduring digital medium. And, it made for a hell of a challenging doctoral research project. But his savings had run out with his senior year of undergraduate studies, and so he'd put those plans on hold to join the ICF, where full-term service guaranteed a trooper funding for up to two degrees. It wasn't a bad life as an assistant gunner in a security platoon. The job was routine and he always had enough 'mental bandwidth' left over at the end of the day to put back into his independent research. At least as long as the Linknet was up and nobody was throttling the connection by downloading tons of vidplay files.

The chirruping icon on the MinMap grew louder as a squat, grey cottage pulled into view ahead of them. It was an older ranch house, formed from overlapping rings of inject-molded alloy. It resembled a large beehive with two chimneys, capped with fresh snow from the night before. A thin stream of steam drifted lazily from one of the stacks for the geothermal generators, the other was empty. Almar eased off the throttle, allowing the MMUTCAT to coast to a stop on regenerative brakes.

"So this is it then?" asked Johnson.

"Yep, Gligman Ranch."

"So how's this work?"

"We go up, knock on the door and wait. Hope they're in a good mood," said Almar unbuckling the harness of his worn, padded seat. "If they're home, we chat, help them unload the crates and leave."

"And if they aren't in a good mood?"

Almar shrugged. "Then we drop the crates and go."

Johnson nodded, unbuckling his own harness. He reached behind the seat for his mask and CWAPL and pulled them on.

The air outside the cab was still, the sun filtering through a haze of receding storm clouds. It was cold for sure, but the troopers took comfort in the knowledge that they wouldn't be there for long. They left the MMUTCAT running, and headed towards the cottage door. Along the way, they noticed a thin whine lingering in the air. A shrill sound, metal on metal, but faint, as if it had been tired out by carrying on for so long. The snow crunched under their heavy boots as they walked to the door, failing to notice the darkened windows or the looseness of the door in its frame.

Johnson stepped up first, wiping his boots on the worn mat on the front step. He knocked on the door through a thick thermal glove. They waited for a response; hearing none, he knocked again. Johnson looked back at Almar, who offered a shrug. It would be a lot easier if they had help unloading the truck, especially if the Gligmans had a MechLift to do the big work. Johnson knocked again, the door echoing under his fist. He turned to Almar and shook his head, and they both turned to walk back.

Johnson had taken a few steps in that direction when he heard the door creak open behind him. He froze in place, turning abruptly to greet the Gligmans. What he saw was an empty doorway, with darkness stretching behind it into the house. He looked back at Almar, who shrugged again and began walking back to the cottage. As they entered through the doorway, they announced their presence and called out to the Gligmans. It took their eyes a few seconds to adjust to the gloom inside, and a few more seconds to fully register the scene inside the beehive cottage.

It was a charnel house. The furniture was scattered about in the wide living room, torn and slashed. Blood clung to the walls in wide, frozen streaks. Bullet holes peppered the domed ceiling, courtesy of the ancient rifle lying on the floor. The previous owner still clung to the rifle, her dismembered arm attached by a frozen and bloody hand, still curled in the trigger guard. The weapon's action was open, having run dry in the course of the struggle. A thin rope of icy viscera dripped from the lamp in the center of the room, the only furniture left standing in the house. Snow drifted in from a huge hole in the back wall, long gouges surrounding the edges of the shredded alloy.

Almar and Johnson turned and ran, sprinting away from the scene of the bloodbath. They tripped over themselves as they went, heavy boots sliding on icy ground. They reached the MMUTCAT and doubled over, chests heaving and knees shaking.

"Fuck, dude! Fuck, fuck, FUCK!" gasped Johnson, face pale and sweating behind his insulated mask.

"I know, I know man," said Almar, steadying himself on the MMUTCAT's metal side. "Let's get the fuck outta here."

He swung open the cab door and prepared to climb inside when Johnson grabbed the edge of his CWAPL.

"Wait, wait," said Johnson, catching his breath. "We have to go back."

Almar stopped, hand still on the cab door. "The fuck you mean? We gots to fuckin' *go*."

Johnson shook his head. "We're the closest thing this planet has to police. We have to go back," he said, breath still coming out in pants.

113

Almar took his hand off the cab door, one foot still perched on the edge of the massive wheel. Johnson straightened himself, slowing his beating heart with deep, controlled breaths.

"We have to go back," he said. "We need to find out what happened."

Almar looked from him, to the cottage, and back to the truck, before settling back on Private Johnson.

"We signed up to keep people safe," Johnson added.

Almar swore in two different languages, but he knew the young trooper was right.

"Ok," he said, taking his foot off the wheel. "But we're doing this armed."

The troopers stalked to the house, weapons up as they approached the darkened door. They fanned out into the bloody living room, the muzzles of their R-91s searching the corners and crevices. They flicked on the flashlights embedded under their barrels and swept the circle of light around the house. Almar coughed beneath his mask, swallowing bile as he took in the details of the bloody mess. They swept around the house, cutting a wide circle in opposite directions. Private Johnson passed by the kitchen, an overturned pot on tile floor, its contents frozen and scattered. *Whatever happened, it was quick*, he thought grimly. He panned his flashlight around as he searched, unwilling to leave a crevice unchecked. *Bandits? Outlaws? Why here? Why at all?* Outside of the installation, there were maybe a couple dozen people on the entire planet. He wondered what could drive anyone to commit something so violent. He wondered if the culprits were still in the house.

As they crept around the beehive cottage, they met up by the large hole in the back wall. They peered through it on the snowy valley, seeing only a stocky barn and distant herd of Gluffants. The whine was louder here, originating from somewhere just outside.

"I think it's the generator," Almar whispered.

Johnson nodded. They took a deep breath and together they stepped out, rolling their heels on the snowy ground. They kept tight together, each taking a sector as they moved towards the noise. The generators were clumped by the north wall of the house, two squat round cones connected by venting and wires to the interior of the cottage. They were both smashed, long gouges torn through the metal. The sound was coming from the turbine on the left, still struggling to turn on a broken axis. With that mystery solved they turned away from the house towards the barn, rifles still sweeping across the frigid courtyard. They closed in on a small shed holding an old red truck, searched it and found nothing.

The barn was a similar story, utterly bereft of clues to what might have happened.

Disappointed, they headed back to the house, dropping their weapons to low-ready and passing by a small hill as they did. All of a sudden Almar stopped, catching a faint orange shimmer out of the corner of his eye. He turned towards the small hill, unsure if he'd actually seen anything. *Was that always there?* Johnson stopped as well, sweeping his rifle to cover the opposite direction. Almar stared hard at the pile of snow, studying it for clues. Too late he saw the shift as the hill moved, leaping back in surprise as he called out to Johnson for help. Johnson turned, swinging his rifle around his friend.

Time passed by Johnson in slow motion. He saw the hill open up, the front splitting into a toothy maw, impossibly wide. He pulled the trigger of his R-91, sending a series of neutral ions blasting out of the barrel. The ions hammered into the hill's front, stitching small orange craters above the widening jaws. A sickle claw swung out, arching towards Private Almar. Private Johnson dropped his hand from the foregrip of his R-91, supporting the rifle solely with his trigger hand. He reached his free hand for the drag handle on the back of Almar's CWAPL, grabbing it and yanking him back. The massive claw snaked out, too fast to be avoided, but it cut too short across Private Almar. A wide wound opened up across his front, a bloody diagonal gash from his left clavicle to his right hip. Almar dropped his weapon from senseless fingers, rifle swinging down on its sling to slap him in the thigh.

Johnson pulled hard, still shooting with one hand, his erratic fire peppering the face of the massive creature. The creature bellowed in pain, shaking off the stinging shots. Johnson dragged Almar to the hole in the cottage and pulled him through. Almar's head lolled to the side, a crimson stain trailing behind them. The creature roared, leaping forward and charging after its fleeing prey. It rammed against the side of the house, misjudging its bulk against the hole it had torn before. A ceiling tile shook loose from the impact, slamming into Johnson's head as he dragged Almar to the front door. He doubled over in pain, his vision suddenly blurry. He snapped his rifle to his shoulder, letting off a few shots at the creature through the haze. He shook his head to clear it, dropping the rifle and reaching back down to grab the handle on Almar's jacket. Johnson pulled with all his might, heaving Almar through the doorway as the creature smashed its way into the room behind him.

Almar woke up and caught himself as he tumbled to the ground, staggering upright and clutching at his chest. Johnson picked up one arm and draped it around his shoulder, supporting Almar's weight as they ran to the truck. The short Private yanked open the MMUTCAT door. He pushed hard on Almar's back, helping the wounded trooper to climb into the passenger side. Johnson clambered up behind him, crawling across the injured man to reach the driver's side. He punched the ignition and the MMUTCAT's engines fired up, idling in the arctic chill. Johnson clipped in to his seat's harness before leaning across and buckling Almar in. He heard a crash and snapped his head to look out the open door, catching sight of the creature smashing its way through the front of the cabin. He slammed the throttles forward, the door swinging shut as the massive truck lurched ahead. Johnson spun the vehicle in a wide arc, turning back towards the east and heading for the installation.

As they reached the apex of the turn, the vehicle halted, hung up on something in the rear. Johnson punched the viewscreen to bring up the rearview camera. The picture-in-picture display showed the massive jaws of the creature clamped around the back right wheel. He watched on screen as the creature's clawed forelimbs lashed out, stabbing around the honeycombed wheel.

But the MMUTCAT was designed for much more than that. Johnson turned back towards the dash, searching across the field of buttons and switches.

"Top left," said Almar, pointing feebly at the dash, "the eight square grid."

Johnson nodded, smashing his finger against the bottom right button. A chime sounded in the cabin as the whirr of hydraulics came from the rear. Abruptly the wheel detached, and the creature rocked backwards, tire still clenched in its serrated maw.

They were free, and Johnson slammed the throttle handles, kicking the MMUTCAT forward on its seven remaining wheels. They hurtled along past frozen dunes, pounding over rocks and ice. He looked back at Almar and pumped his fist in the air, letting loose a cry of triumph. Almar gave a weak thumbs-up, before slumping back in his seat with a cough. Johnson turned back to the screen, fighting to keep the swirling blackness from the edges of his vision.

But their victory was short lived. He caught sight of movement in the rearview camera, the charging form of the creature appearing in view. It bounded towards them, leaping over dunes as it chased them across the plain. It kept pace with the massive vehicle, hurtling towards them on powerful legs. Grimly, Johnson clung to consciousness as he nudged the throttles farther forward, alarm bells ringing in the cab as he pushed the MMUTCAT to its top speeds. The blinking dome of AZH-01 grew on the horizon. Johnson watched the rear camera as the creature receded from view, unable to keep up with the accelerated speed. He steered the massive truck towards the installation, vision tunneling as he closed the distance, aiming for the vehicle bay. His last thought before he faded out was of Brent, smiling as he stood in his apartment kitchen with a steaming mug. He could smell the cinnamon and nutmeg of the latte. He reached out a hand, and the world went black.

The MMUTCAT slammed into the bay door at a hundred and fifty miles per hour.

CHAPTER 11:

Special-Trooper Early strained against the monolithic weight of the RationVendor. Braced against the wall, he pushed the back corner of the dingy grey appliance. The RationVendor screeched in protest, digging its stoppered feet into the pale tiles. Sweat dripped down the small of Early's back, veins popping out on his massive forearms. He heaved against the malevolent food printer with all his might.

Slowly, the will of man won out against the inertia of dense machinery, and the RationVendor swung out from the wall. Baring his teeth in determination, Early doubled down in his efforts. He sensed the end was near, that his foe's resolve was weakening. Locking out his arms he pushed until his shaved head flushed red and his legs began to shake. He let out a ferocious, snorting grunt, flaring his wide nostrils as the appliance shifted forward, opening up a two foot gap between the back and the wall. Early collapsed to his knees, chest heaving, he raised his meaty fists to the sky and let loose a primal cry of victory.

"Dude, we could have helped."

Early looked up to see Joelson and Godrey framed in the chow hall doorway. Sponges in hand, they lowered their buckets to the ground, the green cleaning solution sloshing over the sides and splashing on their boots.

"I. Know." Early panted. "This was easier."

Joelson watched a bead of sweat run down Early's forehead and drip off the end of his crooked nose. He looked back at the RationVendor, noting the long gouges in the dirt from its arduous path over the tiles.

"Sure looks easier," he commented dryly.

He walked over to the weary trooper and offered a hand, grimacing a little as Early pulled hard to pick himself up.

"Thanks," said the heavy trooper, sweat running in rivers down his muscled arms.

Joelson wiped his hand on his pants. "No worries."

The three troopers grabbed their cleaning supplies and turned to face their monumental task. The scuffed and dingy chow hall floor stretched before them, a never ending expanse of cheap alloy tile and years of accumulated grime. A few cockroaches frolicked in the corner of the room, chasing each other along the baseboards. Joelson sighed. The line between Buck-Sergeant and Senior-Trooper was finer than he'd previously thought. He'd always been told that good NCOs lead alongside their men, but all he saw was the same sponge and bucket he had as a Private.

A thunderous crash echoed from outside the room, reverberating through the alloy walls. The floor shook beneath the trooper's feet, the green solution sloshing over the edges of their buckets. They ran to the doorway, looking down the hallway towards the source of the noise.

Joelson peered around Early's massive form, he could swear he saw smoke coming from the vehicle bay. He looked back at Private Godrey.

"What the fuck was that?"

The crash shook through the Command Den, dislodging the careful stack of reports on Sergeant Ramos' black-topped desk. The neat pile toppled over, sending a cascade of InReps bumping into the Reed-Sergeant's hand. Sergeant Ramos froze mid sip, looking to Lieutenant Preston over the top of his mug.

"What the fuck was that?"

Lieutenant Preston shook his head, brow furrowing in concern. He reached for the jacket hanging on the back of his chair and they both rose from their desks, heading out the door to investigate.

Private Li bent his back in the tight stall, hands mid scrub on a pernicious piece of bathroom graffiti. He swiped a sponge over the first words of 'I got rammed in the AZH01E,' grinding hard against the plastic. His efforts were rewarded with a clean streak against the dingy wall, only serving to add contrast behind the letters. Li sighed, dropping his sponge and banging his head softly against the lettering. A distant rumble vibrated the wall against his forehead. Confused, he popped his head outside of the stall, calling to Reming from across the room.

"The fuck was that?"

Reming stood back from his own scrubbing, grinding away at the lettering scratched in the counter by the sink ('Sikes watches when I pee'), his Metam ZapGun dangling from a strap on his side. "What was what?"

Li waved his sponge in the air. "The thing. Just now."

Reming set his scrub pad down and leaned against the metal countertop, wiping a sweaty brow with the back of his wrist. "The fuck are you talking about?"

"Never mind." Li threw up his hands in frustration, returning to his stall. Reming stared off at the space the trooper just occupied, shrugged, and picked up his pad again.

Sergeant Sikes sized up Rania from across the expanse of his SimuWood desk. His eyes were wide, pale grey, twinkling as he stared at her. The ever-present grin growing as she looked around his office, her green eyes flitting from plaque to plaque, the monuments to his years of ICF service. He admired her, she was learning firsthand about the ICF legend seated before her. He leaned back in his chair, steepling his fingers.

"Lovely, aren't they?" he asked, breaking the silence between them.

"Huh?" Startled, her eyes widened slightly, shifting from the walls, to him, before settling on the floor. "Uh, yeah, I guess so."

"They're a testament to decades of beneficent service." He waved a hand around the office, highlighting the dozens of offerings in his personal shrine. "The ICF rewards those that take care of it."

"Ah, of course." She looked up from the floor, locking eyes with Sergeant Sikes. "Senior-Sergeant, why am I here?"

Curious but polite, good, he purred to himself. *I'm sure she would benefit from further lessons on the nobility of service. Especially from someone who has given over two decades to that service.* He closed his eyes, inclining his head before speaking again.

"I," he stopped, catching himself as he began.

"We," he corrected, "wanted to check in on you. To further evaluate your integration within the unit." He leaned in, resting his elbows on the desk, the molded rings of the simulated wood grain ebbing out from him like waves against a shore. Rania shifted in her seat.

"I think I–"

"And so we wanted to sit down with you again," he interrupted. "We wanted to see what level your morale was, to ensure you're making connections within the unit.

"And if not," he said, cutting Rania off again as she opened her mouth to speak. "We wanted to assist you in making those connections. Within the unit."

She closed her mouth, trying to piece together what the Senior-Sergeant had said. *Is he asking me if I have friends?* She tried to gauge him, but any reading of his intent was masked by the toothy smile and piercing grey eyes. She had an odd flashback to her middle school science class, when she examined a butterfly pinned under a microscope.

"Well, Senior, I–"

This time it wasn't the Senior-Sergeant that cut her off, but a muffled rumble, like the crash of thunder in the distance. Rania locked eyes with him again, tilting her head confusion.

"What was that?" she asked.

The scene in the vehicle bay was pure chaos. Smoke filled the room, swirling hazily around the wreckage before being sucked out into the frozen expanse through the gaping hole in the bay door. Lieutenant Preston pushed past the troopers in the doorway. Elbowing his way forward, he took in the hell before him. The MMUTCAT lay on its side, acrid smoke billowing out from the motors and carriage. It had tumbled in its passage through the bay door, jackknifing as it slid into the wall of the bay. The truck rested on the passenger side door, roof against the wall, small flames licking out from two of the seven wheels. Lieutenant Preston traced the trail of destruction back to the bay door, noting with mounting dread the second smashed MMUTCAT, sideswiped on the first's path through the door. Sergeant Ramos ran up alongside him, greying hair disheveled from pushing through the crowd of gathered troopers.

"Holy shit," he started, eyes going wide as he surveyed the destruction. "What hap–"

He didn't finish, as Lieutenant Preston rushed off to the ruined MMUTCAT. Joelson and Early had climbed on top, opened the door, and were carefully lifting Private Johnson out of the wrecked cab. Lieutenant Preston stood beneath them, hands stretched out to catch the unconscious trooper as they lowered him to the ground. He caught the small Private as they dropped him, cradling him in his arms and pulling him away from the fiery wreckage. Johnson's head lolled to the side, caked in soot, blood flowing from a gash above his eye. Troopers flowed around the officer, rushing to the crash site to help. Distantly he heard the directions shouted by Sergeant Ramos, muffled under the sound of his own breathing as he carried Johnson to the hallway. He labored with the dead weight of the Private's body, his feet dragging on the ground the last few steps. Once through the door, he leaned Johnson against the wall, crouching down to check out the wounded trooper.

Private Johnson's eyes snapped open, his mouth sputtered open and closed as he clawed a hand on the officer's chest.

"Sir, I, I," he gasped, blood tracing a line through the dirt on his face.

"Shhh, shhh, it's ok." Lieutenant Preston leaned in, holding the trooper's hand and leaning his bloody head against his chest.

"Di-di-did, I?" Johnson stammered, chest heaving as he struggled in the officer's grasp.

"It's ok, you're here." Lieutenant Preston's voice was raw with emotion. "You're safe."

"Al-Almar?" Johnson's eyes looked up, pleading with the officer.

Lieutenant Preston looked through the doorway, watching the troopers pull Private Almar's limp body out of the cab. He nodded to the trooper in his arms, voice catching in his throat.

"He's safe, don't worry. He's going to be ok."

Private Johnson stopped his struggling and closed his eyes, his ragged breathing slow and shallow. Lieutenant Preston held him in his arms as the trooper sagged against him and was still.

A lifetime passed before Sergeant Ramos found him, still holding Private Johnson in his arms. Gently, he placed a hand on the officer's shoulder.

"Sir, he's gone," the Reed-Sergeant said, softly but firmly. "*We* need you now."

Lieutenant Preston looked up at the senior NCO, tears streaking on his face. He swallowed hard and nodded, tenderly leaning Johnson back against the wall. Sergeant Ramos reached out a hand and helped the officer up, a riot of sympathy, guilt, and sadness churning on his face. Lieutenant Preston straightened to face him, wiping his face on the back of his sleeve. Sergeant Ramos put a hand on the officer's back, and together they stepped back into the chaos of the bay.

It was chilly in the bay, the heat draining out through the hole in the door. The troopers' breath fogged as they worked, rushing to clean up the havoc wrought by the crash. Troopers zipped about, carrying wreckage, sorting through debris, or running fire extinguishers to put out the flaming engines. Lieutenant Preston watched the work in a haze, his mind still reeling from the suddenness of it all.

Sergeant Ramos barked orders next to him, at times grabbing a trooper and physically steering them in the direction of their task. There was much to be done, the destruction immense, and it all seemed too much for the Lieutenant to process as a whole. He looked back at the hallway, able to make out the edge of white tarp covering the bodies of the two troopers. *C'mon Douglas, focus. They need you to focus.* He shook his head to clear it, concentrating his mind on two words. *Find. Work.*

He caught sight of the troopers attaching chains to the side of the rolled MMUTCAT. Still in a daze, his feet propelled him forward to assist. He took up a position on the lead chain, directing troopers on the proper attach points for the boxy truck. As the chains clipped into place, the last trooper hopped down, picking up a spot on the far end. Under the officer's direction they pulled in short strokes, rocking the massive vehicle back and forth. They heaved, the chains rattling under the strain of the immense weight. The MMUTCAT groaned as it rocked on its wheels, a piercing creak echoing through the bay as it finally rolled past the point of no return, landing upright with a thud.

Lieutenant Preston lifted the hem of his shirt to wipe the sweat from his face, his jacket lying in a crumpled mess on the ground. He dropped the shirt and walked over to Sergeant Ramos, who was currently directing the sorting efforts with a handful of troopers. The Reed-Sergeant stood with his hands on his hips, scowling at the troopers arranging scraps of metal in piles.

"Damnit Kowalski, I just fucking told you. Bare alloy in that pile, painted alloy in the other, connecting bolts in the third, and miscellaneous material in the fourth. Now that piece in your hand, is it painted or not?" he demanded. The trooper looked at the scraps of metal, staring hard at each hand. He looked back at Sergeant Ramos, confusion etched plainly on his face. The Reed-Sergeant swore, taking the trooper's hand and pointing in the direction of the proper pile. He looked back at the officer, shaking his head as he came up.

"Republic Schools ain't what they used to be," he sighed.

Lieutenant Preston grunted, shrugging on his jacket.

"How come the fire sprinklers didn't go off?" he asked slipping the zipper in its slide and pulling up.

"We shut the things off after the last inspection," answered Sergeant Ramos. "Damn things were too sensitive. Kept getting triggered when we started up the MMUTCATs."

Lieutenant Preston nodded, smoothing out the front of his jacket. "And we still don't know the reason for the crash?"

"No. Not a fuckin' clue," the Reed-Sergeant grumbled. "Sir."

Lieutenant Preston rubbed a hand through his short, red hair, turning around to survey the devastation surrounding them. His shoulders sagged, the full weight of the tragedy settling upon them. He looked to the bay door, snow swirling in through the massive hole.

"What the fuck happened here?" he asked the icy winds.

The answer came sooner than they'd thought. They had just managed to get the fires put out of the smoldering wreckage, the last of the smoke drifting out the door. Special-Trooper Early led the remaining sorting efforts, taking over for the frustrated Reed-Sergeant. Lieutenant Preston, Sergeant Ramos, Sergeant Wingo, and Senior-Trooper Joelson were huddled in the corner of the bay, locked in debate over the best means of sealing the bay door.

"Duct tape?" offered the chubby Buck-Sergeant.

"Don't fuck around," snapped Sergeant Ramos. "We need something durable, we won't get a replacement for a few supply drops."

"What about a welded cover?" asked Lieutenant Preston, drawing circles on the dirty concrete.

"Too heavy," said Sergeant Ramos. "Door motor can't take too much weight or it won't open."

"What's the point?" Sergeant Wingo shrugged. "MMUTCATs are smashed anyway."

Sergeant Ramos pinched the bridge of his nose with two fingers, failing to keep the frustration out of his voice. "Only two are totaled, we can scavenge the heat cycler from one of those to repair the one deadlined in the south bay."

Sergeant Wingo nodded, a glimmer of understanding trickling through.

"What about a light alloy?" Joelson offered. "Something with nanotubes?"

Sergeant Ramos dropped his hand from his face, looking hard at the Senior-Trooper. "That would work, but we don't have nanotube plates just lying around."

Joelson nodded, looking around the open bay. He froze, an idea forming as he stared at the smashed trucks.

"What about the MMUTCATs?" he asked, turning back towards the group. "They have nanotube bodywork. We could scavenge a plate from a door or sidewall."

Lieutenant Preston looked up, first at the MMUTCAT doors and then to the junior trooper. He turned back to Sergeant Ramos.

"That's not a bad idea. Think it'll work, Sergeant?"

Sergeant Ramos mulled it over, rubbing a hand on his soot-marked chin.

"It might," he admitted. "Can't hurt to try. Worst comes we just tear the shit off and we're right where we fuckin' started."

He looked back at Lieutenant Preston, who was still staring straight ahead. The Lieutenant's eyes narrowed, his head turning quizzically. Sergeant Ramos turned, following the officer's gaze to the hole in the bay door. The view from outside was suddenly blocked, obscured by something large and white. He stood up from the group, arching a brow in confusion. He took a step towards the large metal door.

"What the fu–"

He never got to finish his question.

The creature smashed through the door, claws tearing the hole wider as it tumbled into the bay. A shaggy hill of limbs and teeth, it rolled forward, trying to get its bearings in the open room. It righted itself and sat back on four legs, its powerful hind limbs folding up and behind it like the coiled legs of a great bullfrog. The blunt claws of its front legs dug gouges in the concrete floor as it shifted from side to side, sizing up its surroundings. Two sickle claw arms, dainty and slight in comparison to its other limbs, hung loose near the wide-open mouth, clicking as the creature turned in place.

Lieutenant Preston forgot to breathe, taking in the blunt, hill-shaped body covered in mottled white bristles that shifted as it moved, fuzzing the details of the creature's outline. He couldn't make out any eyes, but a faint shimmer of orange could be seen along the creature's side as breathing vents opened and closed. The wide, jagged-toothed maw snapped open and shut in the blunt head, taking in the unfamiliar scents of the air around it. Lieutenant Preston swept his eyes around the room, willing the other troopers to freeze where they were.

The room was silent as the enormous predator padded by, claws rasping on the concrete floor. It seemed disoriented, bumping into the side of a damaged MMUTCAT and upsetting a mobile tool cart. It reeled back from the noise, the sickle claws clicking furiously as it sniffed the scattered tools. The creature turned its head up, and a strange, saddle-shaped structure lifted up from its face. Lieutenant Preston watched as the structure snapped shut abruptly, the creature shaking its head violently and backpedaling into the side of the MMUTCAT. The clicking grew faster as the creature staggered back, knocking into a pile of metal. It turned its head to the sky and let loose a wretched, bloodcurdling screech. Lieutenant Preston clapped his hands to his ears, trying to shut out the creature's cry of pain. He dropped his hands as the screaming stopped, holding his breath as the bay was silent again.

Looking over, he caught sight of Sergeant Ramos furiously waving, marshaling the troopers towards the hallway with his hands. Lieutenant Preston nodded, signaling to the troopers in his eyeline. He kept an eye on the massive creature, still lurching around in the center of the bay. Without a sound the troopers crept around it, seeking cover wherever they could. Lieutenant Preston began making his own way, charting a course around the back of the MMUTCAT. He rolled his feet, heel to toe, taking care not to make a sound as he moved.

He jumped at a crash behind him, wheeling around to see. A hundred feet away a trooper froze, panicking as the tower of honeycombed wheels teetered over, rolling away on the concrete floor. The trooper pinwheeled his arms, anxiously trying to grab the back of a tire before it slipped away. But he wasn't fast enough. Lieutenant Preston cringed as a wheel rolled past, wobbling its way towards the creature. Time stopped as the rubber tread turned, terminating its predestined arc as it nudged the creature's front leg.

The creature stopped, bending over to sniff the tire through its open mouth. It looked up in the direction of the trooper, the saddle-shaped structure on its head lifting just a crack. It clamped shut and the creature charged, barreling towards the trooper. Someone shouted for the trooper to move, sounding tinny and far away as the Lieutenant watched the impending tragedy. It took a moment to realize the person yelling was him. The creature leapt ahead, smashing through the remaining stack of wheels and knocking the trooper off his feet. Lieutenant Preston looked on in horror as the sickle claws lashed out, snagging the trooper and pulling him bodily into the jagged teeth. The jaws swung closed, cutting off the man mid-scream. The blunt head tilted back, the massive gullet working with gravity to swallow the man whole.

The bay was silent once again.

Lieutenant Preston wanted to close his eyes, to shut out the horror before him, but he forced himself steady. He watched the creature rub its blunt head with a heavy front leg, sickle arms clicking slower now, apparently satisfied with its meal. He began his trek again, stepping softly as he put distance between himself and the creature. He willed his legs to move forward, but he couldn't keep the tremor out of his hands. Sergeant Ramos had almost completed his evacuation, with only a few troopers left on the outskirts of the bay. One step at a time the officer worked his way to the hallway, pausing only to stop and check the creature's location.

He worked his way to Private Godrey, crammed under the bumper of the wrecked MMUTCAT. He motioned for Godrey to climb out, extending a hand to help him. The trooper's eyes were wide with terror, frantically darting from the Lieutenant to the hulking predator. Lieutenant Preston continued his prodding, mouthing encouraging words and gesturing to draw him out. Slowly, haltingly, Godrey emerged, pulling on Lieutenant Preston's hand for support. The officer turned back to Sergeant Ramos, who offered them a thumbs-up as they prepared to head his way.

Their progress stopped short when Godrey's pants snagged on the bumper. Caught on a twisted burr of metal, he jerked out of the Lieutenant's hand, turning back and tugging on the fabric of his pants. Lieutenant Preston steadied the trooper, trying to keep calm as they worked to free him. A soft ripping sound rewarded their efforts as Godrey's pant leg tore free. They both froze and looked back at the creature, waiting for a reaction. They needn't bother, the creature was fully occupied with post-meal grooming, digging a sickle claw into the gaps between its serrated teeth. Lieutenant Preston breathed a sigh of relief, and together they turned back to tiptoe to the door.

They took two steps before the bumper fell off. It clattered off the ground, the sound of metal on concrete echoing in the lofty space of the vehicle bay. The creature's head snapped up in their direction, a low growl rolling from its throat. Lieutenant Preston silently cursed, keeping still and hoping the creature would lose interest. He watched the creature turn towards them, dread forming an anchor in his guts. The saddle cracked open again, a thin line like a squinting eye. The structure snapped shut as the creature began bounding towards them, sickle claws clicking furiously. Lieutenant Preston grabbed Godrey by the shoulders and pushed him out of the way, sending him stumbling back behind the MMUTCAT as the creature drew near. He could feel the creature's hunger as it bore down on him, a palpable, terrible need. As the claws rang off the concrete, he shut his eyes and braced for death.

But the impact never came. Instead the creature slowed as a clang rattled off the concrete. Lieutenant Preston opened his eyes, catching sight of an arc welder fizzling on the ground after bouncing off the face of the creature as it charged. He turned and saw Joelson, still unbalanced from his throw. The creature shook its head, a burned patch on its face where the plasma current had impacted the saddle-shaped structure. The arc welder crackled on the ground, its protective housing cracked from its fall. It sputtered and smoked, bolts of electricity snaking out from the ruined device.

The creature stumbled back, sickle claws clicking furiously as it stepped away from the lightning arcing away from the tool. The power supply in the device failed, a last shock crackling out before it was still. Lieutenant Preston was already running, heels pounding on the paved floor as he tore towards the door. Behind him the creature turned, raising the saddle-structure fully open as it turned to give chase. This proved costly for the beast, the sensitive structure overloaded by too much input. It reeled again, emitting the same ear shattering screech as it clawed at its own face. It turned away from the fleeing Lieutenant and charged towards the corner of the bay, shoving over the wrecked MMUTCAT as it ran past. Private Godrey jumped out of the way, narrowly avoiding the rampaging creature.

The creature leapt ahead, smashing a hole through the alloy wall and tearing a path deeper into the installation. Lieutenant Preston slowed his running, stopping as he came up to Sergeant Ramos. The Reed-Sergeant caught him by the arm, and together they made their way to the hole in the wall. They peered into the ravaged trail the creature left behind, losing sight of it amid the chaos and destruction. Sergeant Ramos' mouth hung open as the Lieutenant turned to face him.

"Sergeant Ramos," he said, his voice calm and steeled. "I need you to sound the alarm."

CHAPTER 12:

The cockroach scurried across the bathroom tile, maneuvering around the curved plumbing of the toilet and past the moldering trash can. It summited the damp wall by the sink, clinging to the slippery metal wall as it climbed onto the counter. It halted in its mad dash to take stock of its surroundings, antennae twitching as it tested the air. A whoosh of pressure built up behind it and the cockroach fled, dodging the cacophonous impact of the hand on the counter. It dashed along the counter edge, scrambling on six flurrying legs. It reached the end of the metal ledge, poised in indecision as it determined the safest route back to the moist safety of covering darkness. Wings flexed along a hinged carapace, readying itself to take flight.

"Gotcha, fucker."

Fifty kilovolts arced through the air, descending upon the hapless insect like the wrath of an ancient god. The cockroach was fried instantly, a sliver of flame sprouting along the wingtips of the charred remains. A tendril of smoke coiled up from the incinerated arthropod, undulating and losing itself in the glare of the fluorescent lights. Special-Trooper Reming clenched his fist in triumph, the other hand wrapped around the pistol grip of his Metam ZapGun. He rocked the miniature tesla rifle against his shoulder, turning back to his companion with an ear-to-ear grin.

Li crossed his arms as he leaned against the stall door. "It's still a gimmicky piece of shit."

"*Jealousy is an ugly habit*," Reming sang, admiring the fingernails of his free hand.

Li rolled his eyes, bending over to retrieve his bucket and scrub pad. "C'mon shithead, we've still got the north showers to do."

Reming ignored his squad-mate's envious negativity, clipping the ZapGun's strap to his belt. He picked up his own basket of supplies, preparing to head out the door after his younger compadre. He stopped when the amber lights began to flash along the edges of the wall, the warning siren rising from embedded speakers.

'ALERT, ALERT, CODE ZULU; BASE UNDER ATTACK. ALL TROOPERS TO DEFENSE POSITIONS.'

Li looked back at Reming, confusion crossing his face. "False alarm? That can't be right."

Reming frowned, scratching the back of his head. "Has to be, I've never heard a Code Zulu before."

The automated message continued, expressing a strained edge to its voice typically absent in its usual broadcasts. The klaxon wavered and fell in time with the flashing amber lights. The troopers stared hard at the lights, trying to discern the urgency of the situation. Li looked back at Reming, who shrugged. Whatever was going on, it sure beat the prospect of continued scrubbing. They dropped their cleaning supplies on the tile floor and jogged out to the hallway to investigate.

Rania sat in a lumpy armchair across from Sergeant Sikes, her head resting on the scratchy backing. As near as she could tell from the tiny digital clock on the monitor behind him, he had been going on for an uninterrupted forty-five minutes. His latest topic was the 'Importance of Guided Reconciliation in Bolstering Unit-Mentor Relationships,' and Rania fought against her own drooping eyelids. She bit hard on the inside of her cheek to stay awake. The last thing she needed was to nod off in front of the Senior-Sergeant mid lecture. *He'd probably take it as an insult to the founding principles of the ICF*, she mused to herself, *and then he'd assign me to come back for another round of 'heritage mentorship.'*

She dug her nails into the palms of her hands, fighting against her body's natural instinct for preservation from auditory bullshit. Not for the first time, she wished she was more like Private Belle. *Regina always knew how to keep it together around leadership.* She had a knack for flattery and a practiced method for feigning interest in her chain of command. Rania tried hard to remember the advice the seasoned Private had given her when she'd first arrived on station, when Sergeant Ramos had assigned her a cleaning shift after he'd caught her 'moving too much' in formation. *'Just tilt your head and keep your eyes focused on the space between their cheek and their ear when they talk. Then smile, nod and say 'mhmm' when they pause. They'll think you're hanging on every word.'* Rania shifted in her seat, trying to put her friend's advice into practice. She couldn't help thinking that she was doing it wrong, that she was staring too intently at Sikes' ear, or her head was tilted the wrong way. Her eyes began to water when she forgot to blink and she shook her head, desperate to regain focus before he noticed her drifting off.

Not that it made a difference, Sergeant Sikes seemed to carry on regardless of what she did, relishing the opportunity to share his opinions on the beauty of ICF service with a captive audience. She realized he had asked a question when the room went quiet for a second. Her eyes went wide as she snapped back into the conversation.

"Mhmm!" She nodded, forcing a smile as she tilted her head. He watched her carefully for a moment, staring right through her. She forced the smile wider, tilting her head further and praying that he didn't call her bluff. Another moment passed and he nodded, picking up the lecture where he'd left off. Rania breathed a small sigh of relief, briefly turning her attention to the walls crowded with ICF awards. *Why would anyone bring this much shit out on a remote tour? And how does someone like this win so many awards?* She pondered these mysteries as the Senior-Sergeant droned on, oblivious to the distraction of his 'mentee.'

Her efforts at feigning attention were gratefully disrupted by the flashing of amber lights and a wailing siren. Sergeant Sikes paused in his delivery and looked up, clearly irritated at the interruption. Rania watched him carefully as the automated message played. Confusion danced across his face, chased narrowly by a twinge of fear behind his pale eyes. The message repeated two more times before subsiding, leaving only the flashing of amber lights to guide them.

She coughed, drawing his attention back to her. "Senior, this sounds serious. I think we should be going."

He stared up at the ceiling, his mouth still slightly agape.

"Yes," he nodded, his mouth suddenly dry. "I do believe you're right."

Reming and Li jogged along the metal corridor, heels ringing on the scuffed tiles. The ominous automated warning message had stopped repeating but the amber lights continued to flash up and down the hallway. Most alarms continued to sound up until situation termination, ensuring that every trooper received the message regardless of what they were doing beforehand. The unusualness of this message, combined with its abrupt silence added to the growing sense of unease experienced by the two troopers.

Reming and Li made their way down the empty hallway, periodically stopping to check around for any other troopers. They were alone as they trekked to the armory, the maze of corridors silent except for the sound of their breathing and the dull thud of rubber boots. Reming stopped abruptly, silhouetted in the low flash of the amber lights. He waited at the intersection of two halls, staring down their length, searching for something.

Li caught up with him. "What's u–"

Reming cut him off with a wave of his hand. He cocked his head, listening intently. Li followed his example, straining to pick up what had disturbed the Special-Trooper.

After a moment the young Private began again. "I don't hear any–"

But then he stopped, catching the faintest sound in the distance. It was odd, like something scraping against the metal, but it was rhythmic, a repetitive clanging growing steadily louder as it approached. Li locked eyes with Reming, opening his mouth to speak.

"What is tha–"

His words were cut off by the sudden appearance of Private Konrad, diving out from the shadows and tackling them to the ground. The heavy-set trooper bowled them over, his knee, knocking the wind out of Reming as he carried them back from the hallway intersection. Reming sputtered and cursed, gasping for breath as the scarred trooper pinned them to the dingy tile. The three troopers struggled in the hallway, wrestling in the amber flash of the warning lights. Li managed to catch his breath, poking his head out of the tangle of thrashing limbs.

"Konrad? What the fu–"

A massive hand clamped over his mouth, stifling his words. Li fought against the giant Private, but the hand only gripped tighter, and he was no match for the hulking trooper's immense strength. He paused, holding still long enough to realize that the scraping noise was louder, the source of the sound almost upon them. He smacked Reming on the shoulder to get his attention, the Special-Trooper's head currently being crushed in the crook of Konrad's muscular armpit. Reming stopped struggling, and Konrad loosened his grip, allowing him to pull his head out and look down the hallway in the direction of the sound.

It was on them in a moment. A mountain of teeth, hunger, and claws rushed past them, an expanse of bristling white filling the corridor floor-to-ceiling as it bounded by. It tore down the hallway, knocking into walls as it leapt along, claws digging long gouges in the alloy tile. It swept past them without noticing, rushing headlong towards some unknown destination. Reming and Li shared a look of shock as the creature rolled beyond their sight, the rhythmic scraping fading into the distance.

With the hallway silent again Konrad released them, rocking back on his heels and standing up in one smooth movement. Reming and Li staggered upright, brushing off their uniforms with shaking hands. Reming turned back towards Konrad, noticing for the first time how heavily armed the neanderthalic trooper was. An R-91 was slung on each shoulder, and a P-3 Sonic Pistol strapped to each thigh. His broad chest was crossed by a bandolier of spare batteries and another of trip-flares and portable pyrotechnics. His pockets bulged with grenades and a long knife hung from a sheath on his belt. He was missing his uniform jacket, his muscled, veiny arms bulging out through the thin undershirt. Reming stared, unable to look away from the craggy-faced trooper's chiseled chest, stretching the confines of the thin grey shirt. Reming shook his head, focusing his thoughts away from Konrad's bewilderingly statuesque physique and onto his rapidly forming questions.

He shifted his eyes, looking pointedly at the ceiling as he addressed the trooper. "Konrad, what the fuck was tha–"

The hulking Private cut him off, shutting him up with a wave of his hand. He unslung the rifles and leaned back into the intersection, staring down the hallway in the direction of the creature. He walked across, an R-91 gripped in each meaty hand. Konrad moved with a purpose, striding swiftly and silently. As he headed back in the direction he had come, he spoke to them without looking back.

"Come with me if you want to live."

Reming rolled his eyes hard enough to shake the world. He looked to Li, cocking an eyebrow in disbelief. Li shrugged, turning away to head after Konrad. In imminent danger of being left alone, Reming sighed through the entirety of his being, his hands and his shoulders sinking backwards to the ground. He looked back down the hallway in the direction of the creature, grabbed the ZapGun from his belt, and chased after the two Privates.

Rania and Sergeant Sikes wandered the hallways in the intermittent glow of the amber lights. He hadn't said a word to her since the alarm message had stopped, and though initially grateful for the reprieve from his institutionalized preaching, she couldn't help but find the withdrawn silence to be unnerving. They walked together, heading towards the control center to piece together what was going on. It was eerily quiet, the hallways empty of the usual response sounds of troopers running by or marshaling to their posts. The only thing Rania heard was the soft sound of their boots on the tile, and the shallow, pinched breathing of the Senior-Sergeant.

"Is this another false alarm? Where is everyone?" she asked, breaking the silence at last.

She waited for an answer, but Sergeant Sikes stared straight ahead, ignoring her as he kept on walking. Rania stopped and frowned, trying to get a read on the Senior-Sergeant. He was poor company, but she knew she didn't want to be left alone. She hustled to keep up with his long strides, tapping him on the shoulder when she caught up with him. He flinched away from her touch, stopping only long enough to peer anxiously around the corner of an intersection. Rania chewed thoughtfully on her lower lip. Whatever was going on had clearly spooked him.

"What's up with a Code Zulu?" she asked, still trying to keep pace with him. "How come there haven't been more instructions? What are we supposed to do for it?"

Her questions were met with silence as he continued down the corridor. Sergeant Sikes looked up and down the hallways they passed, clearly looking for something. She shook her head, determined to get some solid answers out of the senior NCO. She grabbed him by the arm, stopping him in his tracks. He turned towards her, his stare glacial, looking first to her hand on his arm and then to her. He jerked his arm out of her grasp, staring through her with his most imperial and withering glare. She stood firm, planting her feet and returning his gaze, defiantly staring him straight in the eyes.

"Sikes," she said, enunciating clearly and with a careful, level tone. "What did we do for the last Code Zulu? What happened then?"

Sergeant Sikes' eyes glazed over as he struggled with the directness and impertinence of her question. He was silent, looking straight out in the distance above her head. After a moment he composed himself, shifting his gaze back to her.

His lip curled in a faint sneer. "There's never *been* a Code Zulu before."

He turned away from her, striding down the hall with his nose in the air. She wrestled with herself but kept after him; he was still her best shot at figuring this out. He froze ahead of her, poised on the edge of another intersection in the tangled web of the installation's crisscrossing hallways. His eyes were closed as she stopped alongside him, as if concentrating on hearing something far away. It took her a moment to catch it as well, a rhythmic, repetitive scraping coming from the hallway on their right.

As the sound began to grow, Sergeant Sikes snapped his eyes open. He flattened himself against the wall, drawing back from the intersection. Rania copied him, trying to decipher the source of the noise. The scraping grew louder, accompanied by a series of irregular crashes and whumps, like something very large knocking into the alloy walls. Rania waited with baited breath as Sergeant Sikes peeked his head around the corner. He drew back suddenly, smacking his head against the metal wall, his eyes wide and fearful. The sound grew louder, Rania tapped him again, trying to get the Senior-Sergeant's attention as he closed his eyes, a riot of emotion passing over his face.

"Sikes, what is it?" she whispered forcefully. "What did you see?"

He muttered something to himself, the source of the sound was almost upon them. He opened his eyes suddenly, staring down directly at her. A chill slid down her spine as they locked eyes.

"I'm sorry," he said softly. "But you should really see for yourself."

Grabbing her forcibly by the shoulders, he pushed her out into the intersection.

She stumbled forward, pinwheeling her arms and fighting for balance as she processed the suddenness of his treachery. Her eyes were wide with shock as she caught sight of something huge and white barreling towards them. She looked back at Sergeant Sikes, a smile of quiet sadness drawn across his face.

Her foot caught on the edge of a loose tile and she tripped, rolling forward into the hallway beyond. She caught herself on the dingy floor, snapping her head back to see Sergeant Sikes, the smile fading from his face. Her eyes blazed with fury, but she never got the chance to curse him. The creature rushed by, a blur of ferocious, predatory hunger leaping through the narrow corridor. A sickle claw swung out, hooking through the air as it swept past them. It sliced into Sergeant Sikes, opening up a violent, spraying gash across his abdomen. His intestines tumbled to the floor in a bloody pile as the creature sped down the hallway.

Sergeant Sikes sank to his knees, his pale eyes wide in terror as he fell forward onto the pile of his own gore, his mouth gasping open and closed. Rania looked away, shutting her eyes from the horrible sight. She willed herself to stand, gritting her teeth as she turned and fled, the image of Sikes seared into her mind as she ran.

Sergeant Ramos stood over the screen embedded in the top of the table of the Command Den, drawing circles on the digital map with the point of his finger.

"That's the West Bay." He pointed to the map, tapping the screen to zoom in. "It came in through the hole in the door and took off towards the Northeast quarter, tearing ass deeper into the station."

Lieutenant Preston nodded, waiting for the Reed-Sergeant to cover something he didn't know.

"Now we got some reports of the fucking thing in Sector 2, Sector 3, and heading towards Sector 6." Sergeant Ramos drew on the screen, circling the areas of the creature's sightings. "But we don't have any hard clue as to where it fucking is."

Lieutenant Preston frowned. "And why is that? I thought the internal cameras automatically engaged during emergency responses. Why don't we have a live feed for tracking?"

Sergeant Ramos snorted. "Camera systems operate off an internal processing circuit. Proprietary system. ICF lost the software license about three tours ago during contract negotiation. They haven't worked since."

The officer's frown deepened. "Well what about the internal alarm message? Can I broadcast clearer instructions?"

Sergeant Ramos shook his head. "The pre-recorded audio is also specifically licensed with the alarms outlined in the contract. The system isn't programmed to deliver unique messages."

The officer gaped, amazed at the petty incompetence of the grand military machine shaping their lives.

"Well, what *do* we have?" he asked, scratching the back of his head. "We need some options."

Sergeant Ramos stood back, sweeping a hand to encompass the troopers filtering in and out of the room. "Word of mouth is all we got right now. At least when we get everyone together, we can plan to get someone skilled to the control center and broadcast a distress call."

Lieutenant Preston leaned back in his chair, rubbing his chin as he surveyed his options. Troopers were flowing in, receiving a quick situation briefing before being assembled in the back of the room. Once they had a full crew together they'd be able to get organized, marshaling the soldiers to arm and hunt the beast down. The whole operation hinged on getting a technically proficient trooper into the control center, but Rania and Sergeant K were still unaccounted for and Joelson had taken off with Early to round up the remaining troopers. Lieutenant Preston sighed. It was a shit hand to be dealt, but it seemed that the only thing they could do was wait.

A low rumble shuddered through the room. The lights flickered and the table screen went black. Lieutenant Preston looked to Sergeant Ramos in alarm, the Reed-Sergeant already scanning the room to assess the situation. A moment passed and another rumble shook the room. The lights flickered and went out, plunging the Command Den in utter darkness.

"Of course," Sergeant Ramos sighed. "That plan is entirely contingent on having power."

Another moment passed as they waited in the dark. A small chime sounded from a speaker in the wall and the emergency lights flickered on along the edges of the ceiling, bathing the room in a dim red glow. As their eyes adjusted to the low light, Lieutenant Preston smiled at Sergeant Ramos.

"At least that's one contract we did right."

Sergeant Kyrghizwald awoke in a fog, trapped in the sweaty confines of his tangled sheets. The room was dark, illuminated solely by the soft red lights along the edge of the ceiling. He struggled upright, thoughts turning slowly as he processed the information filtering in to his syrupy brain.

"Lights on," he groaned, arching his back as he stretched on the bed. He blinked in consternation as the room remained dark.

"Lights!" he called out. "Lights on!"

But still he remained in darkness. A creeping unease spread through him, a cold wave growing up from his guts. He kicked the sheets off and swung his legs to the edge of the bed, his mind viscid and cloudy. He groped in the dark for his dresser drawer, pulling it open. He reached inside, pulling out a water bottle and his goggles in a case. He set them down on top of the dresser and reached back inside, feeling blindly for the hidden latch in the bottom corner. He felt it click as the false bottom slid back. Sergeant K grunted in satisfaction as his fingertips brushed the soft cloth bag with thin cord drawstrings. He pulled the bag out, cradling it gently as he set it on the bed.

He'd been introduced to NorCan during his first deployment as a young trooper on Farnis. Riding in a turret for days, ducking insurgent snipers and garbage thrown at him from ungrateful colonists. He'd struggled to stay awake during the thirty-six hour security patrols, let alone focus on his surroundings long enough to pick out an ambush from the empty desert. He'd been lost amid the swirl of sand and broken rocks, his mind baking in the intense heat of the alien sun. It was his driver who introduced him to the potent stimulant, sharing it with him continuously throughout the year-long tour.

And the five years since. Even though he'd switched into remote tours after his time on Farnis, he'd kept his use going. Expensive though it was, Sergeant Kyrghizwald relished the warm feeling and sharpened senses that accompanied the immediate use of the pharmaceutical. At least initially, he'd told himself he'd wean down, using just enough to keep himself alert and focused until he could kick the habit entirely. That hadn't happened yet, but he'd gotten extremely good at planning his fix, rationing his supply over the course of each two-year stint at AZH-01. It was a pain in the ass to find a new supplier in the six months of leave between tours, but there was always a market for the drug in his hometown of Kiev.

He reached a hand into the cloth bag and pulled out a syringe and glass bottle filled with tawny liquid. He swirled the fluid in the tiny vial, noting with some dismay that it was already half empty. He needed this supply to last him for another year, but he was always greedy with it at the start of a tour. He'd needed to focus on conserving the precious fluid, perhaps spacing his use to every three days. He blanched at the thought; he drifted through the days between fixes already. He dared not face withdrawal if he ran out before the tour was up.

He dipped the syringe in the bottle, drawing back the stopper and filling it with a few ccs of liquid. He set the bottle down on the bed, leaning back and lifting the syringe up. Holding very still, he inserted the syringe in the corner of his eye, careful to aim for the space between the white and his tear duct. With practiced care he squirted a few drops, feeling a spreading warmth as the powerful drug traveled up the optic nerve. He withdrew the syringe, careful to deposit the rest of the liquid back in the flash before packing it all away in the secret compartment of his drawer.

He stood up, shaking his head as his thoughts raced into overdrive. He pulled on a uniform, stopping in front of the mirror by the door to smooth out his appearance. Satisfied, he pulled open the door and stepped out into the hallway to investigate.

CHAPTER 13:

The rifle entered the maintenance room first, square-cut barrel dappled in the low red light. Shortly behind the rifle was Private Konrad, stepping lightly on the balls of his feet. He peeled left as he came through the door, sweeping the narrow circle of his weapon's light from corner to corner in the dark room. His footsteps were silent as he maneuvered along the wall, holding fast as he came upon a narrow desk. He froze, his grip on the R-91 light and controlled. He canted the rifle around the desk, searching the backside with quick, deliberate swings.

"Hey fucknuts!" Reming shouted. "The thing was huge, remember?"

Konrad tensed, swiveling to face the doorway. Reming stood with one hand still cupped to his mouth, the other on the pistol grip of the tiny ZapGun. Konrad watched through narrowed eyes as Li tripped into the back of Reming, sending them both stumbling into the room.

"Quiet!" he rumbled, grip tightening on the particle rifle.

"Yeah man, shhh!" hissed Li, holding an accusing finger to his lips.

Reming rolled his eyes. "Calm your shit, it was fuckin' huge. If it was in this room we'd know."

Konrad grunted and continued his search, cutting the flashlight across the remaining nooks and crannies. Li followed after him, sticking close to the musclebound trooper's lithe movements. Reming shook his head and fell in behind them, dragging his feet on the floor as loudly as possible.

The doorway to the generator room loomed before them, a well of darkness, vast and imposing. Konrad froze, halting them with a fist in the air. He described a plan through a series of elaborate hand gestures, furtive, quick, and silent.

"We don't know what that fucking means, man!" Reming called from the back.

Konrad turned to glare at him. Reming returned the look, chin up and defiant. Konrad sighed, stepping back from the edge of the door.

"I'll punch in left. Li tags right. You hold center and rear. We'll push center room and regroup. Sweep the generator housings together."

Reming snorted. "No way, tacti-cunt. I know you're a fuckin' Raider and all, but that's dumb as hell. All I've got is my ZapGun and Li doesn't have anything." He panned his flashlight over the hulking trooper, shining a light past the pistols on his thighs and lingering on the spare R-91 strapped to Konrad's back. "We're not doing shit unless you'd like to share."

Konrad frowned, the low light deepening the shadows on his scarred face. The muscles in his jaw clenched and twitched as he worked through a series of violent alternatives to the problem before him. Reming folded his arms and waited, taking small satisfaction in watching the struggle play out in the boorish trooper. After a moment, Konrad shook himself and relented. He unclipped a Sonic Pistol and reluctantly handed it to Li, stopping just short and forcing the young Private to stretch to reach it.

"Happy?" he grunted, and turned back to face the doorway.

"No," muttered Reming, taking up his position in line. "But we're doing this shit anyway."

Konrad held up a hand, counting down from three with his fingers. As the last finger dropped, he swept in, clearing left and rolling in on smooth, even steps. Li was close behind, trying and failing to mirror the poise of the other trooper. Reming brought up the rear, hooking in just past the door and dropping back to hug the wall. The flashlight was small in his hands as he swung it around, its pale circle of light paltry in the vast room. Near the center of the room, the tiny circle caught the edge of something huge and white, covered in mottled bristles.

"Oh, shit!" he cried, fumbling to bring his ZapGun up.

Konrad and Li turned in his direction, their lights joining his in illuminating the mound of bristling white. They opened fire, peppering the beast from all sides. The pistol kicked in Li's hands, reciprocating action sliding back and forth as the sonic blasts erupted from the barrel. Lightning crackled from the end of Reming's ZapGun, arcing away towards the center of the room. Konrad unslung his spare rifle, cradling one in each hand as he unloaded on the mass of fur and claws. The mound shuddered under their combined assault, shots tearing holes straight through the white hide. They pressed in on the center of the room as it crumpled under the weight of their ferocity. At last it toppled over, collapsing in a pile of smoking white and burning hair.

"Was that it?" asked Li, lowering the pistol in his hands.

The troopers approached the beast with caution, alert for the slightest movement.

Konrad kicked a heavy foreclaw with the toe of his boot. "Not so tough."

Reming drew closer to the smoldering mass, studying it intensely. He poked the creature's side with his finger, encountering little resistance as he dented the thick hide.

"Guys, I don't think this is it," he said, voice trailing off in thought.

"What do you mean?" asked Li. "The fuck else would it be?"

Reming pulled on a rubber cleaning glove from his pocket, crouching down to examine it further. He hooked a finger in one of the wounds caused by an R-91, smoke still curling along the edges of the hole. He drew his arm back and the skin came out with him, tenting under the pull of his hand.

"It's hollow," he muttered, releasing his grip and letting the hide fall back in a pile.

Li cocked his head in confusion, the pistol loose in his hands. "It was empty the whole time? Like a balloon?"

"Balloons don't kill," Konrad snorted in derision.

Reming ignored them both, pivoting around the carcass and peeling back the hide. He opened the remains along a wide split in the back, revealing layers of rubbery hide and thick fat. "See what I mean? There's no organs or muscle. I think this is just skin." He shook his head, puzzling over the alien anatomy. "It's like it molted, or maybe metamorphosed."

Li rolled his eyes. "Is that your professional opinion, Doctor Dumbass? I thought you dropped out of xenobiology."

"I passed my classes," Reming shot back, still poking around the pile of leftover creature. Mumbling to himself, he added "At least until midterms."

Konrad shifted his weight back and forth, realizing how exposed they were in the center of the room. "So we don't know where it is." He turned around abruptly, panning his rifles as he searched around the room.

"Or what it looks like," Reming replied, standing back from the smoking remains. He pulled off the glove and tossed it onto the pile. "It might look like anything now."

"Even one of us?" asked Li, tightening his grip on the pistol. Konrad scoffed, but Reming shrugged, picking up his flashlight and joining in the trooper's search. A chill crept down Li's spine. He moved to join the other two, giving wide berth to the creature's remains.

They cleared through the rest of the generator room, lingering a little longer than before in each nook and cranny. They said nothing as they swept past the towering cones of the geothermal generators, pupils widened under the soft red glow of the emergency lights. The beam of Li's flashlight shook a little in his hand as they approached the power coils in the back of the room. The shadows were deeper there, plenty of places for someone or something to hide. He stabbed the light around the imposing coils, flicking it into the spaces between them, so intent on not being caught off guard, he almost missed noticing the coils themselves.

"Holy shit, guys, look!" Li cast the flashlight over the coils, illuminating the claw marks and gouges in the metal stacks.

"So much for the power mystery," Reming remarked dryly.

Konrad let out a low whistle as they took in the scope and magnitude of the destruction. The generators were torn apart, savaged and mangled by the creature's attack. They stood in twisted ruin, a silent testament to the fury of the beast. Quietly, the troopers turned and pressed on, leaving the shredded machinery behind as they searched the remainder of the room. They halted by the rear doorway, Konrad peeking around the corner into the hallway beyond. Reming opened his mouth to speak but the hulking trooper cut him off, a finger to his lips as he leaned back into the room. Reming nodded and they readied themselves, listening for the sound of movement.

It wasn't long before they heard something coming down the hallway. It was quieter than before, no longer rhythmic. The troopers waited in the dark, steeling themselves to strike first as it approached. The clodding sound grew louder, a soft thud against the tiled floor. The troopers tensed, weapons gripped tightly in their hands. They flicked their flashlights off, not wanting to draw any attention from the creature as it drew closer. They held their breath as the clodding stopped just short of the door. Konrad looked back at the other two troopers, nodded once, and together they swept into the hallway, kicking on their flashlights as they brought their weapons to bear.

"Fuck man!" Private Smith threw up his hands, blinking in the sudden glare of their lights.

Reming lowered his ZapGun. "Ah shit, it's just Johnson."

"Smith!" snapped the trooper, shifting a hand to block the light in his eyes.

"Whatever," rumbled Konrad, lowering his rifles. He slung one over his right shoulder and turned away to face down the hallway.

Li kept his pistol firmly pointed at the dark-haired trooper.

"Or is it?" he asked, uncertainty creeping into his voice. "How do we know for sure?"

Reming sighed, but Li had a point. "Fine, ask him a question. Ask him something you know about Smith."

"Something...about Smith...." Li lowered his pistol, shifting his weight back and forth. "Uh..."

He looked back at Reming, who shook his head, then to Konrad, who shrugged.

"Fucking really?!" Smith shouted, dropping his hands. He glared at them as the troopers exchanged looks. They deliberated in silence, struggling to recall anything specific about the short Private. Finally, Konrad nodded, the glimmer of an idea sparking in his thick head. He walked over to where Smith was standing, drew back his arms, and slammed the butt of his rifle into the trooper's groin.

Smith's eyes bulged out as he doubled over in pain. He gasped for breath, wheezing as he struggled to stand on shaking legs.

"Guess that solves that," quipped Reming, turning away with Li to head down the hallway. Calling back over his shoulder, "He needs a gun too, Konrad."

Konrad grunted. He unclipped the other pistol, handing it gently to the distressed trooper and turned to walk away. Smith took the P-3 in trembling fingers, staring daggers at the receding back of the hulking Private. He breathed slowly as he straightened up, shaking out the dull ache spreading through his body. He press-checked the small pistol, double checking the magazine and capacity. Smith shook his head and marched after the others, muttering curses the whole time.

Rania ran down the dimly-lit hallway, heart pounding in her chest as her heels echoed off the tile floor. The ghost of Sergeant Sikes pursued her, the lingering image of his death clawing at her every time she shut her eyes. She wasn't sure where she was going, but she knew that if she slowed down the fear might consume her, might wrap around her with its choking grasp and paralyze her on the spot. And so she ran, putting as much distance between her and whatever the fuck it was that killed Sikes.

The walls blurred at the corners of her vision. Her breath came out in gasps timed with the rhythm of her feet. She rounded the corner, arms pumping as she ran. Rania turned her head to look behind her, convinced she'd heard the echo of something behind her. She whipped her head back just in time to stare down the cavernous barrel of the SLW-18 in Early's hands.

She slammed her heels into the ground, digging in and slowing down to avoid smashing into Joelson and Early. She backpedaled, boots skidding on the dingy tile as she slid to a stop in front of the two troopers.

"Oh fuck, it's Rania!" Early lifted the bulbous laser to his shoulder. "Damnit girl, I coulda shot you."

Rania doubled over with her hands on her knees, trying to catch her breath.

"I'd... appreciate... if... you didn't," she panted.

Joelson smiled and extended a hand to help her up. Rania waved him off, straightening up and bracing her hands on her heaving sides. She walked a small circle, trying to calm her rapidly beating heart. She eyed the two armed men, piecing together the situation as she composed herself.

"I take it you know about the... thing?"

Joelson nodded. "Where did you see it?"

She jerked a thumb behind her. "Back there past the storage lockers. We were coming from Sikes' office."

"We?" Joelson looked down the hall behind her. "You and Sikes? Where is he?"

Rania shook her head, casting her eyes to the floor. Early reached out a heavy hand and placed it on her shoulder.

"It's ok," he said. "You're safe now."

She looked up at the muscled trooper with a half-smile. She patted his hand, taking comfort from the gesture. Rania turned to look at Joelson. "So how many are there? Where is everyone? What's the plan here?"

"Just the one so far, came in the bay door after the crash."

She arched a brow in confusion. "What crash?"

"MMUTCAT," answered Early. "Smashed a hole in the door."

"Almar and Johnson, from the supply drop," Joelson added. "It came after that. Ate Suzettes and then took off through the base. We're rallying people up in the Command Den. LT and Ramos are getting a plan together. When the power cut out we decided to swing by the generators."

Rania nodded, piecing together everything she knew so far. Her head swam in a flood of thoughts, questions, and worries, all churning in a roiling torrent. She struggled to stay afloat amid the raging deluge, the indelible picture of Sikes' pale, sightless eyes floating to the surface like a log adrift in a flood. She shook her head to clear her thoughts, blinking back the images of horror. *Not now*, she thought, swallowing the lump in her throat. *Later.*

"Alright," she said at last. "The generators are two hallways over. We can cut left by the laundry room to save time."

"Sounds good," agreed Joelson, brightening to a smile. "For what it's worth, I'm glad you're ok."

"Oh, I'm pretty fucking far from ok," she said, pulling her tangled hair back with the elastic band around her wrist. "But I'm alive, and right now that's the next best thing."

Early laughed, a rumbling sound emanating from deep within his thick chest. He patted her again on the shoulder, and they headed down the corridor.

Reming and Li were laughing together as they walked through the hallway, locked in a heated discussion with Smith over his many distinctions from Private Johnson.

"Whatever, man, you're both new," Reming said. "How am I supposed to remember that you're the one that plays cello?"

"*You were at my concert on Tamarin!*" bellowed Smith, a throbbing vein standing out on his neck.

"Yeah, but there was that time you guys switched jackets," Li added, bobbing his head as they walked along. "Pretty confusing if you ask me."

Smith sputtered into incoherent rage, waving his hands wildly in the air. His mouth opened and closed as he fought to find a more salient point, pausing only when he noticed that the two troopers had stopped short, ignoring him and looking straight ahead. He turned around, bracing himself for whatever lay before them.

"I didn't know you played the cello," Rania said with a smile. "If we live through this, I'd love to hear it."

The anger drained out of Smith, replaced with relief at the sight of the others. He dropped his hands, grateful to see more inclusive company.

Reming lowered his ZapGun, waving to the other group. "Nice day for a walk?"

"Fuckin' sweet. Early brought the *Slaw*." Li eyed the massive laser cannon with excitement.

"Where are you guys coming from?" asked Joelson, dropping his rifle.

"Generators," answered Li, thumb in the direction behind them. "The three of us found Smith just outside there, we're heading to the Command Den."

Joelson furrowed his brow. "Three of you?"

Reming read the confusion on the Senior-Trooper's face. He looked around before letting out an exasperated sigh. "Konrad you cock-operator, get the fuck out here."

Konrad slunk out from behind a narrow inlet, his rifle still leveled at the group. "Can't take chances."

Reming rolled his eyes. "Will you put that down? It's not them you fucking savage."

"What's not us?" asked Rania, raising an eyebrow.

"We found the creature's skin back in the generator room," Li said. "We think it might have transformed or something."

Reming pinched the bridge of his nose. "These idiots think it might have taken human form."

"Ah," said Rania. "Then how do you know who's who?"

"Like this," grunted Konrad, slamming his rifle butt into Smith's groin. Smith fell over, clutching himself as he rolled on the ground.

"*Why?*" he squeaked, his face clenched and red. "*I was with you the whole time!*"

Konrad shrugged, turning back to face the main group.

Rania put up her hands. "I'm good, trust me, you don't need to check."

Konrad nodded, stalking past them to set up a position further down the hallway. Rania bent down, lending a helping hand to the wounded trooper.

Joelson turned back to Li. "So you came from the generators then? Did you see why they're not running?"

"Smashed to shit," answered Li. "Had to be the creature."

Joelson scratched his head, puzzling over this new development.

"How would it know to cut the power?" he asked the group.

Early nudged him before they could brainstorm further. "We should go. We got our answer."

Joelson accepted his squadmate's wisdom with a shrug of his shoulders. "Alright then, I guess it's back to the Command Den."

Joelson rallied the group together, marshaling them down in the direction they had come. They rolled in a loose formation, with Konrad far out front, Reming just behind, Early and Li hanging in the rear. Walking along in the center clump, Rania felt oddly exposed, out of place. She was acutely aware that she was the only one unarmed, a thought not helped by the fact they no longer knew what the creature looked like. They made slow progress as they backtracked down the hall, with Konrad halting the group to check down every intersection. Still, they marched on. There was an element of danger in any squad movement.

As they cleared down another corridor, they walked past the laundry room. It stretched beside them, sunken and dark, without even the faintest glow of the emergency lights to plumb its impenetrable depths. For the fifth time in ten minutes, Konrad halted the group, clenching a fist and dropping to a knee. The group did the same, each settling into a position along the wall.

Reming caught up with the sullen trooper, dropping to a crouch alongside him. "What the fuck is it this time, Konrad?"

Konrad shushed him, pointing a finger into the dense gloom of the laundry room. Reming stared into the black obscurity, frustration mounting with the hulking Private. He squinted as he leaned forward, accidentally knocking the tip of his ZapGun against the tile floor. It rebounded in his hand, his finger slipping off the guard and onto the trigger. A thin arc of electricity crackled forth, surging through the air and into the alloy wall.

"Oh shit," whispered Reming, scrambling back from the doorway. For the briefest of moments, the thin bolt of lightning had illuminated the dark room, revealing a crouched form and glinting rows of sharp teeth. Reming dove out of the way as the creature launched itself out of the shadows, a mottled blur of orange, black, and claws. Konrad tucked his shoulder into a tight roll, swinging his rifle up and pulling the trigger.

But he was a second too slow.

The creature bowled him over, knocking the R-91 from his hands. Joelson shouted for the others to open fire as the sickle claws swung out, hooking into the screaming Private and dragging him headfirst into the toothy maw. Shots peppered the lean, striped side of the creature as the jaws swung down, muffling his screams as it closed around his midsection. It swung its arrow-shaped head back and forth, silencing Konrad's screaming with a final, violent shake. It weathered the troopers' fire, lifting its head and swallowing him down.

Joelson looked up from his rifle, still firing as he searched around his gathered forces. On his left, Rania clapped her hands over her ears as she crouched by Smith, letting him steady his Sonic Pistol on her shoulder. Behind them Early and Li struggled to catch up, abandoning their position in the rear to bring the heavy SLW up.

Joelson watched as the saddle-shaped structure lifted up on the creature's striped face. It snapped shut and turned in their direction, sickle claws clicking as it readied itself to charge. Joelson gritted his teeth, bracing himself as he feathered the trigger on his R-91.

But the impact never came.

A bolt of lightning arced out from the end of Reming's ZapGun as he crouched against the wall by the laundry room doorway. It zig-zagged through the air, a sputtering chain of pure electricity, fifty kilovolts surging forth and into the saddle-shaped structure on the face of the creature. The creature lifted its head and roared in pain, an ear-shattering scream in the tight confines of the hallway. It stumbled back away from the troopers, scratching at its wounded face as it steadied itself. The creature shook its head and fled, leaping away on long, powerful hind legs.

Reming took up a post at the edge of the intersection, watching as the creature disappeared down the darkened hallway. He looked back at the huddled troopers and gave a thumbs-up, letting them know the coast was clear.

Joelson stood up on jellied legs, hands still shaking from the adrenaline pouring through his body. He swept a hand in the air to gather his squad, steadying himself by leaning against the cool alloy wall. He brought them in close, rubbing a hand across the stubble on his upper lip. He forced his voice level as he addressed the group of troopers.

"Alright, new plan," he said, pushing his glasses up the bridge of his nose. "We keep it tight, as close as possible so it can't pick one of us off. It's smaller now, and fast. We treat every opening as a potential hazard."

Reming pushed his way through the group, Konrad's R-91 held out in his hand. Joelson stared hard at the dead Private's rifle, his thoughts turning to molasses as he contemplated the trooper who had last held it. A cough from Rania snapped him out of his reverie. He blinked his eyes and took the rifle from Reming's hands, passing it over to the female trooper. Joelson surveyed his paltry forces, pausing to look each one of them in the eye. He pushed himself up from the wall, rolling his shoulders as he straightened up.

"Everybody armed? Good." He turned to face their original heading, staring down the dim-lit hallway. "Let's get this shit-show moving."

CHAPTER 14:

Sergeant Kyrghizwald made his way by the dim red glow of the emergency lighting. Despite his earlier dose of NorCan, his brain still felt foggy, the wheels and cogs turning slowly as he wound his way through the maze of darkened hallways. *Must have misjudged the dose*, he thought, stumbling his way through the dark corridor. It happened from time to time, especially towards the middle of a tour, when he was more cautious about expending his supply.

The hallway was empty, entirely absent of the usual sounds of troopers hustling to and fro during an emergency. There wasn't even an alarm announcement to indicate where he should be going or what was happening. Enough turns through the darkened hallways, and he wasn't even sure where he was. His world spun for a moment, tipping over at the edges of his vision. Sergeant Kyrghizwald closed his eyes, placing a hand against the alloy wall to steady himself.

The metal was cool under his fingertips, and he used it as a guide. His hands slapped against the dull metal as he felt his way forward. His fingers pricked the edge of a thin metal plaque, halfway up the wall. Opening his eyes, he focused on the letters inscribed on the aluminum sign. 'AZH-01 Sector 3' it read, with a smaller inscription marking the directions of the Command Den, Med Center, and chow hall. He smiled as he continued on his path. Someone had taken time to carve the letter 'E' on the sign, right at the end of the installation's name.

Sergeant Ramos bent over the thin polymer table of the Command Den. His tongue was in his cheek as he pored over the spindly ink of the installation blueprints, stopping periodically to brush aside dust and eraser rubbings from the page. Found in a tight roll tucked behind a network cabinet, it was a testament to the military's hoarder mentality; 'save everything, as long as it's stamped with official markings.' He scrutinized the ancient map, yellowed around the edges, as he worked to mark sightings of the creature's location. There were two columns written on the wall behind him in shaky ink letters, scribbled out with an antique marker they'd found in the bottom of a sticky desk drawer.

"You almost seem to be enjoying this," remarked Lieutenant Preston.

"Analog skills, LT. No school like the old school." Sergeant Ramos stepped back from the paper map, surveying the intersecting drawings of circles and lines. "Just like Avina."

Lieutenant Preston stood beside him, reading the blueprints over the Reed-Sergeant's shoulder. He traced a finger along the paper, connecting the creature's path through the circled locations. "It zig-zags a bit, but it's headed towards the center of the station."

"Now that doesn't make full sense," said Sergeant Ramos. "Why would the fucking thing go further in? Why wouldn't it just back out and run away?"

Lieutenant Preston folded his arms. "Hunger? More food?"

Sergeant Ramos shook his head. "No, sir. It had plenty of opportunity to eat us in the bay. If it was just hunger, it would have stayed put."

Lieutenant Preston ran a hand through his hair, rubbing the back of his head as he thought. "So it was trying to get away from the bay. But deeper in? Why?"

They both turned towards the wall, reading over the jerky columns of block-printed writing. One side detailed the timeline of events, beginning with the MMUTCAT crash and extending through half-hour increments to their present time. The other side listed all of the installation personnel, carefully tallying them as dead, injured, or missing. A small 'D' was placed by the names of Privates Johnson, Almar, and Suzettes. Four names were noted with a small 'I,' but nearly a dozen were still marked with an 'M,' including two NCOs.

Lieutenant Preston frowned, trying to process the situation as a whole. He found his mind slipping as he tried to piece together the animal and its motives, his thoughts continuing to turn towards the growing casualty list before him. *Focus, Douglas*, he chanted to himself. *What does it want? And why is it here?* He reached back to the table, retrieving the primitive marker and uncapping it. He leaned against the flimsy plastic table, staring at the wall ahead. After a moment he bent forward and started a new column on the wall titled 'Creature.'

"Let's start over. What do we know about it?" he asked the Reed-Sergeant.

"Fuck-all," Sergeant Ramos grumbled. Lieutenant Preston stared at him, marker still in hand. The marker tapped against the empty column as a few seconds of silence stretched between them.

"Fine!" the Reed-Sergeant relented. "It's big. And white."

The officer nodded, jotting down notes on the beast's description. "Right, it was white, so what does that tell us?"

Sergeant Ramos shifted where he stood. "That it was meant for the snow, camouflaged."

Lieutenant Preston continued to write, fleshing out notes about 'shaggy coat,' 'carnivorous,' and 'snow camo.'

"And hungry. With multiple sharp claws, and big teeth," Sergeant Ramos added.

"So it's a predator for sure." Lieutenant Preston looked up from his notes. "Natural or bioweapon?"

"You've been watching too many vidplays, LT." Sergeant Ramos stroked his broad chin. "Nobody does bioweapons, not since the Europa incident in 2275. Too damn costly. The programs take decades to get right and the things are always too fucking fragile. It would take millions of credits to custom design a monster, and even then, they'd have to tailor it to survive in this fucking snow pile."

He stared at the growing list of characteristics. "No, sir. This thing is too well put together. It fits this place, even if no one's seen anything like this in the sixty years this station has been here."

Lieutenant Preston turned back towards the list, adding 'Native?' to the end. "Ok, so if it's indigenous, how come we didn't know? We sent survey drones when they were first scouting this planet. How come they didn't pick this thing up?"

"That was seventy years ago, LT. Who knows how detailed their scanning tech was back then." Sergeant Ramos leaned back against the plastic table. "It's any one of a hundred reasons why we didn't catch it earlier. It's a big planet, and we only use a small part of it.

"Besides," he added, "we've been here for decades without running into it. Maybe it's rare, or it sleeps for a hundred years."

Lieutenant Preston considered this as he finished up a final few notes on the wall. He capped the marker and stood back.

"I didn't see any eyes, just that saddle part on its face."

Sergeant Ramos nodded. "Same, it looked like it used it for hunting. And it freaked out when it opened up all the way, like the bay was too bright."

"So it uses the saddle to see, but we don't know how or what it senses," the officer mused. "Echolocation? Thermal? Some kind of radar?"

Sergeant Ramos shook his head. "Can't be radar or anything it puts out. It wouldn't get overwhelmed if it was controlling its sensor input." He pointed a tan finger at the column. "Heat's not a bad idea, everything in here is warmer than the environment it's used to. But there were lots of hot things in the bay, hell the MMUTCAT engines caught on fire. No reason it would bypass those and go after you."

"Or Suzettes," the Lieutenant added, staring down at the ground.

"Right," the Reed-Sergeant nodded, his voice softening. "Or him."

Their conversation was cut short by the panting arrival of Sergeant Wingo and two other troopers, dragging a nylon sack behind them. He dropped the strap he was pulling as soon as he entered the room, forcing Godrey and Kowalski to push the massive green bag the rest of the way through the door. Sergeant Wingo walked over to the map on the table, sweat bubbling up on his pudgy face.

"Armory's cleaned out," he said, wiping his nose on his sleeve. "Early and Joelson already took one *Slaw*, but I grabbed the other one and the assistant gunner bags. I also cleared out the rest of the R-91s and P-3s."

Sergeant Ramos walked over to assist the struggling troopers, while Lieutenant Preston picked up the marker and started jotting down their inventory.

"Fourteen…fifteen…sixteen. Sixteen rifles, LT," Sergeant Ramos called out, thumbing through the nylon bag. "And nineteen pistols."

Lieutenant Preston marked the numbers on the wall, looking up when he was done. "Grenades? Pyro?"

"Lemme check." Sergeant Ramos lifted up the edges of the bag, pawing deep within its contents. "None, just two trip-flares."

"They were gone before I got there!" Sergeant Wingo held up his hands, cutting off the Reed-Sergeant before the accusations could begin. "Konrad or Sikes must've grabbed 'em already."

"God help the poor bastard that tries to use them," remarked Sergeant Ramos, standing up from the bag. "Grenades don't mix well in tight quarters. If the shrapnel doesn't get you, the overpressure will."

Lieutenant Preston offered him the marker as he walked over to the wall. The Reed-Sergeant deliberated a moment before settling in to assign weapons among the accounted troopers. He broke down the men by squads, designating those remaining into six-man fireteams, complete with a team lead and deputy. It was a pitiable force, and he knew it. The installation equipped for detecting deep-space fleets and repelling skirmishes with small-team raiders, not combatting large scale engagements.

He sighed. If there was one thing his fifteen years in the ICF had taught him, it's that you always work with the tools you have. *And you never get the tools you want*, he thought, ruefully eyeing the sweating Buck-Sergeant. He opened his mouth, ready to issue orders and distribute their remaining weapons, but he was cut off by the sudden arrival of Private Darnis and Special-Trooper Almsted. They stopped just in front of him, their faces pale and eyes wide.

"S-s-sergeant," Darnis stammered, sweat beading on his forehead. They were both out of breath, having plainly run to the Command Den. Sergeant Ramos waited for the troopers to continue but they both fell silent, trembling at parade rest.

"Well? What is it?" The Reed-Sergeant crossed his arms, staring down the two shaking troopers. "What the fuck happened?"

It was Almsted who finally spoke up, swallowing hard before he answered. "Sarge. It's Sikes, we found him."

Sergeant Ramos read well enough between the lines to know that the Senior-Sergeant wasn't going to be walking through the door after them. "What happened?"

"Thing got him," Almsted said. "In the hallway by the air filters."

Lieutenant Preston chewed on his lower lip. He shifted his weight back and forth on his heels as he watched the shaken troopers.

"Show me," he said at last.

Darnis and Almsted's eyes went wide. Almsted looked at the floor as he answered. "Sir, you...you don't want to see. He was damn near cut in half."

The officer stared straight past them to the column on the wall, his eyes on the list of names marked with a small 'D.'

"Show me."

Rania crept through the dark hallway with the other troopers, concentrating on keeping her footsteps as quiet as possible. She attempted to remember her field craft lessons from basic training. *Was it heel to toe or was that just for marching? Should I be tiptoeing?* She became acutely aware of both the existence and exact positioning of her arms and legs, and she struggled to keep them all in steady motion at the same time. She looked on in envy at Joelson and the others, watching them roll forward as a smooth, contiguous unit. *How do these security troops make it look so easy?* She watched them closely as they walked, analyzing and trying to mimic them mid-stride. Her ankles crossed as she focused too hard, tripping her up and sending her stumbling forward. She recovered in a few steps, snapping her head left and right to see if the others had noticed. If they had, they ignored her out of sheer politeness, continuing forward as if nothing had happened and scanning ahead for potential threats.

She shifted her grip on the R-91, the blocky particle rifle feeling clunky and awkward in her hands. *Haven't used one of these since basic either*. The molded metal frame and checkered polymer grips felt foreign to her, like a left hand tool being held by the right. *It's lighter than I remember*, she mused, playing with the balance of the weapon. *And a lot more complicated.* She eyed the assortment of instruments clustered around the barrel, trying to discern the flashlight from laser indicator. Joelson had tried to give her a quick rundown of the optical scope mounted on the top of the weapon, but he'd dropped the subject in the interest of time when it took her four tries to locate the power button. She sighed softly and returned her attention to the dim hallway ahead. *Guess I'll figure it out when I need to.*

They slowed their pace as they came up to the south side of the chow hall, the scant red lighting casting deep shadows in the gloomy room. Joelson paused, holding up a hand to stop the group. They flattened against the wall as a unit, with Rania moving a half second behind. Joelson tapped Smith on the shoulder, using two fingers to point to the door. Smith nodded and together they stalked ahead, pie-ing the corners of the doorway as they moved to look inside. They peered around the edges of the doorframe, straining to penetrate the deep shadows of the room beyond. The dining facility was wide and open, but full of nooks and crannies cut off from their view in the doorway. Clearing the puzzle-piece shaped room was far from ideal, but it was their only way to reach the Command Den from this side of the installation.

Joelson locked eyes with Smith, conferring with the Private about his view of the room. Smith shrugged; he couldn't see anything from his position, but the reality was that they didn't have much choice either way. Joelson nodded, waving a hand and drawing the rest of the group to his position. They stacked up behind him, tapping him on the shoulder once they were in place. He let out a deep breath, in through his nose and out through his mouth. He dropped his hand, and the troopers filed in.

They fanned out as they entered the room, each trooper taking a slice of the large dining facility. At Joelson's command they formed a line stretching across the chow hall. He waved them forward, and slowly they made their way through the room. They flowed around long tables and bench chairs as their eyes adjusted to the low light, taking care to move quietly and touch nothing.

It was Joelson who saw it first, crouching in the deep shadows by the alcove of weights in the far left of the room. At first he thought he was mistaken, just an illusion reflected in the lens of his glasses. He stared hard, eyes straining in the murky light. Gradually the creature's outline revealed itself, sleeker and smoother than when it had burst through the bay door. Its mottled stripes concealed it perfectly, obscuring it in the darkness of the little alcove. He could just make out a slight gleam off the sickle fore-claws, shifting slightly up and down as the creature breathed.

He halted the group, making a quick motion with his hand to draw their attention. They stared in the direction he was pointing, twelve eyes struggling to see through the gloom. One by one they saw it, clutching their weapons a little tighter when they did. Joelson raised a hand showing three fingers, they held their breath as he counted down. As the last finger dropped, the troopers opened fire.

The crackle of rifle fire split the air, the silence of the room shattering under the troopers' withering fire. Neutral ions erupted from their barrels at super speeds, a small burning crater forming at the impact site of each round. The flash of light as ions collided with solid matter and exploded lit up the dark room in strobing bursts of light. Sonic blasts erupted from the pistols carried by Li and Smith, the action of their P-3s cycling in rapid succession.

"Ho! Ly! Shit!" Li shouted, his mouth agape as he pulled the trigger as fast as possible.

"Fuckin-A, right?" yelled Reming, feeling himself swept away in the heat of the fight.

The creature roared. Teeth glinted in the flashes of light as rounds peppered the walls around it. It backpedaled suddenly, surprised by the aggression of its former prey. The Creature knocked into the wall of free weights behind it, sending plates of heavy iron crashing to the floor. The trooper's fire chased it as it leapt across the room, smashing into the RationVendor and knocking the heavy appliance over. The onslaught continued, small orange craters stitching the back and sides of the beast as it scrambled around the open room.

Rania struggled to bring her rifle to bear in the flashing glare of the firefight. The cacophony of fire was deafening, echoing off the metal tables and walls in the wide chow hall. She fought to hold the boxy weapon steady, green splotches obscuring her vision from the flashing light. The creature dodged around the room, forcing her to hustle to keep it in her sights. It settled in one place long enough for her to get a bead on it, and with a breath and a quick prayer, she pushed a button.

And ejected the battery from the back of her rifle.

"Fucking really?!" snapped Reming, lightning arcing away from the ZapGun's tiny muzzle.

"I'M A SENSOR TECH!" she shouted, scrambling to retrieve the power pack and insert it into the mag-well of her rifle.

"The hook-thing is the trigger! The button-thing is the mag-release!" Li called out from the edge of the line.

"I know that now!" she hollered back, slamming the battery in with fumbling fingers.

The creature tumbled by, ducking around the trooper's fire and kicking over tables as it passed. It smacked into the wall at the edge of the room, powerful legs scrabbling for purchase amid the alloy and tile. It found its footing and turned towards them, roaring a challenge at the grim-faced troopers.

"Gotcha, bitch," said Special-Trooper Early, pulling the trigger on his SLW-18.

The room brightened, bathed in the red glow of the portable laser cannon. A fist-sized beam of light blasted out from the weapon, clipping the creature on the haunch and stabbing into the wall behind it. The beast screamed in pain, leaping away from the searing beam. The mighty thunder of the SLW's laser drowned out all other sounds in the wide-open room. Early grunted as he shifted the immense bulk of the weapon, dragging the beam after the escaping creature and cutting a line through the alloy wall as he trailed. Just as a small alarm chirped in the cannon's buttstock, the creature found the edge of the chow hall's north door. It flung itself through the doorway, tearing down the hallway to the right.

Early released the trigger, gasping as he lowered the heavy rifle. Vent flaps opened up along the weapon's side as Early dropped the muzzle to the ground, leaning on the cannon for support. The troopers around him cut loose in cheers as the sounds of the creature fleeing faded down the hallway. Early mustered a shaky thumbs-up, his shaved head flushed with effort.

"Nicely done, E." Joelson patted him on the back, turning to gather the troopers.

"Nothin' to it, but to do it," said Early, panting as he stood back up and shouldered the hefty cannon

They rallied by the door, buoyed by their recent success. Reming and Li exchanged high-fives, a grin stretched across the younger trooper's face.

"Fuckin' owned that shit!" Li crowed, bobbing his head in a victory dance.

"Shit-yeah we did," agreed Reming, blowing on the barrel of the tiny ZapGun.

"Fucking *smooth*, fucking *clean*," Li sang.

"Like a death-dealin' sex machine!" they finished together, slapping palms once again.

"Not bad gents, went pretty well overall," said Joelson, nodding as he stood on the edge of the group.

"Pretty well?" Reming laughed. "Fuckin' Raiders couldn't have pulled that shit off better."

The smile slipped off Joelson's face, Konrad's death still fresh in his mind. Reming saw the shift in his friend, dropping his eyes to the floor as he walked back his comments.

"I mean, you know, even Raiders get unlucky," Reming conceded.

"What do you mean?" asked Smith, wandering into the back half of the conversation. "What about the Raiders?"

"Konrad, dude," Li shook his head. "Try to keep with it."

Smith looked back at them, confused. "Konrad wasn't a Raider."

"Yeah, he fuckin' was," said Reming. "Why do you think he was such a fucking asshole all the time?"

Catching sight of Joelson out of the corner of his eye, he muttered an apology. "I mean, rest in peace, proud soldier."

But Smith refused to back down. "Konrad wasn't a Raider. He and I were both in the selection pipeline but he quit training after week four, knee injury or something. He actually washed out a few days before I did, when I got that concussion falling off the climbing wall."

Reming's eyes bugged out of his head. "You mean that taint-licker acted so big and bad, and he didn't even make it through the school?! Son of a–"

A stern look from Joelson cut him off midstream. He remembered the circumstances of their conversation, and forced himself back into the mindset of solemn remembrance. He stared straight at the ground, adding, "I mean, God bless his soul. He was a good man."

He was spared from wedging his foot further into his mouth by a sharp gasp from Rania, staring down the hall as she leaned out the doorway.

"Guys, quick!" she called, running out the doorway to the left. "Someone's hurt!"

The troopers rushed after her, boots thudding on the tile. As Joelson turned the corner he saw Rania crouching over something slumped against the wall. As he neared them he saw it was Sergeant Kyrghizwald, his chest heaving slowly as he clasped his hand in hers. Joelson rushed in to help, stopping himself as he took in the full scope of the Buck-Sergeant's injuries. A fist-sized chunk was missing from the side of his chest, punched clean through. There was surprisingly little blood, the vessels along the edges burned shut, as if seared by an incredible heat. Joelson didn't need to be a doctor to know this man was drawing his last breaths, and as his blue eyes looked straight into Joelson's, it appeared that he knew he was dying as well.

Sergeant K closed his eyes, his breath coming in halting, shallow gasps. His chest caught once, and he spasmed, struggling out of Rania's grasp. He let out a sound like a strangled cough, and then settled back against the wall. Rania looked back at Joelson, tears ringing the edges of her eyes.

"Do we know what happened?" asked a voice behind him, causing Joelson to nearly jump out of his skin. He had forgotten about the other troopers for a moment, hadn't even heard them approach, he was so focused on the wounded man. He shut his eyes as he considered how to answer, the Buck-Sergeant's injuries matched the fist-sized gouge through the alloy wall, still molten around the edges from the beam's extreme heat.

He heard Early gasp behind him, the sharp intake of breath signaling that he too, had put everything together. Joelson didn't say a word as the Special-Trooper broke down, leaning against the wall as he buried his face in his hands. A few moments passed in the red-lit hallway, the only sound coming from the muffled sobs of the burly trooper. Joelson let out a deep breath as he composed himself, resting a hand on the trooper's trembling shoulder. He steadied himself, looking straight into Early's tearful eyes.

"Not now," he said, keeping his voice level and calm. "We're almost there. We have to keep moving."

Early stopped shuddering for a moment, wiping his eyes with a meaty hand.

Joelson kept his eyes locked with the Special-Trooper, dropping his voice to a whisper. "I need you to keep going."

Early nodded, sniffing once and standing up from the wall. Joelson stepped back, suddenly shaky on his feet. He steadied himself, but couldn't keep the weariness from his voice as he turned down the hallway.

"We have to keep moving."

CHAPTER 15:

"So you're saying it's black now?"

Joelson nodded, swallowing a mouthful of SimuCaff. "Yes sir, and thinner. Sleek."

"Huh."

Lieutenant Preston leaned back in his chair, absentmindedly toying with the cap of the marker. He looked up at the ragged troopers gathered around him. It had been about a half hour since they'd dragged themselves through the threshold of the Command Den, haggard and exhausted from their trek across the installation. He and Sergeant Ramos had immediately cleared space for them, pushing Sergeant Wingo out of his comfy seat on the nylon weapons bag to make room for the exhausted troopers. They settled Joelson's squad at and around the Command Den table, with Sergeant Ramos jumping at the chance to brew a fresh pot of SimuCaff. They looked like they'd been through hell and back.

Lieutenant Preston turned in his chair, looking back to the wall to the column marked 'Creature.' He sighed, standing up from the table and uncapping the marker. He crossed out the lines about the creature's size and coloration. "I guess we're back to square one."

"Not really, sir," Joelson shook his head. "It looks different, but it acted more or less the same. Still fast, still hungry. Just smaller, and dark instead of white."

"With orange stripes," said Li, speaking up from the rim of his mug. "Like a tiger."

"Tigers are orange with black stripes," Reming corrected. He ignored the death glare Li shot him as he sipped his cup of the dark, bitter beverage.

Lieutenant Preston nodded, adding 'Stripes' to the new description on the wall. He stepped back from the list, an uncomfortable idea forming in his mind. "Are we sure this is the same one? Maybe there's two, and this one snuck in while we weren't looking?"

The group considered the realities of the officer's unpleasant scenario. Sergeant Ramos scratched his chin, chewing it over before speaking. "No dice, LT. Lean and black wouldn't have survived outside. It's negative sixty degrees out there, and everything's covered in snow.

"Besides," he added, folding his arms. "Reming and Li said they found its skin. In the generator room."

"Right," admitted the officer, turning back towards the group. He pointed at the two troopers. "What was it exactly that you found? Can you tell us more about it?"

Reming and Li froze mid sip as the room turned their attention towards them. Reming swallowed hard, the burning, bitter liquid scalding the back of his throat on the way down. As he broke out into a series of sputtering coughs, Li covered for his squad-mate.

"Yessir, we found it in the generator room like Sergeant Ramos said. It was weird and hollow, just a big empty pile of skin and hair."

Reming managed to recover from his coughing fit, clearing his chest with a thump of his fist. "It was definitely a shed molt, sir. Maybe even a full ecdysis or metamorphosis. The dermal layers were thick and covered with white hair, probably to trap heat and break up the outline. Below that was a good four or five inches of subcutaneous fat, definite insulation against the cold."

He set his mug down on the table, continuing his train of thought without missing a beat. "It might be a multi-latitude predator, probably ranging up to and just above the polar line. The pre-molt creature is probably its winter form, something it builds up and sheds in the warmer climates. That might explain why it's been so aggressive, it burns a lot more energy now that it's lost its fat reserves."

The room stared at him in silence. Reming stared right back, crossing his arms over his chest.

"What? I went to college."

"Yeah, for a semester," muttered Li, stealing a sip from his mug.

"Better than you, uneducated fuck!" Reming shot back, stabbing an accusing finger back at Li. "At least *I* didn't think it transformed into Smith."

Li slammed his mug down on the table. "That was a serious threat and you know it! You were the one that said we didn't know what it looked like!"

"Both of you, shut the fuck up!" barked Sergeant Ramos, interrupting the squabbling troopers.

Lieutenant Preston whispered as he leaned into Joelson, "They thought Smith was the monster?"

Joelson nodded behind his mug. "They did. Smacked him right in the balls to make sure he was human."

A half smile crept over the officer's face as he leaned back in his chair. "You know, that reminds me of a movie I once saw. Some researchers were trapped in the arctic with an alien that looked just like them. They tested their blood to make sure–"

His musings were interrupted when he realized the group's focus was back to him. He cocked a brow as he stared back at them. "What'd I miss?"

"They want to know if you agree," Sergeant Ramos answered, reiterating for the group. "About what Reming said."

Lieutenant Preston leaned back in his chair, picking up his own cup of SimuCaff.

"Hell if I know," he said, swirling the liquid in his cup. "I studied film history."

Reming whooped, pumping a fist under Li's nose.

"Yeah, yeah," said Li, pushing the hand out of his face. "But we sure as fuck aren't going with that dumbass name you want."

"What name?" asked Rania from across the table.

"The Dreadnot," pronounced Reming, waving his hands to underline the majesty of the name. He was met with a collective stare of nonplus from the gathered troopers. Lieutenant Preston silently mouthed 'Dreadnaught?' to Sergeant Ramos. The Reed-Sergeant shrugged, returning his attention to his mug.

Disappointed with the reaction of his peers, Reming repeated the name with greater emphasis, elaborating further on the accompanying hand gestures. His efforts were met with continued silence. Early coughed in his hand from the corner. Reming opened his mouth to repeat himself for the third time before he was cut off by Li.

"It's from *Altar of Combat*," the Private explained with a sad shake of his head. He jerked a thumb at Reming. "This dumbass thinks the monster looks like one of the mini-bosses in the game."

The group's focus swung back towards the Special-Trooper.

"It does!" he exploded, throwing his hands in the air. "Except it doesn't have tentacles. And it's black instead of green. And it isn't stuck in one place. And it can't shoot rockets. And…"

He lapsed into silence under the crushing weight of their stares. His eyes were pleading as he looked from trooper to trooper. The quiet in the room stretched before him. Early coughed again from the corner.

Sergeant Ramos broke the stillness with a derisive snort.

"Well that's it then, the dumbest shit I'll hear all day."

Reming hung his head in shame as the room broke out in laughter. Lieutenant Preston stood up from his chair, patting the Special-Trooper on the shoulder on his way to the writing on the wall. He let a few minutes pass as the room sorted the giggles out of their system before letting loose with an authoritative 'ahem.' A hush fell over the room again. He drew their attention back to the task at hand.

"Alright, we'll put that at the top of the 'Good Tries' list," he said, uncapping the marker in his hand. "But it's still out there. It's still a threat. And we need to make a plan."

The problems facing the beleaguered troopers were staggering, but not insurmountable. With the arrival of Joelson's squad they had finally succeeded in gathering and accounting for the remaining troopers on the installation. Lieutenant Preston had paled at the news of Konrad and Kyrghizwald's losses, robotically forcing himself through the motions of changing the letter by their names to 'D.' He had slumped in his chair afterwards, numb to the discussions in the room for several minutes. It was Sergeant Ramos who brought him back to the moment, touching him on the elbow and pointing at the map spread out on the Command Den table.

"So as I was saying, sir. We're going to have to add to the emergency power." The Reed-Sergeant gestured to the low red lighting emanating from the edges of the walls. "Right now the basic subsystems are going. We've got the crisis lighting, and mild heating with the O_2 rehabbers."

He pointed on the map to a small room in the center of the station. "The emergency generators are insulated, the core room is blast-shielded, lead-lined, and enclosed with a faraday cage. It was made to survive the worst attacks, but it wasn't built to power the station for longer than seventy two hours. After that, you either bring main power back online, or add something to offset the power drain."

He looked up at Reming and Li. "Now, they're saying that the creature knocked out the main generators."

"Totally fucked," Reming nodded. Li made explosion sounds with his mouth, gesturing with his hands to indicate the exact degree to which the main generators were fucked.

Sergeant Ramos silenced them with a look, clearing his throat before continuing.

"So bringing the main power back online isn't an option. That leaves us with augmenting the emergency generators. Sergeant Wingo thinks he can hardwire some of the MMUTCAT batteries and extend the power supply. If we get two or three wired in, we can extend the power to last us another week, maybe two if we cut down the heat and air to only one or two main rooms."

He paused to take in a breath, holding it in his chest for a moment before letting it out. "Here's where we start getting into the sticky wickets. Each MMUTCAT has eight batteries, so supply isn't a problem. But those batteries weigh around three-hundred and fifty pounds each, so it'll be damn hard work to get them in place. We already figured on two teams, one to each vehicle bay. Early, Reming, and Li on the team to the West Bay. Kowalski, Darnis, and Almsted to the South Bay. That cuts our mission time in half and splits our chances of getting the batteries without taking casualties."

Lieutenant Preston nodded, his mind drifting back to the rising death toll written behind him. "And Wingo? I take it he's going directly to the emergency room? Waiting for the teams to show up with batteries?"

"Yessir," confirmed the Reed-Sergeant. "Him and Leonard are moving out after the other teams leave. We're staggering the teams by twenty minutes to space out our presence a bit. We don't want to draw attention to the Command Den."

Lieutenant Preston considered this, running a hand through his hair. "So that buys us more time, but for what? We need a way to call for transport. How do we get a signal sent off the emergency power?"

Sergeant Ramos frowned, stroking his chin. "I don't have an answer for that, sir. Even with batteries we won't have enough power to boost a signal into deep space."

The room went quiet, the holes in their plan revealing themselves with startling clarity.

It was Rania who spoke up, the glimmer of an idea forming while Sergeant Ramos was speaking.

"What about using a sensor tower?" she asked, rising from her chair and addressing the group. "They run off their own power from the methane vents. I could fly my *Solo Skimmer* to Alpha-03, run a line of code and trigger the alarm. I can rig the tower to bounce a message from our dome antennae to the sub-orbital tether. It won't be enough to reach back to ICF command, but that'll put it in reach of any ships passing by through the system."

Lieutenant Preston cocked an eyebrow at Sergeant Ramos, gauging the feasibility of the Special-Trooper's plan. Sergeant Ramos mulled it over, folding his arms across his chest as he chewed on it.

"It's risky," he said at last, the frown deepening on his face. "And someone will have to program the message through the link in the control room."

He looked back at Lieutenant Preston. "That's either you or me, sir. No one else has the required clearance codes. That also means forming another escort team to get her to the hangar, as well as letting her engage in a solo flight when we don't have full weather data."

"Even with the *best* pilot," the Reed-Sergeant sniffed, "that's a difficult feat to pull off."

The officer nodded, weighing the risks at hand. He looked back at Rania, the bags under her eyes betrayed her exhaustion, but below them there was a determined clinch to her jaw.

"You understand the dangers here?" he asked, staring her straight in the eyes. "Once you take off, you'll be on your own. We can't be sure what the situation is outside, or even the situation in here when you make it back. This whole plan revolves around you rigging a tower alone. The truth is you might not make it back, or even get that far in the first place. Even if you do get back, there's no guarantee your security escort will still be waiting for you. I need you to know this. I can't authorize this mission unless you understand the risks involved."

She blinked once, the reality of the odds against her settling in. She returned his gaze, nodding emphatically as she accepted the weight of her responsibility. Lieutenant Preston let out a slow breath, puffing out his cheeks as he turned to face the room.

"Then I guess we've got our orders. Let's make it happen."

Rania pulled the CWAPL over her head, the insulating outer garment hanging loose and baggy around her petite frame. She'd had to borrow it from the Lieutenant; hers was still hanging off the back of the chair in her room. She cinched it down around the waist and cuffs. *That'll have to do.* The facemask hanging around her neck was similarly borrowed, offered up by the Reed-Sergeant with barely a grunt of acknowledgement. It wasn't quite the right fit. Hers was GP-Small, while his was GP-Medium, but like the rest of her cobbled-together gear, it would have to do.

She stood up after making her adjustments, stretching her back to the tune of a few satisfying pops. She breathed in slow and deep, mentally preparing herself for the task ahead. Across the room, Joelson caught her eye, the look of concern plain on his face as he picked up his R-91 from the table. She offered him a thumbs-up, projecting a confidence far beyond what she felt. A half-smile came to his face, but his eyes were filled with worry. She looked away and shouldered her bag. Most of her tools and climbing gear were already enclosed in molded storage compartments on the DC-12, but she needed a tablet and an interface cable to write the programming necessary to rig the sensor. She rotated her shoulders, settling the bag in the small of her back.

Rania walked to the door, tapping Smith on the shoulder as she passed. He and Joelson were to form her security escort there to ensure that she made it to the hangar in one piece. It was small comfort with the creature still roaming the station, potentially lurking around each dark corner, but she took solace in their enthusiastic volunteering for the mission. She hadn't been at the station very long and was still trying to find her role in the big security platoon. She was grateful to find someone willing to watch her back.

She offered a hand to Smith, helping him up from his spot on the floor. She held out her R-91, pointing to his pistol in exchange.

"What for? You need it too," he said, uncertain as he eyed the outstretched rifle.

"I'm not very good with it, and I won't have room in the cockpit," she said, favoring him with a smile. "Besides, a Raider needs a rifle."

He returned her smile, reaching out a hand and taking the R-91. He toyed with the particle weapon, playing with the balance in his hands. Sweeping it up to a shoulder, he eyed down the optical sight. He nodded once and lowered it, turning back to Rania and offering her the P-3. She took it gently in one hand, patting him on the shoulder with the other as she turned back to the door.

"Ready?" asked Joelson, joining the two of them at the doorway.

Rania sighed. "As much as I can be."

Joelson unshouldered his rifle to low-ready, poking his head out the door as he peered down the hallway. He pulled back into the Command Den when he saw that the coast was clear.

"Then let's do this."

They walked down the hallway in silence, footsteps muffled as they made their way to the hangar. They crept along, the beams from their weapon lights crisscrossing in the dim-lit corridor as they scouted ahead for a sign of the creature. Their progress was quick, hurried by their awareness of their imminent exposure in the empty corridors. They slowed only when they crossed dark rooms, clearing just the edge of the doorway before darting across to continue their mission. The clock was ticking, and every minute was too precious to waste.

They made their way through the station, acutely aware of the sound of their own breathing. The entrance to the hangar was only a few hallways over, just two straight-aways and a left from their current position. Their nerves tightened as they drew nearer to the hangar, each stop at the dark rooms along the way becoming more furtive and rushed.

They hustled as quickly as they could, pulses quickening with their pace. They could see the jutting latch on the door to the hangar, midway down the hallway as they turned. Only two rooms lay between them and their final destination. A quick poke with their flashlights and they cleared the first, holding their breath as they made their way to the second door.

Joelson and Smith stalked up to the edge of the frame, peering around into the dark room beyond. Their hearts were in their throats as they swept their lights through the corners of the room. Rania pressed herself against the alloy wall, making herself as small as possible while she waited for them to finish. They breathed a sigh of relief when nothing was revealed in their cursory search. Joelson and Smith stepped back from the edge and prepared to move on. They were almost to the hangar door.

The hair rose on the back of Joelson's neck as he heard a slight rasp behind him, the muffled scrape of heavy claws on alloy tile. He turned in time to see the creature creep out of the first room they'd cleared, its belly low to the ground, striped flank rippling in the low red light. Fear tightened its icy claws around his brain as he grabbed Smith by the arm, spinning him around to face the creature. Smith's eyes went wide as the creature sniffed tile in the narrow hallway: the tile they had walked across only moments before.

The saddle-shaped structure above the wide jaws raised up, snapping shut abruptly as it took in its surroundings in the dim, red light. It turned towards them, the sickle-shaped claws clicking softly as the creature bunched up on its powerful haunches. Joelson and Smith steadied their rifles, their hearts pounding in their chests.

Rifle still facing towards the creature, Joelson turned his head to look back at Rania.

"Go!" he whispered, his eyes wide behind the thin glass lenses. "You're our only shot!"

Rania swallowed hard and nodded, her heels ringing off the alloy tile as she ran down the rest of the hallway. She yanked open the insulated metal door and swung around the narrow doorframe. She sprinted across the hangar to her skiff, the sound of gunfire erupting from the hallway behind her. Rania slid into the side of the DC-12, fumbling to raise the latch on the bubble cockpit. She lifted it open, swinging a leg over the molded seat as she yanked the poly-plex canopy down over her. She powered up the Solo Skimmer, snapping toggle switches up as she readied it for flight. Easing the throttles forward, she felt the skiff vibrate as it lifted off the ground.

She craned her head in the tiny cockpit, catching sight of Joelson and Smith walking backwards past the hangar door. Their faces were a mask of grim resolve, lit up in flashes of particle explosions. Rania watched as they moved beyond her line of sight, the hallway lighting up in strobing light. She slammed the throttles forward and sped off into the snowy wastes.

CHAPTER 16:

Early heaved against the linking chains with both hands, dragging the battery behind him on four spindly wheels. The MMUTCAT battery was cumbersome, a four foot cube of dense alkaline metals, unwieldy in the narrow corridors of the station. They'd been fortunate enough to find a mechanic's creeper in the vehicle bay, lashing the heavy battery to the tiny platform with some leftover chain they had found. It lightened their load for sure, but brought with it a whole new series of complications. The creeper was designed to support a mechanic lying on their back, the three-hundred and fifty pound battery stretching the weight limits of the tiny platform. It creaked in protest when they placed the battery on it, the thin metal frame straining against the tremendous weight. Every now and then it creaked again as the cargo shifted, breaking the silence of the dark hallways with the errant protest of a squeaking wheel.

It also had a tendency to understeer, momentum carrying the cumbrous load forward in as straight a line as possible. Whenever they found themselves at a corner, it took the full effort of all three troopers to force the battery to turn. Reming and Li pulling back hard on the chains wrapped around the cube, while Early pushed back from the front, slowing the battery down to a complete stop. The three troopers then worked in concert to spin the top-heavy cart around the curve, with Reming and Li straining hard in the back to start the encumbered creeper moving again. It groaned at every turn, the omnipresent threat of the cart tipping over present every time the weight shifted or slowed.

Their progress was challenging, but relatively quick. Reming and Li walked behind the MMUTCAT battery, a guiding hand placed on each of the rear corners. Their other hands were clenched around the knurled grips of their Sonic Pistols, the knobby polymer lending itself comfortably to the contours of their palms.

Early still carried his SLW-18, the bulky laser cannon slung across his broad back. He ignored the blocky metal stock as it knocked into the back of his knees, a constant reminder of the weapon's presence as it hung from his back. He'd hesitated a little in carrying it, wincing

168

whenever he caught sight of the bulbous cannon in the Command Den. Still, the squad needed the penetrating power of the portable laser, and he was one of the few troopers strong enough to heft it. And so, he resumed his duties, slinging the long-barreled weapon up and over his shoulder, out of sight, and out of mind.

Or so he'd hoped, gritting his teeth as the square buttstock smacked him again in the back of the leg. The integrated optical sight dug into the small of his back, nagging him with its continued existence. The big trooper sighed, a rush of air expelled from his flaring nostrils. *Nothin' to it but to do it*, he chanted, over and over again in his mind. He tried to beat back the harpies of guilt circling in his head, drowning them out with his father's favorite mantra. *Nothin' to it but to do it, nothin' to it but to do it.* He forced himself to focus on the task at hand, on the feel of the links of the chain he dragged behind his back, on the simple mechanics of putting one foot in front of the other. *Nothintoitbuttodoit.*

He stopped, unsure if he'd imagined that sound up ahead. The MMUTCAT battery bumped into his back as he stood, in spite of Reming and Li's desperate attempts to slow it down. Early ignored both it and them, straining hard to listen down the hallway.

There it was again, a rasp or scrape on the tile-- something he couldn't quite make out. It repeated itself once more, just detectable on the edges of his hearing. It seemed to be coming from far ahead, moving towards them. He flagged Reming and Li, pointing first to his ear, and then to the dark end of the hallway. They nodded, fanning back from the battery to hug the edges of the alloy walls.

Gently, Early pulled the chain at the front of the battery, easing the cart around perpendicular with the narrow hallway. His makeshift barrier in place, he set the steel links down, careful to ensure they didn't clink together. He worked his way around the battery, unslinging the SLW and cradling it in his meaty hands. He eased the cannon onto the battery top, careful to avoid the exposed contacts as he rested it on its metal bipod. He breathed slowly in and out, calming himself as he settled in behind the rifle.

The rasping came again, a little louder this time, definitely on the approach. He looked back at Reming and Li, both leaning against the alloy walls, steadying their pistols on their knees. Early rested his cheek against the square buttstock, one half of his vision filling up with the red arrow of the optical sight. He held his breath for a moment, letting it out slowly through his mouth. They waited in the dark as the sound grew closer.

Rania hung from the side of tower Alpha-03, suspended by a narrow metal ladder. She hooked one arm through the icy metal rungs, a ScanTool connected to the sensor's interface clenched in her hand. Her free hand tapped away at the small touch-screen tablet, scrolling through lines of amended code. A frigid wind whipped by, pelting her with snow and rattling the spindly metal tower. She clung tighter to the frozen rung. All alone, even with the deep snow around the tower's base she couldn't risk the fifty-foot fall.

She clicked her tongue softly as she worked, running through a last check of her patchwork programming. It was irregular for sure, stretching the limits of her coding knowledge. *I doubt they cover THIS in the developmental studies volumes.* The wind whipped by once more, pelting her with another flurry of snow and bits of ice. She shivered behind the baggy CWAPL, the outsized garment only succeeding in keeping the worst of the cold at bay. She tapped the ScanTool to upload her programming, willing the progress bar to move faster as it grew in length across the screen. She could only hope that the new sensor program would work as intended, and with her DC-12's power at just below half, she wouldn't get a second shot to make it right. *And too many sacrificed just to get me here*, she thought, flashing back to Joelson and Smith.

Not for the first time in the past twenty-four hours, she found herself praying, beseeching an almighty god to look after her friends in harm's way. She wished she'd been more spiritual, more connected to what lay beyond. Prayer and worship had always been her father's thing, the last practicing Muslim in her family. As a girl he'd tried to teach her, showing her how to kneel in prayer and taking her to *Jumu'ah* every Friday. But just like the mosque's dwindling attendance, she too felt herself slipping away over the years. Now, as with the Arabic her father slipped into whenever he got excited, she only remembered the bits and pieces. *Bismillah ir-Rahman, ir-Rahim*, she recited to herself, the line that opened every *surah*, the ones she struggled to connect with when she meditated. *Bismillah ir-Rahman, ir-Rahim.* She knew it wasn't a true prayer, but like the hastily written program she'd put together to broadcast their signal, it would have to do.

The progress bar completed its journey across the screen, flashing once before turning into a small green check-mark, indicating the program had loaded. Rania snapped the ScanTool shut, unhooking it from the tower and clipping it to her belt. The wind picked up again as she made her way down the ladder, the thin metal shaking in the winds and threatening to knock her off her perch. Her knuckles were white inside her gloves as she climbed down the spindly sensor tower, the ground inching closer with each step.

A storm was rolling in, the sky beginning to darken with the shifting winds. She moved quickly, hopping off the last few rungs into the snow below. Rania trudged over to her *Solo Skimmer*, her body bent against the wind. As she swung her leg over into the narrow cockpit, she hoped she hadn't waited too long to leave. The poly-plex canopy closed around her, the wind howling just outside the bubble cockpit. She was reminded of the Lieutenant's words of warning as she sealed the tiny skiff. *No guarantees I'll make it back.* She powered up the DC-12, feeling the ultra-light ship rock beneath her in the rising winds. Rania eased the dampener stirrups with her feet, lifting the craft and turning back towards the installation. She whispered a prayer as she nudged the throttles forward, chasing away from the encroaching storm.

Early tucked in behind the bulbous laser cannon, the four-foot-long barrel stretching for miles in front of him as he waited in the dark. The scraping sound was almost upon them, just around the corner. Early clenched the SLW's molded handgrip tightly, veins popping out of his massive forearm. The glowing red arrow of the optical sight filled his world, drowning out everything else around him. The rushing roar of blood filled his ears as he poured his focus through the rifle sight. A bead of sweat broke on the edge of his shaved scalp, trickling down the back of his thick neck.

Sergeant Wingo turned the corner.

Early gasped, releasing the molded handgrip and pushing back from the rifle stock. He stood up panting, broad shoulders heaving up and down in time with the pounding in his chest. He wiped the cold sweat pooling on his brow, catching the water building in the corners of his eyes as he did. Reming and Li relaxed on either side of him, lowering their pistols and standing up from their positions against the alloy wall.

At the sight of the troopers' makeshift barricade, Sergeant Wingo broke into a wide smile. The portly Buck-Sergeant rushed over to meet them, sucking in his belly as he scooted through the gap between the battery and the wall.

"Nice hasty ambush fellas," Sergeant Wingo said looking over placement of their barricaded position. "Good line of sight with the *Slaw*."

"If I wasn't more careful, you mighta gotten me instead of the monster," he laughed, clapping Early on the shoulder with a pudgy hand.

Early's breath caught in his throat, he choked back the bile rising from his stomach with a retching cough. Sergeant Wingo carried on, oblivious to the sudden onset of the trooper's coughing fit.

"You two though," he said, pointing to Reming and Li. "Not so much. I know this thing can't shoot back, but in a *real* fight, you want to tuck in to the cover, bunch in by the barricade instead of the wall."

Reming and Li looked at each other, rolling their eyes as the sloppy Buck-Sergeant continued his critique.

"What are you doing here?" interrupted Reming, eyes narrowing as he stared down the hallway past Sergeant Wingo. "Shouldn't you be in the emergency generator room, hardwiring the batteries?"

"Nah, son. We finished that up thirty minutes ago," Sergeant Wingo replied, sidestepping the Special-Trooper's accusatory tone. "Kowalski and Darnis brought three batteries in one go, daisy-chained them together on a series of creeper carts."

"Multiple carts," groaned Li, smacking his forehead. "Why didn't we think of that?"

By this time Early had recovered, wiping the bile from his mouth on the back of his hand.

"Where's Leonard?" asked the burly Special-Trooper. "I thought he was with you."

The smile dropped from Sergeant Wingo's face.

"He, uh, he didn't make it," Sergeant Wingo said after a beat. "We were heading towards the EM room when it came up behind us. Grabbed Leonard before I could react and ran off."

He shifted where he stood, his eyes downcast as he spoke. "I, uh, just barely made it away."

Reming and Li shared a look of confusion. Early arched a brow as he stared at the Buck-Sergeant. Something wasn't adding up. He kept his tone level and clear as he turned towards the Buck-Sergeant.

"Came up behind you and grabbed Leonard? And then just ran off?" He bit back on the notes of accusation, his voice neutral and deep as he addressed the NCO.

"Well yeah," answered Sergeant Wingo, avoiding Early's eyes. "There was a noise behind us. I turned and saw the thing. It grabbed Leonard, and ran off."

"No firefight or nothing?" Reming questioned, his brow furrowed and steeped. "What was the noise you heard?"

The Buck-Sergeant fidgeted in place, his eyes on the floor as he answered. "You know, a noise. Like a clang behind us."

"The creature doesn't clang," said Early, his voice rising as he rounded on Sergeant Wingo. "Did you actually see it grab Leonard?"

"I, uh, I," the chubby NCO sputtered, chins quivering as he put up his hands in defense. "*I will not be interrogated by a bunch of junior troopers!*" he snapped, his voice sharpening as he stamped a boot heel on the floor.

He jabbed a finger under the nose of the hulking Special-Trooper. "I have been at this post too long to be questioned by the likes a' *you*. You will remember *my* rank and *your* place."

Flecks of foam built around the corners of his mouth as his voice rose to a shout. He backed away from the troopers and their barricade, finger in the air as he continued his rebuke.

"I've been an NCO longer than you've been in. I've been at this station more than ten fuckin' years! If I say the thing grabbed Leonard, then that's fuckin' what happened!"

Sergeant Wingo swelled in righteous fervor as he walked backwards down the hall. He ignored their looks of wide-eyed shock, no doubt awed by the authoritative fury he wielded against them.

"So when I tell Ramos what happened, you all fuckin' nod an' agree. No backtalk, no questions. Fuckin' nothin' but smiles an' nods." He jabbed a commanding finger at them, his back to the hall. They stood agape and nodded, with Reming and Li slowly backing up around the barricade.

This puzzled the pudgy Buck-Sergeant, his voice faltering a bit. He hadn't expected his reprimand to go over so well, least of all with Reming. The jaded Special-Trooper was a famously snarky pain in the ass. Sergeant Wingo scratched the top of his close-cropped hair. Early seemed to be staring right past him, the look of fear plain across his face.

Still confused, Sergeant Wingo continued in his rant, some of the fire dying out at the edges of his voice. "An' so I expect a bit more fuckin' respect when I say things. It ain't your place to say otherwise. I–"

He stopped midsentence, silence stretching between them as he looked from Reming, to Early, to Li.

"What the fuck is goin' on with you guys?"

His question was answered by the soft clicking behind him.

Sergeant Wingo wheeled around, a scream catching in his throat as he saw the creature a few feet from him. The sickle claws clicked around the black, arrow-shaped head. The wide, toothy mouth split open, and for a moment Sergeant Wingo had a glimpse into the gates of hell. Then the creature lunged for him, claws hooking into soft flesh and dragging him headfirst into the hungry mouth.

Early, Reming, and Li watched as the jaws swung down on the pudgy Buck-Sergeant, half of him still dangling from the creature's wide mouth. The creature snapped its head back and forth, the motion smacking Wingo's legs against the walls of the narrow hallway with the sound of a dull thud. The troopers looked on in horror as the creature seemed to struggle with swallowing its heavy meal.

It was Early who recovered first, reaching slowly for the SLW resting on the battery behind him. His fingers closed around the blocky stock and he pulled, dragging the weapon towards him across the makeshift barricade. He froze as the metal bipod rasped against the top of the battery. The creature stopped its thrashing, turning towards them with Wingo's limp legs still swinging from its mouth. The saddle-shaped structure lifted up as it looked straight towards them.

"Shit," was all Early could manage to say as Reming and Li opened fire on either side. The concussions from their Sonic Pistols deafened them in the narrow confines of the hallway as Early heaved the massive laser cannon around. As the blasts peppered the creature's face it bellowed, disgorging Wingo's limp body on the dingy tile. Early swung the SLW up and pulled the trigger, the fist-sized beam cutting too high into the ceiling over the creature's sleek form.

The mighty *Bwwwrrrrrrmmmm* of the cannon drowned everything else out as the hallway lit up in a red glow. The creature ducked away from the searing beam, kicking out with a powerful hind leg. A massive clawed foot slammed Early against the MMUTCAT battery, crushing his ribs and whipping his head against the dense metal. The SLW slipped from his unconscious fingers as he sagged to the floor, the beam cutting off as soon as he released the trigger.

Reming and Li stopped firing, dropping their pistols to drag the hulking trooper behind the makeshift barricade. The creature turned back towards them, saddle-shaped structure raised and powerful legs bunching as it prepared to charge. Reming released his grip on Early, scrambling to pick up his pistol from the scuffed metal tile. His fingers closed around the knobby grip, a trifling sliver of hope as death approached with open jaws.

Joelson emerged from the darkness of the hallway behind them, running with Smith in tow. His uniform jacket was bloody and torn, the lens of his glasses cracked as they sat askew on the bridge of his nose. Smith loped along behind him, his right leg sporting a deep gash held closed by a hasty tourniquet made from his uniform belt. Smith dropped down to assist Li, lifting Early by the shoulder as they dragged him back down the hall.

Joelson caught up with Reming as the creature charged, knocking his pistol down and yanking him back. His other hand was clenched around the twisted metal of his rifle's lower receiver, shattered and ruined from the firefight before. Reming pinwheeled his arms as he stumbled back, pivoting on one foot and running after Smith and Li. As the creature bore down on them Joelson lifted the gnarled metal high before slamming it down, bridging the exposed contacts of the MMUTCAT battery.

He covered his eyes as he reeled back, sparks dancing across the cube's surface as the battery discharged. He felt, rather than saw, as the creature smacked into the other side of the makeshift barricade, chains rattling from the impact. He heard the scrabbling of claws around the dense cube, but he was already gone, tearing down the hallway as the battery melted down behind him. There was a flash of light and a thunderous pop as he rounded the corner, and then a screech of pain. He glanced behind him and saw the creature reeling back, a tendril of smoke rising from its singed jaws. It tumbled over, kicking the ruined battery as it fled down the hall in the opposite direction. Joelson didn't stay to watch it go. He turned back instead and ran to catch the others.

CHAPTER 17:

The DC-12 tore across the arctic sky, pursued by the growing snowstorm. The sleek, single-seat skiff was buffeted to and fro by the howling winds. The long, angular prow pinged with the impact of hail in the winding airstream. Rania tucked in close to the molded plastic seat, her grip tight against the knobby throttles.

The light craft shook, nose vibrating angrily in the turbulent windstream. Rania tucked her tongue into her cheek, concentrating hard on keeping the skiff level and straight. ICF regulations required command approval for flight in wind conditions over thirty knots, with anything over forty-five strictly forbidden. Her onscreen weather monitor helpfully informed her that the gale whipped up by the snowstorm behind her was in excess of sixty-five knots. A small exclamation point lit up with an angry chime each time the DC-12 was knocked sideways by an errant gust.

Alright, alright, it's windy, I fucking know! she shouted in her head as the little exclamation point chastised her again. She clung tightly to the contoured seat, delicately trimming throttle and adjusting the ailerons with a light twist of her wrists. The steady clatter as bits of ice smashing against the poly-plex cockpit added to the cacophony inside the tiny bubble canopy.

She forced herself ahead of the darkening sky, the snowy dunes blurring below her as she hurtled by at mach five. She dug deep as the *Solo Skimmer* was batted about by the frigid wind. Even prayer was pushed out of her mind as she mustered all of her focus on keeping the small craft in the air. She breathed a sigh of relief as the curved edge of the installation dome appeared in view. Rania backed off the throttle, fanning the ailerons to slow down as she approached. She eased the skiff into the open hangar, landing gear bouncing lightly on the frosted concrete floor. The DC-12 touched down minutes ahead of the encroaching storm.

Rania left the cockpit open as she hurried to the hallway entrance, the snowy wind picking up inside the open hangar. The door to the hallway was still open as she'd left it, a thin layer of frost forming on the edges of the frame. Quietly she pushed it closed, shutting out the growing wind. She pulled her mask off in the frigid hallway, eyes readjusting to the dim light.

To no surprise, she was alone, Joelson and Smith having retreated somewhere else during their fight with the creature. *If they're even still alive.* She shook her head, banishing the morbid thought to the edges of her mind. A quick rummage through her CWAPL pockets yielded a small flashlight. She clicked it on, sweeping the tiny beam up and down the length of hallway. *Back to the Command Den? Or on to the control center?*

She weighed her options in the red gloom of the hallway. The Command Den was closer and safer. She'd be able to meet up with the remaining troopers. On the other hand, she had no guarantee that anyone had actually made it to the control center to encode the emergency message. With the main power knocked out throughout the station, the installation's broadcast unit didn't have enough power to push the signal into orbit by itself. Her work on Alpha-03 reconfigured the sensor tower to relay a message from the installation's short-range antennae, tapping into the sub-orbital tether. But someone still had to punch in at the control center and code the broadcast message or the signal would remain static. Emergency messages required command authorization from Sergeant Ramos or the Lieutenant, and she'd never had to work around that kind of access limitation.

Never had to completely rewrite a PMZ to receive instead of transmit, she mused, *and I never had to fly through a fucking blizzard, either. So I guess I'll figure this out, too.* A half-smile crept over her face as she turned down the hallway towards the control center.

She had only gone a few steps when her foot connected with something in the dark, sending it skittering across the grimy tile. She swept the flashlight down, searching for whatever she had kicked. The edge of the beam just caught the knurled handgrip of her P-3, resting against the base of the alloy wall. She bent down and retrieved the Sonic Pistol, examining the weapon in the tiny circle of light. The slide was scuffed and scratched. She remembered dropping it as she ran from the creature earlier. She clenched the flashlight in her mouth to free up her other hand. A quick pull on the weapon's reciprocating action showed it was chambered with a full magazine. She turned it over, checking for any loose parts or warped metal.

After they'd made it to the Command Den, Reming and Li had spent an almost insulting amount of time covering the basic functionalities of the small pistol. She'd rolled her eyes as they took great pains to point out the trigger, over-enunciating their words and exaggerating the curling motion of their index fingers as they talked her through the mechanics of firing. It had taken all of her will not to slug one of them, but she had to admit that she felt slightly better about carrying the little handgun. It was still a tool made for someone else, but at least she knew how to turn it on.

Satisfied with her inspection, she took the flashlight from her mouth and continued down the hall, one hand curled tightly around the pistol's knobby grip.

Rania crept along the dimly-lit hallway, her footsteps soft in the hushed silence of the empty corridors. She kept her senses taut, alert, straining at the very edge of their ability to distinguish the real from the imagined. She paused every few steps, listening closely for the tell-tale scrape of clawed feet on tile. Her eyes peered out over the pale circle of her flashlight, searching every shadow for the outline of an arrow-shaped head.

She stopped ahead of the door to a darkened room, flattening against the alloy wall. She slunk forward as she'd seen Joelson and Smith do earlier, creeping around the edge of the frame. Rania panned her tiny light around the room, lingering in the crevices and corners. She pulled back from the threshold, taking a shallow breath. In. And out. She turned back to the doorway, craning her head as she scanned the room again with the little flashlight. Finding nothing, she pulled back from the door again. Breathe in. And out. She snapped her attention forward and stepped deliberately past the door, relaxing only once she had put it firmly behind her.

She swung the flashlight down the length of hallway, the thin beam dissipating into the darkness well before the curve at the end.

Only four more rooms to go.

Rania froze, poised at the corner of a hallway intersection. She craned her head around the corner, looking down one hallway, then the other. Another sweep of her flashlight and she was across.

She sighed when she reached the other side of the intersection, releasing a breath she hadn't realized she was holding. She rested against the alloy wall, the metal cool against the side of her head. She knew her progress was slow, her pace alternating between furtive crossings and glacial sneaking. The further she'd traveled through empty quiet of station, the tighter her nerves had stretched. Even now, she imagined she heard a faint scraping behind her, the phantom rasp of the creature stalking her.

She closed her eyes, pushing back on the edges of her fervent imagination. *I have to keep moving.* She pushed off from the wall, steeling herself to continue on.

She passed by scratches in the flat metal of the wall, tracing her fingers along a deep, trailing gouge. It terminated in a thick dark stain that dripped to the floor. She drew her hand back sharply, she didn't need a closer look to tell her it was blood. *I HAVE to keep moving*, her inner voice becoming more insistent and pitched. She forced herself to keep walking, counting out twenty steps between each pause.

She stopped to listen at the edge of another doorway. The quiet in the hallway was absolute, she could almost hear her own heartbeat in the unbearable stillness. It was broken by a soft whimper from inside the room. Rania pulled back, pressing herself flat against the wall. She held her breath, listening closely to the dark room beside her. The sound came again, a hushed bleat almost rising to a sob.

She wrestled with her own fears in the dimly-lit hallway. It didn't sound like anything the creature had made before. The sound was smaller, and weak. It could be someone hurt and hiding in the dark. *Or it could be the monster's babies, just waiting for me to stumble into their nest of human bones.* The whimper came again, sounding a bit more human this time. She made up her mind and went into the room.

The room was dark, without even the dim red glow of emergency lighting. Gingerly, Rania stepped through the doorway, casting the small circle of her flashlight around. It was surprisingly crowded, filled with tables and stacks of chairs. *Another unused office, now just packed with crap.* She turned the flashlight to the corners of the room, passing by a pile of buckets and mops. She skirted around the edge of the clutter, searching intently for the source of the sound. *No nest of bones*, she mused, *so at least I have that going for me.*

"Help," a voice called from the far corner, ragged and weak.

Rania charted a path to the voice, stepping around dusty cabinets and over upturned tables. She made her way toward the far corner, pistol and flashlight trained towards the dark. As she cleared a mound of tangled coat racks, she stepped into a small clearing near the back of the room. She swept the flashlight in the corner, casting light on a figure curled in a ball in the corner. The figure held a hand in front of his face, shielding his eyes from the sudden burst of light. Rania turned the flashlight towards the floor, lessening the glare on the man huddled in the corner. The trooper dropped his hand, blinking sheepishly in the dark and staring up at his rescuer. Rania got a good look at his face and recoiled, stumbling backwards onto the pile of coat racks.

Senior-Trooper Leonard rose from the corner, stepping towards her in the path of her shaking flashlight beam.

"Please help," he whispered, dragging his left foot behind him. "He left me."

It took every fiber in her being not to scream. Rania untangled herself from the pile of coat racks, her pistol and flashlight still leveled at the greasy Senior-Trooper. He was saying something to her. She watched his thin lips open and shut. She heard nothing over the roar of blood rushing to her head, her pounding heart blanketing her ears with a rapid, staccato beat. Flashes of that day two months ago cut back and forth in her mind. *The damp tile squelching beneath her bare feet, feeling her confusion turn to momentary shame when she realized he was seeing her naked, the chill running down her still wet back when she watched him lick those thin lips.* Leonard raised his hands in the air, his eyes wide with fear. She stared hard at those hands, a slight tremble as he held them up. *The grout-line of the tile wall grinding into the back of her head, the straining muscles in her shoulders as she pushed back from the cold wall, his unkempt nails digging into her wrists as he pinned her back against it.* His mouth was moving faster now, he was pointing urgently at the pistol in her hand. The gun aimed straight at him. *The fear that filled her as she realized he was stronger, the disgust pouring through her as she felt his wet tongue on her bare cheek.* He was stepping back away from her, butting up against the corner of the room. She could feel the pistol's knurled grip digging into her palm. *Jerking away from his touch, the sudden movement allowing her to slip out under his arms.* She stared at the unfamiliar weapon in her hand, watching it shake under the tightness of her grip. She looked back at Leonard, his eyes were pleading and afraid. She connected the two in her mind, suddenly processing where she was and what she was about to do.

She flinched, lowering the gun with a gasp. Her heart was pounding in her chest, as fast and loud as it had been two months ago when she'd finally made it back to her room, still naked and dripping with sweat from her sprint down the hall. The sound in the room came roaring back, her ears open once again to the tearful begging of the man before her.

"Shut up. Shut up!" she snapped, cutting him off. She grit her teeth as she looked back at him. Tears welled in the corners of her eyes as she stared at Leonard, still shaking against the room's dark corner. A silence stretched between them as she wrestled with what to do next. He opened his mouth to break it, but she cut him off again.

"No! I don't care!" She shook her head. "Whatever it is, I don't care."

The room fell silent once again. She pushed back the torrent of roiling emotion, shoving it down, deep within her. She turned away from the quivering Senior-Trooper, making her way back to the door.

"I'm going to the control center." Her voice was icy and calm. "Come with or stay here."

They walked through the halls in near silence, the only sound coming from Leonard's wheezy breathing or the slight scuff of his left foot dragging on the tile.

He'd tried to tell her as she waited on the edge of the room's doorway. He'd been partnered with Sergeant Wingo to go to the emergency generators and hardwire in the MMUTCAT batteries. They'd been moving right along, just past the linen closet by the south supply room. Something crashed behind them and they took off, running down the hallway in a blind panic. Leonard had tripped and rolled his ankle, calling out for help. But Sergeant Wingo had kept on running, turning the corner and leaving him behind. He'd gotten to his feet, realizing both that the creature wasn't right behind him and that it hurt too much to walk. He'd shuffled his way down the hallway, hiding in the storage room and waiting for someone to come along.

Rania ignored his plaintive story as she peeked around the door, looking left and right down the dim hallway. She didn't even spare him a glance as she stepped out, leaving him behind as she turned down the hall. Leonard swallowed hard as he watched her go, looking back once more on the cluttered room. He made up his mind and limped along after her.

She tried to ignore him as they made their way through the maze of dimly-lit hallways, pausing only briefly to listen for the creature when they reached another intersection. The smell hit her every time they stopped, the cloying, sickly-sweet stench that accompanied the greasy man. She breathed through her mouth to spare her nose, walking a little faster to keep some distance between her and the limping trooper.

Relief washed over her as they turned another corner, the swinging doors to the control center coming into view. She hurried over, Leonard struggling to keep up, and pushed her way in.

The room was lit by a portable spot-lamp trained on the ceiling. Lieutenant Preston was hunched over a monitor by the door, his shadow magnified on the wall by the bright white light. He was studying the tablet in his hand, a pile of cords on the desk beside him. He looked up as

Rania made her way through the door, a weight lifting from his shoulders as he saw who it was.

"Thank god you're alright," he said, a relieved smile on his face. He held up the tablet and pointed to the mess of cords. "I need someone to show me how to hook up this mess."

Rania smiled back, taking the tablet from the beleaguered officer's hands. "Of course, sir. But you should really be using the signal desktop for that."

She pointed across the room to a computer monitor by the doors on the other side. "That one over there."

Lieutenant Preston chuckled, picking up the tangle of wires and turning to head over. His laughter stopped a moment later when Leonard walked through the door. Confusion crossed his face, and he looked back at Rania.

"Wingo?" he asked.

She frowned and shook her head, returning her attention to the coding on the tablet. Lieutenant Preston looked back at Leonard, concern on his face as he drew connections between the two. A host of terrible scenarios unfolded in his mind as he pictured what must have happened to bring the two of them together in the control center. A cough from Rania shook the officer out of his thoughts. With a shake of his head, he picked up the portable light and walked over to help.

It only took a few minutes for Rania to work through the messaging software on the tablet. She walked Lieutenant Preston through the coding process, helping him input his access codes on the proper screen. They relegated Leonard to the task of splicing in the actual connection, the trooper fumbling with wires underneath the monitor desk.

His task complete, Leonard stood back from the cables, bumping his head on the underside of the desk as he straightened up. He rubbed the back of his oily head as the monitor flickered to life, bathing the three of them in a blue glow.

Rania relaxed as the tablet screen was duplicated on the monitor, the splicing process proving successful. She walked the Lieutenant through a few more programming steps, the two of them sharing a high-five as a loading bar appeared on both screens. Its progress across the dual screens was agonizingly slow, but it was the final step before their job was done. Six eyes watched as the bar inched across, lengthening bit by bit on the twin screens. As it reached the halfway point, the officer nodded, heading to collect the spot-lamp in the center of the room.

Off to their left, there was a sound by the door. The three of them turned, catching sight of a slight swing from one of the hinged doors.

Leonard was the closest. He walked over to investigate, still rubbing the back of his head. Leonard reached the door, pushing it ajar with an outstretched hand. Lieutenant Preston's eyes went wide as his mind processed what he was seeing.

"No, don't!" he called, a split-second too late.

Leonard ducked back in the room, the hinged double door swinging closed behind him. He turned back towards the other two, a look of confusion on his face. Lieutenant Preston let out a sigh of relief, bending over once again to retrieve the metal spotlight.

The hinged doors swung open as a sickle claw pushed through, snagging Leonard around the waist.

Time seemed to stop as he was yanked backwards through the air. Rania dropped the tablet in her hands, rushing over to grab him as he was pulled to the doors. He got caught in the gap between them, fingers scrabbling for purchase on the metal handles. The sickle claw pulled hard around his waist, fighting against the inward-facing hinges.

Rania reached him a moment later, grabbing Leonard by the wrists as the creature slammed him against the doors. His skin was slick with sweat and his eyes were wild with fear. There were tears running down his cheeks as he fought to hold on to her.

"Don't let me go!" he begged, gasping as the claw tightened around his waist. "I'm sorry, I'm sorry. Just please don't let me go!"

This close to him, the rotting lavender smell hit her again, putrid and cloying at the same time. *Like dead flowers*, she thought. She stared at him directly in the eyes, trying to keep her grip on his clammy wrists. But her mind kept flashing back, back to that day two months ago. Back to when he cornered her, naked and wet from the shower. Back to when he held her down against the tile wall. *Back to when he made me so afraid...*

But then he was gone, torn from her grasp and pulled through the doors, the creak of the tearing hinges mingling with his screams.

Rania fell forward, catching herself on the floor. Lieutenant Preston was there a moment later, stepping past her to bar the doors. He pulled them shut on grinding hinges, threading the lamp through the handles and securing them closed. Rania stared at her hands as he helped her off the floor.

"C'mon!" he shouted, grabbing her by the arm and pulling her to the back of the room. The monitor dinged behind them, letting them know that the upload was complete, the emergency message now bouncing from the station, to Alpha-03, and on into space through the suborbital tether.

"We'll take the access tunnel," he said dragging her towards the far wall. "It connects to the Command Den. Ramos found it on the old map."

She nodded slowly, letting herself be pulled forward to the back of the room on unsteady, stumbling feet. Lieutenant Preston released her arm, motioning for her to follow as he crawled through the entrance by a tipped-over cabinet. She bent down after him, numb to the world around her. A single thought chased itself over and over in her head, accompanied by the fleeting sight of Leonard's wide eyes as he was yanked through the doors.

Did I let him go?

CHAPTER 18:

Sweaty, grimy, the legs of their uniform pants shredded and torn, they crawled through the access tunnel into the Command Den. Sergeant Ramos lent a hand on the other side, helping Lieutenant Preston to his feet as he emerged from the hatch in the wall. The officer straightened up, wiping the dirt and grease from his palms on the sides of his ruined pants.

"Long way, sir?" asked Sergeant Ramos, sizing up the panting Lieutenant.

"At least a full klick," he replied, sweat tracing rivers through the dust on his face. He wiped his forehead on his sleeve. "I haven't crawled that far since... well, since ever."

The Reed-Sergeant snorted. "They don't put you through low-crawls in the Officer Training Academy?"

"*Hell* no," he said, stretching the kinks out of his back. "But I took a class in *supervising* tactical movement."

Sergeant Ramos laughed, dusting off the officer's shoulders. Behind them, Rania made her way out of the tunnel, chest heaving, her curly brown hair tangled and matted with grease. She crawled out on her hands and knees, eyes wide as she adjusted to the brighter light of the Command Den. Sergeant Ramos crouched down, looking past her into the dark tunnel.

"Any others?" he asked, looking up at the officer.

Lieutenant Preston shook his head, a pained expression on his face. Sergeant Ramos nodded and stepped back, ignoring Rania as she stood up from the floor. He closed the hatch behind them, lowering the full-length ICF service poster that had previously covered it up. Lieutenant Preston let out a deep breath, puffing out his cheeks as he took stock of the room around him.

"Everyone make it back ok?" he asked, taking a quick tally of the troopers lounging around the room.

"Batteries are in place, sir. The hardwire was successful," the Reed-Sergeant answered, dodging the question. "We were also able to barricade the hallway by the condenser room, so we've got free access to the food storage unit and the formation room."

Lieutenant Preston nodded, processing what the Reed-Sergeant had left out. He looked at him sharply, his voice firm as he repeated himself. "How many?"

Sergeant Ramos sighed. "One dead. four injured, one in critical condition."

He gestured to a desk in the corner of the room. Special-Trooper Early lay stretched out on top, an assisted-vitality unit wrapped around his shattered ribs. The thick gray bandage beeped as his chest filled with air, his oxygen intake and vital functions monitored by a flexible monitor screen positioned on top. He slept a dreamless sleep, held in an artificial coma by the black stasis mask clamped around his face. The three watched as the monitor beeped again, compressing his chest and venting the air with a flat hiss. For a moment they stood in silence, watching the mechanical rise and fall of the injured trooper's chest.

Lieutenant Preston broke the silence, his voice barely rising above a whisper. "Who else?"

"Smith's got a nasty gash in his leg, he's limping but we got it sealed up." Sergeant Ramos continued, counting out the injured on his fingers. "Kowalski got his hand smashed between a battery and a creeper cart, and Joelson got pretty cut up on his chest."

Rania shot the Reed-Sergeant a look, her eyes wide with concern.

"He's fine, he's fine," he said, waving her off before she could ask. "Just some surface lacerations. He'll have some nasty scars, but he'll be ok."

Lieutenant Preston walked over to the table in the center of the Den, his eyes trained on the list of names written on the wall. He picked up the marker from the table, uncapping it as he moved to update the list. He drew a little 'I' beside the injured troopers, his hand still hovering over the wall as he looked back at the senior NCO.

"Wingo, sir," Sergeant Ramos answered. "We lost Sergeant Wingo."

Lieutenant Preston nodded, his eyes watery as he turned back to the list. He scribbled out the 'A' by the Buck-Sergeant's name, drawing a small 'D' with shaking hands.

"And Leonard," he said softly, doing the same for the deceased Senior-Trooper. He stepped back from his work, capping the marker with a click of finality. His back turned to the other two, he walked stiffly to the installation map spread on the table.

"So the batteries are in place, and the distress signal is broadcasting." His voice was flat as he tapped a finger on the yellowed paper, pointing out the circles traced around the control room and emergency generators. He continued without looking up from the map. "So where does that leave us?"

Sergeant Ramos joined him on the other side of the table. "Well, sir, we're in a pretty good spot, all things considered. We've got e-rations from the storage room, enough to last a few weeks. We've got bed-down space in the formation room, and an empty office to use as a latrine. With the barricade in place we've got some maneuver room between our current spot and the West Vehicle Bay, so we have an evac route as soon as help arrives."

He paused before continuing. "Honestly, sir, we could hunker down here. Post watch and wait this thing out. It's a fucking siege, but it's one I think we can survive until a ship arrives."

Lieutenant Preston looked over his shoulder to the columns on the wall. His vision swam as he traced a path down the growing list of dead and injured. He closed his eyes and blinked back tears, his hand curling into a fist as he composed himself.

"No, Sergeant," he said, his voice level and calm. "We end this now. On our terms."

The troopers gathered in the Command Den, loosely circled around the map on the table. Sergeant Ramos stood at the head with Lieutenant Preston and Senior-Trooper Joelson on his sides. With the Buck-Sergeants gone, Joelson had been shocked to find himself as the ranking trooper, third in command behind Sergeant Ramos. *Mom always said 'Authority comes in times of need,'* he thought as the Reed-Sergeant began outlining the plan. He glanced over to the troopers hanging around the outskirts of the table, then back to the officer standing to his right. *It's been a weird fucking week.*

"Alright folks, listen up," Sergeant Ramos barked, drawing the attention of the room. He drew a circle on the map with a laser indicator stripped from the barrel of an R-91. "We're here, in the Command Den." He traced a few more circles in key locations on the map. "The creature has been sighted here, here, and here. We don't know where it is currently, but all sightings indicate it's sticking around in the southern half of the installation. Not coincidentally, since that's where we've been hanging out as well."

All eyes were on him as he took a breath before continuing.

"We've rigged a signal through the suborbital tether. It's not strong enough to reach back to ICF command, but we should catch a ship if they pass through the system. We've got food and power for about two weeks, especially if we conserve."

He locked eyes with Lieutenant Preston. The officer nodded, and the Reed-Sergeant pushed ahead.

"Now it does us no good to huddle in the dark, waiting for this thing to pick us off one by one. We're fuckin' IFC troopers, we take the fight to the enemy, and we burn their hungry ass to the fucking ground."

He paused, casting his eyes to the troopers around the room.

"The hallways are too narrow, too dark, and there's too many places to hide. Even if we split up we'd have too much ground to cover if we go out hunting for it. So we're going to bring it to us." He drew a circle around the vehicle bay with the laser. "Ambush it here, on our turf."

He looked up at the group. "Now we know that small arms don't do much except piss it off, but we've got a *Slaw* and that should have enough punch to get through. We'll set up a crossfire with two squads of small arms to push it into the objective here, giving the *Slaw* a clear shot on the target. Reming, Li," he pointed at the two troopers, "You're our gunner and AG. You'll set up a base of fire on the smashed MMUTCAT."

Li whooped, high-fiving the Special-Trooper.

Sergeant Ramos sighed. "Just try not to fuck this up."

He shook his head and turned back to the table.

"Lieutenant Preston will have fire control over the *Slaw*. Joelson and I will each take squad of riflemen. Our job is harassing fire to push the creature into place." He dragged the laser over two X's drawn on the map, indicating the positioning for the two squads. "Joelson, you take the east squad, I'll take the south. Once the creature enters into the bay, I will give the command to fire. My squad will engage, stop, then your squad engages." He looked up at Joelson. "Understood?"

Joelson nodded, making mental note to double check the status of his squad's weapons.

"Once the creature is on the objective, LT's squad will engage with the *Slaw*. Now it will probably take repeated shots. This thing is damn tough, so Joelson's squad will need to continue to engage to pin it down on the objective. If we hit it enough times, we should be able to take this fucker down."

Sergeant Ramos concluded his speech, making eye contact with each trooper in the room. Their expressions ranged from fear and anticipation to grim resolve. He ended on Reming and Li, the ear-to-ear grin on the young Private's face bringing him no small irritation. Curiously enough, Reming didn't share his squadmate's exuberant glee. He frowned as he stared at the map, digesting the elements of the Reed-Sergeant's plan.

"Excuse me, Sarge" the Special-Trooper said, raising a hand. "But doesn't this whole thing ride on the monster getting into the bay in the first place? How do we even know it'll come here?"

Sergeant Ramos glared at Reming, opening his mouth to offer an acerbic rebuke.

Lieutenant Preston interrupted, cutting off the ornery Reed-Sergeant. "The best we can say is that the creature should come because we're all gathered in one place, a concentrated food source."

He sighed, crossing his arms over his chest as he looked down at the map. "But the truth is we don't know enough about this creature to tell if it'll work. We don't know how it hunts or why it's even here." His shoulders dropped as the hopelessness of the situation settled on him. "I couldn't begin to tell you what might attract it."

Joelson looked up from the map at the officer, tuning out his own thoughts and tuning back into the conversation.

"Electricity," he said, blinking at them from across the table. "Through the saddle-shaped thing on its face."

The others just stared at him.

"It came to me when I was thinking about the generator coils, how it attacked those first even though they're not the warmest or loudest thing here." He adjusted the warped glasses on the bridge of his nose. "It's why I shorted out the battery when it attacked Early, I had a hunch the creature would focus on that instead of us."

"Right!" interjected Reming. "Kind of like how it freaked out when I hit it with the ZapGun."

"Exactly," nodded Joelson. "So if we get something with electricity we—"

"We can draw it to the ambush," Lieutenant Preston finished. "And kill this thing once and for all." He looked back at Sergeant Ramos. "What do you make of it?"

Sergeant Ramos' eyes were on the map as he chewed it over.

"It beats sitting around with our dicks in our hands." He said at last, scratching the underside of his broad chin. "But we'd need something that puts up a strong current. We can't use another battery, it'll melt down too fast."

He looked up at the officer and shrugged. "I got nothing, sir."

A gloomy silence settled back over the group as they sat in thought.

After a few minutes, Reming smacked his palm to his forehead.

"My Zapgun!" he shouted. "I've still got it!"

He eagerly unclipped the diminutive pest weapon from his belt, tossing it on the table for all to see. Lieutenant Preston picked it up while Sergeant Ramos looked on with disdain.

"Son, I take back what I said earlier," he sniffed, *"That* might be the dumbest thing I'll hear all day."

Lieutenant Preston played around with the tiny tesla rifle, turning it on and watching the crackle of voltage from the coils at the end of the barrel. He looked back at Sergeant Ramos as if to say, *'Do you have a better idea?'* The Reed-Sergeant sighed, loathe to admit that he did not, in fact, have a better idea.

"Fine," he grumbled. "But we can't just leave it in the middle of the bay and hope for the best. It's not powerful enough to draw the thing out."

"So we'll need a rabbit," the Reed-Sergeant said, fixing an eye on Reming. "Is that gonna be you?"

Reming blanched. "I, uh, I would, Sarge. But you know I got a 'moderate' on my last physical test." He swept a hand down a body beginning its journey to flab. "Made for shootin', not for runnin'."

Sergeant Ramos snorted, turning back to address the group. "Anyone else? We need–"

"I'll do it," said Rania quietly.

Sergeant Ramos stopped midsentence, turning back to look at the Special-Trooper. It was the first thing she'd said since emerging from the tunnel, the mug of SimuCaff shaking in her hands as he watched her. He looked over to Lieutenant Preston. Their eyes met and the officer shifted uncomfortably where he stood.

"Out of the question," replied Lieutenant Preston, still looking at the Reed-Sergeant. "You've done more than enou–"

"I'll do it!" she repeated, more forcefully this time. Standing up from her chair, she set the mug down on the table, pointing to the X's on the map. "I'm the fastest runner here, and the only one without a weapon cert."

She stared them both in the eye, one by one. "If it's going to be anyone, it's going to be me."

Lieutenant Preston looked at Sergeant Ramos, taken aback by the fierceness in her display. Joelson stared at Rania, his brow steeped in worry.

"She is the fastest," Sergeant Ramos shrugged. "And that frees up another trigger puller."

Lieutenant Preston set the ZapGun down on the table, uncomfortable at the thought of another plan hinging on the risks taken by the lone, female Special-Trooper. He turned it over in his mind, giving up when he saw no other options. He looked from Rania, to the ZapGun, before settling on the map.

"Alright then," he said at last, his voice tinged with doubt. "I guess we have our rabbit."

They firmed up the finer details of the plan, settling on a start time of 0600 the next day. Nobody complained about getting a full night of rest. Sergeant Ramos assigned watch duties, and then they broke for the night, each splitting to prep weapons, grab chow, or catch up on sleep. Joelson caught up with Rania after they broke in the Command Den as she bent over the sink to rinse out her mug

"Rania wait," he said, catching her by the arm. "What's up with this plan?"

She stopped and turned back towards him. There was worry in his voice and she was touched. *Too bad he doesn't know the truth. About the control room. About you.* She set the mug down in the sink, crossing her arms over her chest.

"What do you mean?" she asked, feigning ignorance.

"It's risky. I don't like it."

She stared at the floor, her voice sounding flat, almost bored. "You heard Sergeant Ramos. Someone has to run the bait. Someone has to be the rabbit."

"Yeah, but why you?" he asked, his eyes searching her face from behind the cracked lenses.

"Because I'm the fastes–"

"Bullshit!" he snapped, his voice carrying across the room. Reming and Li looked up from the SLW-18 they were fussing over, suddenly much more interested in what was going on by the sink. Joelson glared at them and they ducked back down, preoccupied once again with the massive squad weapon. He lowered his voice as he turned back to Rania. "That's bullshit, and you know it. Darnis is fast too, ran his three-miler in sixteen minutes. He could do this instead."

She stared at him for a moment before looking down again. "I don't have a weapon cer–"

He cut her off again with a sharp wave of his hand. "Kowalski got his hand smashed, so you're at least more capable than he is."

He kept his voice to a tight whisper. "What is this about? I understood Alpha-03, you're the best programmer we have, but why this? Why you? Why again?"

She shifted her weight on the balls of her feet, hugging her arms to her chest.

"Everyone else has their role," she said, her voice flat once again. "I'm just finding mine."

He stared at her in incredulous silence.

"Is *that* what this is?" he exploded, his voice rising once again. "Some kind of '*I have to prove I belong*' bullshit?"

She refused to look at him. "No, I, uh–"

"'Cause that's *settled*," he continued, interrupting her again. "You have a place. You proved that with the sensor."

"No, but–"

"And *again*, with the fucking control room. You were the one that got the signal programmed for the LT."

She hugged her arms tighter. "But, I–"

"And now *this*!" he said, waving his hands in the air. "This bullshit suicide mission for who? *What could you possibly have left to prove?*"

"*I WON'T LET ANYONE ELSE GO!*" she shouted, stunning him to silence.

"It has to be me," she said, sinking to the floor, her voice ragged and raw. "I can't let anyone else go."

Joelson looked at her, dumbstruck. The Den was silent, save for the tone-deaf whistling coming from across the room as Reming and Li pretended to focus on their work. Joelson's mouth opened and closed several times before he spoke.

"But why you?" he asked, shaking his head.

She stepped past him, heading for the door. She walked stiff-legged past Reming and Li in the corner, still bent over the SLW. Joelson watched his friend go, a powerful sadness descending over him as she disappeared out the door. He took her mug out of the sink, shook it dry, and put it away in the cupboard above.

A few hours passed, and the Command Den was quiet, the troopers having bunked down to sleep or posted as fire watch. Lieutenant Preston stood over the map on the table, alone except for his thoughts. He rehearsed the plan, time and time again, running through the sequence in his mind. The circles and X's on the map blurred in his vision. He rubbed his bleary eyes and slumped into his chair. He spun around idly, turning back to reread the columns on the wall, studying the loadout for each trooper and their role in the attack the next day. As far as operations go, it was relatively straightforward. He'd had to perform far more complicated movements during his time at the Officer Training Academy. *But no Academy mission ever had this much riding on it.*

Lieutenant Preston sighed, breaking the hushed stillness of the empty room. He knew he should get some rest, it was close to 0300 already and their start time was fast approaching. *They need you to be sharp, focused*, he thought, but his stomach lurched, churning with acid.

His reflection was interrupted by Sergeant Ramos, whistling to himself as he strode through the doorway on his way to the SimuCaff maker. Lieutenant Preston watched the Reed-Sergeant from his chair, envying the NCO's calm composure. He cleared his throat, the whistling halting abruptly as the Reed-Sergeant noticed he was there.

"Guarding the map, sir?" Sergeant Ramos asked, searching for his mug in the cupboard.

Lieutenant Preston shrugged. "Beats wandering the halls. I think the troopers are sick of me checking in on them."

The Reed-Sergeant nodded, punching the buttons on the maker to start a new pot. He looked back at the young officer, noting the deep bags under his eyes. "You should get some sleep, sir, be fresh for the morning."

"Same goes for you," Lieutenant Preston shot back. A little softer he added, "I couldn't."

A smile of sad recognition played across the Reed-Sergeant's face. It had been almost a decade since he'd last seen combat, but he hadn't forgotten the anxiety and anticipation that builds before a mission. The waiting was the worst, worse than any bomb exploding or bullet overhead. It was the waiting that always set his teeth on edge. An angry chirp arose from the SimuCaff maker, breaking him from his thoughts. He turned back, irritation spiking as he read the text on the tiny touch screen.

"Organic supply expended?" he exclaimed, smacking the top of the appliance. "Mo-ther-*fucker!*"

"Wait, just wait!" Lieutenant Preston interrupted the Reed-Sergeant's building tirade. He rose from his chair, dashing over to his desk in the corner and rifling through a drawer. "I've got something better!"

Sergeant Ramos looked at him dubiously as he emerged clutching a shrink-wrapped, sealed box, waving it in the air triumphantly as he marched to the sink. The Reed-Sergeant watched him peel off the box's packaging, discarding a label marked 'Colombia, Dark Roast.'

"I've been saving this for the right occasion!" The Lieutenant positively shook with glee as he punched instructions into the appliance. The SimuCaff maker whirred and sputtered, filling a pot with boiling water.

"None of that simu-swill you normally drink," said the officer, almost beside himself as he prepared two mugs. "Tonight, we drink the good stuff."

He handed a mug of coffee to Sergeant Ramos. The Reed-Sergeant took it in a skeptical hand, sniffing the steaming contents once before taking a quick, furtive sip. Lieutenant Preston beamed at him, waiting on the NCO's reaction as he took a hearty swig from his own mug. Sergeant Ramos swallowed hard on the burning liquid, mustering up a small grimace of thanks.

That was all the encouragement Lieutenant Preston needed, rushing back to his seat by the table. The Reed-Sergeant followed grudgingly behind, downing a few more sips of the bitter, black coffee. Lieutenant Preston reclined in his seat, propping his feet up as Sergeant Ramos joined him across the table. They sat in silence, alternating drinks from their mugs.

"Is it always like this?" asked Lieutenant Preston. "The worrying?"

Sergeant Ramos nodded from behind his mug. "Always, sir. Same as it was on Avina."

Lieutenant Preston swirled his mug in his hand, watching the waves of coffee tumble and turn.

"You never told me about Avina," he said after a moment, his eyes still on his mug. "By all accounts you did good work. Rallying your troopers against the Troubs, carrying out raiding missions on their weapons caches from your ad-hoc firebase. You got two stars out of that campaign. How'd you end up doing five tours here on the ass end of the outer rim?"

Sergeant Ramos took a long sip, staring at the officer from behind his mug.

"Avina was some real shit," he said at last, setting his mug on the table. "We were running security for the shipping terminal there. The Troubs were deep with the locals though. We never knew who was going to pull a gun as soon as we looked away. We were getting hit every day, portable artillery, harassing fire when we left the gate. The kicker came when they detonated a passenger shuttle at the main terminal. They'd gotten our access codes and docked like any other ship. Two of mine went to check their access creds. Then, boom." He drew his hands back, mimicking an explosion.

"Fuck," Lieutenant Preston said, watching the Reed-Sergeant's hands.

"Yep," Sergeant Ramos replied. "It was the sickness, had everybody scared. Desperate. Then the power went out and everything went dark."

Sergeant Ramos took a hard look at his mug, taking a deep swallow before he spoke. "You know, I met James there. My husband."

Lieutenant Preston nodded. "The reporter right? You met him on Avina?"

"Yeah," Sergeant Ramos answered, a wistful look in his eye as he stared off at the wall. "He was young, ambitious. He had this fire in his belly. I was a cocksure Buck-Sergeant back then, newly sewn. So sure of myself, so convinced I had it all figured out. Nobody else could tell me different."

Lieutenant Preston hid a smile behind his mug, some things never change.

"He was attached to our station, running a story on the insurrection. After the shuttle blew up, James got embedded in our unit. We spent quite a bit of time arguing over the ICF's involvement in the conflict."

The Reed-Sergeant paused in his story, a wain smile on his face.

"We got married at the station, just after the power went out. We were dumb, we didn't think we'd get out of there alive."

Sergeant Ramos took another drink, watching the steam rise.

"After we evac'd, a story broke about the Coalition Republic covering up the sickness on Avina. The pressure to retract it was huge. I told James he never should have printed it. He kept insisting it was the right thing. 'The people deserve to know,' he'd always say."

His brown eyes tracked the rising steam until it faded away.

"I was transferred to remote assignment a week later."

"Fuck," was all the Lieutenant could say.

Sergeant Ramos shrugged. "It's not so bad. I liked it here. Every day is simple, and every day makes sense. Truth is I was never good at playing house. And James was always better with the kids."

Sergeant Ramos took a long pull from his coffee.

"Besides," he said, wiping the drip off his chin. "Every time I left he got a new cat. And I fucking *hate* cats."

Lieutenant Preston giggled, coffee spilling as he shook. Seeing the officer break, Sergeant Ramos joined in as well, their laughter echoing off the alloy walls. They settled down after a few minutes, their sides heaving.

Lieutenant Preston wiped a tear from the corner of his eye. "Thanks, Sergeant."

Sergeant Ramos nodded, lifting his mug in cheers. "Anytime LT. It's what I'm here for."

Lieutenant Preston returned the cheers, downing the rest. They lapsed into silence again, the empty room returning to its stillness. Sergeant Ramos stared down at his cup, swirling the last dregs of his coffee.

"You know, sir," he said at last. "I appreciate the gesture."

He set the mug down, pushing away from the table.

"But this coffee tastes like shit."

0600 came quietly that morning. The troopers rose without a word, eating a cold breakfast of rations or double checking their weapons. As they made their final preparations, Lieutenant Preston gathered them in the formation room. He was an officer, and his rank carried with it certain obligations.

"Men," he said, addressing the gathered troopers. He was interrupted by a small 'ahem' from the back of the room.

"Uh, and women," he corrected, a slight flush to his cheeks. "We stand on the precipice of battle. The enemy has pushed us, wounded us, and driven us back."

He paused, the room was silent as the troopers waited on his words of inspiration.

"But no more!" he declared, a little too loudly, his voice echoing in the open room. "We stand today, united in our fight, united against a foe of tooth and claw."

He paused again, the quiet broken by a trooper coughing into his hand.

"No more shall it come for us, no more shall it take from us," he said, his voice rising with passion. "Today we shall fight back! Today we strike back!"

He paused again, the dramatic effect impressing his gathered troops.

"We are the best of the ICF. We are troopers. We are proud! And we are brave! And though we face annihilation, I know." He punctuated his words by pounding his fist in his hand. "That. We. Can. Crush. It!"

He was shouting at the very end, the last few words hanging over the gathered troopers, moved to silence by his speech. He surveyed the room, reading the impact he had on them. The troopers stared back at him, stunned hope and inspiration radiating on their faces.

And then the room erupted in laughter.

Giggles broke out across the formation room, troopers snickering and holding their sides. In the front, Reming and Li were the worst, the two troopers doubled over in laughter.

"Was. That. From one. Of your. *Films*?" Reming gasped, tears streaking from his eyes as he laughed.

Lieutenant Preston turned bright red beneath his freckles. His shoulders slumped as he stormed away from the group. Sergeant Ramos caught him as he passed, stopping him on his way out the door.

"Thanks, sir," the Reed-Sergeant said, patting him on the shoulder. "They needed that."

CHAPTER 19:

Dawn broke across the snow-swept plains, bathing the tundra in a warm, amber glow. The bull Gluffant awoke with the sunrise, letting out a rumbling, low bellow, announcing to the world that it was, in fact, daytime. The great bull rose on broad, umber hooves, carrying his seven-ton bulk deftly as he stretched. A mighty shake of his shaggy head loosed the snow deposited on him from the blizzard the day before. He cast an imperious eye towards the sun, confirming its continued place in the sky above, and its continued, orange, brightness.

The Gluffant king surveyed his domain, the glittering icy plains stretching forth in all directions. The sunlight glinted off his curved horns, horns that stretched a full half-inch larger than any in his herd. They marked him for his regal lineage, assuring his rightful place of dominance among his kind. He thanked the auroch gods for their blessings, bowing his massive head as he scraped for lichen on the icy soil.

He chewed thoughtfully on the lichen, ruminating on the day ahead of him. It appeared to be another unusual, extraordinary day for the Gluffant king, though he had yet to determine a reason why. The sun was still bright and still out of reach. The lichen was plentiful around him, but that was not in itself unusual. The great bull had found that he was well suited to finding the plumpest patches of fresh lichen, allowing him to forage and feed well above the other males in his herd. It wasn't even a lingering effect of consuming methane. He had been searching for one of the spindly towers the day before. The great bull had halted his quest only when the snowstorm had forced him to hunker down, weathering the icy gales and whipping snow.

Perhaps it was something on the wind, he mused. There had been a host of unusual smells the day before, drifting fitfully from the west. Acrid smoke, the tang of steel under stress, and another odor the great bull had never encountered before, something aggressive and sour, with an undercurrent of rot. The new smell was distasteful to the Gluffant king, it kindled within him the same feelings as when a younger bull approached his herd. He turned a beady, black eye towards the west, fixing it on the curved, grey dome rising from amid the icy dunes.

The wind shifted again, bringing with it a fresh whiff of the unusual smells. The Gluffant snorted, expelling a great glob of mucus from his flaring nostrils. Curiosity was not a trait given to his kind, but he was no ordinary Gluffant, and this was already an unusual, extraordinary day. He made up his mind, resolving to investigate the dome further. He was a monarch, benevolent sovereign of all he surveyed. And a king must know his realm.

Reming and Li heaved the SLW-18 into place, grunting as they positioned the bulbous laser cannon on its metal bipod legs.

"Now I know why Early lifted so much," griped Li, his arms shaking as they pushed the cannon on top of the ruined MMUTCAT.

"This is what you always wanted," said Reming, sweat trickling down the back of his neck. "You finally get your chance with the *Slaw*."

"Yeah, but not really," Li whined, his breath coming out in short puffs. "I'm just the assistant gunner, you're the one that gets to pull the trigger."

"A little more to the left," Lieutenant Preston called from the floor of the vehicle bay. "I want a sighting line off the stack of tires."

Reming nodded, grunting in acknowledgement as they shifted the massive laser. He stepped back when they were done, wiping the sweat running into his eyes. Lieutenant Preston eyed the gun's placement. Satisfied, he gave them a thumbs-up. The weary troopers returned the gesture and settled in behind the big gun.

Lieutenant Preston walked across the bay to check on the other two positions. Joelson was set with Smith and his other two troopers, positioning themselves behind a barricade of MMUTCAT wheels and spare parts. Joelson gave the officer a wave as he approached, letting him know their position was set. Lieutenant Preston returned the wave, carrying on to Sergeant Ramos and the others.

The Reed-Sergeant was presently engaged in leading his troopers through the construction of their own fortifications, built from a trio of mobile tool carts. The troopers' breath rose in steam clouds in the chill of the bay. The gaping hole in the door proving too much for the meager heat of the emergency generators. Lieutenant Preston caught Sergeant Ramos' eye as he drew near, the Reed-Sergeant pausing in his direction as the officer walked up.

"How're we looking, Sergeant?" he asked, watching Godrey and Darnis lift a tool cart on top of the others.

"Almost done, sir, and not too soon," the senior NCO replied. "I want to get this shit finished quick. This damn cold is getting into my bones."

Lieutenant Preston nodded, looking past the Reed-Sergeant to a trooper standing apart, in the center of the room.

"How's our rabbit?" he asked.

Sergeant Ramos followed his gaze to the other trooper, watching as she fiddled with the strap attached to the ZapGun.

"She's fine," the Reed-Sergeant answered. "Getting ready like the rest of us."

Lieutenant Preston acknowledged the Reed-Sergeant, leaving him to his preparations as he headed over to Rania. She was leaning against the bumper of the MMUTCAT the creature had knocked over when it smashed into the bay. The CWAPL hung over her shoulders like a bulky cloak, but she welcomed the extra layer. Beneath it she was stripped down to the bare essentials, just her uniform undershirt and mottled grey pants cut into shorts. She was focused on the tangled strap, stiff fingers fiddling with the knots forming the loop around her. She clicked her tongue softly as she worked, looking up when she heard the sound of the officer's boots approaching.

"Knots looking good?" he asked, flashing a smile of encouragement.

"So far, just double checking," she said, attempting a smile in return. "I should have a seven-foot tail behind me, enough to make sure this thing isn't knocking me in the back of the legs when I run."

"Good, good," said the Lieutenant, looking over the cord wrapped around her waist. "And it's still one pull to disengage?"

"Should be," she replied, her eyes back on the knot in her hand. "If not, I guess I'd better run faster."

The officer frowned, troubled once again by the risk resting on the trooper's shoulders. "But you'll pull it once you're in the bay?"

She nodded, still fiddling with the cords. "Once I'm in the bay, I dump the ZapGun, and take cover in the back of the MMUTCAT." She flashed a smile as she looked back up at him. "I'm leaving the back hatch open before I go. Can't waste time fumbling for the latch with the creature on my tail."

He nodded grimly, attempting to muster confidence to share with the Special-Trooper. The best he could offer was a forced half-smile, hanging below worried eyes. She forced herself to smile as well, a pregnant pause stretching between them. Finally, the Lieutenant cleared his throat.

"Good to go?" he asked, his voice coarse and strained.

She nodded, returning once again to fiddling with the strap. Lieutenant Preston acknowledged her response with a gruff nod of his own before turning to walk away. He confirmed that everything was in place with the other squads before climbing atop the ruined MMUTCAT and settling in with Reming and Li.

Rania stood on the edge of the hallway, just inside the vehicle bay. She looked back one last time to the troopers huddled around the bay, receiving a wave of encouragement from Joelson. She turned back towards the hallway, an involuntary tremor sweeping over her. She took a deep breath from the frigid air. In, and out. She shed the CWAPL from around her shoulders, it would only slow her down as she ran, and double checked the length of cord stretched behind her. The ZapGun cracked at the end of the tether, sparks of electricity sputtering from the end of the tiny barrel. She could imagine a thousand other places she'd rather be at the moment. She took another deep breath, and stepped through the doorway.

Her eyes adjusted to the darkness of the hallway, illuminated only by the dim, red glow of the emergency lighting. The vehicle bay had been well lit in contrast, sunlight filtering through the hole torn in the bay door. She sighed to herself, checking the strap around her waist one last time. Breathe in. And out. She turned down the hallway, and began to run.

Her pace was leisurely as she jogged along the gloomy corridors. She knew she needed to save her energy as much as she could. The ZapGun clattered on the ground behind her, bouncing along on the dingy tile. The racket rang off the alloy walls, echoing down the stretch of empty hallway. *At least if it doesn't see me, it'll damn sure hear me.* She kept her breathing smooth and controlled, in through the nose, out through the mouth. Her arms swung easily with each step, keeping her momentum as she pushed ahead.

She turned left at an intersection, sticking to a course she'd mapped out for herself the night before. It looped around in figure-eights, the intersection for each corresponding with the hallway for the vehicle bay. She checked left and right as she went, her pace quickening by a half-step each time she passed a darkened room.

She turned down the hallway towards the armory door, passing by Sergeant Sikes' office as she went. Unbidden, an image of pale, sightless eyes arose in her mind. She shook her head, forcing the thoughts deep down. She needed all her focus for the hallways around her.

She slowed down by the armory, passing a length of claw marks etched into the walls and floor. They looked fresh, the gouged alloy glinting in the dim light. She paused ahead of the armory door, jogging in place in the dark hallway. The clatter died down behind her, she paused to listen intently to the quiet of the room beyond.

There, up ahead in the armory. The tell-tale rasp of claws on tile, accompanied with the now familiar sound of hushed, predatory breathing. She didn't stay a moment more, turning back and sprinting down the hallway. The tiny ZapGun bounced at the end of the tether, rattling on the tile. Behind her something big smashed into the wall, the scrape of claws louder and faster as it chased her.

She ran as though her life depended on it.

Her arms pumped furiously back and forth, her heels rang off the dingy alloy tile, her breath came fast and heavy, chest heaving as she forced herself faster and harder than she'd ever run before. She didn't have to look behind her to know it was still on her tail, crashing against the edges of the hallway whenever she turned a corner. She ran, the corners of her vision blurring, foam building at the edges of her mouth. She ran, with the creature close behind her.

The troopers huddled in their posts around the frigid vehicle bay. Their breath rose in clouds in the frosty air, marking the spot of each position amid the clutter. They waited, flexing their numb fingers as they clutched their rifles. The silence in the bay was heavy and poised, hanging over their heads like a gathering storm. They waited, and they listened, watching the doorway to the dark hallway.

They did not have long to wait.

They heard the clanging first, echoing in advance from the hallway door. Then Rania appeared, gasping for air as she turned the corner and tore through the bay. She cleared the point between Joelson's squad and Sergeant Ramos, yanking on the cord around her waist and leaving the ZapGun behind, still sputtering on the concrete floor. She threw herself into the back hatch of the overturned MMUTCAT, slamming the tailgate down behind her. Rania curled up in a ball inside the sparse cargo bed, her face red with exertion and her chest heaving.

Eleven sets of eyes swung from the MMUTCAT and back to the hallway. They held their collective breath as a black, arrow-shaped head pushed its way through the doorway, sickle claws clicking furiously. They watched as the creature stopped abruptly, appearing to get hung up on the doorframe. The angular head pulled back, disappearing into the darkness. Unease gripped the troopers, each fearful for a moment that the plan had failed.

And then the creature smashed into the bay, powerful, clawed limbs peeling the doorway back and forcing itself through. It leapt into the open room, claws scraping on the concrete as it found its footing on the frosty floor. It paused, unsure for a moment as it oriented itself in the new surroundings. A low growl emanated from the toothy maw as the saddle-shaped structure popped open on its face. Ahead of the creature, the tiny ZapGun continued to crackle, electricity arcing from the small coil at the end of the barrel. The saddle-shaped structure snapped shut and the creature crept forward, cautiously stalking the tiny pest gun at the center of their ambush.

Come on, come on. The Lieutenant willed it forward, urging the creature to drop its suspicion and get in range of their crossfire. The creature crept forward, quiet and slow, and the Lieutenant got a good look at it for the first time since it crashed into the bay. It was thinner now, the shaggy white bulk shaved down in favor of an angular, sleeker form. It was black, with vertical orange stripes, breaking up its outline as it moved. It retained the same powerful hind legs as before, folded and hunched as it walked. The clawed forelegs seemed thinner now as it prowled ahead, with a wide-set stance like a bulldog. The skull was a sharp V, ending back in a curved ridge of bone. It was a far cry from the blunt face of the creature's winter form, but it retained the same wide, toothy jaws. The grey, saddle-shaped organ remained in place on top of its head, although it seemed smaller and more shrunken compared to before. Only the two slender limbs around the mouth remained unchanged, each still ending in a clicking sickle claw.

The creature's pace had slowed considerably. It shied up to the sputtering ZapGun, gently nudging it with the end of an outstretched claw. It prodded the diminutive pest gun, but kept it at length of arms reach. Lieutenant Preston realized that they might not get a better shot and waved frantically at the troopers positioned to the south.

Sergeant Ramos was way ahead of him, ordering his squad to open fire. The hush of the bay was broken in an instant, filled with the crackle of rifle fire. Burning craters erupted along the creature's flank, tiny splashes of orange and red against the sleek, black side. The creature screeched in pain, dancing away from the stinging fire. It turned to face the troopers gathered in the south, opening its mouth to roar a challenge.

And then Joelson's forces opened up on it from the east. The withering fire of the four troopers slamming into the creature's wounded side. It screeched again, its cry of pain echoing over the sound of gunfire in the open bay. It leapt away from the crossfire, stopping just in front of a stack of tires.

"Send it," said Lieutenant Preston, squeezing Reming's shoulder.

"Fuckin-A," replied the Special-Trooper, and a fist-sized red beam blasted forth from the long barrel of the laser cannon. The troopers were lit with the red glow of the SLW as the beam surged forth, searing a deep gouge across the creature's back. The creature's howl momentarily drowned out the deep rumble of the laser as it ducked under the burning path of the beam. Lieutenant Preston pulled up on Reming's shoulder, guiding the trooper and the beam to follow the creature down. The laser cut a swathe across the bay, igniting the stack of tires as it chased the creature.

But the creature continued to weave, dodging out of the way of the laser's scorching light. A small warning chirped from the SLW's buttstock, indicating the weapon's rising temperature. Reming hung on, teeth clenched as he followed after the creature with the powerful red beam. Another alarm sounded, a forceful triple-chirp from the buttstock and the beam cut off, winking instantly out of existence. Reming looked down at the bulbous weapon as small flaps opened up along the length of the barrel, venting jets of superheated air to cool the weapon. He looked past it to the creature, hoping that maybe, just maybe, his last shot had been enough.

It was not.

The creature roared at them from the concrete floor, the grey saddle fully open as it searched for the source of its pain. The powerful hind legs bunched beneath it as it prepared to launch itself at the three troopers on top of the MMUTCAT. The toothy jaws opened, wide and hungry. The sickle claws clicked furiously as Reming and Li fumbled to engage the SLW's emergency cooling.

And then a volley of fire slammed into the creature from the east. Joelson barked orders to his four-man squad, alternating fire from each of their rifles. The creature turned towards them, momentarily distracted from the three men on top of the ruined truck. It charged Joelson's position, barreling towards the flimsy barricade of wheels and metal. Joelson clung to his rifle as the speeding black form grew to fill his entire weapon's sight.

The creature was thrown off course by sudden fire from the south, eruptions of orange opening up along its side. Sergeant Ramos shouted at his troopers, a gritted smile on his face as he poured fire into the beast.

The creature hissed, dipping away from this new irritation. It charged the southern position, claws digging into the concrete as it propelled itself forward. The troopers kept up their fire, neutral ions slamming into the creature's front. But it wasn't enough to deter the enraged creature as it slammed into the barricade of tool carts, scattering them and knocking the troopers around.

Sergeant Ramos was tossed high through the air, landing on his right foot with a snap of his ankle. He dragged himself upright as the creature turned towards him. He pulled the pistol from his belt, a grim frown on his face as the toothy jaws opened and the creature began to lunge for him. The Reed-Sergeant blasted away with the tiny Sonic Pistol, anticipating death approaching at any moment.

But the moment never came.

The bull Gluffant slammed into the creature, seven tons of force sending it careening off balance across the bay. Sergeant Ramos lowered his pistol, struck dumb with surprise. The great bull stood proud in the frigid bay, an orange trickle of blood running down the points of its two curved horns. He was the Gluffant king, and no creature alive shall challenge his reign.

The creature reeled back from the sudden attack, it tumbled into a pile of twisted metal, scattering spare parts as it fought for footing on the concrete floor. The bull Gluffant charged again, knocking the sleek predator off its feet. Having shed its winter bulk, the creature was no match for the ferocity and sheer mass of the great bull Gluffant. The creature backpedaled as it slid, claws digging for purchase on the concrete floor.

"Hurry up, man," snapped Li, fumbling with Reming over the SLW's cooling protocols. "It beeped twice already, you need to push that lever down to re-arm."

Reming nodded at his AG's instructions, pivoting the venting lever to close the flaps along the barrel.

Across the bay, Rania huddled in the bed of her own MMUTCAT, watching the action from behind the tailgate. She watched the creature gain its footing, turning back to the Gluffant with a violent hiss. The great bull stamped its umber hooves, snorting clouds of steam from its flaring nostrils. The creature snapped its jaws at the great, shaggy beast, warning it off with the threat of its flashing, sickle claws.

But no one threatens the Gluffant king.

The shaggy head came down, curved horns glinting in the light of the bay. The massive white beast charged, smashing the creature back and sending them both crashing into the burning pile of tires.

Perched atop the ruined MMUTCAT, the SLW chirped in Reming's hands as the last flaps closed, priming the weapon for another round.

"Now!" shouted the Lieutenant, as the monstrous beasts tumbled in front of them.

Reming pulled the trigger, the massive beam surging forth from the barrel and cutting a burning line between the brawling titans. He jerked the laser around, trying to pin down the creature under the searing, red beam.

"Careful around the Gluffant!" warned Li, his grip tight on Reming's arm.

Reming lifted his face off the weapons buttstock, turning to correct the younger trooper. "For the last fucking time, they don't fucking explo–"

He was cut off when the blistering beam of the portable cannon connected with the Gluffant's side. A fireball erupted as massive stores of blubber and marbled fat vaporized in an instant, bursting outwards in a powerful, violent conflagration. The Gluffant exploded, detonating in a flash of heat and light. The creature beside it was incinerated instantly, torn apart by the blast. Troopers ducked down as the concussive wave swept across the bay, rocking the MMUTCAT with a thunderous boom.

As the blast wave passed, the troopers stood up, hesitantly looking for a sign of the creature. Seeing none, Reming let out a whoop, pumping his fist in the air with Li as they reveled in their victory. The Lieutenant scanned the crater as the smoke began to clear, ignoring the celebrating troopers until he could be sure that the creature was gone.

Reming bumped into the concerned officer as he danced atop the ruined MMUTCAT. "C'mon, sir. It's good. We wo–"

He was cut off when a splatter of steaming gore drenched him from above. All around the room the troopers were showered with blood and viscera raining down in the open bay. Reming was caught with his mouth fully open, covered head to toe in stinking, slimy goop. When the main deluge stopped, Rania crept out from her cover in the overturned MMUTCAT. She dodged puddles of blood and chunks of singed hair, as the charred remains of the two great beasts continued to drizzle the troopers from the vast bay ceiling.

Reming and Li wiped the steaming blood dripping in their eyes, their hair matted, covered in meat and singed fur. Reming leaned over as he spit out a mouthful of putrid blubber.

"I fucking hate this place."

CHAPTER 20:

It was a long week before they were rescued. Seven days of waiting in the dark. The four-room complex they'd set up as a base of operations growing smaller with each passing day. The empty office they'd set aside as a latrine growing into a horror they dared not discuss.

The first day after the battle had been relatively quick. After scouring the vehicle bay to ensure the creature had perished in the explosion, the troopers celebrated briefly, retrograding back to the formation room after a quick stop in the showers. Morale was high. They passed around the last bottle of Joelson's SimuChamp, each sharing a sip before the bottle was drained.

On the second day, they awoke to foggy breath and a chill in the air of the crowded formation room. Nearly five kilometers across, the station was far too large for the emergency generators to keep up with the demands for heat and fresh air. An expedition was mounted, led by Joelson, to rewire the emergency generators and constrain their heating and air recirculation to the four-room complex in the western section of the station. They scavenged medpacks from the rooms along the way, using them to treat the wounded from the day before.

On the third and fourth days, their morale began to flag. The immediate high from the battle had dissipated and the busy work of refortifying their positions and salvaging supplies had finished. An unbearable stillness settled over the troopers, the boredom brought on by the completion of all their conceivable tasks and priorities of work. Day and night flowed together in the dim red light of the station, with only their regular turns at posting fire watch to break up the monotony.

On the fifth day, the troopers woke without speaking, chewing their cold rations in silence. Tensions were simmering in the four dark rooms, with Sergeant Ramos' continued insistence on posting watch forming an acute source of aggravation. Reming and Li were not on speaking terms, having had a falling out over who could claim the most important role during the battle in the bay, and therefore most deserved the bunk space directly under the heating vent. Having now spent the better part of a week trapped in close quarters with eleven male troopers, Rania found that being accepted in a male-dominated security unit consisted chiefly with the dissolution of all pretenses of modesty and her constant exposure to the hairy indignity of the human body, as well as all of the sights, sounds, and smells it produces.

On the sixth day, Lieutenant Preston brewed up his last reserve of coffee, ordering it be served to all the troopers to boost morale. This order was quickly rescinded, after he overheard some troopers complaining about the bitter tang and acidic aftertaste of the beverage. Gathering up all the remaining mugs of the hot drink, Lieutenant Preston resolved loudly to never again do anything kind or thoughtful for any trooper ever, or their 'ungrateful, peasant palates.'

On the seventh day, Reming and Li were back on speaking terms thanks to the careful mediation of Senior-Trooper Joelson, who pointed out that the SLW was originally designed for two person operation, and that they could both share the vent if they just turned their bunks sideways. Their plan was thwarted almost immediately by Sergeant Ramos, who having overheard Joelson's carefully reasoned discussion with the two troopers, claimed the spot under the vent for himself on the grounds that he was older, he outranked them, and that they were both 'fucking idiots.' Rania found herself at the focus of a sudden elevation in unit status, when she answered a trooper's question about her 'plans for tonight' with a fart so loud that it echoed off the walls.

On the eighth day, they were spared from the hideous prospect of finally needing to clean out the latrine by the arrival of a rescue shuttle. An Orbyx Mining Barge had stopped along the planet's orbit to bank sun before their jump to the shipping lane. The barge picked up on the distress signal still broadcasting through the suborbital tether, dispatching a surface transport shuttle immediately to pick up the bedraggled troopers. As the first shuttle crewman approached the crudely constructed and graffiti-covered barricade, they were met by a chorus of cheers from the bored troopers still posting fire watch. The word spread quickly through the four-room complex, and the troopers of AZH-01 gathered their meager belongings and prepared to leave.

With the troopers all loaded, the shuttle lifted off from the planet's surface, repulsors firing and rocketing the light passenger craft through the icy atmosphere. The windswept wastes of AZH's polar caps fell away as the ship ascended, the tundra shrinking far below the rising craft. It punched through the thinning, icy air, exiting the remote planet's gravity and powering through to meet up with the barge. The shuttle drifted into the dry dock of the scarab-shaped ship, the bay doors spiraling shut behind it. With a hiss the atmosphere normalized outside the shuttle, and the troopers disembarked.

It was bright within the barge's medbay, the fluorescent lights overhead bathing everything in a cold white glow. Lieutenant Preston squinted against the glare, after nearly two weeks in the darkened station, he was having a hard time readjusting to the light.

"They told me you're doing good, that they'll get you patched up when we stop at the next port," he said, holding Early's hand.

He watched the big trooper's chest rise and fall, wrapped tightly in a beige covering connected by tubes to the monitoring tablet mounted by the bed. He was still in stasis. The on-board medical facility was a recent upgrade and more than capable of nursing the trooper through his fractured ribs. But his most recent scan showed pockets of blood vessels that had burst in his brain, and that required far more delicate medical care than the ship could provide. So he would remain in an artificial coma, awaiting the spectrum of advanced treatment options available at a hospital on Cerulia.

"I know you'll pull through this. You have to." His eyes watered as he looked down at the sleeping trooper. "Everyone keeps telling me about what a singer you are. I still need to hear you play."

There was a knock at the door. Lieutenant Preston looked up as Sergeant Ramos came in, the gruff Reed-Sergeant sporting a fresh shave and a haircut from the grooming facilities on the barge.

"Fuckin' bright in here," grumbled Sergeant Ramos, shielding his eyes against the glare with his hand. "I got a message off to James before our jump to the shipping lanes. He's thrilled I'm coming home a year early." Sergeant Ramos snorted, hobbling into the room on his injured leg. "I checked the job boards on the Linknet, there's a Reed-Sergeant post open on the *Osiris*. Maybe I can swing a transfer when we get to Cerulia."

Lieutenant Preston allowed himself a half of a smile. "Checking in on our injured trooper?"

"Yes, sir," said the Reed-Sergeant. *Among others…*

He'd seen the change in the Lieutenant when they'd boarded the shuttle. The bodies of the fallen were the last on, loaded just before they took off. Five carts draped in white tarps. *And those were just the ones we found.* The young officer had gone quiet as the carts passed, the final count clearly taking its toll on him. Eight dead, nine injured, including Early, who'd require more critical medical care as soon as they reached port. It always hurt to lose your own. *Especially when you were the one giving the orders.*

"How's the leg?" asked Lieutenant Preston, pulling a chair out and gesturing for Sergeant Ramos to sit.

"Stiff," he grunted, but accepted the help nonetheless. The new StimWrap he'd gotten from the barge's crew was doing wonders, the nanotech stimulation in the bandage greatly accelerating the healing process in his shattered ankle. "But it itches like hell."

The Lieutenant nodded, pulling out a chair for himself. He sat down by the senior NCO, his eyes still on the wounded trooper. Sergeant Ramos watched him for a moment, letting the silence between them settle before he spoke.

"You know, sir," he said, clearing his throat a little, "I know exactly what you're thinking. You're running through it in your head, over and over and over again. 'I should've been faster. I should've told them to go left instead of right. I should've given them a rifle instead of a pistol.'"

"I should have been smarter," Lieutenant Preston whispered, still staring at Early. "I should have recognized what the creature was seeking. I should have sent them off in bigger squads. Fewer teams, more men."

"More trips then. That means more time spent where they'd be at risk," Sergeant Ramos nodded grimly. "You've got to quit this shit. sir. I know it's going to eat at you, but you did the best you could."

The Lieutenant's eyes watered, his shoulders quivering slightly as he watched the rise and fall of the wounded trooper's chest. "I should have–"

The Reed-Sergeant cut him off. "'Should have' nothing, sir. You did what you could. You kept your cool, you made a plan with the shit-sandwich you'd been served, and you got as many out alive as you could."

Lieutenant Preston nodded, his eyes far away. Sergeant Ramos reached out a hand, resting it gently on the officer's shoulder.

"I know it's hard to believe, sir," the Reed-Sergeant said. "You couldn't have done it better. Nobody could. Ninety-percent of this business is boring, petty, day-to-day bullshit."

"And the other ten-percent?" Lieutenant Preston asked, turning back to look at Sergeant Ramos.

"*Real* shit," the Reed-Sergeant grunted. Lieutenant Preston laughed, a small half-chuckle as he wiped the corners of his eyes. Sergeant Ramos favored him with half a smile before continuing. "I'm deadly serious. Ninety-percent bullshit, ten-percent *real shit*. Shit like Avina. Shit like what we went through back there. Nobody knows exactly what to do when the bullshit turns to real shit. You just keep your head down, make a plan, and try to get everyone out alive."

Sergeant Ramos removed his hand from the officer's shoulder. He leaned back in his chair, staring at the quietly chirping display by Early's bed. "That's the thing about this business we're in. You never know when the bill comes due, how much it's gonna be. Sometimes you pay it. Sometimes somebody else pays it for you."

He sighed, stroking his broad chin. "But the bill always gets paid, that's the truth about our line of work."

The quiet settled over the room again, stretching for a few minutes as they both watched Early breathing in and out.

"I understand what you're saying," the Lieutenant said at last, "about the nature of our job. And I appreciate your words, Sergeant." He looked back at Sergeant Ramos for the first time since he'd entered the med bay.

"I just don't think that's a price I can pay again."

Rania sat alone in the ship's cafeteria, nursing a cup of cooling SimuCaff. The half-eaten omelet on her tray, her third one that day, had already gone cold. The ship's commercial-grade RationVendor was several steps down from the deluxe, gourmet models installed on passenger ships, but after months of eating military grade cubes and a week of cold emergency rations, she would have devoured anything that had a recognizable shape that matched its flavor.

She stared at the monitor mounted on the wall, admiring the view of the stars outside the ship. The view was static, flat, the same view she'd had for months when she first traveled to AZH. But there was depth behind that frozen image, a field of possibilities stretching before her. She sighed, taking a sip from her cup.

She looked up from the monitor to see Joelson walking through the door. He grabbed a tray of his own, punching his selection of the enchiladas verde. He walked over to her table, balancing his tray in one hand and a mug of SimuCaff in the other. He looked refreshed from his stop in the showers, almost entirely clean-shaven.

"You kept the mustache?" she said as he sat down across from her.

"Yeah," Joelson chuckled, running a hand over his fuzzy upper lip. "It really filled in after not shaving this past week."

"Good for you," she said, taking a sip from her mug. "It suits you, *Buck-Sergeant* Joelson."

He chuckled again as he dug into the food on his tray. "I've got to pick up new ranks and all new uniform tops when we stop in to Cerulia. Lucky enough for me, my pay goes up on the first of next month. No more faded duds for *this* trooper."

"Lucky you," she said, setting her cup down on the table and turning back to watch the monitor. A quiet stretched between them, punctuated only by the clink of Joelson's fork on his alloy tray. He got halfway through his second plate before he paused, putting his fork down.

"Rania," he said, breaking the quiet between them. "I, I never thanked you. For what you did back on the station. For being our runner. For putting yourself at risk to spare others."

She looked back sharply from the monitor, her eyes shifting from him to her tray on the table.

"That's not...that's not why I did it," she said stiffly.

"I know, you had your own reasons," he said, looking straight at her. "But I'm grateful just the same."

She looked up from the table, locking eyes with him for a moment. A shadow of a smile crept over her before she looked away. "Whatever, you saved my life plenty of times as well."

"Yeah, I guess I did," he said, doodling with his fork in the remains of his food. "We've been through some shit over the last few months, huh?"

"We sure have," she said, staring back at the monitor. Memories of the past six months flashed before her eyes. *Sergeant Sikes' sneer as he shoved her into the intersection, the thrill of flying her DC-12 on a cloudless, sunny day, the look of pure terror on Leonard's face as he was pulled through the doors, Li tossing her the pound cake from his dinner rations when he heard it was her favorite.* She blinked, dispelling the images as she picked up her cup. She sipped quietly as she watched the stars outside.

"So what happens next?" she asked. "Think they'll fix the station, and we'll go back?"

Joelson shook his head, leaning back in his chair as he picked up his own mug. "Doubt it. It'll take years to get the station repaired. In the meantime they'll probably reassign us to other posts."

"Ah," she said softly, drinking the last of her cup.

Joelson watched her for a moment before speaking again. "You know, you could always request assignment with another security platoon."

"And you could always cross-train into the Electric Corps," she replied, setting the cup down on the table.

He shook his head, "Nah, *somebody* has to keep these assholes in line."

They shared a laugh, interrupted by the arrival of Reming and Li. They both looked up, watching the two troopers bicker over the serrated teeth Reming had pocketed before they left the installation.

"It's not fair man, you got two and there's two of us," Li complained.

211

"Is so fair," said Reming. "I snagged them fair and fucking square."

"But if I'd known you were grabbing them, I would have gotten my own before we left," protested Li. "Now we're gone and I won't get another chance. C'mon man, just gimme one."

Reming stared down the young Private, his grip clenched tightly over the two teeth in his hand. Truth be told, he was regretting showing them to his fellow trooper. That is, until an amicable idea came to him instead.

"Fine," the Special-Trooper said, a sly grin stretching across his face. He offered up a tooth to the young Private. "But only if we agree on what to call it."

Li threw up his hands, outraged at the obstinacy and audacity of his squad-mate.

"No one is going to call it a fucking *Dreadnot!*" he shouted.

"Then I guess you're shit out of luck!" snapped Reming, drawing back his hand.

"We'll see," Li fumed, storming off to sit at Rania's table. "Joelson! Reming's being a *fucking* child. He won't fucking *share*."

Joelson laughed, turning back to Rania as the arguing troopers sat down beside them.

"See what I mean," he said, his eyes twinkling behind the glass lenses. "You really want to skip out and leave these guys unsupervised?"

"Yeah, you're probably right," she said, a smile stretching over her face. "I should probably stick around."

EPILOGUE:

Captain Daniels ate alone in the empty galley of the *Hendrix*, doodling on the navigational tablet in front of her. She traced her finger over the star map displayed, charting a connecting path for her crew's next mission. The current course had already been set, the central fuselage already loaded down with a mining module for Tamarin, a parabolic deep-space camera for the orbital installation above Karnassus, and some shipping canisters meant for the remote posts along the outer rim. Her finger hovered over a small planet, briefly displaying its name and salient features.

> *PLANET OXT: silica terrain features with heavy mercurial pools. Rich deposits of cadmium, sulfur, and nickel. Temperature range: -10° to 50°, prospective site for Coalition Republic mining colony. Currently uninhabited.*

Figures, she thought. It had been over three-hundred years since mankind discovered space travel, but with so few planets able to sustain life, and so few economic incentives to do so, interstellar colonization had been constrained to only a few dozen planets. *And most of those are just a handful of miners and a few price-gouging corporate overseers*. It was another profound disappointment in her time as the captain of an ICF freighter. An entire universe of possibilities stretched before her on the navigational tablet, but almost the entire universe was empty.

"Captain Daniels." The sound of the intercom speaker cut through her thoughts. "Ma'am, we're nearing another drop point, t-minus seventy seconds."

Oh good, time to exercise my command duties…

Captain Daniels highlighted another planet on the star map with a bored sweep of her index finger. The icon chirruped, displaying a mission tasker alongside the planet's information. Her eyes widened as she read the small text. *Well, well, well, Commando Raiders need another deep-jet run from Anius.* Any mission involving the Raiders was sure to be interesting, and a deep-jet run meant they wouldn't take on any additional stops along the way. A small smile crossed her face.

Senior-Trooper Briggs' voice cut in again over the intercom. "Ma'am? T-minus thirty seconds…"

Captain Daniels pinched the display, selecting a course for Anius on their next run. She stepped away from the alloy bench, picking up her mug of SimuCaf as she looked at the stars on the galley viewscreen.

"Go for launch."

The capsule erupted in a jet of flame, hurtling through the starlit void as the freighter traveled on. The white and grey drum tore through space, an onboard computer guiding and tracking its path to a frozen outpost on the edge of the outer-rim. The parachutes unfolded red and white as the capsule entered the upper limits of the frigid pole, tracing a slow arc towards the planet's surface. It spun lazily as it went, blunted nose cone glowing in the fading twilight.

Far below, a Gluffant scraped for lichen among the ice and snow. It sneezed in the arctic air, long ropes of snot dangling from its flared, black nostrils. It looked up to the night sky, catching sight of a trail of orange blazing across the horizon. The Gluffant shook its head, sending icicles of frozen mucus clattering to the ground, small horns glinting in the waning light. The comet sped on, destined for impact beyond the sightline of the immense, hairy beast. As the capsule burned a course past the Gluffant's view, it gave a last shake of its great and shaggy head, and returned its focus to the lichen.

The capsule impacted the frozen soil, sending up a wave of dirt as the blunt cone dug a crater in the tundra. It came to a rest on its side, 'ICF OFFICIAL' emblazoned in bold, black letters on the grey and white hull. Internal gyroscopes spun, rotating the cargo upright with a light whirr. The capsule settled in place with a slight tremor, and for a moment all was quiet.

Rockets fired from inside, jettisoning the capsule's side panel and launching the cargo out into the snow. It tumbled out, a tight octagonal bundle of wires and jointed limbs. Rolling along the icy ground, the cargo came to a stop at the curved base of a snowy dune. It rocked softly, lights flickering to life along its sides. The cargo shook, booting up with the sound of a muted gong. The Class-II Inspection Drone unfurled, stretching its five multi-jointed arms and lifting its teardrop metal body out of the snow. A shutter opened on the front face, revealing the soft blue glow of the inspector's 'eye.' The drone shook itself, knocking snow from the clipped underside. A second shutter opened up in the metal base, and the drone's hover-fan kicked on.

The Inspection Drone lifted up, stabilizing a few feet off the ground. It hovered in the air, bobbing in the swirling winds. The drone turned left and right, searching for the trooper escort it was programmed to expect. The eye swept its surroundings with its optical sensors, blue lasers sorting and categorizing the empty rocks and snow. The intricate government circuitry and programming registered that it was alone, and the lights along the drone's side flickered in annoyance. It debated among its logic circuits, confusion sown from the egregious breach in courtesy protocols. The drone settled on a course of action, puttering off in the direction of the installation, but made a special point to annotate the lack of proper welcome within its final report.

It drifted alone, arms etching trails through the snow as it made its way to the outpost. The curved metal dome appeared on the horizon, blooming from the empty landscape. The Inspection Drone stopped a quarter mile away, awaiting the unfurling of its welcome procession. It hovered in the frigid air, scanning for the lines of assembled troopers and enthusiastic, smiling leadership. Finding none, the lights along its side flickered again. Logic circuits traced an argument back and forth, a decision was made and the drone swept on to the outpost entrance. Another note was added to the report.

The Inspection Drone floated through the hole in the vehicle bay, scanning left and right. It noted with some confusion that the bay was dark, without overhead or emergency lighting employed. It whirred disdainfully to itself before switching to night-vision. Another note was added to the report.

The drone hovered through the scorched and ruined bay, maneuvering past the charred carcasses of damaged MMUTCATs. It scanned the piles of twisted metal, noting the irregular and disheveled placement of spare wheels. The lights flickered on its side as the eye scanned past a splatter of frozen gore dropping from the ceiling lights. It whirred and chirped, taking in the gouges and scorched crater on the concrete floor. Another note was added to the report.

The drone passed into the narrow hallway, sweeping past scrapes along the alloy walls. Still no troopers lined up to greet it. No post briefings offered, no demonstrations of knowledge or functional capabilities. It was alone as it turned the corner into the dining facility. The chow hall was dark as the drone floated by, eye scanning the overturned benches and smashed RationVendor lying on its side. A tangle of cockroaches splashed in a pool of organic residue leaking out from the ruined appliance. Another note was added to the report.

The Inspection Drone worked its way to the Control Center, changing course abruptly when its initial entry was barred by a damaged main doorway. It buzzed in irritation, slender arms attempting to shift the dented and scratched doors open. The spindly clamps pushed against the swinging doors, feeble hydraulics sputtering as the drone heaved. The door remained stuck, and the drone gave up its efforts, logic circuits surging as it turned to head to the Command Den. Denying entry to sensitive locations was something the drone had never encountered before, and strictly against ICF inspection regulations. Another note was added to the report.

The drone entered the Command Den, finding it just as dark and empty as the rest of the station. It chirped, furious at the callous disregard of every protocol inscribed within its circuitry. It tilted in place, the shutter on the front closed slowly as lights flickered up and down its sides. The logic circuits within blazed with energy, threatening to melt down in a fit of apocalyptic, mechanical vexation. Decision parameters bounced back and forth in the schema of dense programming, before a single course of action was selected. The teardrop body tremored as a final notation was added. The shutter snapped open and the Inspection Drone wove its way back outside. It climbed to the summit of the rounded metal dome, splicing in to the antennae at the top. It clamped down on the spire, tapping in to the deep-space linkage and transmitted its final report back to ICF headquarters.

The five hundred page document was thorough, detailed, and dense. It outlined the distinct departures from established greeting protocols. It discussed the severe breaches of equipment storage and maintenance regulations. It described the piles of dirt and grunge, noting that the scratches and gouges throughout the installation constituted equipment malfeasance under ICF Consolidated Code 21C-849B. It annotated the piles of garbage left un-incinerated, a particular note of penned horror when it described that an unused office had been filled with human feces. It laid out the complete lack of proper post briefings and personnel knowledge quizzing customary in the course of biannual inspections. Its tone was apoplectic, summarized in the conclusion of its findings on the last page.

AZH-01 INSPECTION 9-18-2332

POST COMMAND: LT DOUGLAS PRESTON

FINDINGS: DISREPAIR, DISREPUTE, DESTRUCTION!

RECOMMENDATION: DISCIPLINARY ACTION!

FORCED RETRAINING IN PROTOCOL AND CLEANLINESS
REGULATION F567-81V. PERMANENT REMOVAL, REPRIMAND,
AND DISCHARGE OF COMMAND PERSONNEL.
REINSPECTION IN 6 MONTHS.

FINAL GRADE: *BELOW MARGINAL*

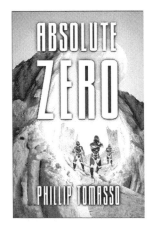

CHECK OUT OTHER GREAT SCIENCE FICTION BOOKS

AGENT PRIME
by Jake Bible

Denman Sno is Agent Prime!

The best of the Fleet Intelligence Service's elite Special Service Division, Denman Sno will need to use all of his skills and resources to stop the galaxy from plunging into another War with the alien menace known as the Skrang Alliance.

Sno's assignment: protect and deliver Pol Hammon, the galaxy's greatest dark tech hacker, to Galactic Fleet headquarters.

Hammon is in possession of new technology that can and will change the landscape of galactic life. The Galactic Fleet will do anything to keep that technology out of the hands of the Skrang Alliance even it it means sacrificing their best agent.

Even if it means sacrificing Agent Prime!

GALACTIC TROOPERS
by Ian Woodhead

For three thousand years, the Terran Empire has ruled the Galactic Expanse with an iron fist, conquering any alien civilisation who dared to oppose the might of their new human masters.

Their grip is about to be shaken apart when an unknown invasion force starts to strip whole planetary populations.

Now humans and aliens must find a way to work together to prevent the Empire and the invaders turning the Galactic Expanse into a graveyard.

CHECK OUT OTHER GREAT SCIENCE FICTION BOOKS

WARNING: THIS NOVEL HAS GRATUITOUS VIOLENCE, SEX, FOUL LANGUAGE, AND A LOT OF BAD JOKES! YOU MAY FIND YOURSELF ENJOYING HIGHLY INAPPROPRIATE PROSE! YOU HAVE BEEN WARNED!

MAX RAGE
by **Jake Bible**

Genetically Engineered. Physically enhanced. Mentally conditioned.

Master Chief Sergeant Major Max Rage was the top dog in an elite fighting force that no one in the galaxy could stop. Until, one day, someone did.

The lone survivor, Rage was blamed for the mission failure and court-martialed.

With a serious chip on his shoulder, Rage finds himself as a bouncer at the top dive bar in Greenville, South Carolina. And, man, is he bored with his job.

At least until he gets a job offer he can't refuse. Now, Rage is headed halfway across the galaxy to the den of corruption known as Horloc Station.

With this job, Max Rage may have a chance to get back to what he was: an unstoppable Intergalactic Badass!

RECON ELITE
by **Viktor Zarkov**

With Earth no longer inhabitable, Recon Six Elite are sent across space to scout promising new planets for colonization.

The five talented and determined space marines are led by hard-nosed commander Sam Boggs. Earth's last best hope, these men and women are the "tip of the spear". Armed with a wide array of deadly weapons and forensics, Boggs and Recon Elite Six must clear the planet Mawholla of hostile species.

But Recon Elite are about to find out how hostile Mawholla truly is.

Made in the USA
Columbia, SC
26 July 2019